Eugène Bersier

Coligny

the earlier life of the great Huguenot

Eugène Bersier

Coligny
the earlier life of the great Huguenot

ISBN/EAN: 9783337332631

Printed in Europe, USA, Canada, Australia, Japan

Cover: Foto ©Andreas Hilbeck / pixelio.de

More available books at **www.hansebooks.com**

COLIGNY;

The Earlier Life of the Great Huguenot.

BY

EUGENE BERSIER, D.D.

TRANSLATED BY
ANNIE HARWOOD HOLMDEN.

London:

HODDER AND STOUGHTON,

27, PATERNOSTER ROW.

MDCCCLXXXIV.

Printed by Hazell, Watson, & Viney, Limited, London and Aylesbury.

CONTENTS.

CHAPTER I.

CHAPTER II.

CHAPTER VII.

CHAPTER VIII.

CHAPTER IX.

CHAPTER X.

CHAPTER XI.

CHAPTER XII.

CHAPTER XIII.

CHAPTER XIV.

CHAPTER XV.

CHAPTER XVI.

CHAPTER XVII.

CHAPTER XVIII.

CHAPTER XIX.

CHAPTER XX.

CHAPTER XXI.

CHAPTER XXII.

CHAPTER XXIII.

CHAPTER XXIV.

CHAPTER XXV.

CHAPTER XXVI.

TRANSLATOR'S NOTE.

I BEG to acknowledge the kind help of the Rev. T. G. Rooke, of Rawdon College, in the revision of the English sheets for the press.

ANNIE HARWOOD HOLMDEN.

CAMBRIDGE,
   July, 1884.

PREFACE.

THIS book might bear as its fitting epigraph the saying of Agrippa d'Aubigné, " The world judges of all by success." Coligny did not succeed. For a long time his name was proscribed, and even now it has received but scant and tardy justice. His mortal remains found their first resting-place at Montfaucon ; thence they were removed to Montauban and to Châtillon, where for greater security the leaden coffin was built up in a recess in the wall. Thence, in 1786, they were again removed to Maupertuis, and finally, on September 29th, 1851, they were laid in their present resting-place, among the ruins of the old Castle of Châtillon, on the very spot where Coligny was born. His name and fame have suffered like vicissitudes. History has been slow to give him his rightful place. Yet a brief survey of his life shows that he is one to whom the world owes much.

Coligny was a born soldier. This was the natural

vocation of the head of the house of Châtillon, and his own bias was altogether in this direction. While still young he rose to a very high position. He owed this rapid rise to his noble birth, to the patronage of his uncle, the Constable de Montmorency, and above all to his own abilities as a soldier, and to the patient perseverance with which he applied himself to the organisation of the French infantry and the discipline of the army. Nothing but the substantial value of his services could have counter-balanced the disfavour which he often drew upon himself by his bluntness of manner, for no man had ever less of the making of a courtier.

His first military success was the taking of Boulogne. After this he distinguished himself in the brilliant campaigns which threw some lustre over the early part of the reign of Henry II. He was made governor of Paris, and, some time after, of Picardy. Then the king raised him to the high rank of Admiral of France. Coligny did not mean that this dignity should be merely an empty name. He dreamed of founding beyond the seas a new France, which might become at the same time a place of refuge for the exiles from the old world. The colonists whom he sent there tried to carry out his idea. For several years there were rivers in Florida called the Garonne, the Loire, and the Seine, and upon their banks rose towns endeared by familiar

names, and hallowed by the sound of psalms.
When France abandoned these colonies, the ill-fated
emigrants fell victims to the fierce hatred of the
Spaniards.

Coligny had been commissioned by Henry II. to
negotiate the peace of Vaucelles. When through
the ambition of the Guises and of Cardinal Carafa,
their accomplice, this peace was abruptly broken off
and the king was plunged into a foolish enterprise,
which was to issue in disaster, Coligny threw himself into St. Quentin, sacrificing his own reputation
to his sense of duty, and by his heroic resistance
saved· Paris, and enabled France to reorganise her
army. Himself made prisoner by the Spaniards at
St. Quentin, the only recompense he received for
his self-sacrifice was the displeasure of his sovereign.

Meanwhile the Reformation was making steady
progress in France, in spite of the severest measures
of repression, and was beginning to gather adherents
not only, as at first, among the poor and lowly, but
from the higher classes of society. Coligny himself
had long been favourable to it. He joined its ranks
at the very time when persecution was at its height.
He embraced the cause with enthusiasm, and served
it with the devotion of a man ready to sacrifice
honours and wealth for conscience' sake. Finding in
his new belief a fountain of the highest moral inspiration, Coligny presented the noble example of a

pure and beautiful home life, in which austerity of
principle was blended with the utmost tenderness of
heart—an example rare indeed in that dissolute age.
The Reformation took him away from the quiet of
domestic life to make him the illustrious leader of a
formidable party, with which the Court was to measure strength. This party had neither the resources
nor the numbers which command success. In order
to supply this deficiency it accepted the aid of
foreigners, thus falling into the fatal error of that
day, which subordinated every other consideration
to the triumph of one religious party. Coligny was
very reluctant to accept this alliance, and did all
that he could to shake it off. If the intrepidity of
the Huguenots had sufficed to secure victory, the
conflict would have been of short duration, but they
had to fight against the *prestige* of the king's name,
against the compact mass of Swiss battalions, which
decided the day at Dreux and Moncontour ; and
against the opposition of Old France, which was
still ardently Catholic.

Often defeated on the field of battle, Coligny was
never more formidable than just after such defeats.
It was by his steady persistence that he at length
obtained for his followers the religious liberty which
he might well think was thenceforth assured. He
was weary of civil war, to which he had an unutter-
able aversion. In order to efface the memory of it,

and to guard against its recurrence, his one thought
was to oppose a united France to the enormous
power of the House of Austria, relying in this project on the enfranchised Low Countries. The idea
was a grand one, to be taken up one day by
Henry IV. Charles IX. appeared to lend himself to
it, and made Coligny his chosen adviser. There was
a moment when "the Admiral," as he was called,
seemed the arbiter of the destinies of France. His
name appears in all the diplomatic despatches of
that day, denounced by the one party, extolled by
the other, respected by all who were not blinded by
fanaticism. While he was forming these glorious
projects, the hatred to his party, which had long
been growing, culminated in the atrocious tragedy
of the 24th of August, of which he was the first
victim. With him disappeared the ideal of the new
policy on which his mind had been set, and France,
wallowing in blood, sank rapidly into anarchy and
into the ignominy which marked the reigns of the
last of the Valois.

From this time the memory of Coligny has been
at the mercy of contending historians.

At the close of the sixteenth century his name
was the signal for an outburst of enthusiasm or of
hatred. In the eyes of the Protestants he was a
martyr invested with an undying halo by the tragedy
of St. Bartholomew. The League, which was the

b

organ of the Guises, called down curses on his memory. The few men who could rise above the spirit of their times, such men as De Thou, who tried to be impartial from a sincere love for justice ; and Brantôme, who was often impartial out of mere moral indifference, show how deep was the impression produced upon them by the severe greatness of Coligny. In the political reaction of the reign of Henry IV., Coligny's vindication is solemnly proclaimed. In the seventeenth century his memory becomes gradually obscured. A veil is drawn over the religious controversies of the past. The ever-growing worship of the monarchy and of Catholic unity, throws into the shade the figures of the great leaders of sedition in bygone days. Coligny is remembered only as the stern sectary, the formidable leader of the party that sought to dismember France. The surprise of Richelieu would have been great if anyone had hinted to him that the vast political projects which he supposed to originate with Henry IV., had been first conceived by the Huguenot Admiral. The official history of that time has long passed its verdict upon Coligny. It forgot all the service rendered by him to the country, and pretended to ignore his patriotism ; and if it did not directly charge him with complicity in the assassination of Francis of Lorraine, it found in his supposed conspiracy against royalty an extenuation of the bloody massacre of St. Bartholomew. The best illustration of this type of writing is to be found in Varillas, historiographer of the Court under Louis XIII. It would be hard to imagine anything more dry, unintelligent, and false than his estimate of the character and conduct of Coligny.[1] It is pleasant to turn from such unfair estimates to the judgment of Bossuet, who, struck with the greatness of Coligny, narrates his death with genuine emotion, and pays a tribute to his patriotism by saying that "all the attempts made to decry the Admiral had only rendered his memory more illustrious."[2]

But we must come to St. Simon, whose clear intellect was so free in many respects from the prejudices of his age, to get a really equitable and high-minded judgment upon the Admiral. I quote from a page of his writings recently given to the public: "Henry IV.," says St. Simon, "had as his master the wisest and most honest man of his age, the greatest captain, and the most skilful in turning to account even adverse circumstances and in rallying his party after

---

[1] *Vie de François II., Vie de Henri III., Histoire des révolutions en matière de religion.* In the writings of the Jesuit Father Daniel, historiographer under Louis XIV., we find a much finer historic sense, which sometimes asserts itself above the prejudices of his cloth and his age.

[2] This passage occurs in *L'Abrégé d'histoire de France*, Book XVII., in a *resumé* of lectures given by Bossuet to the Dauphin. The manuscript of this work, published for the first time in 1747, was revised by Bossuet himself, as we are assured by the edition in 1821.

its falls and heaviest reverses ; the man most able to
hold his followers together and to guard against all
that might arise to divide them ; finally, the most
disinterested and prudent of men, the man most
beloved and esteemed by the party of which he was
always the soul and strength, the man who knew
best how to secure the co-operation of foreigners
and to command the respect of opponents, the man
most generally esteemed and admired for his virtues.
Such was Admiral Coligny (so little favoured of
fortune, yet so worthy of fortune and of a better
cause !), who was the instructor of Henry IV. in
his early years both in arms and politics. Happy
prince to have been trained under the most prudent
captain, the wisest and worthiest man of his time!"[1]

St. Simon alone was capable in his day of writing
words like these. In the eighteenth century the name
of Coligny is often brought up as a protest against
fanaticism. The author of the *Henriade* tells the
story of his death in verses not to be forgotten. As
an historian, he takes an exalted view of him whom
he has called "the greatest of Frenchmen." Montes-
quieu passes his famous verdict : " Admiral Coligny
was assassinated while he had at heart nothing but
the good of the State." President Hénault, in his
drama of *François II.*, puts into the mouth of the

---

[1] *Parallèle des trois premiers rois Bourbons*, published by
M. Faugère.

Admiral language not unworthy of him. Abbé Raynal, who from his own labours in the Indies was in a position to appreciate the work done by Coligny in founding French colonies, does not hesitate to describe him as " one of the most far-sighted, resolute, and active of all the illustrious sons of France." Following him, Abbé Anquetil, in his *Histoire de France*, and at the beginning of this century Lacretelle in his interesting work *Les Guerres de Religion*, and Sismondi in his *Histoire des Français*, all unite in presenting the religious struggles of France in a broader and truer light. But the mass of the public knew Coligny only by a few incidents of his life and by his tragic death. It has been reserved for our day to take up what may be described as the historical vindication of the Admiral.

An enormous mass of documents relating to the sixteenth century has been brought to light in the last fifty years, and we are thus enabled to judge of Coligny with full knowledge of the facts. These revelations greatly enhance the importance of the part played by him. They bring out the great services he rendered to France before the wars of religion, and fully sustain the judgment of St. Simon, proving that Coligny was the true initiator of the new policy, all the glory of which had been hitherto ascribed to Henry IV. The character of Coligny as a private individual, illuminated by all these convergent lights,

and by the discovery of many details hitherto unknown, only stands out in stronger relief against a
dark background.   In the writings of modern historians, such as Guizot, Mignet, and Henri Martin,
Coligny becomes a more and more prominent
personage;[1] but Michelet has been the first to
describe him with that divination of the heart, and
that marvellous intuition, which give him an insight
into the very soul of men and things.   He says :
" No one will accuse me of being a hero-worshipper
in my books, but Coligny is the hero of duty, of
conscience.   Try him by whatever test I will, he
stands firm, nay, he grows ever grander, nobler.
Unlike so many mock heroes, this man, who was
never the hero of success, challenges scrutiny and
puts it to the blush."   Michelet abundantly vindi-
cates this high estimate of Coligny by the proofs
he gives of the breadth of his views, the vigour
and tenacity of his military genius, the integrity of

---

[1] In simple justice we must add here the names of such
German historians as Soldau, Ranke, Polenz, who have treated
the history of France in the sixteenth century with so much
ability and exactness of information. Among the publications
which have done most to throw light upon this great past, we
must mention *La France Protestante*, by MM. Haag ; and
the valuable collection in the *Bulletin de la Société d'histoire
du Protestantisme français*, edited first by Charles Reade,
and of which M. Jules Bonnet, the first editor of the *Lettres
françaises de Calvin*, has been for many years the indefatigable director, always on the watch for anything bearing
on the history of the French Reformation.

his life in an age of singular corruption, his uprightness contrasted with the perfidy around him, his
readiness ever to obey the call of duty.

We can but wonder that such a life has not sooner
found a historian. In the sixteenth century, three
years after the death of Coligny, a biography of the
Admiral appeared in Latin, which is usually attributed to Francis Hotman. At the close of this
preface we give at some length in a note, our reasons
for not endorsing this opinion. We look upon this
Vita Colinii, nevertheless, as a very important source
of information for the biography of the Admiral. A
century later Sandras de Courtils published a *Vie
de Gaspard de Coligny* (Cologne 1686; 2nd edit.
1691). This Sandras de Courtils, formerly a captain in the regiment of Champagne, went to Holland
in 1683, and there published some political pamphlets, memoirs, historical romances, and biographies
of various statesmen. On his return to France he
was imprisoned for nine years in the Bastille as a
seditious writer, and died in 1712. We do not
know whether he was a Protestant, but at any rate
he so describes himself in his *Vie de Coligny*. He
is a sort of literary adventurer, whose fertile imagination adds to the real facts which he narrates,
conversations and details of his own invention. His
biography of Coligny, while it is very favourable to
his hero, is an ill-digested book, and contains many

grave errors and fictitious statements. The military aspect of his subject is better treated than the rest. It must be observed that Courtils was born at Montargis, that is to say, near the birthplace of Coligny. In his preface he says :—" I have in my hands many papers, which give me an assured knowledge of facts. My access to such information will be at once understood when I say that I belong to a family which was always closely associated with that of the Admiral, and to whom he himself often communicated his most secret thoughts." While it is impossible for us to verify this assertion of a writer who proves himself otherwise worthy of little confidence, it would seem unfair to dismiss it summarily as incredible. In the history of the Admiral's youth Courtils mentions many incidents which may probably have been borrowed from family traditions, and which bear the impress of truth. We have refrained, however, from embodying them in the substance of our narrative ; they will be found in notes in the appendix.

It is strange that the Protestant refugees have made no attempt to exalt the memory of Coligny. Bayle's vast repertory, which goes over so wide a range, and critically discusses so many doubtful points, contains not one page about the great Huguenot.

Among the writings of our own day we may mention the notice of Coligny by M. M. Haag in

La France Protestante;[1] M. Jules Tessier's remarkable historical sketch *L'Amiral Coligny*, which, however, touches only on certain portions of his life;[2] and, most important of all, the noble monograph of Count Jules Delaborde.[3] M. Delaborde follows the life of the Admiral day by day, searching carefully all the documents relating to it, whether to be found in the histories or in the diplomatic correspondence of the time (the English Calendar of State Papers, reports and letters of Italian or Spanish Ambassadors, letters of representatives of the Reformed Churches in France and abroad, etc.) M. Delaborde has done more than this. He has collected, with admirable patience, both from the national library and archives, from the archives of the Swiss cantons, of Turin, and the British Museum, all the letters of Coligny that could be found. He has inserted in his book many of these never before published, and has given copious extracts from others. This is a truly noble work, breathing throughout a spirit of filial reverence for the memory of the great Huguenot, and deserving to be carefully studied by all who wish to understand his inner life.[4]

---

[1] This paper has been enlarged and completed by M. H. Bordier, in the second edition of this valuable work, now in course of preparation.

[2] *L'Amiral Coligny, étude historique*, by Jules Tessier. Paris, Sandoz and Fischbacher, 1872.

[3] *Gaspard de Coligny, Amiral de France.* (Paris, Fischbacher, 1879—1882, 3 vols. 8vo.)

[4] While referring to these biographies of Coligny we must

The many quotations we make in this work from M. Delaborde's book show how largely we have availed ourselves of it. In publishing the present sketch of the earlier part of the Admiral's life, we make no attempt to improve on that which has been already done with so much conscientiousness and learning. Our object has been to present Coligny to our readers in the great moments of his life before the wars of religion, endeavouring to describe the environment in which he moves, and the principal personages with whom he comes in contact. Fully appreciating the detailed and conscientious study which M. Delaborde has given us of the thoughts and deeds of the Admiral, our aim has been to draw this central figure in broader outline, and faintly to fill in the more distant horizon of the picture. We

---

not omit to mention the eloquent tribute paid to him by M. de Felice in his *Histoire des Protestants de France*; and by M. Puaux in his *Histoire de la Réformation française*. As a popular publication we may mention *La Vie de Coligny*, by Pastor A. Meylan. We note also that M. Dargand in his *Histoire de la liberté religieuse en France et de ses fondateurs* (Paris 1859), brings into great prominence the life and character of the Admiral. If Protestant writers are sometimes open to the charge of too great partiality to their hero, it appears to us that the Duke d'Aumale, in his admirable *Histoire des princes de Condé*, has yielded to an unjust prejudice when, for example, he attributes the rupture of the Peace of Vaucelles to the ambition of Coligny, or speaks of him as jealous of Condé. We the more regret these blemishes because the general tone of the book is one of such lofty patriotism. In speaking of the Admiral, can we for a moment forget the noble drama in which M. de Rémusat has made him live before us?

do not claim the merit of having brought to light any passage of the history before unpublished, but we do think we have been able to derive some fresh views of the subject, both from the careful study of sources already explored,[1] and from the analysis of documents recently published, the bearing of which upon our subject had not before been shown. To give only one instance. We have been able to throw light on several important points, by the help of the valuable collection of Catherine de Medicis' letters up to the year 1563, recently published by M. de la Ferrière. To these he has added numerous extracts from the correspondence of the Ambassador Chantonnay with the Duchess of Parma. The Latin

---

[1] We cannot attempt to give here a complete enumeration of these sources, but we may indicate some. Besides the letters of Coligny, we have of his own writing only his *Discours sur le siège de St. Quentin* (1622), his *Lois et ordonnances militaires pour l'infanterie*, and his *Testament olographe*, published in the bulletin of the *Société d'histoire du Protestantisme français*. He had written some memoirs which, as is well known, were destroyed after his death. Abstracts of several of his speeches are given by historians of the time The contemporary writers who give us the fullest details relating to him are La Planche, La Place, Castelnau, Brantôme, d'Aubigné, Davila, De Thou, the two Tavannes, and Theodore Beza, of whom we have at length a correct edition, thanks to two of the learned editors of Calvin's works. Then comes the correspondence of the Reformers (published in M. Herminjard's great work), the letters of Jeanne d'Albret, Antoine of Navarre, Catherine de Medicis, Hubert Lanquet, to mention only the principal. Then the extracts from the archives of the House of Orange, published by Groen van Prinsterer, the letters and reports of the English ambassadors (Calendar of State Papers analysed in the *Bulletin de la société d'histoire de Protestantisme français*), the letters and

correspondence of Calvin, now published in its integrity in the admirable edition of his works by Reuss, Baum, and Cunitz, has also been of great service to us. The present volume goes as far as the commencement of the religious wars. Those who scarcely know Coligny, except as the leader of the Protestants in arms, will perhaps be astonished at the importance of the part he took before assuming the military command. Until now he has been supposed to have been nothing more than the lieutenant of his uncle the Constable, up to the time of his espousing the Protestant religion. People spoke of "the Constable and the Châtillons" as though Coligny were a mere satellite revolving in the Mont-

---

reports of the envoys of Florence and Venice, of which we have the substance. We are only acquainted through Ranke and Soldau with the papers of the German ambassadors. In relation to Spain, there are the Granvelle State papers, and the correspondence of Chantonnay and his successors, but there is still much to be found out in the archives of Simancas. Baumgarten's last book, *Zur Bartholomeus nacht*, shows how much light might be derived from this source. Will the archives of the Vatican ever be freely opened? The extracts from these, published by Theiner, relating to France in the sixteenth century, are very meagre, and make one suspect how much is still concealed. The papal policy is still in many of its aspects mere matter of legend. The curious work in which M. G. Durny has just dissipated this illusion on one point, by bringing to light the true Carafa, enables us to trace with certainty the causes of the rupture of the Peace of Vaucelles. As we do not in the present volume go beyond the year 1562, we say nothing here of the sources to be consulted for the later history, that of the religious wars, of the political part played by the Admiral in the last two years of his life, and of St. Bartholomew. The name of these documents is truly legion. •

morency òrbit. No one knew how pronounced had been the originality of the nephew from his very youth. Our readers, as they trace the part taken by Coligny at the time of the rupture of the Peace of Vaucelles, will perceive that even then he dared to hold his own opinion in the face of all opposition, and to counsel a course of policy which would have saved France the terrible disaster of St. Quentin. They will see also that in 1559, when under the influence of Granvelle the Guises turned round so rapidly in favour of Philip II., Coligny stood firm, and foresaw how the country would be engulfed in this vortex to its ruin.

In order to appreciate the man fully he must be known in his inner life, in the ardour of his religious faith, which was so intense even before he became a Protestant. We must understand the strength he found in his new convictions, and the holy enthusiasm with which they fired him. The Admiral was a Huguenot. When a modern writer exclaims, "What grand citizens Coligny, Du Plessis-Mornay, La Noue, even d'Aubigné would have been if they had not been sectaries!"[1] when others, taking the standpoint of free thought, reproach the Protestant leaders with not having reasoned and acted like men of the eighteenth century, we can

---

[1] M. de Meaux, *Lettres religieuses en France au XVI. sièale*, p. 114.

but deplore the prejudices which preclude any just appreciation of men in whom religious faith was the ruling inspiration and the source of all manly virtues.

We know well that the sympathy which gives the intuition of character is apt to degenerate into party spirit, and that it easily transforms its heroes into saints. In the study of the sixteenth century, when there was an incessant conflict of beliefs, the temptation is great to hoist our banner and to fire without scruple upon the enemy's flag. Our readers will see how earnestly we have striven not to yield to this temptation. They will, we hope, be convinced that we have at least sought to be just, and in being so, it seems to us we do most honour to Coligny.

N.B.—We have made it a strict rule not to assert anything without giving our authorities. All our quotations are verbatim. But we have not thought it necessary to reproduce the spelling of the sixteenth century, which varies so curiously in different authors, and sometimes even in the same author. The exact reproduction of orthography is absolutely necessary when a collection of documents is being republished; but we have high authority for holding that this is not required in a history written for the general public. If we had reproduced, for example, the exact orthography of Henry II., of Catherine de

Medicis, and Jeanne d'Albret, with all its eccentri-
cities, we should have imposed on our readers an
arduous task of deciphering hieroglyphics. A glance
at the original texts will convince them of this.
Some historians take a middle course, and while
adopting modern orthography as a general rule in
their quotations, leave a few words of the original
text here and there, to give an archaic turn to the
passages they reproduce. This mixed method may
have its merits, but we have preferred not to adopt it.

NOTE.

Gasparis Colinii Castellonii magni quondam Franciæ amirallii vita, 1575 (without any name of place).

We have before us two different editions of this work, and in both I observe a curious mistake. Coligny was born, we are told, on February 16th, 1517, and when he died, August 24th, 1572, he was fifty-three years, six months, and eight days old. The age is correct, but the date of his birth is obviously wrong. Coligny was born in 1519, as we shall show. In 1576 appeared an English translation of this work under the title, "The Lyfe of the most godly, valiant, and noble capteine and maintener of the trew Christian religion in Fraunce, Jasper Colignie Shatilion, sometyme Great Admiral of France," translated out of Latin by Arthur Golding (imprinted at London by Vautrollier, 1576).

The French translation of the *Vita* did not appear till the seventeenth century, 1643, 1646, 1665, etc. The translator has attempted to correct the error of the Latin text relating to the age of the Admiral, but as he retains the incorrect date for his birth, 1517 instead of 1519, he falls into the fresh error of making him 55½ at the time of his death, a mistake which has since been constantly repeated. In 1783 a learned German named Dassdorf published at Dresden an edition of this French translation, with interesting notes. In all these editions the life of the Admiral is accompanied by his discourse on the Siege of St. Quentin, which has since been printed in several collections of memoirs upon the history of France.

The discourse and the life are even united in the edition of 1665, and following editions, under the erroneous title of *Mémoires de l'amiral Coligny*, and several historians (M. de Felice among others) being unacquainted with the Latin text of the *Vita*, have quoted these memoirs as an original work of the sixteenth century, the authorship of which has been commonly attributed to Cornaton, the Admiral's servant.

Who is the author of the *Vita Colinii?* The sixteenth century gives no exact answer. In the seventeenth century, La Monnoye attributes it to Francis Hotman ; de Tourny, (*Histoire des grand officiers de la couronne*) to John Hotman, Sieur de Villiers, the son of Francis. Nicéron assigns the authorship to Jean de Serres, because the name of Jean de Serres had been written by Pierre du Puy in his copy of the *Vita.* Le Long adopts the same theory, as also does Dassdorf.

The learned editors of *La France Protestante*, M. M. Haag and Henri Bordier, in the new edition of the Coligny collection, pronounce in favour of Francis Hotman, as also does Count Delaborde.

Great as is our respect for these high authorities, we venture to differ from them on this point. Let us first show on what grounds their opinion is founded :—

1st. It is certain that on January 15th, 1573, Jacqueline d'Entremont, widow of the Admiral, wrote to Francis Hotman a letter in which the following expression occurs : " Do not think it strange if I have tried to move you to use your pen to hand down to posterity as many testimonies to the virtue of my husband and lord as our enemies will bear to have depicted in him."

2nd. It is equally certain that Francis Hotman complains in a letter to Cappel that the magistrates at Geneva have forbidden him to publish in that city any writings about Coligny.[1]

3rd. The author of the *Vita*, in quoting in Latin the last touching letter of Coligny to his wife, dated August 18th, says he has the original in his hands, which naturally points to Francis Hotman.

4th. It is certain that the author of the *Vita Colinii* came into close contact with the Admiral, for he says, in describing his life at Châtillon-sur-Loing, " We add briefly that which we have *seen* and heard tell." This again would apply exactly to Francis Hotman.

5th. Lastly, if it is considered that Francis Hotman, especially after the publication of *Franco-Gallia* (1573), was regarded as a sort of revolutionary and republican, and that his very name became obnoxious to many Protestants, we can understand why the *Vita*, if written by him, should have appeared without the author's name.

---

[1] See *France Protestante*, Art. Hotman.

c

These are the arguments in favour of the authorship of Francis Hotman. Let us now weigh what seem to us the graver reasons against it.

Francis Hotman published in 1573, under the name of Ernestius Varamundus, a work bearing the title, *De furoribus Gallicis, horrendâ et indignâ amirallii Castillionei, nobilium atque illustrium virorum cæde sceleratâ ac inauditâ piorum strage passim editâ per complures Galliæ civitates, etc., vera et simplex narratio.* This is a very valuable historical document, of which Crespin, De Thou, and other writers, have made much use, and which is for the most part trustworthy in its statements, though it was written under feelings of burning indignation. A comparison of this work with the *Vita Colinii* makes it difficult, if not impossible, to believe that they are by the same author.

We do not lay much stress on the orthography of names, which often differs, in the one Castellonius, in the other Castillioneus; Cossinius and Cossenius; Thelinius and Thellignius; Benuesius (Besme) and Behemius, etc. In the sixteenth century points like these were not much regarded, nor would we insist too much on the fact that twice over the author of the *Vita* mentions the *Historia furialis carnificinæ*, (i.e., *De Furoribus gallicis*), as one would quote an unknown author. We go deeper :—

1st. The style of *De Furoribus* is precisely that of Francis Hotman, a man of the sixteenth century, who, according to Calvin, wrote Latin with great ease and eloquence. From the first words of the masterly opening, "Optandum esset recentium furorum memoriam," etc., we recognise the man. These are his grand periods. This is his powerful and graphic style. We feel throughout that this is a great writer, with remarkable breadth of view and power of delineation. With a few bold strokes he brings before us all the details of circumstance and character, as in the gloomy dialogue between Henry of Guise and Besme: "Absolvisti-ne Benuisi ? At ille : Absolvi, inquit."

In the *Vita* there is nothing like this. A quiet continuous narrative style, not an eloquent word, no generalisations, nothing which suggests an actor in the great crisis. The author's one idea seems to be to exhibit Coligny in his edifying life as a faithful subject of the king. The language is simple, without fervour ; there is not a phrase which recalls, however remotely, the *verve* and brilliancy of Hotman.

2nd. Here and there we meet with assertions which are incomprehensible on the part of a man initiated as Hotman was into the life of the great Admiral. We are told, for instance, that when Coligny was brought into the Protestant faith, "in a few months the whole aspect of his home at

Châtillon was changed, and his two brothers, Odet and Andelot, were, *by his example*, stimulated to great ardour in the study of religion." Now Hotman was the intimate friend of Andelot. Could he fail to know that Andelot embraced the evangelical faith before Gaspard, that his conversion to Protestantism lost him his office and drew upon him the public reprobation of the king, and that it was at his instigation that Coligny, then a prisoner at Ghent, turned his attention to the new doctrines?

3rd. If we compare the account given in *De Furoribus* and in the *Vita* of the attempt of August 22nd, and of the death of the Admiral, we find, not indeed any contradiction between the two narratives, but the order is different. The one mentions words spoken which the other omits. The same sayings of the Admiral are variously expressed, and one cannot help asking how the author of the *Vita* could pass over traits which elsewhere he had brought out so forcibly.

Dassdorf, who was familiar with Hotman's style and writings, had already arrived at the opinion that he could not be the author of the *Vita*. Who, then, is the writer? Pierre du Puy, as we have already said, attributed the work to Jean de Serres, and Dassdorf, noticing a somewhat striking resemblance of style between the *Vita* and Jean de Serres' historical writings, concluded without further inquiry that he was the author of the biography. We cannot acquiesce in a conclusion based on such insufficient premises. There is, undoubtedly, a certain analogy between the spirit of the writer of the *Life* and that of Jean de Serres, who was distinguished by his moderation, but this is not enough to sustain Dassdorf's statement.[1]

We believe that Francis Hotman, yielding to the impulse of his own heart, wrote his terrible work, *De Furoribus*, in 1573, and that as Jacqueline d'Entremont entreated him at the same time to perpetuate the memory of her husband, he yielded to this request by devoting some of the most eloquent pages of his work to Coligny's death. We believe that this was the writing which the Geneva magistrates would not allow to appear. It is inconceivable that they could have raised any objection to the publication of the *Vita Colinii*, which contains not a single aggressive passage, and is so moderate in tone throughout.

---

[1] M. Ch. Dardier, who has written a very able paper on Jean de Serres, seems to have reached the same conclusion as ourselves, for he makes no mention of the *Vita Colinii* among the writings of the Protestant historiographer. (See his articles in the *Revue Historique*, 1883.)

The author of the *Vita* is still unknown to us. *In dubio, abstine.* We shall describe him then without naming him. He was a gentle spirit, a friend to peace, who seems not to have known Coligny intimately in the early part of his career. He often quotes the testimony of eye-witnesses. The only passage in which we find any description *ex visu* is in the appendix, in which the domestic life of Coligny is depicted. It is possible that this fragment may be by Francis Hotman. The *Vita* is nevertheless a document of great value, if only from the tone of perfect veracity which characterises it throughout.

CHAPTER I.

THE family of the Coligny came originally from
La Bresse, and their old feudal manor stood at
the foot of the Jura, commanding the approach to
the small town which still bears their name.

This little town is situated on the slope of a wooded
hill, from the top of which, turning to the west, the eye
takes in the great plain of Mâconnais.[1] The castle
stood just on the borders of La Bresse and Burgundy.

The Coligny belonged to one of the oldest families
of the French *noblesse*. Villehardouin mentions, in
the crusade of 1202, one Hugo *de Colenii*, who distinguished himself by his valour. It has been
asserted, and it was the belief of the admiral himself,
that his house had once been independent and
sovereign.[2] This independence was not absolute,

See *La France Protestante*, 2nd edition, Art. Chatillon,
for the interesting description of this spot given by M. Henri
Bordier.

[2] This claim is mentioned in the *Vita Colinii*.

I

however, and it is certain that, about the middle of
the fifteenth century, William de Coligny was fighting
under the banner of Savoy.　After his marriage, in
1437, with Catherine de Saligny, he acquired, as a
marriage portion, the *seigneurie* of Châtillon-sur-
Loing, to the north of the Loire, in Gâtinais, and
this *seigneurie* descended to his eldest son John.
John took up his abode at Châtillon.　The services
which he rendered to Louis XI., in the war with the
"League of the Public Weal," brought his family
into notice.[1]

He had two sons ; Jacques, the elder, died in
fighting before Ravenna (1512) ; Gaspard, the
second son, was made Marshal de Châtillon in 1516.
Two years previously he had married Louise de
Montmorency, sister of the famous Constable Anne,
who was to exercise for half a century such an
important influence over the destinies of France.
Louise was sister to the Seigneur de Mailly.

The Marshal de Châtillon was one of the generals
of Francis I.　Brantôme says that he had "a strong
head and a strong arm."　But we know of no
brilliant exploit performed by him.　On the contrary, it was through yielding to his counsels of
extreme prudence that Francis I., during the war
of 1521, after having crossed the Scheldt in the face
of Charles V. and the Count of Nassau (October 22nd)
refused to enter on a decisive engagement, as urged

[1] The whole subject of the genealogy of the Coligny family
has been thoroughly treated by Jean du Bouchet in his *Preuves
de l'histoire de l'illustre maison de Coligny* (Paris, 1662).
See also M. Edmond Chevrier's interesting paper, *La maison
de Coligny au moyen âge* (Bourg-en Bresse).　M. Delaborde

by the Constable de Bourbon, and thus lost, says Martin du Bellay, "the good fortune which God had sent him, and which was never to return." During this war the Spaniards had taken possession of a large part of Châtillon's estates in Franche-Comté; he received from the king, in compensation, the principality of Orange.[1] He had just been summoned to defend the frontier near Bayonne, when he died, after nine days' illness, of malignant fever at Dax, August 4th, 1522.

Louise de Montmorency was thus left a widow, and though still young, she had seven children to educate, three by her first marriage and four by the second. We shall only mention here those whose names figure in history. The first of these was Madeleine de Mailly, afterwards Countess de Roye, whose daughters became the wives of the Prince de Condé and the Count of La Rochefoucauld.[2] Then followed Odet, Gaspard, and Francis de Coligny.[3] Odet, who became a Cardinal, was born July 18th,

---

and M. Bordier go fully into the subject. M. Bordier justly conjectures that the Admiral lays so much stress upon the sovereignty of his house because of his favourite scheme of making his little principality a place of refuge where the adherents of the Protestant faith might enjoy freedom of worship.

[1] Thus the father of Coligny, by a strange concurrence of circumstances, bore the title of Prince of Orange, which was to be rendered so illustrious by his future son-in-law, William the Silent.

[2] Of the other children of the Sieur de Mailly, one, John, died at the age of twenty-two fighting in the siege of Naples; the other, Louise, became a nun.

[3] An elder son of the Marshal, named Pierre, born in 1516, was page to Francis I., and died in 1534 at eighteen years of age.

1517; Gaspard, the future Admiral, February 16th, 1519; and Francis, who afterwards took the title of Andelot, April 18th, 1521.

Louise de Montmorency was equal to her task. She moulded the character of her sons. To her they owed the strict uprightness, the generous ardour, the moral courage which were such striking traits in her character. Gaspard de Coligny especially was the true son of his mother.

Here we must pause to make one general observation. At no period of modern history was the influence of woman so marked as in the sixteenth century. We are not referring to her hidden influence, which has always been great, but to the brilliant and active part taken by her in outward life. This may explain to some extent the spasmodic character of the policy pursued, which was often determined rather by feeling and passion than by calm statesmanship. In the two rival camps which then divided Western Europe, we shall find, if we look closely, that behind the principal actors, the strings were moved by women. We see the astute and sagacious Margaret of Austria, aunt of Charles V., instilling into him her own crafty taciturnity; Mary Tudor, "Bloody Mary," whose ardent fanaticism failed to melt the cold and arid heart of Philip II.; Louise de Savoie, whose haughty caprice dictated much of the treachery of the Constable Bourbon; Diane de Poitiers, who made the fortune of the Guises, and held in passive obedience his ponderous majesty Henry II.; Mary Stuart, whom we see through an illusive halo of romance, and who would have received sterner justice from posterity but for the pity inspired by her cruel fate;

and lastly, Catherine de Medicis, about whom we are ready to ask if she even knew what remorse meant, and who seems never to have loved any human being but her worthless son Henry III., who bore so strong a resemblance to herself. In contrast with these, and in the opposite religious camp, is Elizabeth of England, sceptical at heart, proud, and often cruel, but in whom no access of passion ever stifled the dictates of sound policy, and whose strong intellect justified the saying that the greatest man in England at that time was a woman. Before her came Lady Jane Grey, that lovely flower so prematurely cut down ; and in France the elder Marguerite de Valois, with her bright intelligent face, her mind eager for all knowledge, and her heart as open to all human tendernesses as it was closed to all bigotry ; Jeanne d'Albret, her daughter, "who had nothing feminine about her but her sex " ; the woman of penetrating intellect and firm will, in a word, a true queen, whose political programme, except in the matter of religious toleration, was almost that of 1789. Of upright conscience, of true and brave soul, Jeanne d'Albret could see with her frank eyes through the intrigues of the Florentine, but she failed to conceive the atrocious perfidy with which Catherine was preparing the crimson nuptials of St. Bartholomew. Henry IV. was wont to speak of her as " my good mother, to whom I owe everything," which was indeed a tribute as true as it was graceful, only that the moral levity of the Gascon detracted somewhat from his greatness as a hero. Side by side with these figures famed in story stand Madame de Roye, Coligny's noble sister ; Charlotte de Laval, his brave companion, and the lovely Princess de Condé, as intrepid under the enemy's fire as she was tender and dignified in her domestic afflictions, and of whom Anne de Rohan worthily sang :

" That she deemed it higher grace,
Though she came of noble race,
To be called a child of God
Than a princess of the blood."

Louise de Montmorency deserves a foremost place in this galaxy of good women. Her high birth, the charm of her person, the honourable position already filled by her as maid of honour to Anne de Bretagne, all fitted her for a life at court. But she preferred to shut herself up at Châtillon, and to devote herself entirely to the education of her sons. In 1530, however, she came to pass some time in Paris with the new Queen Eleanor, who wished to have her about her person. She dreaded the atmosphere of frivolous gallantry which prevailed in the court of the Chevalier King. The Chancellor de l'Hospital has celebrated, in one of his Latin poems,[1] the purity of her character and her virtues as a mother.

Louise de Montmorency had an evident leaning to the new doctrines then being propagated by the Reformation. This predilection was shown in the choice which she made in 1528 of a tutor for her sons. She selected Nicolas Bérauld, a distinguished classical scholar, about fifty-five years of age, and an intimate friend of Erasmus and Louis de Berquin, one of the first martyrs of the Reformation. Louise de Montmorency was tenderly beloved by Marguerite,

---

[1] Liber I., Epist. viii.

sister of Francis I., who was the avowed protectress
of the Lutherans of Meaux. The oldest biography
of Coligny says that Louise de Montmorency gave
her dying testimony to the true and pure religion
she had embraced. She had perpetually on her lips
the words, ". His mercy is from generation to generation upon them that fear Him," and on her death-bed
she exhorted her son Odet, " who was already a
cardinal, and expressly forbade him to bring any
priest to her, saying that God of His singular mercy
had taught her how to fear and serve Him in all
piety, and how to lay down this tabernacle of the
body and to enter the heavenly country."[1]

We can well understand how Father Maimbourg
came to say of her in his *Histoire du Calvinisme:*
" It was Louise de Montmorency who instilled into
her sons the spirit which made them fall so easily
victims to heresy." But it would be erroneous to
conclude that she associated herself directly with the
Reformed Communion. It was not till several years
after her death, that her daughter Madeleine de Mailly
broke openly with Catholicism, thus setting her three
brothers an example which they all afterwards followed, as we shall see, but each in his turn obeying
the dictates of his own conscience.

If Coligny's mother had the most powerful influence on the formation of his character, it was to
his uncle, the Constable de Montmorency, that he at
first owed his rapid advancement.

Anne, first Duke de Montmorency,[2] came of that

---

[1] *Vita Colinii,* 1575, p. 8.
[2] He derived his name from the Queen Anne de Bretagne,
whose godson he was.

ancient family which Henry IV. once called the first house in Europe after that of Bourbon.

Born in 1492, he was educated with Francis I., then simple Count d'Angoulême. In 1515 he fought at Marignan, in 1521 at Mezières, under Bayard, then at Milan under Lautrec. In 1522 he was made Marshal of France. Irreproachable in valour, he yet lacked the qualities of a great captain. Hence he was always ready to temporise, playing in relation to the Spaniards the part of Fabius Cunctator. This caution served him well in 1536 at the time of the invasion of Provence by Charles V. Remembering Pavia, the Constable refused to encounter the enemy face to face. He desolated the country through which the Spaniards were to pass, burning up all the villages and the harvests which might have yielded sustenance to the foe. By this barbaric energy he forced Charles V. to retreat. The king rewarded this service in 1538 by making him Constable. In this position he exercised the function of prime minister. All questions were submitted to him, and his influence was immense. The Sultan himself bought his favour by lavish presents. His natural conceit was fostered by his position, and soon became insufferable. He delighted in humbling all the nobility, and gained the reputation of being the greatest "snubber" in France. If anyone ventured to contradict him he spared no abusive epithets ; his adversaries were fools, asses, calves.[1] As general or statesman he showed not a spark of genius, but he had a strong will, and a power of continuous appli-

---

[1] Brantôme.

cation, which under an impulsive king like Francis I.
was often of service in the conduct of affairs. Ra-
pacious and greedy of gain, he could not bear any
squandering. He set himself to protect and enrich
all his family, though demanding of them at the
same time an activity like his own in the service of
the king. He was the type of those great dignitaries
the race of whom was to become extinct with
Richelieu. Disgraced in 1540 for having too openly
embraced the party of the Dauphin,[1] he turned his
exile at Écouen to account by building there a
splendid mansion. Restored to office under Henry II.,
he exercised a disastrous influence, lost the battle
of St. Quentin, concluded the unfortunate Peace of
Cateau-Cambrésis, and placed himself with Guise and
Saint André at the head of the famous triumvirate.
As the "first gentleman and Christian baron of
France," he was naturally hostile to the Reformation,
which he regarded as merely a revolt. This led to
an open rupture with his nephew, and it was in
fighting against Coligny at St. Denis that he received his death wounds. His piety was of a very
original type. "He would never fail," says Brantôme,
"to perform his prayers and devotions, but of a morning said duly his *Paternosters*, whatsoever might be
his occasions, whether to stay in doors or to ride
forth among his men-at-arms, insomuch that it grew
to a saying among them to beware of the Constable's
Paternosters, for though there were great stir and
confusion he would be still muttering his prayers

---

[1] In the latter years of Francis I. an open contest broke out
between the Duchess d'Étampes, the king's favourite, and
Diane de Poitiers, the Dauphin's mistress.

and telling his beads, and ever and anon broke off with a 'Lay me such an one by the heels ;' 'String me such another to this tree ;' 'To the halberds or the arquebuses on the spot with a third ;' or, 'Put me those knaves to the sword that have thought to hold their peddling hamlet against the king's grace ;' or, 'Burn me down this village, set a torch to everything for a mile about'; and so ran on with such like commands as need was for discipline or warfare, but without ceasing or stinting a jot of his *Paternosters* until he had made an end, holding it a grievous misdoing to put them off to another season, so tender a conscience as he was of."

This naïve description brings the man vividly before us, and we see how the rough soldier was blended in him with the very Christian gentleman. The pitiless cruelty with which he treated the inhabitants of Bordeaux, who in 1548 had refused to pay the salt tax, reminds us of one of those Commissioners to whom the Convention entrusted the pacification of the provinces.

. Anne de Montmorency was, as we have said, much attached to his own people, and the natural patron of all nearly connected with him. His nephews early reaped the benefit of his good will. In 1533, the Pope, in honour of the marriage of his niece, Catherine de Medicis, with the future Dauphin, promised to create four cardinals in France. Francis I. offered a cardinal's hat to Montmorency for one of his family. Montmorency designated his nephew Odet, then scarcely sixteen years of age! He was invested with the purple on November 7th, 1533. This was what is called an anticipated vocation. The same year he was made Archbishop of Toulouse, and prior of a great many abbeys. Two years later he was called to the bishopric of Beauvais, one of the oldest ecclesiastical peerages in the kingdom. In this way the benefices of the Church were often dispensed at that time. At the same period, Calvin, while scarcely more than a child, was, in defiance of all canonical rules, endued with a benefice at Noyon, just as a century later Angélique Arnauld became abbess of Port Royal at twelve years old. These very abuses often stimulated the spirit of reform in those whom they were intended to benefit.

When Odet entered on his career as a churchman, he left to his brother Gaspard the ordering of the house at Châtillon. He also gave up to him and his brother Andelot all the patrimonial estate.

Coligny was a born soldier. In order to prepare himself for this career, he accustomed himself to severe bodily exercise, and finding himself prone to too much sleep, he formed the habit of waking himself up every hour through the night till he felt he was master of his own body. His tutor was, as we have said, Nicolas Bérauld ; his governor, Sieur Guillaume de Prunelay.[1] When Coligny was in Paris he studied with Tagliacarne and William du Maine, tutors of the royal children, and often exer-

---

[1] Sandras de Courtils, who derived many details from the family traditions of the Châtillons, says that Bérauld was very slow of speech, that Prunelay had usually a tooth-pick in his mouth, and that Coligny imitated them in both these respects. The latter detail is confirmed by a proverb long current in the south. If the Protestants said that it was well to beware of the paternosters of the Constable, the Catholics replied that they had to beware of the Admiral's tooth-pick.

cised himself in company with the Dauphin in all knightly arts.

We have a letter in Latin written by him at the age of fifteen, and addressed to Bérauld from Paris.[1] He gives him news of the Conclave of Cardinals and of the Court. He writes: "In the midst of the doubt and anxiety which prevail on all hands, the king does not lose heart, far from it. Just as though he had a good hope to cheer him on, he devotes himself daily to the chase, stalks the deer or slays the wild boars caught in the nets." He goes on to say, "I sometimes join in the same exercise, but for the most part my time is given to the reading of *Cicero* and the study of the tables of Ptolemy, under Du Maine, who, adopting a different method from Tagliacarne, teaches cosmography at the same time, especially in the portion relating to the longitude and latitude of places, with the addition of meridians and parallels." Even at such an early age Coligny thus gives indication of his faculty of observation and devotion to study.

This in no way prevented his joining eagerly in the sports of youths of his age. His brother Andelot was his constant companion, and thus there grew up between them that close affection which united them through life.[2]

The proverb is still remembered. Brantôme quotes it in another form, as already current in his day: "God save us from the smooth tongue and douce ways of the Prince de Condé, and from the wit and tooth-pick of the Admiral."— *Brantôme, Lalanne Edition* (vol. iv., p. 339).

[1] Herminjard, *Correspondance des réformateurs*, vol. iii., p. 219.

[2] See in Appendix A. a curious incident of Coligny's youth,

Among those with whom he was most intimately associated in his youth was Francis of Lorraine, who was born one day later than Coligny, and who was to become his most implacable enemy. Brantôme says : " They were both in their youth such great companions, friends, and allies, that as I have heard from several eye-witnesses, they would dress for the most part in the same habits, be on the same side in jousts and tournaments, racing for the ring, masquerades, and other court pastimes, both of them madcaps, outstripping all others in their extravagant follies, and always doing some mischief in their fooling, so rough were they and unlucky in their sports."

These exuberant spirits, this effervescence of youthful vitality, Coligny learned to keep in check and to transmute into manly energy. Had his will been less firm, he might easily have drifted into evil in that frivolous court, where favourites reigned and where virtue so often made shipwreck. It is a marvel that he stood erect, training himself with stern self-discipline for the hard life of a soldier, cherishing purity of life and that blameless integrity which made him such a power in his generation. Even as a young man he won the respect which followed him to the end of his life.

It was a dangerous age to live in. For thirty years France had been drinking deeply into the intoxicating life of Italy. The *noblesse*, who left their feudal manors for brilliant expeditions beyond the Alps, there

quoted by Sandras de Courtils, and which we only give with the reservation made in our Preface with regard to this author's statements.

caught the manners of the Renaissance, and breathed the atmosphere of a restored paganism. In Rome they met with cardinals who ridiculed the literary poverty of the Gospels and the barbarous style of St. Paul, priests who read Aretino and Boccaccio, and popes who had Machiavelli's *Mandragora* in the Vatican put on the stage. From Rome they carried away visions of the miracles of art, and on their return to France were eager to raze to the ground their gloomy Gothic dwellings, to replace them by light and fairy architecture like that of Chenonceaux and Chambord. They became enthusiasts about music and painting. Francis I. spent enormous sums on singers for his chapel. There was a rage for brilliant costumes, magnificent fêtes and processions, robes of silk, brocade, and velvet. It was a violent reaction against the utilitarian and prosaic age of Louis XI., who hated all pomp and circumstance, and went himself through the provinces in his fur cap and close-fitting suit of grey cloth. Italian scepticism, however, had not yet laid hold of the souls of Frenchmen. Machiavelli, whose *Prince* was only printed in 1531, did not exert any real influence till the middle of the century, when Catherine de Medicis had gathered her Italian favourites around her. The France of 1530 had still its chivalrous impulses. In contrast to the sinister and coldly criminal type of Cæsar Borgia, France could point to the noble Bayard. Her danger lay rather in the direction of the voluptuous. Not indeed in the gross and rollicking licentiousness of the old Trouvère tales, which was the naïve. apology of a gay life in opposition to the monastic austerity of the middle ages. It was rather an access of refined corruption, of unwholesome curiosity, which troubled and unsettled the heart of France. The court set the example. Noble souls like Marguerite, the king's sister, strove in vain to stem the tide, or to turn it in a spiritual and mystical direction by skilfully inweaving moral lessons in tales of the imagination, trying to rekindle the faithful passion of the old romances of chivalry and the love songs of the Trouvères. All these slight and graceful barriers were swept away by the rush of gross sensual passion. Francis I., as Michelet observes, shows in his portraits the traces of this downward tendency of the age. At first he is the gallant and noble.cavalier ; then, little by little, the face assumes a heavy and repellent ugliness ; the bloated cheek, the lustreless eye bespeak a soul swallowed up of the flesh. And the like degeneration goes on from sire to son, till the men of that age furnish the gallery of models which Brantôme describes with the callous facility of the mere chronicler, indifferent alike to virtue or infamy.

The reaction, however, was already going on, and in many minds it took the form of an unconscious but powerful moral protest before it touched on doctrine or religion. Coligny, his brother Andelot, their mother and sisters, and many others whom we could name, had as yet but a vague knowledge of the doctrines of the Reformation. In the year 1540 scarcely more than one or two men of the higher classes could be found who had embraced the Protestant faith, and yet men's consciences were being aroused. There came a moment when this moral

Renaissance seemed about to germinate and expand under the influence of a genial atmosphere. There seemed to be promise of a future for the Reformation in France. All historians have spoken of that unique moment when Francis I., inspired by his sister, resolutely opposed the Sorbonne, and defended, in opposition to it, the claims of Greek and Hebrew, " those heretical tongues " in which great lords and ladies chanted the psalms in the groves of Pré-aux-Clercs. But it was but the hush before the storm. What might not France have become if, following the impulse of her better genius, she had wrought out her own religious renovation ? To what great destinies might she not have attained ? The only response to this question is the sombre reality of that pitiless persecution, which from the first torture of the Lutherans of Meaux to the Saturnalia of the League, checked the impetus of free thought, and forced upon the minds of men by fire and sword the unity so dear to the Latin races. Under its influence France well nigh became a second Spain ; the reformed themselves, finding all their generous and expansive impulses repressed, assumed that stern and rigid puritanical attitude with which they are so often reproached. How could it be otherwise ? How could their soul blossom and fling its perfumes abroad, when it was nipped by the biting winds of persecution ?

Coligny grew to manhood just when this era of repression was at its height. Returning from the fêtes at Chambord or Fontainebleau, or leaving the royal receptions at the Louvre, it was but too common to see on the Place de Grève or in the Rue

Maubert, scaffolds erected, on which men and women of the lower classes were the victims. They were criminals of a strange sort ; of grave and yet joyful mien. They were heard singing with rapture unknown poetry, which all took up in chorus, and the crowd listened. It was an appeal to the God of righteousness ; it was the sublime confidence of the heart that waits for Him ; it was the accent of eternal hope. The flame leapt up. The martyrs, putting aside the crucifix held by the priest before their eyes, gazed up into heaven. One by one the voices sank into silence. The crowd dispersed, and more than one who had joined in the cry, " Death to the Lutherans ! death to the heretics ! " went away quiet and thoughtful. The air seemed full of omens.

CHAPTER II.

COLIGNY began his career in arms in 1542,
just after the disgrace of his uncle the Constable. Failing this powerful protection, he had to
make his own way. As he said, the life of the
Court had little attraction for him, and he " usually
walked abroad where blows were to be exchanged."[1]

The campaign of Luxembourg, 1542, is one of the
numerous episodes in the interminable duel between
Charles V. and Francis I. The latter, on this occasion, took the initiative with great vigour. Attacking
the Spaniards in the north and south, he entrusted
the army of the north to his son, the Duke of
Orleans, but the command really belonged to Claude
de Lorraine, Duke of Guise, a skilful general and
the true founder of the glory of his house. It was
under his orders that Coligny and Andelot fought.

---

[1] Brantôme, Lalanne edit., vol. iv., p. 316.

In a few weeks Damvillers, Yvoi, Arlon and Luxembourg were taken by the French, assisted by the Duke of Guelders.[1]

At the taking of Montmédy shortly afterwards, Coligny received a wound in the head from a ball. He scarcely allowed it time to heal before he took arms again. The results of this campaign were unhappily lost almost as soon as gained, through the folly of the Duke of Orleans, who abandoned his own army, preferring to rejoin the army of the south, where he hoped to win " a greater battle."

The next year (1543) it was again Francis I. who took the initiative in the attack, notwithstanding the powerful support which Henry VIII. of England was lending to the Imperialists. Charles V. had retaken Luxembourg; the principal field of action was Flanders, and Coligny distinguished himself at the siege of Binche, where he was grievously wounded, and in the defence of Landrécy. The issue of the campaign remained doubtful.

In 1544 the contest with the Spaniards was carried on vigorously in Italy, whither the king had sent the young Duke d'Enghien. The old generals of the king, still smarting from the defeats of Pavia and La Bicoque, were inclined to temporise. The Spaniards jeered openly at their caution. Enghien sent Blaise de Montluc to the king to obtain from him " leave to give battle." The Gascon, who was as eloquent a messenger as he was a brave soldier, acquitted himself so well of his task, that the king

---

[1] At the taking of Arlon an incident is recorded which, if true, shows how great was Coligny's moral courage. See Appendix B.

allowed himself to be persuaded.   So soon as it was
known there was to be a battle, more than a hundred
young gentlemen of the first houses in France
hastened to join Enghien.   They offered sums of
money to retain the mercenaries, who always threatened to leave on the eve of a battle.   Coligny and
his brother hastened with the rest to the field of
action, and were attached to the staff of the general-
in-chief.

The encounter with the Spaniards took place at
Cérisolles, on the morning of Easter Monday, April
14th.   Enghien, with his cavalry, carried all before
him ; but he thought for a time that the rest of his
army was defeated, and in his despair was about to
commit suicide, when some one rode up with the
news that the Gascons and the Swiss on their side
had cut to pieces their Spanish and Italian foes.
The Imperial loss was enormous.   France had gained
no such brilliant victory since Marignan.   Unhappily,
as so often happened, Francis I. did not know how
to turn his success to account.   Enghien was soon
recalled.   The Imperialists recovered from their
consternation, and their general offered to sign a
truce, which closed the campaign.   In the mean-
time Coligny and his brother had done important
service in the taking of Carignan.   Seeing their
soldiers faltering, Coligny seized the standard, flung
it into the counterscarp, and compelled his men to
follow him to recover it.   The affair was so brilliant
that the king, offended as he was with the
Constable, did not hesitate to publicly thank the
Châtillons.

It was Francis I.'s imprudence which nullified the

advantages of this victory. He had as opponents
the Emperor of Germany and the King of England.
These were attacking him in the north, and it was
to oppose them that he recalled his troops from
Italy. Charles V. had secured for the first time the
support of the whole Germanic Confederation against
France, so great was the indignation felt at the
alliance of Francis with the Turks. Henry VIII.
landed with 30,000 English troops, who were joined
by 25,000 Netherlanders. He laid siege to Bou
logne. At the same time Charles entered Champagne
with 50,000 men. The little town of St. Dizier
made a heroic resistance, and thus retarded the
advance of the Germans for forty days. It surrendered August 17th, 1544. Charles V. advanced as
far as Château-Thierry. The Parisians were panic-
struck, but Francis I., though much reduced by illness, was roused to some of his old energy by this
crisis, and offered such a resistance that Charles
thought it best to treat with him. Peace was concluded September 18th at Crépy-en-Laonnais, in
spite of the protest of the Dauphin, who had hoped
to win laurels in the campaign. Coligny took part
in this expedition as Colonel, and distinguished
himself by the rigid discipline he enforced in his
regiment.

Henry VIII., however, continued the siege of
Boulogne, which fell into his hands by an unexpected
capitulation at the end of the year. Francis now
determined to turn all his efforts against the English.
During the winter of 1545 the taxation was increased by one quarter; fresh troops were levied;
the Mediterranean fleet was called home, and the

strongest trading vessels of Bordeaux, La Rochelle, Bretagne, Normandy, and Picardy were added to it. The fleet was intrusted to Admiral d'Annebaut. He was to land in England, and there to be joined by the Scotch.

The French fleet sailed for the Isle of Wight, and tried in vain to provoke the English to fight. Coligny commanded one galley. He sailed up to the enemy and opened fire, but Peter Strozzi, who was to have supported him, held back, and compromised the attack by his pusillanimity. Coligny reproached him bitterly, saying he would rather have died than have acted thus.[1] This is the first and only occasion on which Coligny commanded at sea, and we see how bravely he did his part. Annebaut abandoned the project of landing, and returned to France about the middle of August. Thus ended this expedition, the only result of which was to show that if France could muster a fleet, she did not yet know how to use it to advantage.

It was then decided to re-take Boulogne. The Marshal du Biez commanded the besieging army ; but he set to work badly, and wasted time in building a fort at Outreau, which was at too great a distance from the sea for the firing from the fort to prevent the re-victualling of the town by the English. An Italian engineer, named Melloni, wasted enormous sums of money on this construction, and the siege made no progress.

Coligny took part in the siege, and had frequent

---

[1] The account of this is given at length in Delaborde, vol. i., App. XIV. M. Delaborde is the first who has mentioned this fact.

skirmishes with the enemy.   In one of these en-
counters Francis of Lorraine received a thrust from
a lance, which entered his head a little below the
right eye.   He was healed by the skill of Ambroise
Paré, who was just rising into repute.

Henry VIII. grew weary of this long campaign,
and made proposals to Francis, which he received
eagerly.   On the 7th of June, 1546, a treaty was
concluded, by which France was to recover Boulogne
at the end of eight years, on consideration of a
payment in gold of 2,000,000 crowns.   It was
understood that neither side was to commence any
new fortifications in the County of Boulonais ; but
this stipulation was practically nullified by the permission granted to each to " continue and complete
any intrenchments or fortifications already begun."

Coligny was twenty-seven years of age when this
peace was concluded.   In the correspondence of
Catherine de Médicis we find a letter[1] which intimates
that at this period he made, or at least planned, a
journey into Italy.   She writes to Cosmo, Duke of
Florence, September 28th, 1546 : " My cousin, the
brothers Châtillon and Dandelot, gentlemen in waiting of my lord the king, and others of their company,
have undertaken to journey to you, for the great
desire they have to see our city of Florence and the
antiquities of it.   I pray you, my cousin, receive
them well for my sake, and I will pray the Creator
to grant you all you desire."   No historian, as far as

---

[1] *Lettres de Catherine de Médicis*, published by M. le
Comte Hector de la Ferrière.   We shall often refer to this
valuable collection, which contains 1,000 letters, many of
them here published for the first time.

we know, makes any allusion to this journey, and it
is impossible to tell whether the project was carried
out or not.

Francis I. died at the age of fifty-three, after a
painful illness. His latter years were embittered
by the loss of his favourite son, and by the fearful
tragedy of Cabrières and Mérindol, where 3,000
peasants were butchered on a charge of heresy.
The Duke d'Enghien, the brilliant victor at Cérisolles,
had died before the very eyes of the king, from an
accident, the cause of which was never explained.
The king had loved to pit him against the Guises,
whose ambition already began to make him uneasy.
He knew that his son Henry was rejoicing at the
prospect of his death, and was already distributing
in anticipation the principal offices of state among
his own favourites.[1] On January 28th, 1547, he
heard of the death of his old rival, Henry VIII., and
it seemed to him a presage of his own. On the
31st of March he died at Rambouillet, unmourned
and unpitied even in his death agony. " He is
going ! he is going ! the old gallant !" said Francis
of Lorraine ; and the king's son, Henry, could
scarcely conceal his joy at his father's funeral. Thus
sadly ended a reign which had begun with such
brilliant promise. Through sheer lack of moral
force, Francis I. had shown himself incapable of
fulfilling the splendid destiny which seemed to await
him. Yet the sorrow and shame which his children
brought upon France have made posterity lenient to
his memory. Even the Huguenots, to whom he

---

[1] *Mémoires de Vieilleville.*

showed no pity, could not forget the services rendered by him to science and letters, and Beza has given him a place in his *Icones*, as one who "chased away the darkness of barbarism and opened the gates of the new temple of light."

One of the first acts of Henry II. was to reinstate the Constable Anne de Montmorency; but at the same time he gathered around him the Guises, who had always adroitly courted the favour of the new king's all-powerful mistress, Diane de Poitiers. The king was consecrated on the 26th of July, 1547, by Charles of Lorraine, who received a cardinal's hat for the service.[1] Writing on this occasion to Diane de Poitiers, the astute cardinal says : " I cannot refrain from thanking you again for the special favour you have shown me, feeling myself so singularly contented therewith, and being desirous to serve you more and more, *having a good hope of thus reaping a harvest not less for you than for myself*, since it is impossible henceforth that my interest should be other than yours also."[2]

Some time after, Charles of Lorraine repaired to Rome. It is curious to note the daring ambition of this young prelate, then only twenty-three years of age. He does not shrink from suggesting to Pope Paul III. the scheme which, ten years later, was to cost so dear to France. He proposed to form a league between the papacy and France against Spain. He tried to stir up the old pontiff by reminding him

---

[1] He was called Cardinal of Guise until the death of his Uncle John, Cardinal of Lorraine.
[2] *Bulletin de la Société d'histoire des protestantisme français*, vol. ix., p. 216.

of the great popes of other times who had resisted the emperors. Forgetting that he was a Catholic and a priest, he boldly counselled an appeal to the Turks. Finally, writing from Rome to the king, he intimates that the kingdom of Naples might be conquered, and lets slip this phrase, which betrays the secret thought of the Guises : " They tell me that if you will not undertake this enterprise, and will say so to me or to one of my brothers, they will raise men and money for me, and will put me in the said kingdom *to hand it over to one of my brothers.*"[1]

The ambition of Charles of Lorraine did not stop even here. He asked the king to use his influence to secure the tiara for his Uncle John after the death of Paul III. He utilised the same journey to negotiate the marriage of his brother with Anne of Este, daughter of the Duke of Ferrara.

Ambitious souls find each other out by mutual affinity. In Rome, Ignatius Loyola met Charles of Lorraine. He saw at once what an auxiliary he could find in this unscrupulous cardinal, only eager for prey. Without any hesitation he asked him to become the patron of his order in France, a request which was granted " with a truly cordial affection." [2]

Francis of Lorraine, on his part, was only too ready to follow suit. This cadet of the house of Lorraine cherished boundless hopes. Possessed of high military genius, he was to render eminent services to France. L'Aubespine, in his history of Henry II.,

---

[1] Bouillé, *Histoire des ducs de Guise*, vol. i., p. 179. It was not then Cardinal Carafa who first suggested this conquest to the Guises in 1547. The project was their own.
[2] *Ibid.*, vol. i., p. 178.

says that it was the ambition of his brother which was his ruin. The verdict is partially true ; for Francis had generous thoughts and magnanimous impulses, such as the Cardinal of Lorraine never knew, but both were equally ambitious. Francis aspired from the very first to hold a sovereign position in France. His slightest acts betray this. On the day after the famous duel at Jarnac, he caused a magnificent tomb to be erected at Vivonne. The inscription runs that " it was erected by a great *French prince*." The nobility protested, but the king let it pass, and the title was assumed. Just so with the name of Anjou, which gave him eventual rights over Naples. He contrived to slip it into his marriage contract in spite of the objections of the lawyers. His brother in Rome assumed in the same way the title of Cardinal of Anjou.[1]

In Dauphiné, of which he was governor, he often signed his edicts simply "Francis," as though he were a king ; he sometimes used seals of gold, which the king alone was entitled to do ; he wore his sword

---

[1] M. de Bouillé, in his *Histoire des ducs de Guise*, says that Francis I., by his imprudence, did much to foster this ambition. In the letters patent, by which in 1544 he raised the marquisate of Claude de Lorraine, father of the two Guises, into a dukedom with a peerage attached to it, he allowed a clause to be inserted to the effect that " our said cousin, the Duke of Guise, is of *the house of Lorraine, and is descended by marriage and by alliance from the house of Anjou, and from our predecessors the Kings of France*." These letters patent were not registered till May 8th, 1553, consequently under Henry II., who raised no objection. The fact stated by M. Bouillé is substantially correct, but there is a mistake in the dates. The dukedom of Guise was created in 1527.

in parliament, and took precedence of the princes of
the blood.[1]   To this, whether from want of percep-
tion or, more likely, from weakness of character,
Henry II. raised no objection.

It was easy to foresee what would come of the
alliance of these two young ambitious souls, who
never knew what a scruple meant.[2]

Francis of Lorraine, in order to strengthen the
bond with Diane de Poitiers, desired that his brother
Claude should marry one of the daughters of the
Duchess de Valentinois.   He made the mistake of
consulting Coligny on this point, who replied that he
esteemed a little good repute more than much riches,
an answer very galling to both brothers.[3]   Words
like these are not soon forgotten, and though Brantôme says that the difference to which this incident
gave rise between Guise and Coligny lasted but a
short time, and they were again friends as before,
there may well be some doubt about the sincerity of
the reconciliation.

Coligny and his brother Andelot soon felt the
effects of the Constable's protection.   They were
both named gentlemen-in-ordinary of the king's
bedchamber.   Andelot was sent to Charles V. to

---

[1] This precedence of the princes of the blood was only
definitely fixed by an edict of Henry III. passed at Blois in
1576.

[2] We may quote one incident which shows to the life the
ambition of the Cardinal.   Francis of Lorraine had just had a
daughter.   The Cardinal in congratulating him adds : " *This
daughter, please God, shall make a good match ; and if we
play our parts well we shall have our choice, and shall have
time to think it well over.*"—*Mémoires-journaux du duc de
Guise*, published by A. Champollion.

[3] *Vita Colinii*, 1575.

thank him for his message of congratulation to Henry II. on his accession.

On April 29th, 1547, Coligny was made "colonel and captain-general of all the French infantry." The extreme importance of the infantry at this period shows how great was the trust reposed in this young captain of twenty-eight. Coligny soon had occasion to show that he was equal to his new functions.

This elevation of fortune in no way changed his serious habit of life.[1] He was at this time just contemplating marriage.

His mother, Louise de Montmorency, died on the 12th of June in the same year (1547).[2] The Constable had brought up, in his household at Chantilly, Charlotte, daughter of Guy, Count de Laval. Her father had been married three times ; his first wife was daughter to the King of Aragon ; the second, sister of the Constable ; the third, the mother of Charlotte, was Antoinette de Daillon. The young

---

[1] See in Appendix C. very curious details as to the life then led by him in court and camp.

[2] The following words, taken from an epistle addressed by Michel de l'Hospital to Odet, show in what esteem Louise de Montmorency was universally held : " How happy was thy mother ! She could look without fear all around her, and into the recesses of her conscience. Her life, both before and after her marriage, was above suspicion. She married a man who, having often to lead the armies of France, won many victories over her enemies. Louise de Montmorency gave birth to children worthy of her beauty, nourished them at her own breast, and saw them grow up to man's estate. Having thus fulfilled her duties as a mother, she watched with fond pride her children and grandchildren, who surpassed even her fondest hopes. In a good old age, in full possession of her faculties, and strong in hope of a better life, she passed to heaven."—*Poésies*, by Michel de l'Hospital.

child, who was soon left an orphan, was educated at
Chantilly from the year 1540, and Coligny had long
had the opportunity of knowing her. Their marriage
was celebrated at Fontainebleau, on the 16th
October, 1547. Shortly after Andelot married
Claude de Rieux, cousin of Charlotte de Laval,—a
union which drew still closer the bonds between the
two brothers.

CHAPTER III.

COLIGNY was soon recalled to his post before
Boulogne. We have already said how ambiguous was the treaty concluded with the English.
It was agreed that the two armies confronting each
other might go on completing the existing fortifications, but that no new ones were to be begun. This
was a contradiction in terms. The English had not
failed to set to work, and had built what was really
a new fort close to the harbour, in spite of Coligny's
remonstrances. The king grew impatient. After
visiting the French camp in person, he sent written
orders to Coligny, under date May 19th, 1548, to
construct the forts needed to prevent the re-victualling
of the town. Coligny at once took steps to put
these orders into effect. He called together 6,000
sappers and miners, and with great sagacity decided
to throw up a huge earthwork upon a tongue of
land facing the very entrance of the harbour. Two
months later the fort was finished and supplied with
artillery. It was called Fort Châtillon.

While superintending these works Coligny was also actively engaged in disciplining his troops. He wrote out and enforced in his corps the famous military regulations which three years later were adopted throughout the kingdom. These formed a new military code which was intended to protect the peaceful inhabitants from the license of the soldiery. " It was Coligny," says Brantôme, " who introduced decency and order into the whole French infantry by his wise regulations. They were the best and most politic ever made in France. And I believe that since they have been passed the lives of millions of persons have been saved, as well as their honour and goods ; for before these regulations there was nothing but pillage, robbery, plunder, ransoming, murders, quarrels, and ravishing among the bands, so that they rather resembled companies of Arabs and brigands than noble soldiers."[1]

A brief glance at these regulations will suffice to show what were the evils Coligny was trying to remedy.

It was necessary, for example, to ensure stated and fixed terms of service, to guard against desertion, and to enforce instant obedience. The punishment annexed to disobedience was severe, but sometimes moral only, not corporal, as for instance :—

" If a soldier, without just cause given, shall say anything against the honour of another, the said calumny and dishonour shall return upon himself, and shall be proclaimed before all the companies."

---

[1] M. de Chastillon in *Les couronnels français.*

And again :

"If a soldier, without due cause, shall give the lie to another, he shall be made to stand in the public square, and with ensigns unfurled and uncovered head, shall ask pardon of his colonel, and of the man to whom he gave the lie."

Rape and pillage were forbidden under pain of death. This and the following article show the stern morality of Coligny :

"The soldier who blasphemes the name of God shall be put in the stocks in some public place for three separate days, for three hours at a time, and at the end of the same shall, with uncovered head, ask pardon of God." In this enforcement of a severe morality we catch the spirit of the future Huguenot.

Brantôme tells how Coligny applied these regulations, and how he succeeded in controlling the lawlessness of his troops.

Such a task required unflinching severity, but severity alone would not have sufficed. "His soldiers," says Brantôme, "were neither his subjects nor his vassals, neither his hirelings nor his mercenaries ; and yet when they were in his presence the slightest word of reproof was rarely needed, and in his absence his signet alone was enough to enforce obedience. So completely had he acquired the habit of ruling them, that it seemed as if he was born to command and they to obey. If any of his soldiers or other subordinates gravely offended he never spared to punish. Yet he was beloved and honoured by men of all ranks, and when any of his soldiers had a private interview with him they were as pleased as if they had had audience of the king."[1]

The siege of Boulogne still dragged on wearily. On September 6th, 1549, the king appointed Coligny his lieutenant-general in the Boulonais. Coligny having now the command of all the resources he needed, was able to press the siege more closely, and to shut the harbour against all hostile vessels. At the end of September the English began to speak of surrender. The negotiations went on for some months. At length, on the 19th February, 1550, the French and English plenipotentiaries assembled at Fort d'Outreau.[2] It was agreed that Boulogne should be given up on condition of the payment by France of a sum of 400,000 crowns. Andelot carried the draft of the treaty to the king, and it received his sanction on March 19th. Henry II. sent Coligny, du Mortier, and Bochetel to England, " to convey his ratification, and to receive that of the king and his solemn oath and covenant."

On the 25th April the French entered Boulogne. Henry made his own formal entry on May 15th. The English had often learnt to their cost how impetuous a people were the French ; this time they had encountered a tenacity of resistance like their own.

While Henry II. was taking possession of Boulogne, his ambassadors repaired to London, where they met with the best reception. Three English

---

[1] *Hommes illustres et grands capitaines français*, M. de Chastillon.

[2] A letter from Paget to the Earl of Warwick shows with what haughtiness Rochefort treated the English envoys. *Froude's History*, vol. v.

ships came to meet them at the mouth of the
Thames. The day after their arrival they were
received by Edward VI., who invited them to dine
with him. The young king was only twelve years
of age, but he already showed a very lively wit,
and unusual thoughtfulness, and charmed all who
approached him by his gracious manner. His coun-
sellors were carrying forward zealously the work of
religious reformation begun by Henry VIII., and
the French plenipotentiaries were present at the new
Anglican service performed in the vulgar tongue,
at the close of which the king publicly swore to
observe the treaty of peace. Coligny seems to have
been much attracted by the fair, pure face of this
prince, scarcely more than a child, who, occupying
the throne of England between the coarse and
violent king, his father, and his sister, " Bloody
Mary," stands out like a heavenly vision against the
dark background of one of the most troubled epochs
of history.

The taking of Boulogne brought Coligny into
great prominence. His uncle, the Constable, thought
he had a right to ask the government of Piedmont
for him from the king, but the more powerful
influence of Diane de Poitiers prevailed, and Brissac
was made governor. This proved to be a fortunate
choice.

Coligny, however, was rising more and more into
favour. This is evident from the terms in which the
king speaks of him in a circular dated March 20th,
1551, which extended to the whole army the
military regulations introduced by Coligny.

Three months later, Coligny's niece, Eléonore de

Roye, contracted a brilliant alliance with one of the first princes of the blood, Louis de Bourbon, Prince de Condé, and younger brother of Antoine de Bourbon, then governor of Picardy, and subsequently King of Navarre. But this alliance met with the strongest opposition from the Guises, and Diane de Poitiers their patroness. Thus the antagonism between the houses of Lorraine and Châtillon became gradually more pronounced.[1]

On the 9th of September in this year, Coligny was made governor of Paris and of the Île-de-France, in place of his uncle De Rochefort. In the royal letters investing him with this office, reference was made to the great services rendered by him.

It was an important appointment, and Coligny's investiture with his new functions was celebrated with all due solemnity on Tuesday, February 9th, 1522, in the Hotel de Ville, in Paris, in presence of the dean of the merchants' guild, the sheriffs and leading citizens, and the civic guards.

After a long panegyric on the Constable de Montmorency, the dean of the merchants' guild said that Coligny had shown "himself a diligent imitator of his uncle in his generosity and noble enterprises." He referred to his successful campaign in the Boulonais, and bade him welcome to Paris.

---

[1] Though they were the first princes of the blood, the Bourbons did not hold a position corresponding to their rank. Since the revolt of the famous Constable Charles, their family had always been looked on suspiciously by royalty. Louis de Bourbon was poor at the time of his marriage, and held no office. All that is known of his youth is given by the Duke d'Aumale in his *Histoire des princes de Condé.*

Coligny replied :

" Gentlemen, I thank you for the honour you have done me. As to this office to which it has pleased the king to appoint me, I take it to be due not at all to my own merits or efforts, but solely to his liberality and goodness. I am assured that you have had heretofore as governors, persons of great virtue and experience, to whom I must in all reasonableness yield in all things save one, of which I pray you rest assured, namely, in my good will to exert myself with all the understanding God has given me (though it be but little) for the good and advantage of this city. And where my own judgment does not suffice, I would borrow of men whom I know to be of greater experience, wisdom, and competence, promising you, gentlemen, that no effort of mine shall be wanting to promote the good of this city, both in general and in particular."[1]

After this exchange of courtesies, the sheriffs made the customary presents to the governor— basins, cups, and ewers of silver, " all silver gilt, gilded and engraved, weighing altogether forty-four marks and some ounces, with which present the said governor was highly pleased, and thanked the said city." [2]

---

[1] See all the details of this ceremony in Delaborde and in Appendix XXVI.

[2] Godefroy, *Le cérémonial francais*, vol. i., p. 1009.

CHAPTER IV.

Campaign of 1552.—Alliance of Henry II. with the Protestants of Germany.—Brilliant campaign of Les Trois-Evêchés.—Maurice of Saxony goes over to the French.—Treaty of Passau.—The Emperor besieges Metz.—Determined resistance of Guise.—Part taken by Coligny in the army of observation.—He is made Admiral of France.—Duties of his new office.

COLIGNY'S residence in the capital was not to be of long duration. His presence soon became necessary with the army. Before following him further we must glance at the new phase of the conflict between France and the Empire.

In the year 1550 Charles V. had reached the zenith of his power. He had crushed the Protestants of Germany, and quelled the revolt in the Netherlands. He had gained the support of Julius III., one of the most worthless of all the bad popes of that age. In order to secure the possession of Italy, he endeavoured to prevent the French, who occupied Piedmont, from advancing further into the peninsula. He already held Milan, Genoa, and Piacenza, and coveted Parma. Ottavio Farnese, Duke of Parma, placed himself under the protection of France, and this was the spark which kindled the conflagration (July, 1551). In one of the skirmishes in this first campaign, Andelot, whom Henry II. had sent to fight under Brissac, fell into an ambuscade, and the news of his captivity, which threatened to be long and cruel, reached Coligny at the very moment when he was raised by the king to the governorship of Paris.

War had begun in Italy, but it did not spread far. The real battle-field was to be elsewhere. Ever since his accession Henry II. had been eager to commence hostilities with Charles V. Defective as he was as a ruler, he had devoted much attention to military affairs. He had surrounded himself with able generals—Brissac, Francis of Lorraine, Coligny. He cherished a deadly hatred to the emperor on account of the harsh captivity in which Charles had kept him and his brother in Madrid. The idea that in fighting the emperor he would also be resisting the pope presented no obstacle to him. He renewed the former alliance with the Germans and the Turks, and, as if to quiet his conscience as a Catholic, he redoubled his cruelty to the Protestants.

On October 5th, 1551, a secret treaty was signed between the king and the chiefs of the Lutheran states of Germany. The signatories engaged to resist "the practices used by Charles of Spain to reduce Germany to a state of abject, insupportable, and perpetual servitude, such as he had already introduced into Spain and other countries."

Henry promised 240,000 crowns in gold for the first three months of the war, and 60,000 crowns a month afterwards, so long as the campaign lasted. The German princes on their side recommended that "the king should make himself master of certain imperial cities in which the German tongue was not spoken, such as Cambray, Toul, Metz, and Verdun."

When it was known, on January 15th, 1552, that the king had declared war on Charles V., there was an outburst of enthusiasm throughout France. Gentlemen of good position entered the army as simple privates, the youth of the cities ran away to enlist, and even artisans forsook their work for the camp. The army, swelled by German mercenaries, crossed the Meuse. Toul and Metz opened their gates to the French; but Henry presented himself in vain before Strasbourg, which received his advanced guard with a volley of cannon. He proceeded as far as Wissemburg; then feeling that he should have to encounter too strong an opposition, he decided to retrace his steps, taking possession of Verdun on his way. Such was the brilliant campaign of *Les Trois Evêchés*, in which Coligny took an active part, "not sparing himself," says Brantôme, "any more than his lowest subaltern."

Meanwhile Charles V. was undergoing the most humiliating affront which had yet touched his pride. Knowing nothing of the treaty concluded between the Protestant princes of Germany and the French king, he was at Innspruck watching the deliberations of the Council of Trent when the storm broke. At the very time when Henry II. declared war on him, Maurice of Saxony deserted him. Maurice had been his *protégé*, and had been in high favour ever since, four years before, he had betrayed the Protestant party and joined the Duke of Alva in exterminating his co-religionists at Mühlberg. But, far-sighted as he was ambitious, Maurice observed the growing hatred of the Spaniards in Germany, and suddenly facing round again, he threw off the mask, revealed the alliance concluded with the French, and issued a manifesto in which his name appeared joined to that of Henry, surmounted by a cap between two daggers. " Some say that this device was found on some old coins, and had been adopted by the murderers of Caius Cæsar."[1] " Thus," says Henri Martin, " it was a king who, under some strange impulse of the genius of the Renaissance, unearthed that terrible *bonnet rouge* of liberty, before which the old monarchy of France was one day to fall."

The soldiers flocked around Maurice. He swept through Germany like a torrent ; entered Augsburg on April 1st, terrified the Fathers of the Council of Trent, who fled like a cloud of birds at his approach, and advanced upon Innspruck. Charles, who was suffering from a sharp attack of gout, aggravated by the treachery of Maurice, had to flee over the mountain in the middle of a night of drenching rain, and thought himself fortunate to have escaped a shameful captivity.

It was a terrible humiliation for the monarch who had just reconstructed the empire of Charlemagne, and who a few months before had seen all Western Europe at his feet. Charles saw the urgent necessity of appeasing Germany, and by the treaty of Passau (1552) he guaranteed to the Lutheran princes the free exercise of their religion. He was eager to re-instate himself in the eyes of Europe, and the surest way of attaining this end was to march at the head

---

[1] Sleidan.

of Germany and to recover from the French the three imperial cities which had just been taken from him. He had no difficulty in mustering a formidable army, and at the end of September he advanced upon Metz.

Francis of Lorraine was awaiting him there, and had been fortifying the place ever since August. He held his ground with the greatest courage and determination. It was no easy matter to resist a besieging army of 60,000 men, with 114 pieces of artillery and some of the best infantry in Europe.

The emperor had declared that he would not raise the siege of Metz if he had to use up three armies one after the other. Guise showed himself equal to his task. He was, moreover, admirably seconded by Peter Strozzi, of Florence, the first military engineer of his time. They did not hesitate to destroy all the public buildings that stood in the way of the defence. They sent away all the inhabitants who could not fight. The first lords of France, following the example set by Guise himself, worked like sappers, and carried the hod as an example to the rest.

Coligny had sent a part of his infantry to join Guise in Metz. He himself remained outside the town, under the orders of the Constable, who was in charge of an army of observation. In the letters which he addressed to Guise from his camp, we still trace the old affection which past misunderstandings had failed to destroy. Writing on October 15th, Coligny says :

" I would it were my fortune to be near you when the Emperor comes to besiege you, for though you have many good men, I flatter myself that my men" (referring to his infantry, whom he had sent into Metz) "would do none the worse for having me among them, and by the same occasion I could let you know by experience the desire I have always had to find myself in a position to do you service. Since this cannot be now, it shall be at some future time."[1]

The army of observation under the command of the Constable had to watch the Margrave Albert of Brandenburg, one of the German princes, who the previous year had signed an alliance with the King of France, and who had not joined the emperor. The Margrave, at the head of a large body of lanzknechts, was occupying Pont-à-Mousson. It was suspected that he would lend the support of his troops to whichever side bid highest for them. Henry II. thought he had got him out of the way by offering him 100,000 crowns if he would fall back upon Belgium, doing all the harm he could to the emperor on the road. The Margrave accepted these conditions, and began his retreat, closely followed by the Duke d'Aumale. But all at once, throwing off the mask, he declared for the emperor, threw himself (October 28th) on d'Aumale's corps, made the duke prisoner, and then went to join the besieging forces before Metz. At the same time one of Charles V.'s lieutenants, Antoine de Croy, advanced into Picardy with 15,000 Belgians, and surprised Hesdin.

The king lost not a moment. Having received

---

[1] Delaborde, vol. i., p. 111.

from Guise the assurance that Metz would hold out against Charles, who had been besieging it since October 18th, he left one army corps in Lorraine and resolved to cover Picardy. With this view he sent for Coligny, and in consideration of the good and continual services which he had rendered, and was daily rendering, to the king, he bestowed on him the honourable title of Admiral of France,[1] and at the same time made him his lieutenant, to conduct his army from Lorraine into Picardy.[2] Coligny immediately joined Antoine de Bourbon, Duke de Vendôme, then governor of Picardy, and marched upon Hesdin, which surrendered (December 19th) after two days' siege. This rapid success not only saved Picardy, but decided Charles V. to raise the siege of Metz. The emperor was really afraid that he might be attacked in his entrenchments by the forces of the Constable. His furious assaults upon Metz had been unavailing. In vain had he cannonaded the old city ; the crumbling ramparts were built up again every night by the besieged, whose sorties became more and more frequent. The icy temperature of the beginning of December, followed by a heavy fall of snow, had cruelly tried his army, whose camping-ground was reduced to a mere swamp. Typhus was raging ; it was reckoned that a third of the soldiers had died. Charles V. himself was paralysed with gout. In despair he gave the order to raise the siege, January 1st, 1553. "I see," he exclaimed bitterly, "that fortune is of the feminine

---

[1] His predecessor, Annebaut, had just died of fever at La Fère, in Picardy, which he was defending against the enemy. Rabut in, *Guerres de Belgique.*

sex, and likes a young king better than an old emperor." He fell back upon Belgium.

The year 1553 opened under happy auspices for Coligny. The brilliant success of the campaigns in Lorraine and Picardy had filled France with joy, and Henry II. celebrated the beginning of his reign by a succession of fêtes, which recalled the palmy days of Francis I.

On the 12th of January Coligny, who, as we have said, had just been made Admiral in place of Anne-baut, was to take the oaths of his new office in a solemn session of parliament. Étienne Pasquier has handed down to us an account of this assembly, at which he was present. Christophe de Thou spoke first as advocate of the Admiral, and praised Coligny's ancestors. Then Pierre Séguier, first advocate to the king, made an attempt at wit, after the style of the Renaissance school. " He began by playing upon the name Admiral—'*Admiramur cælum, admiramur terram, admiramur marem,*' and from this proceeding to the estate of admiral, introduced by a thousand fine reasons which he enumerated, he concluded not to hinder the verification of the letters, the adminis-tration of the oath, and the reception of the Sire of Châtillon into this estate." After which, M. Gille Lemaître, the first president, " bade him, on the authority of the court, to come up and take his place among the highest seats, not, however, as Admiral, since his predecessors had never occupied such a position, but as Governor of Paris and of the Île-de-France."[1]

---

[1] Est. Pasquier, *Recherches de la France*, vol. ii., ch. xv.

In accepting these functions, Coligny did not give up those of colonel-general of the French infantry, but he retained them, says Brantôme, with a view to handing them over to his brother Andelot, who was still a prisoner in Milan.[2]

---

[1] The French fleet, which played so important a part in the fourteenth century, and which almost disappeared in the fifteenth, only came into notice again under Francis I. We have spoken already of the abortive attempt made by that monarch to organise a descent upon England, under the command of Admiral Annebaut. On this occasion he had got together 150 large ships, 60 small vessels, and 25 galleys; but it was all an illusive show. France, in the sixteenth century, could only man small fleets. It was under Richelieu that she became again a great maritime power. In the curious sketch of the state of France under Francis II., given by the Venetian Michele Loriano, we feel in what slight estimation the French fleet was held. As to the office of Admiral (the word, according to Littré, comes from the Arabic *amir*, commander), it was in existence in the time of St. Louis. It became one of the highest offices in the kingdom, and in the fifteenth century, when the fleet was at such a low ebb, it was often given to men who had never commanded a vessel. Under Francis I. Chabot and Annebaut played a part of some importance. Francis I. defined the duties of an Admiral. He was to have absolute jurisdiction over all the seaboard of France (the maritime provinces retaining their vice-admirals); he was to command the fleets and the marines, and to appoint the officers. After the disgrace of Chabot, however, this right of appointing the officers went back to the crown. The Admiral had, moreover, the first claim on all prizes taken at sea. In Vieilleville's *Mémoires* of the year 1553, I find a very curious conversation of the Marshal with Saint André. The king had offered the title of Admiral to Saint André before offering it to Coligny. Saint André consulted Vielleville on the subject, and he in his reply shows with amusing *naïveté* the opinion then entertained of the future of the French navy. "In truth," he said, "the sea does not suit us Frenchmen. If we were in Spain, Portugal, or England, you should by all means accept the post of Admiral, for there it is the highest of all, inasmuch as their great strength is their navy. But being a Frenchman, I pray you, sir, change not your lance, your war-horse, and your gilt spurs for the sail, the wheel, or the mast."

CHAPTER V.

HENCEFORTH Coligny will appear in our
pages under the title of Admiral, by which
he is best known to the public. Is it true, as has
been often said, that the title was a purely honorary
one, and that there was nothing in the services
rendered by him to justify it? In order to answer
this question, we must slightly anticipate some events
which transpired later in the life of Coligny. Though
somewhat out of order, this seems to us the best
place for giving an outline of the first colonial expedition which he attempted to organise.

It is certain that Coligny never exercised any
great naval command. The only action in which he
was directly engaged was the attack on the Isle of
Wight, under his predecessor, Admiral Annebaut.
He was then twenty-five years of age, and, as we
have already said, commanded a galley. It was
also due to his energy that on August 11th, 1555,
the sailors of Dieppe won a brilliant victory over
twenty-four Flemish vessels;[1] and fifteen years later,

---

[1] The Spanish Government had seized and confiscated all
the French ships in the ports of the Low Countries. Henry II.

during his last sojourn in Rochelle, the attention he gave to maritime affairs there made that port afterwards the Carthage of the Huguenots.

It was in another branch of service that Coligny vindicated his right to the title of Admiral. He was the first French statesman who thought seriously of founding colonies, and if success did not crown the enterprise, it was through no fault of his, for he threw himself into it with all his characteristic tenacity of purpose.[1]

Beside his desire to extend the influence of France, two other motives impelled him to this attempt at colonisation : first, his wish to spread the faith of Christ far and wide ; and second, to provide a place of refuge for those who were persecuted for the reformed religion. Long before he himself threw in his lot with the Huguenots, Coligny, as Beza tells

---

was greatly embarrassed how to find a fleet which should avenge this injury. Coligny formed the idea of appealing to the patriotism of the shipowners of Dieppe. In a short time they had equipped nineteen vessels, at the head of which Coligny placed Louis de Bare, Sieur d'Épineville. Though with so small a fleet, he boldly attacked twenty-four Flemish vessels, August 11th, 1555, and completely scattered them. (See the full account of this engagement in *Les Batailles navales de France*, Troude, vol. i., p. 73.)

[1] We are not forgetting the earlier attempts—unhappily without result—made by some of our seamen to get a footing in the new world. Captain Denis, of Honfleur, touched at the Brazils in 1504 ; Captain Parmentier, of Dieppe, at Madagascar and Sumatra in 1529. In 1506 the same Denis discovered Newfoundland. In 1524 the Florentine Verrazano, in the service of Francis I., discovered the coasts of Florida. In 1534 the Breton Jacques Cartier, of St. Malo, discovered Canada. The whole of North America was called New France ; but the only colony, properly so-called, which can be mentioned is that which Francis I. founded in Canada in 1540, under Roberval, which came to a miserable end.

us, "favoured their cause as far as possible." His
first relations with Geneva arose in the following
manner.

Nicolas Durand, Sieur de Villegagnon, a distinguished seaman, who had taken part in the
expedition sent by Charles V. into Africa, and to
whom the king had confided the charge of conveying
Mary Stuart from Scotland to France, was made
Vice-Admiral of Brittany by Henry II. He was of
a hasty and irritable temperament, and encountering
opposition to his orders at Brest, he resolved to quit
Europe and to go and found a colony in America.
Villegagnon opened his project to Coligny, and
"told him that his intention was to find some place
in America which he could fortify as a place of
retreat for those of the Protestant religion who were
willing to repair to it, so that the country might
be gradually peopled, the Church of God extended,
and the inhabitants brought to a knowledge of the
truth." [1]

This, then, was the first of those emigrations for
the sake of religious liberty, which a century later
were to people great districts of North America with
English fugitives, and to scatter French Huguenots
all over the world.

Was Villegagnon sincere in the outset of his
enterprise ? We see no reason to doubt it. He had
joined the Protestant party, but he was, as Beza

---

[1] Theodore Beza, *Hist. Eccl.*, 1883, vol. i., p. 185. As this
is our first reference to this history, we cannot forbear expressing our high obligations to MM. Baum and Cunitz, who
have prepared this edition of the work which bears Beza's
name.

says, a "creature of impulse," whose disappointed ambition soured his whole nature. Coligny entered into his project with eagerness. He spoke of it to the king, "urging him," says Beza, "not for the sake of the kingdom of God, but for the sake of the advantage which might accrue to his own kingdom, as it had done to Spain, from such colonisation." Henry took no interest whatever in a Protestant emigration, being always very bitter against his heretical subjects; but the renown of the Spanish colonies tempted him, and he gave Villegagnon the command of two vessels.

They sailed from Havre in the middle of the summer of 1553. On the 15th of November following, they cast anchor in the bay of Rio Janeiro. Villegagnon took possession of a small island, to which he gave the name of Coligny. He began to erect a fort, and wrote to the Admiral to ask him to send him some more colonists and two Protestant ministers.

Coligny forwarded this request to the Consistory of Geneva, through one of his old neighbours in the Gâtinais, a Huguenot seigneur, the Sieur du Pont, who lived in the territory of the Republic. Jean de Léry [1] says: "The Church of Geneva returned thanks to God for the extension of the kingdom of Jesus Christ in such distant countries, in so strange a land, and among a people who were wholly ignorant of the true God." It was decided that the emigrants should be placed under the conduct of the Sieur du

---

[1] Jean de Léry was one of the emigrants who joined Villegagnon, and who has left a very interesting account of his voyage to Brazil, from which we quote.

Pont. Two ministers of religion, Richier and Chartier, were sent with them, and some skilled workmen. Villegagnon's letter warned the colonists of the difficulties and dangers of the voyage. He told them "they must be content to eat, instead of bread, a kind of flour made from a root, and as to wine they must look for no new wine, for none grew there." "All those, therefore," says Jean de Léry, "who loved the theory better than the practice of these things, and did not care to change worlds or to encounter the dangers of the sea and the heat of the torrid zone, or to see the antarctic pole, refused to enter the lists and would not enrol themselves or embark on such a voyage." Fourteen emigrants started from Geneva. They passed through Châtillon-sur-Loing, where they found Admiral Coligny in his house, which was one of the most beautiful in France. He not only encouraged them to pursue their enterprise, but also promised to assist them in the matter of a vessel. "Setting before us many reasons for going, he gave us hope that God would grant us to see the fruit of our labours."

When they sailed from Honfleur, November 28th, 1556, the emigrants numbered 290. Among them were six boys whom they took, that they might learn the language of the barbarians. They embarked in three vessels.

On the 9th of March, 1557, they arrived at the Island of Coligny. Villegagnon received them with open arms. "My children," he said, "for I mean to be a father to you ; as Jesus Christ, when He was in this world, did nothing for Himself, but all that He did was done for us, so having a hope that God will preserve my life till you shall have established yourselves in this country and are able to do without me, all that I seek to do here is for you and for those who shall come after for the same end that you have come. For I purpose to make here a retreat for the poor of the faith who are persecuted in France, in Spain, and elsewhere beyond the sea, so that without fear, either of king, emperor, or any other potentates, they may serve God according to His will."

Nothing could be more edifying at first than the attitude of Villegagnon. He would pour forth sighs and prayers to God that He would " give His blessing to this Island of Coligny, and to the whole country of Antarctic France. He would discourse excellently of religion and of the Christian reformation. But the impression of him soon changed. It was seen that he had the spirit of a despot. Not only did he exact from the colonists herculean tasks of manual labour, but he attempted to force upon them his theological views. On two points he was at variance with the Huguenots—the episcopate and the Lord's Supper. In these respects he adhered more closely than they did to the Catholic tradition. Any opposition exasperated him. To these disciples of Calvin he declared that Calvin was " a wicked heretic who had erred from the faith."

His companions, indignant at this change of attitude, supposed that they had been duped ; that Villegagnon had sold himself to the Cardinal of Lorraine, and had only assumed a Protestant mask. But if he really wished only to injure the Huguenots, why need he have made so great a venture, and

risked his own life at the very outset? There is a
simpler explanation. Villegagnon was one of those
tyrannical and impulsive persons whom contradiction
exasperates, and passion easily misleads. He died
insane, and his conduct from the arrival of the
Genevese colonists betrays already some degree of
mental aberration. This unsoundness of mind soon
led him to commit an act of atrocious perfidy.
Some of the colonists, especially the strong Calvinists
of the party, could not endure the yoke laid upon
them, and declared their intention of returning to
France. Villegagnon encouraged them to do so.
But among the papers which he entrusted to the
captain of the ship which took them back, "there
was," says Jean de Léry, "an indictment which he
had framed against us without our knowledge, and
an express charge to the first judge to whom it
should be handed over in France, that in virtue of
the same he should detain us and have us burnt
as heretics, which, said Villegagnon, we were."
Happily the fugitives on their arrival fell into the
hands of good and humane magistrates, who gave
them a kind reception, and supplied them with
money to continue their journey. "Thus," says the
simple chronicler, "does God take the crafty in their
own net; for by the means of these good men He
not only delivered us from the danger into which
Villegagnon had brought us, but furthermore the
treason which he had plotted being discovered, the
whole turned to our comfort and to his confusion."

Unhappily five of the colonists, who had started
to return to France, being terrified at the bad state
of their vessel, decided to get into a boat and

go back to the Island of Coligny. Villegagnon had them arrested, and brought against them a charge of heresy. After a mere form of trial he chose out three of them, Du Bordel, Vermeil, and Bourdon, and had them strangled and thrown into the sea.

It is easy to see that acts like these were of a nature to ruin the colony. Soon after, Villegagnon conceived the unfortunate idea of leaving the island and going with some of his companions in search of more fertile lands on the shores of Brazil. This would have been certain death. The Portuguese would have soon exterminated them. Villegagnon returned to France, turned against the reformers, and published violent controversial articles against Calvin and Coligny. But, suspected by the Catholics, and despised by the Protestants, he ultimately lost his reason, and died in 1571.

Jean de Léry asserts that if Villegagnon had accomplished his mission and stood firm at his post, "there would have been more than 10,000 Frenchmen, who beside the good use which they by this time would have made of our island and fort against the Portuguese (who would never have been able to take it, as they have done since our return), would have been now holding for the king a large district of land in Brazil, which might then still have been called Antarctic France."

We shall see presently that this failure, disastrous as it was, did not put an end to the Admiral's schemes of colonisation. He returned to the project in 1560, and again in 1564, at the close of the first war of religion. None of these attempts were successful. The French government never really looked on them with favour. It seems even that their collapse was hastened by treachery. Nevertheless truth compels us to say that in Florida, even more than in Brazil, " the misfortune was that those who could not be quelled by fire or water, fell victims to their own folly."[1] The colonists were themselves mainly responsible for the failure of their projects.

[1] René de Laudonnière, *Hist. notable de la Florida*, p. 53. Laudonnière was commander of the expedition of 1564.

CHAPTER VI.

WHILE the ill-fated expedition to the Brazils was going on, events of importance were transpiring in Europe, to which we must now revert. Let us go back to the year 1553, the year in which Coligny was made Admiral.

Charles V. had but one idea at this time—to avenge the humiliation to which he had been subjected before Metz. He had just appointed to the command of his troops Philibert Emmanuel, Duke of Savoy, one of his bravest captains. Poor as a Savoyard, and dispossessed of his estates by France, Philibert Emmanuel had his fortune to make, and he was soon to be successful enough to marry the sister of that King of France against whom he was taking up arms. The soubriquets of the *Iron Head* and the *Prince of the Hundred Eyes*, given him by his soldiers, indicate his characteristic firmness and vigilance, of which France was to have bitter experience. In a single month the Spanish army took Thérouanne and Hesdin, two of the most important fortresses in the north. In the taking of Thérouanne Francis de Montmorency, son of the Constable, was made prisoner ; and at Hesdin, the same fate befell Robert de la Marck, Duke de Bouillon, Marshal of France. These startling tidings fell like a thunderbolt upon the effeminate courtiers of Henry II., who thought of Charles V. as already dead with chagrin at having been forced to abandon Lorraine. Henry himself went north with a small army, in which Coligny commanded the infantry. He succeeded in arresting the progress of the Spaniards without gaining any decisive advantage over them. Winter came on, and the resumption of hostilities was deferred till the spring of 1554.

In the month of June the King of France advanced as far as Namur. Dinant surrendered after a furious assault, in which Coligny was wounded. On August 8th the French took up a position before Renty. The Spaniards charged them, and at first had the advantage. They were skilfully massed in a wood, called the Bois-Guillaume, which completely foiled the charges of Guise's brilliant cavalry. Coligny saw that here was the nucleus of the action, and marching at the head of his infantry, he dislodged the enemy, who were then pursued and scattered by the cavalry.[1] Brantôme says : " The Admiral advanced with from a thousand to twelve hundred men, some armed with arquebuses and others cuirassiers,

---

[1] M. Delaborde has with justice given prominence to the Admiral's share in this affair, the credit of which has been too largely assigned to Guise and Tavannes.

himself marching at their head, halbert in hand, and fell with such fury upon the enemy, that in a twinkling he had broken the Spanish arquebusiers and driven them from their position in the wood, though their numbers were twice as great as his. This was no small service."

On the evening of this battle, and in the presence of the king, a sharp altercation took place between Guise and the Admiral. Guise was describing the combat. At one point Coligny felt constrained to contradict him ; whereupon Guise exclaimed angrily : " Mort Dieu ! do you cast a slur on my honour ?" Coligny replied : " I do no such thing." " Nor could you," said Guise. The king commanded them to make peace ; but this quarrel brought to light the mutual aversion which had long been growing secretly, and their contemporaries, De Thou, La Place, and Brantôme, date from this time the breach which was for ever to divide the two great captains.

The battle of Renty was the most important engagement of this year. The two armies remained face to face till they went into winter quarters. The king, in token of his satisfaction, gave Coligny a company of a hundred men-at-arms, which Coligny made one of the best corps in the army.[1]

The year 1555 found the Imperialists and the French face to face on the northern frontiers of the

---

[1] The companies of orderlies, or men-at-arms, were fifteen in number, and each one included a hundred *lances garnies*. A *lance garnie* consisted of six men, viz., the man-at-arms, a page or valet, three archers, and a cutler, or man armed with a knife. " Coligny," says Sandraz (book ii., p. 142), " was careful to fill his company with gentlemen of proved military service, so that it put to shame all others. This

kingdom. Antoine de Bourbon, Duke de Vendôme, husband of Jeanne d'Albret, was, as we have said, Governor of Picardy. The death of his father-in-law, Henry of Navarre, compelled him to remove to the states of his wife, and he resigned his office.

The King of France, without hesitation, gave the post of governor to Coligny. This favour was the result of a secret engagement between the king and the Constable. Montmorency had asked the governorship of the Isle of France for his son, Francis de Montmorency. Francis was still a prisoner in the hands of the Spaniards ; but it was an understood thing that on his return from captivity Coligny should give up the governorship to him.

In his new position Coligny at once displayed his extraordinary activity. But he had a difficult task. The state of the public finances scarcely enabled him to provide adequately for the fortification of a province which he regarded as the true bulwark of France, for he was wont to say that the smallest village of Flanders or Artois was more important in his eyes than a province in Italy. Heavy as were his duties in Picardy, Coligny contrived to go to the east of France at the end of the year, to hold out a helping hand to the Duke de Nevers, who was revictualling Marienbourg and Rocroy, which were threatened by the enemy. "The Duke de Nevers," says Brantôme, "did the king good service in the

---

was not done, however, without expense, and beside the king's pay, he gave to every such soldier one hundred crowns yearly from his own purse. The Duke of Guise, who watched all Coligny did, seeing that by this he had made so fine a company, offered even a higher price, and the rivalry between them was the cause that never were seen such splendid troops."

victualling of Marienbourg, aided by the Admiral,
who had come to join him in Champagne. Their
united forces succeeded in victualling the place, but
with all the trouble in the world, through the worst
rains and frosts that winter ever brought (for it was
the beginning of November), and in the teeth of the
Prince of Orange, who was sent by the emperor and
Queen Mary with a good army to oppose them.
Yet the duke and the Admiral brought their task to
an excellent conclusion, to the great admiration of
the king and of every one, for they had to fight
against heaven, which is a great impossibility."[1]

Charles V., however, had just come to a great
decision. In a solemn assembly convoked in Brussels
on the 25th of October of this year (1555) he had
announced his intention of soon abdicating, and of
handing over to his son, Philip II., the sovereignty
of the Low Countries.[2] At the same time he showed
a desire to conclude a treaty with the King of
France, and as a preliminary he offered an exchange
of prisoners.[3] Henry II. looked favourably on these

---

[1] Brantôme, *M. de Nevers, François de Clèves.*

[2] The news of this abdication took every one by surprise.
Henry II., writing to Coligny and Nevers, November 5th, to
congratulate them on having saved Marienbourg, adds: "The
emperor is much disturbed in mind, so that he has little or no
resolution left, and, in truth, his acts show there is more amiss
with him than he says." Paul IV. came to the same conclusion, and in the Consistory in the following December
declared that it was notorious that the emperor was *impos
mentis.* (Letter from Cardinal du Bellay, in *Lettres et
mémoires d'état,* vol. ii., p. 623.) The pope and the king
were soon to learn to their cost that Charles V., in his pretended retreat, was the secret and watchful instigator of the
Spanish policy. It might well be thought, however, that he
was weary of war.

Charles V. was not influenced simply by a desire for peace

proposals, and charged Coligny to carry on the negotiations. The Sieur de l'Aubespine was associated with him in this trust.[1]

They were to meet the envoys of the emperor, the Count Lalaing and Councillor Simon Renard, at Vaucelles, on December 13th.

Two questions were to be decided by them—the exchange of prisoners and the conclusion of a truce. The French looked upon these two points as inseparable ; the envoys of the emperor wished to treat on them apart. Among the prisoners there were men of the highest rank : on the French side were Andelot, Coligny's brother ; Francis de Montmorency, his cousin ; Robert de la Marck, Duke de Bouillon and Marshal of France. On the Imperial side were Count Mansfeld and the Duke d'Arschot.

The envoys of Charles V. and of Philip II. demanded as a condition of the release of the Duke de Bouillon, that his principality, then occupied by France, should be restored to the empire. The duke on this occasion showed a rare disinterestedness. " He implored Henry II. not to consent to surrender Bouillon, urging him to hold that and all the duke's other possessions as his own, and declared that he would rather remain a prisoner another ten years or

He had learned that just at this time (October 14th, 1555) the Guises were negotiating in Italy a secret alliance with the pope, an alliance the terrible consequences of which France was to experience two years later.

[1] As soon as the Guises knew that this task had been entrusted to the Admiral, they worked upon the king, through Diane de Poitiers, to get d'Estrées appointed in his stead, but in this intrigue they were not successful. See a *Letter from Francis of Guise to the Cardinal of Lorraine*, quoted by Delaborde, vol. i., p. 155.

all his life, and endure whatever ill-treatment they might choose to inflict on him, than he would consent that any one of the said places should be given up to the prejudice of the king's service and of his kingdom."

It was not till February 5th, 1556, that the plenipotentiaries were prepared to sign the Peace of Vaucelles. The question of the prisoners remained in abeyance, owing to the delays which Philip II. (who now appeared for the first time on the scene) introduced into the negotiations. Throughout the discussions Coligny showed the utmost firmness. This the king acknowledged in writing to him on January 25th. "My cousin," he writes, "having seen the despatch of your last day of negotiations, I would say to you, apart from the memorial I send you containing my final intentions, *that I could not be more satisfied and well-content with any servant than I am with you*, who have so well and skilfully conducted this negotiation, that never was service done more to my pleasing," etc. Anne de Montmorency confirmed this testimony in writing to his nephew, under date February 6th : "You have done so well that the result is far better than we thought or could have dared to hope. . . . I assure you the king is as satisfied and pleased as he can be, knowing that you have so well carried out his mind in all things, both small and great, so that nothing has been forgotten."[1] The treaty which was concluded

---

[1] We may note here one point of detail which shows the Admiral's greatness of soul. One of Guise's first concerns at the time of the signing of the treaty was to get rid of the German auxiliaries who were quartered in his town of Guise

on February 5th arranged a truce of five years between " their imperial majesties, the emperor, his son, the King of England, and the very Christian King of France." During these five years all things were to remain as they were, and each power pledged itself not to undertake any enterprise which could damage the other powers, and not to give any succour to their enemies. As to the prisoners it was agreed, in a general way, that they should be set at liberty on both sides, on payment of a ransom, to be fixed after a declaration made by each one in writing, of the value of his yearly rentals, estates, etc. In the case of the Duke de Bouillon, Francis de Montmorency, and the Duke d'Arschot, it was stipulated that their ransoms should be fixed within a term of three months. It now remained for the sovereigns to ratify the treaty. Coligny and l'Aubespine were designated to go to Brussels to receive the oath of Charles V. and Philip II. Lalaing undertook the same mission to the King of France.[1]

and on his lands. He wrote to Coligny on the subject. Coligny replied, under date of February 12th, 1556, that he had already himself provided for that, having sent the said Germans to another garrison, "*out of the desire I had to relieve your town and spare your wood.*" And he added: "And you may be sure, that in all other matters in which I see that I can secure your advantage, profit, and commodity, I shall not wait for your commands, but shall act with all promptness, out of the desire I have to do you service." It would be difficult to conceive a more generous return for the hostility which Guise had just manifested to Coligny.

[1] The negotiations relating to the Peace of Vaucelles are given at length in M. Delaborde's book (vol. i., ch. vii.). The curious narrative from which we give extracts is obviously written by an eye-witness. It is found in Ribier's excellent collection, *Lettres et mémoires d'état, etc., sous les règnes de François I., Henri II., and François II.* (Paris, 1666).

In March, Coligny left for Brussels, with an escort of nearly a thousand persons, including men of high rank and captains of various places in Picardy. But at Cambray the Count de Bossut, grand equerry to the emperor, informed the Admiral that Charles V. had already convoked an assembly at Brussels of all the orders of the Low Countries, and that it would be impossible for him conveniently to receive so large a suite. Coligny therefore sent back nearly all the captains who had accompanied him. On March 25th the Admiral arrived in Brussels. The next day it was curious to note the contrast between the light-hearted gaiety of the Frenchmen and the Castilian solemnity which reigned in the court of Charles V. "These French gentlemen who accompanied the Admiral being assembled in the great courtyard of the house, while he was despatching some business, were of so lively a disposition (for 'the French mind is, like the course of the heavens, in perpetual motion) that they could not be quiet, but began most of them to play at 'leap-frog,' which, when it was noised abroad, many Flemish gentlemen and others of quality also came, and found it such good sport that they did the same; but ours carried off the palm, for it belongs to Frenchmen alone to do things with a grace."

Philip II. awaited the Admiral in the castle. He had had the incredible indelicacy to have the great hall hung with tapestry representing the defeat of Francis I. at Pavia. Even this rudeness could hardly astonish those who remembered the petty affronts to which the emperor had subjected his royal prisoner during his long captivity in Madrid; but on an occasion like the present, it seemed almost like a studied insult.

Brusquet, Henry II.'s fool, who had come in the Admiral's suite, took it upon himself to avenge the affront.

The next morning, after mass, just as Philip II. was about to swear on the Gospel to observe the treaty, Brusquet began to cry in a loud voice, " Largess, largess ! " and opening a bag of crowns, threw it into the midst of the assembly.

The avarice of Charles V. had passed into a proverb. He was not one of those who, on the occasion of any public rejoicing, threw money among the people. Every one asked in whose name Brusquet was acting. There was one moment of dumb surprise. Philip II. looked at the Admiral. The Admiral did not know what to say, and presently perceived that the fool meant to give the Spaniards a lesson of generosity in their own palace. But " those present, in number about two thousand, thinking that it was the Prince's liberality, rushed eagerly forward to snatch up the crowns, the archers of the guard being among the foremost, and even pointing their halberds in the struggle. The rest of the crowd was thrown into such confusion that ladies had their hair dishevelled and their purse strings cut, and men and women were tumbled together in so strange a medley, that the Prince had to lay hold of the altar to keep himself from falling down with laughing, and so had the Dowager Queens of France and Hungary, Madame de Lorraine, and others."

A comic scene indeed, and a truly French method of retaliation, which relaxed into momentary laughter even the haughty and sullen face of Charles V.'s sinister son !

On the following Sunday, being Palm Sunday, the Admiral went to pay a visit to the emperor, who was then residing in the Park of Brussels, in his small house, where, while already assuming the guise of the hermit life he was about to lead at Yuste, he nevertheless continued to direct all the affairs of state, having for his sole counsellor the Bishop of Arras.

Charles V. was dressed with the extreme simplicity which he had always affected. Gout obliged him to remain seated on a reclining chair. The room where he was, was hung with black cloth, and all the furniture was draped in black.

" Sire," said the Admiral, " the greatest wish of the most Christian king, my sovereign liege, has always been that it might please God to bless his reign with perfect peace and friendship with all the Christian princes, his neighbours. The germ of this blessing has been laid in a peace concluded with you on the 5th day of February last, which, if God please, shall bring forth a lasting peace between you, your kingdoms, estates, and subjects. It has pleased my lord the king to send me to you to witness the customary oath, which you shall be pleased to take for the observance of the said treaty, as you will see by the letters which he has written, and which it is my honour to present to you on his behalf."

The reply of Charles V. was courteous and noble. He held out his hand to receive the letter from the king. But when he tried to unseal it, his fingers stiffened by the gout, could hardly manage it. Granvelle stepped forward to help him. But the emperor, with the good grace which he knew so well how to show at times, said, " How now, Monsieur d'Arras, would you rob me of this duty which I owe to the king, my good brother ?   Heaven forfend that any one should do it but myself."   Then turning to Coligny, " What say you of me, M. l'Amiral ?   Am I not a brave cavalier to dare to break a lance, who can but barely open a letter ? "

After reading the message of the king, the emperor entered into friendly talk with Coligny.   He prided himself on being descended, through Marie de Bourgogne, from the House of France.   " I hold it much honour," he said, " to have sprung on the maternal side from the stem which adorns and sustains the most famous crown in the world."   He asked news of Henry II., whom he had seen formerly in Spain, when France had sent him thither as a hostage in the place of his father.   " It seems," he went on to say, " but two or three days since he was in Spain, a little prince without a hair in his beard."   He then asked if Henry was beginning to get gray. Coligny said, " Sire, in truth the king has two or three white hairs already, but so have many younger than himself."   " Oh! do not trouble about it," replied the emperor.   " That is less than nothing. I ask after his condition, and I must tell you of my own.   When I was about the same age, and came from Tunis to Naples,—M. l'Amiral, you know the loveliness of the town, the beauty and the grace of the ladies in it ; I am but a man, and would deserve their favours like the rest,—the day after my arrival, in the morning, I called my barber to shave, curl, and perfume me.   I am given a mirror.

I see myself in the same state as the king, my brother. Astonished, I ask, 'What is that?' Says the barber, 'Two or three white hairs.' There were more than a dozen. 'Take them away,' I said to the barber; 'do not leave one.' Now, would you guess what happened?" Addressing himself to the French gentlemen : "A little while afterwards, looking at myself again in the mirror, I found that for one white hair I had taken out three more had come ; and if I had had all these pulled out, in less than no time I should have been as white as a swan."

The rest of the interview was spent in the same free-and-easy talk. The emperor, recognising Brusquet in the Admiral's suite, asked him if he remembered a certain battle in which Marshal Strozzi, to whom Brusquet then belonged, fled before him. "Yes, sire, I remember it well," replied the fool. "It was when you bought those fine rubies and carbuncles which you have on your fingers." All eyes were turned to Charles's fingers, which were swollen and inflamed with the gout ; and even the emperor's attendants could not refrain from bursting out laughing. "I see now," said Charles V., "that one must not judge people by appearances ; thou playest the fool, but I swear thou art no fool."

On March 29th, the emperor was to take the oath to observe the treaty of Vaucelles. Coligny then had another opportunity of seeing Charles V., and it was, no doubt, in this interview that a conversation took place which Brantôme reports, in which Charles gave his opinion of the military leaders of the day. He "placed himself first as a matter of course, then the Constable, then the Duke of Alva."

This high estimate of the military capacity of the Constable may seem strange on the lips of so good a judge. Perhaps Charles V. only intended by it to pay the Admiral a compliment, or perhaps he was thinking of the obstinate and successful resistance Montmorency had made to him in Provence.

Nothing more than these commonplaces passed between the emperor and Coligny.

It was a singular coincidence which thus brought face to face the old monarch who had so long swayed the destinies of Catholic Europe and the young captain who, a few years later, was to be the leader of the Protestant party. Not a word was exchanged between them on the great controversy which was dividing Europe into two hostile camps.

Coligny had no idea as yet of the great part he was to play in history, and Charles, whose sagacity has been somewhat overrated, never suspected that the future of the world would be decided in that religious struggle, the first champion of which, the little Augustine monk, had stood before him thirty years previously at the Diet of Worms, and had been regarded by him as beneath contempt.

Coligny did not hold his mission fulfilled till he had settled the question of the prisoners of war, among whom was his brother Andelot. He broached this subject with Granvelle, Philip II.'s sinister counsellor, whose perfidious and cruel policy was to crush the heart out of the unhappy Netherlands. Granvelle met him, says the Admiral, with "preposterous interpretations," which reopened questions that had been held to be already settled.

At the end of April Coligny returned to France.

After a short stay in Picardy, he went to Chambord, where Henry II. was then residing. The king, in recognition of the great services he had rendered to France, went the month following to spend a few days at Châtillon-sur-Loing. This visit probably marks the zenith of Coligny's fortunes. He took an important part in the deliberations relative to the release of the prisoners. Philip II. had sent Councillor Renard to the French Court as his representative in the matter, and an understanding was at last come to with him.

At the beginning of July Andelot returned from Italy, where he had undergone a long and severe captivity, sometimes even close confinement, without the privilege of corresponding with his friends.

The day after his return, Coligny handed over to him his office of Colonel General of the French infantry.[1] It was at first feared that the captivity of Francis de Montmorency would be still prolonged ; for the Duke d'Arschot, the imperial prisoner whose position corresponded most closely with his, had effected his escape from the Fort de Vincennes. Montmorency, however, also succeeded in obtaining his freedom on payment of a heavy ransom, and on August 17th he entered on his office as Governor of Paris and of the Isle de France, which Coligny had only held that he might transfer it

---

[1] M. Delaborde gives a touching incident which shows how deeply the brothers were attached to each other. On July 12th Coligny wrote a letter about affairs in Picardy, but he did not sign it as governor, that his brother might add his signature of Colonel General (vol. i., p. 228). This office had been promised to Andelot by the king when Coligny was made Admiral.

to him. The unfortunate La Marck, Duke de Bouillon, also recovered his liberty, but he died a few days after, and rumour accused the Spaniards of having poisoned him.

CHAPTER VII.

IN concluding the Peace of Vaucelles, Coligny
thought he had done an important service to
his country. He deemed that France needed time
to recover strength. Anne de Montmorency was
of the same opinion, and on this occasion his long
experience of affairs of state guided him wisely.
Renard wrote to Philip under date of June 24th,
1556 : "The Constable, who is old, far-sighted, and
intimately acquainted with the affairs of the King of
France, who knows just how far he can safely go,
and understands the humour of his lords and their
dangerous cliques, is anxious to maintain the peace
and to build up the reputation of his house as the
author of it. The Guises, on the other hand, are
equally eager to recommence hostilities."[1]

Unhappily an alliance, fatal in its results to
France, was being formed between two ambitious
houses—those of Guise and Carafa.

---

[1] Granvelle's *State Papers*, vol. iv., p. 605.

Francis, Duke of Guise, whose defence of Metz had covered him with glory, was the idol of one party of the French noblesse. His brother, the Cardinal of Lorraine, one of the restless and designing spirits of the age, had his own no less ambitious dreams of the future. Had not *parvenus* like the Sforza, the Medici, the Farnese, quite recently divided up the States of Italy among themselves and taken rank among the reigning families of Europe ? Might not the younger branch of the Lorraines also hope to find its place in the firmament of princes ? We have said that as early as 1547 the Cardinal of Lorraine had dreamed of conquering the kingdom of Naples for one of his brothers. The Guises were descended from the house of Anjou, the former possessors of that kingdom.[1]   The house of Lorraine went back to Charlemagne, and the Guises would presently try to make this a pretext for laying claim to the throne of France. Just now it was Naples that attracted them. But Naples belonged to Spain, and in order to secure this shining toy they were ready to declare themselves the implacable adversaries of that Philip II. whom, three years after, they were to astonish by their servile devotion.

The Carafa were a family of the kingdom of Naples, who had an hereditary hatred of the Spaniards. Pietro Carafa had just been raised to the papacy,

---

[1] Louis (son of Jean le Bon, King of France, who died in 1364) was Duke of Anjou. He had married Marie de Châtillon, Countess of Guise. From this marriage sprang Louis II., King of Sicily, who held the dukedom of Guise, as did his son Réné. Réné of Lorraine, grandson of Réné of Anjou, died in 1508, leaving his son Claude, father of Francis of Lorraine, as his heir.

May 25th, 1555, under the name of Paul IV. Already advanced in age, an ascetic in his habits, and founder of the Theatine order of monks, he was the implacable enemy of Charles V. Irascible, passionate, incapable of forgiving an injury, he gave himself up to the guidance of one of his nephews, Carlo Carafa.

This Carlo Carafa is one of the most prominent personages of the sixteenth century.[1] A man of no character, who led in his youth the life of a *condottiere* and a pugilist, he entered the Church when his uncle became Pope, and was made a cardinal by him June 7th, 1555. From that time he had but one thought—to raise his family to sovereign power in Italy; and for this end he sold himself first to France and then to Spain. Cool-headed, in spite of the ebullitions of passion characteristic of his race, of keen intellect, skilled in all seductive arts, elated by success but never cast down by reverses, he was to be for years the evil genius of his uncle, and in the end to be solemnly condemned by him. After the death of his uncle, Carafa managed to reinstate himself, was foremost in the nomination of the new Pope, and, after making everyone his dupe, died at last in the Castle of St. Angelo, strangled by the very pontiff who owed everything to him.

---

[1] This strange character has just been described very vividly by M. Georges Duruy in a most interesting volume, *Le Cardinal Carlo Carafa*, a study of the pontificate of Paul IV. (Paris, Hachette). By the aid of documents, many of them unpublished, and by a patient analysis of the various texts, M. Duruy has brought the character of Carlo Carafa out in its true light, and has dispelled the legendary prestige with which ecclesiastical panegyrists had invested Paul IV.

Carlo Carafa was so subtle a diplomatist, that he would have been capable of carrying through the most difficult enterprises if he had had any high inspiration. As it is, he figures on the page of history only as a consummate actor, who for more than a year decoyed France to her bitter shame and loss. It is one of Coligny's merits that, from the very first, he clearly saw the true character of this man, and augured the evil he would work.

Paul IV. had only been four months Pope when, under the influence of his nephew, he turned to France and entered into a secret league with her to deliver Italy from the Spaniards.

One question arises here which has always been a great embarrassment to historians. How could Henry II. lend himself to such negotiations at the very time when he was preparing to conclude the peace of Vaucelles? Must we believe, as has been said, that this treaty was only a feint on his part to conceal his real designs? We cannot admit this. The care with which the treaty was prepared, the stress laid upon it by the king, and his explicit approval of Coligny's negotiation of it, show that he was desirous of peace. But it must not be forgotten that there were two rival influences in Henry's Court— that of the Constable, which was favourable to the peace ; and that of the Guises, especially of the Cardinal of Lorraine, who was from the first the tool of Carafa. Diane de Poitiers was anxious for anything that could favour the fortune of the Guises Carafa, while paying court to the mistress, was mindful also of the legitimate queen, and Catherine de Medicis had felt her pride as an Italian flattered by the prospect of freeing her country from the heavy yoke of Spain.

The negotiations were conducted with such rapidity by Cardinal Carafa that on October 13th, 1555, a full treaty of alliance between France and the papacy was drawn up in Rome, and ratified by the King of France. Every possible provision was included in this treaty: the military contingents and the contributions in money to be supplied by the contracting parties, the alliance of some Italian princes and the neutrality of others, the territory of Milan and Naples, which the King of France was to claim; and lastly, the principality which he was to offer to Carafa and his brothers.[1] Evidently the Cardinal had not forgotten his own family; indeed, such was the avidity of these *parvenus*, that they formed a project of marriage between Marie, daughter of Count Montorio, and the Duke d'Alençon, the last of Henry II.'s sons.[2]

Carafa thought he had gained the day. He was already expecting the French army to arrive in Italy, but Henry II. oscillated between two policies. At the very time when he was approving the secret treaty (which he seems, however, not to have communicated to all the members of his privy council), he was pressing Coligny to carry on the negotiations at Vaucelles. This treaty was signed, as we have said, on February 5th. When, ten days later, the

---

[1] The Cardinal had two brothers; the elder, Montorio, to whom Paul IV. had just given the duchy of Pagliano, taken by him from the Colonna family, whom he thus made his mortal enemies; and the second, the Marquis of Montebello.

[2] See the document quoted by M. Duruy (Appendix, p. 354, No. 15).

news of it reached Rome, Carafa was confounded, and the pope flew into one of his terrible fits of rage in which he showed what he really was.[1]

The Cardinal soon recovered, however, from his consternation. He knew that he had allies in the Court of France, and he asked the pope to send him to Paris. As it would have been too great a scandal for a pope to appear to be inciting to war, the ostensible mission of the legate was to strengthen the peace between France and Spain ; but while he was thus to use fair and pacific speech, he had secret instructions from Paul IV. to look after all the necessary military preparations.[2]

The journey of Carafa through France was a triumphal progress. At Fontainebleau and in Paris the great lords, no less than the common people, threw themselves at his feet. The king asked him as a favour to be the godfather of one of his children, and knelt before him to receive the sword blessed by the pope, which Paul IV. had sent him. Everywhere splendid fêtes were given in his honour, while

---

[1] Such facts as this must be borne in mind if we wish to know what Paul IV. really was, divested of the halo of legendary tradition, in which he appears as a pattern of monkish austerity. Read, for example, the account of the reception which he gave, after hearing of the peace of Vaucelles, to MM. de Selve and De Lansac, the king's envoys. After describing the peace as an invention of the devil, and saying that whoever advised it was a servant of the devil and a minister of iniquity, he threatened the ambassadors, if they went through with it, that he would *make their heads fly off their shoulders;* and, growing more excited, he said that he would *strike off hundreds of heads like theirs,* and repeated it several times, choking with rage. (*Lettres et Mémoires d'état servant à l'histoire de Henri II.,* vol. ii., p. 665.)

[2] In M. Duruy's work, p. 160 and following pages, there is abundant evidence of this duplicity of Paul IV.

he, wholly bent on the object of his journey, lost no time in gaining the ear of the king and his councillors, and persuading them to break off the peace. So completely were they carried away by him, that all yielded, not excepting the Constable, who felt that his influence would be endangered if he made much show of resistance. Montmorency's weakness in this way was well known, though he tried to conceal it by an affectation of bluster. The lion's skin, in which he enwrapped himself, did not always hide the old fox. As an excuse for his defection, he alleged the enormous sum which Spain demanded for the ransom of his eldest son, who was still a prisoner. Coligny, and with him a little group of patriotic lords, alone expressed their detestation of the comedy he was playing. An old member of the parliament, and a true Frenchman, Étienne Pasquier, has recorded, with caustic humour, the impression made upon him by the position of affairs.[1] He writes: "Captain Carafa, the pope's nephew, has been made Cardinal by him, and suddenly sent over here to bring to us, not the keys of St. Peter, that he might open to us the gate of heaven, but the sword of St. Paul. You think mayhap that I am jesting. But he has in truth brought the king a gift of a very fine sword, and therewith a challenge to recover the State of Naples, which is the toy of the popes, and the playground of foreign princes. . . . Gentlemen of the house of Guise hold out the hand to this new legation, having, as they deem, some part in the quarrel." With prophetic good sense Pasquier adds : " In brief, it bodes us no

---

[1] Etienne Pasquier, *Œuvres*, vol. ii., p. 73.

good that he who, as head of the Church, should be the first father of peace, should be the first author and promoter of war among Christian princes."

Carafa obtained from the king an explicit assurance that the peace should soon be broken. He asked that the army to be sent into Italy should be entrusted to the Duke of Guise ; he promised the assistance of the Dukes of Ferrara and Parma, and guaranteed a very large levy of soldiers by the pope. On the eve of his departure, intoxicated with his success, and in one of those accessions of pride and folly which reveal his true character, he assembled all the foreign ambassadors, and in their presence heaped all manner of insults on Charles V. and Philip II., saying that the hour of vengeance was at hand. This was so great a scandal, and so enormous a blunder, that he is supposed to have done it in a state of intoxication. Of what avail was all the studied dissimulation he had practised, and the pacific language which he had at all times used in public, when at the last moment he thus betrayed his secret to Spain ?

Coligny had watched with a deeply wounded spirit this new turn of affairs. He had just laboriously concluded the treaty of Vaucelles. All this work done with so much patient effort was now to be thrown away. And why ? No one could allege that it was in the interest of France. The Guises alone were to profit by it. And was the country to be imperilled in an enterprise which might end in disastrous failure, just to secure to them a coveted appanage ? How could such an enterprise be entered on ? Only in defiance of the plighted faith of the nation and the solemn oath of the king, "so that by this counsel of the Guises the peace, which a few months before had been solemnly entered into, would be violated, to the great dishonour of the French nation, and to the regret of the Admiral, who could not cease from foretelling disastrous issues from such perfidy, since God is always and everywhere the Avenger of perjury."[1]

At the end of June, as we have said, the rupture of the peace had been determined. The king, however, thought himself bound to keep it a secret, so that he might choose his own time for attacking the Spaniards without any previous declaration of war. It was the pope who gave the signal for hostilities to commence. At the end of July he accused Charles V. and Philip II. of having given their support to the Colonna in Rome, who were then in revolt against the holy see. Under this pretext he arrested the Spanish ambassador in Rome, and threatened to excommunicate Spain itself. Seeing this, the Duke of Alva, who was then governing Naples, advanced with an army into the 'Roman territory, and took several towns, but did not dare to pursue his advantages, probably remembering the odium cast upon Charles V. in the Catholic world, when in 1527 his soldiers had laid siege to Rome. The pope, in alarm, implored Henry II. to keep his promises, and towards the close of the year the Duke of Guise crossed the Alps. We shall see presently what was the issue of this campaign. We must notice that in sending Guise into Italy, Henry II. had not yet de-

---

[1] *Vita Colinii*, 1575, p. 13.

clared war on Philip II. The Treaty of Vaucelles was not yet broken.

The energy with which Coligny had urged the maintenance of peace, and the firm stand taken by him against the general infatuation about this deplorable enterprise, had irritated the king. Coligny saw this, and feeling himself no longer the man for the position, he wished to resign the government of Picardy. The king begged him not to do so. Coligny obeyed ; but in writing to his uncle the Constable, August 26th, 1556, he let it be clearly seen that for himself the era of royal favour was over : " You know, Monseigneur," said he, " that the recompense which God gives and that which man gives are wholly different ; for God recompenses us after death, and the world during our lifetime. And those whom God loves best are often most tried in this world ; but those whom princes love are signalled out by favours and benefits, else men think nothing of it. *I tell you this because, on my late journey to Paris, I had no gracious word, nor any other mark of favour, by which I or any one else might think that the king was well pleased with me.*" He spoke, moreover, of masters who want to be served " *according to their way of thinking, not according to ours.*"

Evidently Coligny felt that the hour of his disgrace had come, yet his only fault had been that he had dared to give preference to the interests of the country over the king's favour. As to the Constable, though he was, in truth, as opposed as Coligny to the war, he had decided, like an old courtier as he was, to fall in with the prevailing opinion, thinking, no doubt, that the approaching

6

departure of Guise for Italy would leave him master
of the situation at home.[1]

---

[1] At this time (October 1556) we must note an incident in
the life of Coligny which shows that while he had courage to
oppose the king when the welfare of the country demanded it,
he was equally ready to resist his uncle, the Constable, when a
question of morality was involved. Francis de Montmorency,
the Constable's eldest son, and consequently first cousin to the
Admiral, and to whom he was much attached, had fallen in
love with Mademoiselle de Piennes, maid of honour to the
queen, a woman "whose nobility, virtue, and beauty made her
well worthy of his love." He had promised her marriage, and
had made Coligny his confidant. The old Constable, who
knew nothing of this, had himself formed a project to marry
his son to Diane, widow of the Duke de Castro, and illegitimate
daughter of Henry II. His pride as a courtier was much
flattered when the king gave his consent to this union. The
Constable never doubted that his son would be of the same
mind as himself. Driven to despair by this proposal, Francis
de Montmorency at once implored Coligny to interfere on his
behalf, to tell the king the real state of affairs, and entreat
him not to be angry at his refusal. Coligny undertook this deli-
cate task. The Constable had prepared a great feast, to which
the king had consented to come. "As his majesty entered the
house with his retinue of gentlemen, the Constable said to him
that he would God had granted him so much grace that he
might be able to show to the world the obligation he was
under to his gracious majesty for the honour of his permission
to marry his son to the king's bastard daughter. Coligny, on
a previous occasion when there was some talk of marrying a
daughter of Diane de Poitiers to d'Aumale, had expressed himself on this point with uncourtly frankness. He did not think,
like his uncle, that such alliances brought much honour, or gave
much occasion for speaking of the grace of God. The king
having been told by Coligny the state of affairs with Francis de
Montmorency, took the Constable apart just before sitting down
to table and told him how matters stood, saying that he would
not cross the love which his, the Constable's, son bore to
Mademoiselle de Piennes, to whom he was betrothed. The
Constable was so annoyed at this that he was quite melancholy
throughout the whole supper.

"The next morning he was full of the idea of getting this
marriage broken off, saying that he would have recourse to
the pope if necessary. Francis resisted, and appealed, as a

man of honour, to his love and his plighted troth. The Constable would hear nothing. He flew into a rage, and in spite of Coligny's entreaties, he loudly asserted his paternal authority. He even proceeded to violent measures, obtained from the pope the sequestration of the property of Mademoiselle de Piennes, alleged (which was false) that he had received from the pope a letter annulling the promise of marriage, forced his son to break off his engagement, and finally succeeded in getting him married to the Duchess de Castro. Such was the domestic tyranny of the man whom Henry II. was wont familiarly to call his compeer, and to whom he could refuse nothing.'' (See *Le Laboureur, De Thou, Brantôme,* and *La Place* on this incident. See also a letter from Renard to Philip II., quoted by M. Delaborde, vol. i., p. 237.

CHAPTER VIII.

COLIGNY had gone into Picardy, whither Andelot had followed him. He watched anxiously the attitude of the Imperialists, and made every effort to strengthen the places on the frontier. As soon as Francis of Guise had arrived in Italy, taking with him the flower of the French army, Henry judged that the moment had come to throw off the mask, and he commanded Coligny to cross the frontier without any declaration of war, and to seize one of the enemy's strongholds. To violate in this way a solemn treaty was an act of base perfidy, and we know how repugnant it was to Coligny. Nevertheless his sense of duty as a subject and a soldier prevailed. He resolved to surprise Douay. In this city there lived an Italian, formerly a banker at Lucca, a ruined and miserable man, who had built himself a sort of hermitage at the gates of Douay. Clothed in sackcloth like a hermit, he went from door to door begging his bread, but in reality he was ready to sell himself to any bidder. He knew perfectly all the approaches to the city, and came to the French camp to offer his services as a spy. Guided by him, the French army approached Douay in the night of Epiphany, January 6th, 1557, the hour when the Feast of the Kings was being celebrated in every house. But an old woman, whose window looked over the ramparts, saw the French advancing through the dark, and shrieking out "To arms, to arms!" she gave the alarm to the garrison.[1] The Admiral retired and threw himself upon Lens in Artois, which he captured and burned. The king's will was done; and it was upon the most honourable of his captains that the shame fell of carrying out this ill-advised and perfidious scheme. For a moment the king repented and tried to draw back, but it was too late. The Imperialists in their turn had crossed the frontier at many points, and committed depredations in Picardy and Champagne. On the 31st of January, Henry II. declared war against Philip; several months passed, however, before any decisive action took place.

Coligny lost no time, but troops were wanting. The attention of the king was fixed upon Italy, and thither he sent his best forces. No reinforcements reached the Admiral.

Very different was the attitude of the enemy. Philip II. kept up a constant correspondence with his father. He even urged him, on the declaration of war, to quit his retreat at Yuste, thinking that the mere rumour of such an event would strike consternation into the enemy. Charles V. would not leave his solitude, but he displayed the utmost activity in

---

[1] La Popelinière, *Hist.*, vol. i., book 4.

his son's service, raising troops for him, and extorting fresh imposts and large loans of money from Spain.[1] Philip's general-in-chief was Philibert Emmanuel, of Savoy, of whom we have already spoken. Beside his Spanish infantry, the best in Europe, he was enrolling Germans, and had at his disposal the vast resources of the Low Countries, and the excellent cavalry of the Netherlands, led by chiefs young and eager to distinguish themselves, such as Horn, Egmont, and William, Prince of Orange. Not content with this, Philip went over to England to persuade his wife, Queen Mary, to join the alliance against France. The English had no real reason for taking part in this contest. But Mary was devoted body and soul to her husband, whose cold and selfish heart never knew a throb of affection for her. The fanaticism of Philip was akin to her own ; he was the "*preux chevalier*" of her dreams. She therefore obtained from parliament a declaration of war against Henry II., June 7th, 1557, and sent a herald-at-arms to notify him of the fact. Henry received him at Rheims, and told him that he only treated him with courtesy because he was sent by a lady. He complained bitterly of the perfidy of England, as if he had any room to reproach others, when he himself had just violated his treaty engagements. Hostilities being thus declared, the queen sent an army of 8,000 men from England. Among them were the Earl of Pembroke, Lord Clinton, the three sons of the Earl of Northumberland, and many other scions of the English nobility. The Duke of

---

[1] On this point see Mignet, *Charles Quint; son abdication*, etc., p. 269.

Savoy had thus under his command more than 50,000 infantry and 12,000 horse.

The French army numbered only 23,000 in all, and of these one-third were German mercenaries. It had very few *gendarmes*, for the king had sent all the best of his forces into Italy to serve under Guise. Pending the arrival of the Constable, the king had placed at the head of the army the Duke de Nevers, governor of Champagne, a good general, but not a match for his powerful adversary. Nevers led his army to Pierrepont, but there he learned that the enemy had suddenly marched upon St. Quentin, and was likely to take it. Should he succeed, the road to Paris would lie open before him. Coligny saw the danger, and at once undertook the perilous mission of throwing himself into St. Quentin. He knew that if he could detain the enemy some weeks before its walls, France would have time to recall her armies, and to save the capital ; but he was equally sure that this result would only be obtained if he thus threw himself into the breach. In fact, St. Quentin had no garrison. Its citizens had always refused to receive one, on the ground of their municipal franchise. Its fortifications only consisted of an old wall without bastions, which could be commanded by the artillery of the besiegers, and which in many places was crumbling to ruins. A prolonged defence was impossible ; the place must be taken. The Admiral knew this perfectly well, so that his throwing himself into it was an act of noble self-sacrifice.

On August 2nd, at daybreak, Coligny left Pierrepont with only a few companies. When he reached

Ham he commanded his captains to send back their orderlies, since they were about to shut themselves up in a place where provisions would have to be eked out.

Taking with him therefore only 450 men, the next night he entered the city, which covered so large an area that, according to the testimony of one of the enemy's officers, it would have required at least 8,000 soldiers to form an efficient garrison.[1] The governor was a Captain de Breuil, a Breton, but he had only been in office ten days, and had himself but a small number of men. There was first what was called the Dauphin's company, consisting of a hundred soldiers, then forty gunners from among the citizens, and as many archers. The town possessed only fifteen cannon and twenty-one wall-pieces.

The Spaniards had invested it from August 2nd, and had even made one unsuccessful attack upon the Faubourg d'Isle, which was repulsed by the city militia, into whom the mayor, Gibercourt, had succeeded in instilling some of the courage by which he distinguished himself to the end.

St. Quentin is situated on the right bank of the Somme, to the north-west of the river. There was one bridge communicating with the Faubourg d'Isle on the left bank, which was only protected by a low wall. On the south-west the city was surrounded by great marshes, which rendered any attack impossible; the enemies had invested it on the north, east, and south. On the east the wall extended in

---

[1] Ch. Gomart, *Récit du Siège de St. Quentin, par un officier espagnol*, p. 411.

a straight line, forming a succession of curtains without bastions, and flanked with simple round towers
projecting for two-thirds of their thickness. The
absence of bastions enabled the enemy to come right
up to the foot of the curtains. Saint Rémy, an
engineer, who was with the Admiral, and who had
gone through several famous sieges, declared frankly
that " he had never been in so bad a place."

Such was the town into which Coligny threw himself, and where he was to sustain a siege famous in
history. We shall try and follow him through it by the
aid of his own journal. This journal is a sober, plain
narrative of about fifty pages, given in true military
style. It does not contain one word written merely
for effect ; not one self-complacent reflection. It
breathes throughout the spirit of a true patriot and
hero.[1]

As soon as he entered the town, Coligny repaired to the Faubourg d'Isle, and decided to
defend it as long as was at all possible, so as to
preserve on the left bank a position from which he

---

[1] Coligny's *Discours sur le Siège de St. Quentin* has often
been reproduced. In order to form a true idea of the whole
situation, Coligny's narrative ought to be supplemented by the
records of the siege taken from the town archives and reproduced by Gomart, *Extraits originaux d'un Manuscrit de
Quentin de la Fons* (St. Quentin, 1856), and *Siège de St. Quentin
et bataille de St. Laurent* (St. Quentin, 1859). The differences,
which are only slight, between these manuscripts and the
Admiral's narrative, refer chiefly to the part taken by the
inhabitants. Coligny, writing as a soldier, does not attach
much value to the services rendered by the city militia. The
Mémoires quoted by M. Gomart, on the other hand, lay great
stress on the courage of the inhabitants. We would draw
attention to an extremely curious document published also by
M. Gomart, *Récit du Siège de St. Quentin, par un officier
espagnol.* A remarkable work of unknown authorship.

could hold out a hand to the French army. The boulevard which formed its boundary was commanded by houses situated just outside, and these were already occupied by the Spaniards. On August 3rd the besieged made a sortie to dislodge them, but they only succeeded in setting fire to some houses.

The same day the Admiral assembled the principal inhabitants at the Hotel de Ville, and ordered them to get together all the tools, hods, and baskets which could be used in repairing the ramparts ; told them to form all the inhabitants, men and women, into companies ; and, last, to make an inventory of all the arms and provisions to be found in the town. He also took measures to secure the safety of the flour mills, and to prevent any waste of the munitions of war.

This done, he summoned the captains, and divided the quarters of the town among them. " One thing I implored of them all, namely, that every man who knew or thought of anything that it might be well to do, should tell me of it, and I promised always to receive such suggestions in good part. And as there might be men in the companies who had had much experience in other sieges, I desired they should be told that they would do me a pleasure in telling me of anything they thought might be of service." [1]

He then ordered that all the trees near the ramparts should be cut down. He mounted the clock tower of the great church and studied the position of the enemy's patrols, and the likeliest place for getting

----

[1] *Récit du Siège de St. Quentin*, 1665, p. 192.

supplies brought into the town. While he was doing this, Jarnac, Téligny, and Luzarches made a sortie from the side of Rémicourt as a sort of diversion on the east. On August 4th there was another sortie, which the Admiral had to entrust to Téligny, for he says, " I had so great a pain in the head that I was forced to throw myself on a bed in M. de Jarnac's house."[1]

But the reconnaissance was not successful. Téligny, seeing his men being put to the rout, rushed out to join them, "all unarmed and badly mounted as he was." He was at once surrounded by the enemy and left for dead upon the spot. Hearing this, the Admiral vowed that he would have him "dead or alive." They went out to look for him, and brought him in, but he died immediately. For some days after this there were no great engagements. A Scotchman, whose name we do not know, had invented some fusees full of pounded sulphur and gunpowder, which *were to explode with the shock* ; by this means they were able to set fire to the houses which the Spaniards had occupied ; and from which they were able to fire upon the ramparts. The Admiral meanwhile had been busily employed in making enquiries on the subject of provisions. The inhabitants had declared there were only provisions for three weeks in the place ; Coligny found enough for three months.[2]

---

[1] Although Coligny looked strong, he often suffered from severe indisposition and from attacks of fever, in which his life was in danger.

[2] This is what Coligny says ; but, as Gomart points out, this calculation supposed that they would get rid of all useless inhabitants, a cruel necessity to which Coligny was twice reduced.

He felt, however, the absolute necessity of rein-forcements, and succeeded in sending a message to this effect to the Constable. On August 6th the Constable sent his brother Andelot to him with 4,000 men. Andelot approached by the Gate de Pontoilles on the west, which the enemy had not yet invested, having reserved that position for the 12,000 English sent by Queen Mary, who were expected from day to day. But the Spaniards got wind of the arrival of Andelot, and he had only time to beat a retreat, and on August 8th to make in return a valiant offensive attack, which enabled him to escape. The same day the English arrived with a large train of artillery, and the town was closely blockaded at all points.

In the night of August 8th-9th the Spanish batteries were placed in a commanding position opposite the Faubourg d'Isle. The Admiral then decided to evacuate it, which he did, after first setting it on fire. At daybreak, just as the batteries were about to open fire all along their line, a dense cloud of smoke rose, hiding the retreat of the French, who, crossing the Somme, fell back upon the town. A serious accident happened, to add to the difficulties of their retreat. A powder magazine, situated in a tower which flanked the Porte d'Isle, exploded. The explosion killed forty soldiers, and made a breach by which twenty-five men could have entered abreast. Happily the thick smoke from the burning faubourg prevented the Spaniards perceiving it ; and the French, whose energy seemed inexhaustible, soon built up the breach.

The Admiral next called together all the inhabitants who knew anything of the art of war, and who could be trusted to bear arms. He thus got together " 220 men, fairly armed and equipped." Many of the countrymen, who had taken refuge in the town, refused to work on the ramparts. Coligny made a proclamation that any who refused to work should for the first offence be whipped through the streets, and for the second should be hanged ; that all those who preferred to leave the town might do so that evening by the Porte de Ham, which would be opened to them for that purpose. Seven or eight hundred left accordingly.

"At this time," says the Admiral, " one of the things on which I thought the most, as it was of such pressing necessity, was by what means I could get succour." After well examining the approaches to the place, he observed a marsh, which he told his men to sound, and over which he endeavoured to make a passable way, and by this way he urged the Constable to try and send him reinforcements.

The situation was, in truth, becoming very grave. Coligny had scarcely any artillery. He had found in the town only fifteen cannon and twenty wall-arquebuses. It was impossible therefore to reach the enemy at any distance. On the other hand, with the small number of men at his command, it would be folly for him to attempt to make sorties. He was therefore reduced to defending the ramparts, but the enemy's artillery kept up so hot a fire upon them, that the workmen refused to repair them, and had to be kept at their work by dint of blows.

CHAPTER IX.

ON the 18th of August, the Feast of St. Lawrence, the Constable left La Fère to advance
upon St. Quentin. He had under his command
12,000 Germans, fairly good soldiers, and fifteen
companies of French infantry, in all 16,000 foot-
soldiers and 5,000 cavalry. His plan was to
approach St. Quentin from the south-east, by the
Faubourg d'Isle, and to cannonade this faubourg,
which had just been taken by the Spaniards. While
the enemy was thus engaged, he proposed to get
some flat boats which he had brought on wagons
from La Fère, set afloat on the water on the marshes
to the south of the town, below the faubourg, and
by these he hoped to get 2,000 men within the walls
to reinforce the garrison.

Resolutely executed, this plan might have been
successful. But Montmorency was not the man to
carry out a rapid and effective *coup de main*. He
did not reach the Somme till nearly nine o'clock,

and his army was encumbered with a crowd of menials and wagons, who impeded the march. They surprised the Spaniards, however, who under the fire of the artillery fell back upon the Faubourg d'Isle. Marshal St. André, who was entrusted with the feigned attack on the left, did his part with such effect that the balls reached the camp of the Duke of Savoy, who fell back on the north of the town. The time was come to launch the boats, but the operation was a slow one. It was found very difficult to get them to float, and the Spaniards from the faubourg kept up a sharp fire on all who attempted to cross the marsh. Only 400 men succeeded in reaching the town ; happily Andelot was among them.

The Constable had made one fatal mistake. A little way above St. Quentin there was a road which crossed the Somme by a narrow bridge. This the French ought to have occupied at all costs. The Duke of Savoy saw their mistake, and leading his army to the east of the town, he took possession of this road, by which his troops quickly gained the left bank and advanced upon the Constable's right, setting fire to the stubble fields as they went along, so that the smoke might cover their movements. It was not till two in the afternoon that the Duke de Nevers, whom the Constable had sent out to reconnoitre, became aware that their army was thus being turned. He at once saw that they would be forced to give battle to an army twice as large as their own, and containing some of the best soldiers in Europe. The young Count Rochefoucauld, who was in the advanced guard on the right, seeing their danger,[1] sent messenger after messenger to the old Constable. But he was obstinate, insisting that there was nothing to fear, and that he would give the Spaniards a taste of his metal. Condé attempted to make head against the enemy. He begged Nevers, who was commanding the cavalry, to charge with him, before the Spaniards had crossed in too great numbers. It was too late. The Flemish and Netherlandish cavalry, led by the impetuous Count Egmont, came down the road like a torrent, carrying all before it. Condé and Nevers were quickly out-flanked, and separated from the centre. Enghien, Condé's eldest brother, exclaimed that he would not be wounded fleeing from the enemy ; he turned and sought a glorious death in the midst òf the foe. The Constable, when it was too late, tried to beat a retreat, but he lacked the genius of command, and his undoubted valour could not make up for this deficiency. Thus he had never thought of occupy-ing the Mill of Tout Vent on his right, where fifty arquebusiers could have detained the enemy a long time. His French infantry kept a steady front throughout. They advanced in good order along

---

[1] The Duke d'Aumale, in his *Histoire des princes de Condé*, attributes to Coligny these wise warnings sent to the Constable. But we find from the *Mémoires* of Mergey, who was an eye-witness of all that occurred, that it was La Roche-foucauld who warned the Constable of his danger, entreating him in vain to stop the enemy at the bridge, and meanwhile to send his infantry into the woods, where the enemy's cavalry would not be able to follow them. " I was with La Roche-foucauld all the time," says Mergey, " and heard all that passed between him and the Constable, who either forgot or failed to send his arquebusiers to stop the enemy's cavalry, and thus caused us to be put to the rout."

the road to Grand-Essigny to reach the woods of
Jussy, where the cavalry would not be able to attack
them.   As they retired they presented a forest of
spears, against which the Flemish cavalry and the
German gunners dashed in vain.   Philibert Emmanuel
saw that he could only break their lines with his
artillery.   He therefore brought up his cannon, which
opened great breaches in the compact mass, and
through these the enemy rushed in like a torrent.
The German auxiliaries turned their horses' heads ;
some companies of English light-horse in the service
of France went over to the enemy.   In vain the
infantry tried to re-form.   The greater part of it was
mown down where it stood.

In a few minutes the victory of the allies was
complete.   Half the French army was destroyed ;
the other half taken prisoners or in flight.   The
Duke de Nevers alone succeeded in cutting his way
through at the sword point, and when he reached
Laon he had only 6,000 soldiers left.   Among the
prisoners were the Constable, the Dukes de Montpensier and de Longueville, Marshal St. André, and
many great French nobles.   Philip's army, it was
said, did not lose more than fifty men.   When the
king arrived in the camp the next day, all the
French standards were placed in his hands.

It was the most brilliant victory which Spain had
won since Pavia.

Philip II. showed himself for the first time on a
battle-field.   He was never seen there again.   It
was not that he had a horror of blood.   Few
men shed more blood than he.   But his cowardly
nature recoiled from the dangers of war.   He

7

ascribed to St. Lawrence the honour of this victory, and in memory of the day he afterwards built
the vast and dreary palace of the Escurial in the
form of a gridiron, to suggest the mode of the
martyr's death.

It was thought that the Spaniards would march
upon Paris. This was the advice of their best
generals. The capital was wholly undefended, and
panic reigned. Charles V. was so confident that
they would take this course that he could not conceal
his anger when he heard that his son was remaining
before St. Quentin. Philip was not willing to run
any risks. Moreover, the Duke de Nevers, who had
assembled the relics of his army, put on a bold face,
sent to treat for an exchange of prisoners, and
seemed to suggest by his attitude that France was
still in a condition to fight.

Coligny did not learn at once the whole extent of
the defeat sustained by the Constable. He had seen
him retreat after the four hundred men had entered
the city by means of the boats. " Still," he said,
" although all the forces that were to have come
into the town had not arrived, being prevented by
the enemy, it may be imagined what pleasure I felt
in seeing those who had entered, and most chiefly
my brother Andelot, who came to me like a *second
self* on whom I knew I could rely."

The next day the Spaniards let the besieged know
of their victory, and hoisted, in view of the ramparts,
the banners taken from the French. The inhabitants
were struck with consternation, and most of the
garrison were utterly disheartened. The workmen
hid themselves in cellars and garrets to escape being

sent again to the ramparts.[1]   The leaders had to
redouble their energy.   Happily Andelot was there.
" I can truly say," writes the Admiral, " that but for
him I should have sunk under the burden, for I
could not satisfy alone all the demands made upon
me ; but from the time he entered the town he took
the heaviest share."

This is no exaggerated praise. From the moment
of Andelot's arrival he showed what spirit he was
of.   Having swum across the stream, he scarcely
took time to dry his clothes before he was out
inspecting the ramparts.

We have said that the wall was most endangered
on the east.   Since the Spaniards had occupied the
Faubourg d'Isle, they had set up batteries which,
reaching across the Somme, took this wall obliquely,
and swept it so completely that no cannon could be
mounted there.   Andelot immediately had boats
placed on the top of the ramparts, and these he
filled with earth, so that they formed a parapet,
behind which the French artillerymen and gunners
could find shelter.

Every day gained was one more chance of salvation for France.   This Coligny thoroughly realised,
therefore he went on multiplying the means of
resistance, though he was under no illusion as to

---

[1] This failure of the inhabitants to do their part is not
admitted in the MS. of the town.   According to these, it was
the situation of the ramparts which were raked by the enemy's
fire, which prevented the besieged from remaining on them.
M. Gomart shares this view.   It is difficult to believe, however,
that Coligny would have charged the inhabitants unjustly.
He does not hesitate to admit, moreover, that it was not their
fault, but the fault of the regular soldiers of the Dauphin's
company, that the breach was finally abandoned to the enemy.

what the final issue must be. St. Rémy, a very
skilful engineer, constructed counter mines to meet
the covered ways by which the Spaniards approached
to the very foot of the curtains. The great thing
lacking for the defence was arquebusiers. Nevers,
who had been told of this by the Admiral, promised
to send in three hundred. These stole by night up
to the marshes on the Somme, and tried to cross in
flat boats; but the alarm was given, and only one
hundred and twenty effected an entrance. This was
on the 22nd of August. The evening before, the
Spaniards, who at length had command of fifty siege
pieces brought from Cambray, had opened a terrible
and ceaseless fire upon the east wall. On the north
and west the Flemish batteries and the English
cannon were in play. The masonry of the walls
was so bad that it could not stand the balls, and
gave way in all directions.

On August 24th the besieged were obliged, from
scarcity of food, to send out of the town six hundred
useless mouths. It was a cruel necessity, for the
unhappy fugitives had to fear all kinds of violence on
the part of the besiegers, who were rendered furious
by the unexpected resistance.

The consternation of the inhabitants redoubled.
Coligny went about at night, mixing with the people'
and receiving any suggestions.

Seeing the general despondency, he assembled all
his captains, and told them that " he was fully determined to hold the place, and that if any should
hear him say one word that seemed like giving in,
he implored them to throw him as a poltroon from
the top of the walls into the foss; and if any made

any such proposal to him, he should treat them in like manner."

On the 24th of August, Philip ordered the English archers to shoot eight arrows into the town. Around each arrow was a piece of paper, by which his Majesty promised the inhabitants, if they would surrender, that he would spare their lives and allow them to go wherever they liked, without being despoiled of their possessions. He warned them that the Admiral was deceiving them by false promises, and that if, as was certain, the town was taken by assault, they would all be put to the sword. These arrows were given to the Admiral, who, having read the papers, replied by the same means. The papers which he sent into the Spanish camp contained only these words, "*Regem habemus !*"[1] This reply was sublime in its heroic simplicity. It truly expressed his loyalty to his country, which he identified with loyalty to his king. He himself never mentions this incident of the siege. It has been handed down to us by a Spanish officer.

On the 27th of August the situation had become very serious. The enemy's artillery had made eleven breaches in the walls, but Coligny remained immovable. "You see," he said to his men, " how the enemy are strengthening their batteries, and it is likely they may make a great onslaught to-day. I pray you, let every man prepare himself to give them a good reception this first time, and then God shall show us what we are to do next."

But his admonitions were vain. Coligny could

---

[1] Ch. Gomart, *Récit du siège de St. Quentin, par un officier espagnol,* p. 394.

not infuse into the souls of all the defenders of St. Quentin his own heroic spirit. The fatal instant was at hand.

That very day, as had been foreseen, a general assault was made. The Admiral had divided the eight hundred men at his command in such a way that they could defend the eleven breaches already made by the enemy's artillery.

At two in the afternoon, when the fire of their batteries had swept the ramparts as far as possible, the Spaniards advanced. Coligny was fighting valiantly in his breach, when, turning round, he saw the soldiers of the Dauphin's company fleeing into the town, and the enemy already almost up to the tower which had been in so cowardly a way abandoned to them. Panic had seized these young and undisciplined troops. Furious at such cowardice, Coligny threw himself into the midst of the fugitives, and tried to lead them back to the ramparts. But it was too late. In an instant he saw himself surrounded by the enemy, and deserted by his followers, with the exception of a young page named d'Aventigny, and two of his servants. A Spaniard, named Francisque Diaz, attacked him, and exchanged a few sword thrusts with him. But one of the servants having told him it was the Admiral, he changed his attitude, struck aside the weapon of an arquebusier, who was about to fire upon Coligny, and summoned him to surrender himself as his prisoner. He then brought him to the Spanish camp, passing out through the very breach which the Admiral had defended, and by which, as he proudly said, no foe had entered.

As he left the town, Coligny could see in the

distance Andelot's company still fighting. It was the last struggle to hold this bulwark of France. St. Quentin was in the hands of the enemy!

Francisque Diaz brought the Admiral to the Duke of Savoy, who, after surveying him from head to foot, committed him to the charge of Cazères, one of his staff officers.

The next day the Duke invited Coligny to dine with the Count de la Rochefoucauld, but it was only to insult him. The character of Philibert Emmanuel was not worthy of his genius as a soldier. His hatred to France was intense, and his avarice proverbial. When despoiled of his duchy he had taken as his motto, *Spoliatis arma supersunt*, and he made the profession of arms a means of enriching himself. Following the practice of many generals of his time, he made a traffic of his prisoners, demanding enormous sums for their release. All his campaigns were pecuniary speculations, and it is said that by his victory over St. Quentin he made more than five hundred thousand crowns.[1] A general of a nobler spirit than he might well have felt indignant with the French for the manner in which they had broken the peace, and might have thrown the responsibility on Coligny. But Philibert Emmanuel avowed the most open scepticism in relation to these engagements, which, according to him, were only held binding by the weak.[2] He ought then, at least, to have done justice as a soldier to the valour Coligny

---

[1] This is said by a historian who is favourable to him,— Guichenon, *Histoire de Savoie* (vol. ii., p. 245).

See Motley's *Foundation of the Dutch Republic* for the character of the Duke of Savoy.

had just displayed. But he chose to humiliate him, making him sit at the bottom of the table, and "not addressing to him a single word, nor, indeed, appearing even to see him." [1]

Andelot determined not to be again taken by the Spaniards, remembering his harsh captivity in Italy. He therefore risked crossing the marshes, and, though he had to wade breast-deep, he reached the French camp in safety.

The Admiral's first anxiety was naturally to clear himself in the king's eyes in regard to his defeat. He knew that he was no longer in favour with Henry II., and that his enemies would not fail to try and damage him in the king's estimation on account of his ill-success. "I deeply regret," he wrote to the king on August 28th, "not to have been able to carry out my good will and large obligation to do you service, but my comfort is that your majesty is so reasonable, that you will be satisfied when you learn that to the last I did all that became a gentleman and a man of honour." He related how the town had been surprised through the desertion by the Dauphin's company of the post they should have defended. "It is reasonable," he added, "that those who had the charge of that breach should be heard and should state their reasons. For myself, from what I saw and know, I am of opinion that if they had been as resolute to defend it as were those who kept the other breaches, I should be still in St. Quentin to do your majesty service. My heart is very sore to think that we were stormed

---

[1] *Mémoires de Jean de Mergey.*

at one of the strongest points, and almost without resistance, while at the other breaches the enemy was partly repulsed, so that our men there were taken in the rear."

These are the natural regrets of a brave soldier, but even supposing that this attack of the 27th of August had been repulsed, it is certain that the place could not have held out long under the ceaseless fire of the enemy's artillery, and with no hope of receiving further succour from France, Coligny had done all that it was possible to do.

M. Delaborde says : "With a mere handful of men Coligny detained the great army of Spain for seventeen[1] days before the walls of a dismantled town, and thus saved Paris, and gave the French army time to rally from its discomfiture and re-organise itself. Only a man of his indomitable energy could have accomplished such a prodigy, and history has but done justice to the Admiral in recording that by his heroic resistance at St. Quentin he saved France. But Henry II. was incapable of appreciating such faithful service, and he vouchsafed no reply to Coligny's letter."

The nameless Spanish officer who has left so interesting a record of the siege of St. Quentin, mentions one touching incident of this time of captivity : "One of the Spanish soldiers placed near the Admiral said to him one day, 'Why is your grace so silent ?' (he never spoke). 'The affairs of France are going well, and we have yet to take the king.' The Admiral replied : 'Before thirty days

---

[1] It was really twenty-five days, from August 2nd—27th.

the king will come hither with a powerful army, and thou shalt see what will happen.' 'Within thirty days,' replied the soldier, 'we shall have taken La Fère, Guise, Le Catelet, and Péronne.' 'Thou sayest not, "And God please," even in this time of misfortune,' said the Admiral bitterly." [1]

St. Quentin was given up to pillage and carnage for two whole days. All the inhabitants who could not pay a ransom were put to death. As the town was rich, the booty was large, and many soldiers boasted of having had as much as 12,000 ducats for their share. Philip II. gave orders that the lives of the women should be spared, and the cathedral was thrown open to them as a place of refuge. But before bringing them thither, the soldiers took away all their clothing that was of any value, and struck them with their swords, wounding and bruising them to make them confess where they had hidden their money and jewellery. Some women took refuge in the camp, where they claimed the protection of the Bishop of Arras, who accompanied the king. On the evening of the 28th the town was set on fire from end to end. Then Philip, who had left the wretched inhabitants exposed to all manner of outrage, piously busied himself in saving the body of St. Quentin and other relics contained in the churches.

On August 29th the king proclaimed that before he made his solemn entry into the town it must be completely evacuated. The 3,500 women who remained were led away to a distance on French territory. It was pitiful to see the long and mournful procession ;

---

[1] *Récit du siège de St. Quentin, par un officier espagnol,* Gomart, p. 410.

many of the women had horrible wounds ; some,
more than eighty years of age, had their white hair
saturated with blood ; others were carrying their
little children, and uttering cries of anguish as they
passed in the streets the dead bodies of fathers,
husbands, and sons.

On the 30th of August the king made his entry
into the ill-fated town, which a month before presented the spectacle of a busy and prosperous place.
Corpses were heaped among the smouldering ruins,
filling the air with pestilential odours. " I walked
through the place looking around me," says the
Spanish officer whom we have already quoted, " and
it seemed like a second destruction of Jerusalem.
What was strangest of all was that not a single
citizen was to be found, not one person who was or
dared to own that he was French. ' How vain and
transitory are the things of this world ! ' I said to
myself ; ' six days ago what wealth was in this
town, and now not one stone is left upon another.' "[1]

---

[1] Quentin de la Fons, in his *Histoire particulière de la
ville de St. Quentin,* says that the ramparts long remained
overthrown, so that in winter the wolves sometimes came into
the city, and at the time when he writes—that is, ninety years
after the siege—St. Quentin had not recovered its former
prosperity.

CHAPTER X.

PHILIP II. seemed at last to have decided to march upon Paris. But he was not a man of rapid action, and the habit of temporising, which characterised all his policy, lost him, on this occasion, the result of his immense success. He knew that France was arming in all directions; that Paris, recovered from her stupor, was organising a determined resistance, thanks, it must be owned, to the initiative given by Catherine de Medicis. This is the fairest page in her life. The king was at Compiègne; she was left alone in Paris. Panic had seized all minds.

Of her own instance Catherine repaired to the Parliament, and there making an urgent appeal to the patriotism of its members, she spoke, says the Venetian ambassador, with so much feeling and eloquence, that a subsidy was voted by acclamation, and the leading men of the city offered three hundred thousand livres. She thanked them in words so full of feeling that all present were moved to tears.[1]

---

[1] Hector de la Ferrière, *Lettres de Catherine de Médicis*, Introduction, p. 52.

Philip II. knew that the Duke of Guise, who had been recalled from Italy, was about to land at Marseilles. Philip's own army was composed in great part of mercenaries, who, gorged with booty, were threatening to desert. The English and the Spaniards hated each other. Philip heard from Queen Mary that Scotland was attacking England, and that she must recall her troops. His vast army seemed melting from his grasp. He contented himself with occupying some towns in Picardy, and did not go further. Early in October he returned to Brussels, and from there gave the order to disband the troops. This abandonment of an invasion which had loomed so threateningly over France shows how much there was that was factitious in the seemingly imposing array of Philip II.'s forces.

But all this time what had become of Coligny?

On the 31st of August, 1557, two companies of arquebusiers conducted the Admiral to Lille, and thence to Sluys, a little military port near the mouth of the Scheldt, on the borders of Zeeland, where there was a gloomy castle, in which he was confined.[1] The Duke of Savoy had consented to his retaining about him those of his domestics whom he absolutely needed, on condition that they should hold no communication with the outer world. All letters received or sent by Coligny were to be submitted to Philibert Emmanuel. The Admiral was to be made to undergo the irritating *surveillance* which Philip II. loved to exercise over his state

---

[1] The Constable, who had been wounded and made prisoner in the battle of August 10th, had been taken to the Castle of Ghent.

prisoners, and of which we find traces in every line of his voluminous correspondence. He was more adapted truly to the profession of a detective than of a monarch.[1]

Hardly had he reached his place of imprisonment when the Admiral, who was always subject to attacks of fever, fell dangerously ill. The strain upon mind and body which he had endured was enough to undermine a more robust constitution. For forty days his life hung in the balance.

As soon as he recovered his strength, he set himself to the task of writing his *Memoir of the Siege of St. Quentin,* from which we have so largely quoted. He wrote it in self-vindication. He knew that the king had condemned him without a hearing, and he learnt, by the news which reached him from France, that the fortunes of the Guises, who had become his avowed enemies, had rapidly advanced during the disasters which had befallen the kingdom. We must here give a brief outline of the part which Francis of Lorraine was now called to play.

We have mentioned that he went to Italy at the close of the year 1556. We need to know something of the state of that country at the time, in order to judge how much truth there was in the brilliant promises with which Carafa had dazzled him.

Naples and Milan belonged to Spain. The Duke of Alva was occupying Naples with an army, small,

---

[1] In proof of this, note the refinement of cruelty with which Philip afterwards treated the illustrious Lanoue, in his five years' captivity.

no doubt, but comprising several corps of the formidable Spanish troops, which were then deemed
invincible. The Duke of Parma, Ottavio Farnese,
was a feudatory of Spain; so was the Duke of
Genoa. Venice, in spite of all Carafa's efforts, stood
firm in a prudent neutrality. Florence sought only
her own interests, and Philip II. held sway there
through his ambassador. In view of all these hostile
or neutral states, what had Carafa to offer to France?
The alliance of the pope, that of Hercules of Este,
Duke of Ferrara, the husband of Renée of France,
and father-in-law to Guise. Beyond this he had
promises of risings in Sienna and Naples, but this
was all. The pontifical army counted for nothing.
It had been beaten every time it had met the
Spaniards in open fight; and if the Duke of Alva
had not yet entered Rome, it was solely from
religious scruples. Many of the Roman nobles,
moreover, and among them one of the first rank,
Marco Antonio Colonna, were serving under the
banner of Spain. The papal treasury was empty,
and Carafa had been obliged to raise a loan in
France at the exorbitant rate of twenty-two per
cent. interest. This was the true position of things.
The Cardinal of Lorraine, if he had not been
blinded by his ambition, might have seen it, for
he had come to Italy to try to move the Senate
of Venice, and had met only with a courteous
refusal. Francis of Lorraine, who had so lightly
lent himself to the comedy which Carafa had just
been playing in France, might have suspected that
the crafty Italian might one day practise the same
arts upon himself. In truth, on the very eve of

Lorraine's arrival in Italy, the cardinal was privately intriguing with the Duke of Alva, and offering him peace on condition of the cession of Sienna to the Carafas.[1] So much was this ally worth, who talked of delivering Italy from the Spanish yoke !

Guise knew nothing of all this, and perhaps expected an easy campaign. He brought with him 12,000 foot-soldiers and a brilliant company of cavalry. As Savoy belonged to France, he easily crossed the Alps. It would have been well for France if he had come into collision there with the Duke of Savoy, Philibert Emmanuel, who at that very time was preparing on her northern frontiers the crushing victory of St. Quentin.

At Reggio Lorraine met his father-in-law, the Duke of Ferrara. Brissac, governor of Piedmont, advised him to take Milan. He would then have a compact basis of operations in Piedmont, Milan, and Ferrara. But this plan did not suit Carafa, who wanted his principality; nor Lorraine, who coveted Naples. They went further south. From this time the disillusion began. Hercules of Este kept back his army, not wishing, naturally, to leave his frontiers unguarded.

Paul IV. had scarcely any soldiers to give to Guise, but he solemnly excommunicated Charles V. and Philip II., and on Good Friday, when the Church prays for infidels, Jews, and heretics, he refused to pray for the Emperor. Lorraine would rather have been supported by the carnal weapons that had been promised him.

In order to effect an entrance into Naples, Guise

---

[1] This fact is distinctly stated by Pietro Norres. See G. Duruy (p. 202).

attacked the little town of Civitella on April 24th. The place was bravely defended. The besieged had only two cannon to oppose to the French artillery, but they were bravely served, and every assault was repulsed. Weeks passed, and Guise was still detained before this citadel, which set him at defiance. In vain he looked for the promised rising of the population in his favour. One day, seeing the pitiful state of the troops brought to him by Montebello, Carafa's brother, he accused him to his face of pocketing the pay of the soldiers, and of not having his full complement of effective troops. He even went further, and hinted that Carafa might be playing him false. In order to calm him, Carafa was obliged to send his two sons as hostages to Paris. On May 15th, Guise was compelled to raise the siege of Civitella, which had detained him twenty-two days. He gave up the attempt to enter the kingdom of Naples, and assumed a defensive position, feeling that with so small a number of troops he could not venture to take the field. The Duke of Alva, who was naturally of a prudent disposition, observed him closely. While the two armies thus remained confronted, Paul IV. brought over 3,000 Swiss, and sent them to Paliano, the patrimony of one of his nephews, in order to protect it at any rate against the Spaniards. With a view to encourage these Swiss to fight, he gave them the name of angels sent from heaven ; but on the 27th of July the so-called angels were cut to pieces to the last man by the terrible Colonna. Paul IV., in great alarm, summoned Guise to fall back upon Rome. Guise obeyed, but unwillingly. He seemed to have become indifferent about this campaign, and had just sent off several detachments to Ferrara to protect his father-in-law. The Spaniards took possession of the town of Segni before his very eyes.[1]

On the 23rd August the terrible news of the disaster at St. Quentin reached Rome. It produced indescribable consternation. Paul IV. was about to find himself left alone, face to face with a victorious enemy. But Cardinal Carafa, who knew that the Duke of Alva would never be induced to undertake another sack of Rome, such as had brought such execration upon the Bourbon name, at once entered into secret negotiations with him. France being defeated, he had nothing more to expect from that quarter, and without hesitation he was about to sell himself to Spain. On September 14th he signed a convention, which satisfied the Duke of Alva, but in order to spare Paul IV.'s pride he concealed from him some of the stipulations to which he had been obliged to submit.[2]

Henry II. immediately wrote to Guise to return to France. He told him the whole extent of the disaster of St. Quentin, adding: "Keep a good heart, and fear nothing."[3] The Valois were always ready with brave words after disasters brought about by their own blundering. We may well suppose that Guise was only too glad of such a way of escape

---

[1] Segni was taken on August 15th. It will give an idea of the atrocities of these wars when we say that the entire population was exterminated with every refinement of cruelty.

[2] It was this deception which, coming subsequently to the knowledge of the old pontiff, opened his eyes, and led him to abandon and denounce his nephew.

[3] Ribier, vol. ii., p. 700.

from his false position. His last interview with
Paul IV. is historical. "Begone, then," said the old
pontiff, "you have done little enough for the service
of your king, still less for the Church, and nothing
at all to your own honour."[1]

The remains of the brilliant army which Carafa
had summoned into Italy six months before, were
seen trailing back along its northern frontier. The
soldiers were in such pitiful plight that the Duke of
Guise offered to pledge the whole of his possessions
to the Duke of Ferrara for a loan of 100,000 crowns,
"the soldiers being forced to go about in their shirts
and barefoot, begging their bread from town to
town."[2]

Such was the miserable end of the enterprise into
which Paul IV., counselled by an intriguing cardinal,
had plunged France—the country was invaded, one
army destroyed at St. Quentin, and another fleeing
out of Italy.

But France knew nothing of what was passing
beyond the Alps. Altogether stupefied by the
disaster of St. Quentin, it was clamouring for an
army and a leader, and when it learned that Francis
of Lorraine had landed at Marseilles, it welcomed
him with acclamation. Was he not the saviour of
Metz? Was he not the one man who could repair
the disaster which had befallen the unhappy defender
of St. Quentin?

With the levity natural to Frenchmen, they made

---

[1] Fra Paolo Sarpi, *History of the Council of Trent*, book v.,
p. 415.
[2] Letter from Guise to the Duke of Ferrara, Rome, September 4th, 1557, Ribier, vol. ii., p. 703.

a superficial comparison of the two sieges, without
taking at all into account the difference of the circumstances.   At Metz, Guise occupied one of the
strongest places in the kingdom, with excellent
troops.   He had no doubt a formidable foe to contend with, but the besieging forces were decimated
by such a terrible winter, that one of those who were
in the city at the time said with truth : " I was at
the siege of Metz, and I shall always testify that
M. de Guise did right good service there, but it must
be confessed the severity of the winter did the best
service of all to France."[1]   At St. Quentin, Coligny,
with a handful of men, defended a dismantled town
against 60,000 assailants, with everything in their
favour.   In the first of the two sieges the relieving
army, by its able diversions, made Charles V. so ill
at ease that he abandoned his enterprise.   In the
second siege the relieving army was crushed as soon
as it came in sight.   What matter ?   Francis of
Guise was hailed as the great conqueror of the
Spaniards, and much as Henry secretly dreaded the
house of Lorraine, he was obliged, by the pressure of
public opinion, to make Francis his lieutenant-
general, with almost unlimited powers, and to entrust
the finances and administration to his brother the
cardinal (October 5th).

Francis of Lorraine had energy enough to acquit
himself worthily of his new trust.   On arriving at
Compiègne, followed by the soldiers he had brought
back from Italy, he found there a regular army,
which the Duke de Nevers had re-formed from the

---

[1] Le Vidame de Chartres in La Place. *Comment*, quoted
by M. Delaborde.

relics of the army of St. Quentin. He occupied the attention of the enemy by manœuvres along the Meuse ; then suddenly, at the end of December, he led his troops by forced marches into Flanders, and presented himself before Calais.

The idea of attacking Calais had not originated with him. It was a plan which Coligny had carefully prepared, and about which he had given directions to his lieutenant Senarpont. More than two years before, the Admiral had spoken to the king about it, and had even confided to him that he had so studied the approaches to the place that he would be able to take it by surprise. Henry II. remembered this interview. Hence Brantôme is right when he says that Coligny was " the originator of this enterprise." The king despatched Feuquières to Châtillon-sur-Loing with an order to demand of the Countess de Châtillon the Admiral's papers relating to this subject. They were found. The Admiral advised the attack to be made in winter, because at that season the English, trusting to the waters, which ebb and flow more strongly than in summer, did not send over any large number of men, and the garrison was very weak. These calculations were perfectly correct. Queen Mary never dreamed that Calais could be threatened just after the crushing defeat of St. Quentin. For two hundred and ten years it had belonged to England, and it was supposed to be so strong that one of its gates bore this inscription :—

> " When iron and lead float like cork on the sea,
> Then may Calais perchance besiegĕd be." [1]

M. de Bouillé, *Hist. des ducs de Guise*, vol. i., p. 723.

Guise pushed the attack with great vigour. He was well provided with artillery, and had entrusted his left wing to Andelot. On the 3rd January, 1558, the French attacked simultaneously the two forts of Nieullai and Risbank, which guarded the town. The well-directed fire of the besiegers speedily dismantled them, and the French took possession of the two the same evening. For the next three days they opened a steady fire on the town itself and its castle. On the 4th of January Andelot was entrusted with the difficult task of crossing by the shore between the sea and the town, at low tide, with one thousand five hundred arquebusiers, and of making, under the enemy's fire, a channel into which the water might be diverted from the moat which the French must cross to make the assault. This all but impossible work upon marshy and shifting ground was only accomplished by means of hurdles covered with pitch which Senarpont had prepared, and upon which the soldiers walked, so as not to sink into the marsh. When the moat was emptied at break of day, January 6th, Guise advanced with his troops, crossed an arm of the sea where the water came up to their waists, entered by the breach and occupied the town. Lord Wentworth, who was commanding the citadel, obtained an honourable capitulation, and on the 9th Calais was evacuated by the English.[1]

---

[1] M. de Bouillé, in his book on the Dukes of Guise, which is generally so remarkable and so exact, supposes very gratuitously that it was out of spite against Francis of Lorraine that the honour of having planned the taking of Calais is attributed to Coligny. On the contrary, this fact is well established, and Brantôme speaks of it as a thing generally known. At the same time he in no way depreciates the skill

Guise did not sully his victory by any cruelty, and the conduct of the French presented a striking contrast to the hideous scenes which had disgraced the taking of St. Quentin. The garrison and the inhabitants were given their lives, and were allowed to retire into England or Flanders, but they were to abandon their arms and possessions to the conquerors.

Fifty English officers alone were retained as prisoners with Lord Wentworth. A few days later the fortress of Guines also surrendered, and the English ceased to possess anything in France. Following so rapidly on the catastrophe in which Paris itself was threatened, the effect of this victory was immense. Francis of Lorraine was regarded by all as the saviour of his country. "The people forgot that while the lucky adventurer had been just before compromising France in the heart of Italy, a man of honour had saved it by accepting with full knowledge of the issue a hopeless task." [1]

Another event was shortly to enhance still more the glory of the Guises, placing them, as it were, on the very steps of the throne. Their eldest sister, Mary of Lorraine, had married James V. of Scotland

---

and energy with which Guise executed the plan. The charge of malice might indeed be thrown back on the Guises, for it is certain—(1) that Coligny alone had prepared the attack on Calais, which Guise could not have originated, and which he only executed according to the Admiral's plans, and with the valuable aid of Coligny's lieutenant, Senarpont; (2) It was Andelot who, by his valour, played the principal part in the attack; (3) Some months later, the Guises, forgetting all this, acted as spies on the Admiral's correspondence, denounced Andelot to the king, and deprived him of his post of colonel of the French infantry. These are the simple facts of the case. *Cuique suum.*

[1] Henri Martin.

in 1538.   Left a widow in 1542, and declared
regent of the kingdom in the name of her daughter
Mary Stuart, she had sent this daughter in 1548 to
the Court of France.   Mary Stuart had been warmly
welcomed by Henry II., and had received a brilliant
education.   She was devoted to the fine arts, particularly to music.   All contemporaries, even the
grave chancellor l'Hôpital, tell us that at fifteen
years of age her beauty exercised an irresistible
charm.   "Our little Scotch queenie has but to
smile," said Catherine de Médicis, "and she turns
the heads of all Frenchmen."   It is easy to understand then what a spell she exercised over the
Dauphin Francis, to whom she was betrothed.   The
Guises were impatient to conclude this marriage,
and they succeeded in getting it fixed for the spring
of this year, in spite of the feeble health and extreme
youth of the prince, who was only fourteen and a-
half.   The Scotch parliament conferred on the
dauphin the title of King of Scotland.   The Guises,
who had their niece completely under their sway,
made Mary sign a secret deed making a gift of her
kingdom to the crown of France, and this they
induced her to do some days before the public act of
her marriage (April 27th, 1558), in which she and
her husband solemnly swore to maintain the liberties
and independence of Scotland.   It was by this act
of perfidy and treason against her own people that
this fascinating child, acting under the influence of
her uncles, began that tragic story in thinking of
which one is at a loss whether most to pity or to
blame her.

The Guises were now at the zenith of their fortune.

The Constable and Coligny, both prisoners, could give them no umbrage. Andelot had, indeed, just rendered Francis of Lorraine the most signal service by his valiant conduct at the siege of Calais, but the suspicious spirit of the Lorraines was in no way disarmed by such obligation. At the very time of his attacking Calais, Francis of Lorraine had made use of his position as lieutenant-general to act as a spy on all the correspondence between the captive Admiral and his family,[1] and we shall presently see by what cunning devices his brother, the Cardinal, endeavoured to damage Coligny with the king.

---

[1] On this point see a characteristic letter from Guise to M de Humières, published for the first time by M. Delaborde.

CHAPTER XI.

TO return to Coligny. The blow which had fallen on him was heavy enough to crush the bravest and to embitter the most generous spirit. He had been defeated ; he was being subjected to a rigorous imprisonment ; he felt himself misunderstood and dishonoured by the king whom he had so heroically served, and he had at the same time to see his rival triumphantly carrying out plans which he had devised with long, patient thought. His cup of bitterness was full to the brim.

But no complaint escaped him. He seemed dead to earthly ambitions and regrets ; his mind was absorbed with new and higher thoughts ; and from this time of retirement and meditation he was to come forth one of the noblest champions of " the religion." His *Memoir of the Siege of St. Quentin* concludes with these words, " All the consolation I have is that which it seems to me all Christians should possess, namely, that such mysteries do not take place without the permission and will of God, which is always right, holy, and reasonable, and which does nothing without just occasion. And albeit I know not the cause, I am not concerned to inquire; but rather desire to humble myself before God in submission to His will."

These words, dated December 28th, 1557, show what was the direction taken by Coligny's thoughts, and this stern sense of the Divine sovereignty reveals how largely he had come under the influence of the reformed doctrine. Whence had he derived this faith? On this point the testimony is unanimous.[1] It was his brother Andelot who, by his conversation, had led Coligny into the new light. Brantôme says, "M. Dandelot, after being taken at Parma, was wedded to the Castle of Milan as his prison." . . . "I have heard even some Spanish soldiers, old pensioners in Milan, say that, during his imprisonment, having no other exercise, he set himself to reading, and had all sorts of books brought to him without any molestation from the warders, for the Inquisition was not so strict then as it has been since; and that he thus became instructed in the new religion, of which he had already gathered some idea, having been in Germany in the war of the Protestants."

Andelot, then, was the first of the three brothers Châtillon to embrace openly the Reformed religion. He was too much attached to his brothers not to

---

[1] We must except the author of the *Vita Colinii*, who affirms that the Admiral was the first to embrace the Gospel, and that the Cardinal Odet and Andelot " were by his example greatly stirred to the study of the religion" (*Vita Gasparis Colinii*, 1575, p. 28). We have said in our preface that such a mistake could hardly have been made by Hotman, who was an intimate friend of Andelot's.

make them sharers in his convictions. We have seen, moreover, that the education they had received fróm their mother was calculated to prepare them to accept the new teaching.

Coligny did not disguise his sympathy with the Protestants, and Beza says that, for several years before this, he had on every occasion tried to protect those of that religion. But it is probable that his life as a soldier, and the many offices he held, had left him no leisure to study the Reformed doctrines. His long imprisonment, first in the fortress of Sluys, and from March 1558 in the castle at Ghent, gave him time to go thoroughly into these questions. Andelot sent him a copy of the Bible, and a book the title of which we do not know, but which was probably some exposition of the new doctrines. Coligny felt himself gradually more and more persuaded of their truth ; but it was not till two years later that, after grave and mature reflection, he determined to attach himself to the new Church. From the year 1558, however, he had belonged to it in heart. His wife, Charlotte de Laval, though separated from him, arrived at the same conclusion, and from this time Calvin kept up a correspondence with them both.

The Reformer had, no doubt, long known that Coligny was in sympathy with the Protestant cause. The Church of Geneva remembered how kindly he had received the emigrants who had left that city to go to Brazil. But now, for the first time, the Admiral entered into direct communication with Calvin.

Calvin was intensely interested in the fortunes of

the Reformation in France. Geneva, that citadel of Protestantism where for thirty years Calvin carried on his great work, was the near neighbour of France and Savoy, which shut it in so closely that sometimes they well-nigh stifled it. In return it was often (as a contemporary has said) "a thorn in the flesh" to its two powerful neighbours. That it maintained its independence is little short of a miracle. For half a century the idea of destroying it was never absent from Catholic diplomacy. Many times the old Spanish troops, passing through Franche Comté on their way to the Low Countries, came within a few leagues of its territory. Philibert Emmanuel, the conqueror of France, was for twenty years its neighbour, and hovered hungrily over it like a bird of prey. Happily the Swiss were there with their formidable infantry, the only infantry in the world at that time which could cope with that of Spain ; and the Bernese bear kept the Savoyard at bay. Geneva had even a better safeguard than this in the indomitable courage of her citizens and the unfaltering ardour of their religious faith.

The Genevese were not a people easy to mould and guide. Calvin often told them so plainly. Driven away by them once, he had constantly to contend with their captious and turbulent humours. In the midst of fightings within the city, and fears of the foreigner without, the Reformer carried on his work. "I do not believe," says Theodore Beza, "that the like was ever seen."[1] He goes on to describe the ordinary labours of Calvin. One sermon every day beside

---

[1] See for these various quotations, *La Vie de Calvin*, by Theodore Beza.

two on Sunday, preached in the great cathedral before immense congregations, composed not only of the Genevese, but of refugees from all countries; his writings and lectures on theology, based on a deep study of Scripture and the fathers; his training of the young ministers whom he prepared for martyrdom. And all this accomplished with broken health, an emaciated body; asthma, which well-nigh stifled him at times; a face pale and wan, but lighted up with a look of calm serenity which bespoke the steadfastness of the soul within. "I know not," says Beza, "if any man of our time has had more to hear, to reply to, and to write, beside matters of greater importance. The quantity and quality of his writings alone suffices to astonish all who see them, and still more those who read them." . . . "We would urge him to take more care of himself; but his usual reply was that what he was doing was as nothing, and that he would that God should find him watching and working as he was able till his latest breath."

This testimony of Theodore Beza is confirmed by the mass of correspondence only recently published.[1] It gives us some idea of the extent of Calvin's ministry, which thus embraced, by means of daily letters, the whole of Protestant Europe, treating of questions of doctrine and discipline, confirming the churches, carrying consolation to the persecuted for the faith. Étienne Pasquier says, "We sometimes had our prisons crowded with confessors, whom he ceased

---

[1] See the edition of *Calvini Opera* by MM. Reuss, Bauer, and Cunitz.

not to exhort, console, and strengthen by letters,
never failing to find messengers, to whom the doors
were opened in spite of the vigilance of the gaolers."[1]

To all who to-day read these letters of Calvin, he
will seem greater than they had thought. One can
but admire a soul so consumed with zeal for the
cause of God and with love to all who did it service.
In all those thousands of missives which were carried
by intrepid messengers all over France, there is not
a line to conceal. Calvin never intermeddled in any
intrigues or plots. Such as he appeared in public,
we find him in his most private life. In writing to
Coligny and the great lords of his party, his great
concern is the salvation of their souls ; not a word of
flattery, of concession to their claims as men of rank,
not a hint of worldly policy or interest. To kings
themselves his honesty is inflexible, and sometimes
amounts to rudeness. He never sacrifices duty to
expediency, and yet this man of iron has accents of
softest pity for the humble and the weak. A poor
artisan or weaver will get words from him that will
strengthen him in the very hour of death. From
end to end of this correspondence there is the same
sublime monotone—*Sursum corda.* Bossuet complains of the melancholy of Calvin's style. The
Bishop of Meaux ought rather to have respected this
sadness, for it was the shadow cast upon his soul by
the tortures and atrocious executions of which he
was for thirty years the witness.

I am not writing Calvin's apology. He had his
blemishes ; he made grave mistakes ; his logic was

---

[1] *Recherches sur la France*, Book VII.

pitiless ; he himself was often hard. He did not understand the meaning of religious liberty. I know that for the death of Servetus the age was more to be blamed than himself ; that Servetus would have been burned at Grenoble no less than at Geneva. But even this does not excuse the fierce intolerance and vindictiveness with which Calvin pursued his unhappy victim, exclaiming, " Vivum exire non patiar " ("I will not suffer him to go hence alive ").[1] Calvin himself on his death-bed reproached himself, not for the death of Servetus (for to the last he thought that heretics ought to be punished by law), but for his own impatience and passionate anger. On this count we cannot hold him guiltless. But history ought, nevertheless, to judge him by the whole tenor of his life ; and that life is a grand one, for it reveals on every page an unswerving loyalty of faith and uprightness of conscience. It is not one of the least glories of Calvin that he was the Counsellor of Jeanne d'Albret, of Andelot, and of Coligny.

The first letter addressed by Calvin to the Admiral bears date September 4th, 1558 :—

" Monseigneur," he writes, " I hope that after reading this present, inasmuch as it will bear you witness of the care I have for your salvation, you will not take it amiss that I have written to you. I shall make no long apology, being well persuaded that the reverence you bear my Master will make you regard favourably that which you will see to have proceeded from Him, and to be set before you in

---

[1] This is what Calvin wrote on hearing that Servetus was coming from Grenoble to Geneva.

His name. Neither shall I use much exhortation to confirm your patience, inasmuch as I believe and have been told that our God has so strengthened you by the power of His Spirit, that I have rather occasion to glorify God for the patience He has wrought in you than to incite you to more.[1] And, in truth, it is here above all that true greatness of soul ought to show itself, in surmounting all our passions, not only that we may be victorious, but that we may offer a true sacrifice of obedience to God, and quietly submit ourselves. Now, seeing He has given you such constancy, we need not to exhort you to it. Only I pray you to think yet again that God, in sending you this affliction, has willed to draw you aside a while, that you might be the better *listened to of Him.*[2] For you know, sire, how hard it is amidst the honours and riches and favours of the world, to lend an ear to Him; so is one driven hither and thither and ready to faint, so to speak, except He use such means to draw to Himself those who are His. Not that dignities and temporal possessions and estates are incompatible with the fear of God, provided that as God raises men, He gives them opportunity to draw closer to Him and to be the more incited to honour and serve Him. But I trow you have had experience that those who hold the highest places in the world, are so occupied with it,

---

[1] From this we infer that Coligny's conversion was already an accomplished and recognised fact.

[2] So runs the text of this letter as published by M. Jules Bonnet, and MM. Baum, Cunitz, and Reuss. It seems to us, however, that there must be a slip of the pen, and that the phrase should read, " that *He may be the better heard of you.*"

and held captive as it were in its thralls, that they scarcely give themselves time for the chief work of all, which is to worship God, to dedicate oneself wholly to Him, and to aspire after the heavenly life. Wherefore, sire, I pray you, inasmuch as God has given you this opportunity of profiting in His school, as though He would speak privately to your ear, be attentive to taste better than ever the sweetness and preciousness of His doctrine, and give heed to the diligent reading of His Word, to be instructed thereby, and to become rooted and grounded in the faith, so that you may be made strong for the rest of your life to do battle with all temptations."

The letter concluded with an exhortation to Coligny not to let himself be drawn away by the corruption of the age, but to persevere in the grace of God.

The same day Calvin encouraged Charlotte de Laval with the like exhortations, pointing out to her the uses of adversity. " In truth," he said, "when we are sailing before the wind, as they say, we are apt to miss the track in our light-hearted ease." He urged her to serve God in spite of the murmurings and hatred of the world. " It is most reasonable," he continued, " that we should dedicate ourselves to Him who has bought us at such a price, and according to the love He has bestowed upon us, should esteem His favour more than all the smiles of the world." He prayed God, in conclusion, to fill her with an invincible constancy.

Let us pause a moment at this turning-point in the life of the Admiral. History is nothing if it does not help us to discern, beneath the surface of

events, the inward motives which influence men.
Let us endeavour to realise to ourselves what is the
new belief which is henceforth to be the inspiration
of the life of Coligny.

The great movement of religious emancipation,
which Luther had commenced in Germany, had gone
on in France also, but on a more restricted scale, and
without that outward show which strikes the imagination and sways the masses. As early as 1512,
when the name of Luther was still unknown, Lefèvre
d'Étaples taught a doctrine in Paris which anticipated
in a less incisive and impressive form the teaching
of the Augustine monk. The first disciples of
Lefèvre, particularly Guillaume Farel, were to become
afterwards the ardent promoters of a popular Reformation. In 1535 this Reformation found in Calvin
the genius who formed the new belief into a system,
and gave to the Church a simple and strong organisation. With all its errors, narrownesses, and defi-
ciencies, this was a colossal work, which was to live
on from generation to generation. From that time
the Church grew up under the cutting blast of persecution, and though the first French reformers were
called Lutherans, the Reformation in France had
from the first its own proper life and original
character.

Those who look upon it as simply a political
insurrection, or those who explain it away as a mere
enfranchisement of the reason wakened into new
energy under the powerful influence of the Renaissance, fail altogether to comprehend it. To be
known aright it must be studied in its authentic
monuments, whether in the confession of faith of

its early martyrs, or better still in the unrestrained outpouring of their souls. It will then be recognised as above all the advent of a new religious life, born of a new conception of the relations of men to God.

What does the Reformation affirm as its very basis? Two things. First, it overthrows the hierarchy and all sacerdotalism, and re-establishes the direct relation of the believer with God, through the medium of the Scriptures, in which alone it recognises a true revelation of Him. Secondly, while the Church makes salvation the chief end to be attained by the meritorious works and expiatory offerings of the believer, who is thus supposed to supplement the work of redemption, the Reformation declares that salvation is a free gift, and thus gives to the Christian life a new starting-point, whence all true holiness springs. The divine sovereignty exercised in the Church and in the individual soul, through the word of revelation and the grace of the Spirit, is the central dogma of the Reformation. This is the belief which became henceforward the inspiration of Coligny's life, and apart from this his character will always remain an insoluble riddle.

We must say here, in passing, one word on a religious problem which lies at the root of all the great struggles of the sixteenth century, a problem strangely evaded or ignored by most of our historians. I refer to the doctrine of the enslaved will, which played a most important part, and in the name of which the greatest religious emancipation known in history was accomplished. To solve this problem by saying that the doctrine is contradicted by the life; that logic asserts one thing and human nature another, is simply to explain a mystery by a paradox, and to abandon the attempt to discover the chain of cause and effect, or the motives which influence mankind. To compare the Calvinistic doctrine of predestination with Mussulman fatalism, when their consequences are so diametrically opposed, implies an entire want of appreciation of the deep spiritual experiences of the men of that age.

It is certain that at its commencement the Reformation denied the doctrine of free-will, and that on this point Coligny was in full accord with his co-religionists. It is no less certain that no men ever realised more fully than the Huguenots of that day the reality of moral responsibility, or fought more valiantly for liberty. How can we explain this contradiction ?

Let us observe first that the word liberty has a very extended and variable signification. In current language we speak of a man as free who can do what he will. He is free, then, who chooses a life of sensual pleasure and moral degradation, and if he gives himself up to it wholly, so that conscience is silenced, he seems to enjoy complete liberty. But put before him another aim—some high ideal of justice, duty, obedience, sacrifice, and at once he becomes conscious of hindrance and moral impotence. He begins to doubt whether he is free after all. The higher the ideal he sets before himself, the stronger this sense of bondage becomes. The good that he would, he cannot do. Suppose the ideal before him to be absolute perfection, he feels that he cannot attain to it. In vain you tell him his will is free ; he only answers with the bitter sigh of failure.

We may then lay it down as a principle that the higher the moral ideal set before a man, the less can he reckon upon its attainment by the mere exercise of free will. Hence authentic Christianity, not toned down by philosophy, speaks with the utmost plainness of the moral bondage of mankind, for the very reason that it never presents to man anything lower than the absolute ideal of perfection. From St. Paul to Augustine, from Augustine to the Reformers, from the Reformers to Pascal and Arnauld, there is an unbroken chain of Christians, who speak in the same terms of the natural state of man as a slavery from which grace alone can release him.

Does this imply any denial of moral freedom in its very essence? Is there not rather in this stern denunciation of man's slavery an implied tribute to the grandeur of his true destiny? Liberty, in the Christian sense, means the possibility open to man to fulfil the whole law of his being, and this law enjoins moral likeness to God. Whether this ideal be thought to be chimerical or not, it is at least a grand and lofty one.

This freedom, moreover, is to be recovered. It is not a boon which man has lost for ever. God restores it to His elect. Here we touch on the stern and hard side of the Calvinistic theology. Undoubtedly the idea of predestination underlay the Christian doctrine from the beginning, and we know in what terms St. Paul expressed it. But the error of Calvinism is that it makes this the central doctrine of the Christian system, and carries it out with a pitiless logic, which sadly restricts the Divine mercy, and is derogatory to the very character of God.

Here, however, we must make one reservation.
There is an essential difference between a new conviction taking hold of the human soul for the first
time as a living reality, and the same belief reduced
to an intellectual formula or abstract dogma. To the
Protestant, deeply conscious of his moral misery and
enslavement by nature, predestination meant primarily the grace of God taking possession of his soul.
It was the joyous affirmation of Divine sovereignty
ruling over him as its empire, and restoring his filial
liberty and the faculty of obedience prompted by
love. Hence this belief became a fountain of new
morality. Man has found his God again, or rather
has been conquered afresh by God. He no longer
thinks of salvation as an end to be attained by
means of penitence and expiations. Salvation is to
him a realised fact. He knows himself saved,
reconciled to God, and this strong conviction rightly
becomes the mainspring of his whole conduct in life.
He ceases from monastic asceticism, and from offering expiations of his own for the sins of the flesh ;
he casts off the leading-strings of the casuistry which
would hold his soul in bondage. Conscience, set
free, finds its law in the will of God. Obedience
is then the consecration of the nature to God, with
all its legitimate joys, and foremost among them
all, the holy ties of family. In that strange
century in which exalted mysticism was often
found allied with the moral degradation of the
paganism of the Renaissance, this beautiful plant
of the Reformation grew up, producing as its
flowers the Protestant family home, and men and
women of so grand and true a type that they

make the name Huguenot for ever fragrant in the field of history.

Nor must we fail to notice one other significant fact. In the very face of the Reformation arose Jesuitism. Both belong to the same era. The Reformation proclaims man's moral enslavement, and the necessity of grace to set him free. Jesuitism, on the contrary, declares that man's freedom of will is scarcely at all impaired. But the one emancipates men and nations ; the other brings both into bondage. The one gives birth to the grandest characters in French history ; the other would have made France a second Spain, but for the powerful reaction of the Gallican spirit and of the national loyalty to truth. We leave this problem to be solved by all candid and thoughtful minds. The more they reflect on it, the more will they be convinced of the formative influence exerted upon nations by those religious convictions, which superficial students of history too often ignore.

CHAPTER XII.

WE have endeavoured to explain the nature of the change which was wrought in the soul of the prisoner in the Castle of Ghent. But it was, as we have said, only by slow degrees that Coligny yielded to his new convictions. It was not till the year following his leaving the prison that he took his place decidedly in the ranks of the Reformers.

His brother Andelot had taken the same step before him, and many suspected Odet, the Cardinal, of sharing like opinions. During the captivity of the Admiral in Belgium two events happened which should be mentioned here.

Francis of Guise and his brother, the Cardinal of Lorraine, had both initiated themselves into high favour with the king, the one by his brilliant military services, the other by his diplomacy. The marriage of their niece to the Dauphin Francis raised their fortunes to the zenith : and the captivity of the Constable and of Coligny left them without a rival in their influence over the king. Yet they knew that Henry II. had no love for them, and that Anne de Montmorency was still the counsellor of his choice.[1]

The two brothers saw clearly, therefore, that the surest way for them to secure their authority and to win general favour was boldly to take the lead of the Catholic party, and to make the king suspicious of the Châtillons, rumours of whose heresy were already afloat. The Cardinal of Lorraine devised a very astute plan. He asked the pope to issue a brief establishing the Inquisition in France as it already existed in Spain. Paul IV. was a fanatic, and always ready to act in this direction. On April 25th, 1557, he published a pontifical brief, appointing three Grand Inquisitors in France : the Cardinals of Lorraine, Bourbon, and Châtillon. The Parliament of Paris was weak enough to approve this brief, January 15th, 1558, though the Inquisition was odious to the French. Theodore Beza, speaking on this subject, says[2]:—" The Cardinal of Lorraine thus laid a crafty snare for the Cardinal of Châtillon, for he knew well that one against two would be utterly powerless, and he hoped in this way to entangle him, so that if he ventured to show any favour towards those of ' the religion,' it might be a pretext for bringing suspicion and discredit not on himself only, but on his brothers also." Odet at once perceived the snare laid for him. If he accepted the offered post he would be compelled to be a party to the cruel repression of the reformed religion ; if he refused, he would in some sort denounce himself

---

[1] La Place says that even during the Constable's absence and captivity the king still consulted him about everything.

[2] *Histoire ecclesiastique des églises reformées.*

before the eyes of Catholic France. At this time his new convictions were not sufficiently formed for him to take a decided step. It was not till three years later that he openly embraced "the religion." But he contrived to elude the perilous distinction which the pope had sought to thrust upon him ; and the project of establishing the Inquisition in France was soon set aside by the pressure of popular disfavour.

Not being able to succeed in their schemes against the eldest Châtillon, the Lorraines next tried to denounce Andelot. "Francis of Guise," says De Thou, "was anxious to get Coligny's brother deprived of his office as Colonel and Captain-General of the French infantry, one of the most important posts in the kingdom."

His boundless ambition made him forget all that he owed to the brave soldier to whom, more than to anyone else, the taking of Calais was due. It was not difficult to find occasion for denouncing Andelot. His was a singularly frank and upright nature. He had made no secret of the Protestant beliefs which he had brought back with him from his captivity in Italy. The Cardinal of Lorraine was the very man to conduct an intrigue like this. In May 1558 he had the opportunity of meeting Granvelle, Bishop of Arras, formerly councillor of Charles V., now the guiding spirit of Philip II. Granvelle was lamenting to the Cardinal the war which had separated two great kings who had to contend with a common enemy, equally formidable to both, namely, heresy. "This common foe," he said, "had allies in the very court of France," and on being asked to say to whom he referred, he strongly denounced Andelot. The

Cardinal of Lorraine did not fail to report this interview to Henry II. Now it happened that at this very time Andelot was residing on his estates in Brittany, and with his sanction the reformed doctrines were being boldly preached there by two ministers, Carmel and Loiseleur, with great success. The king was much irritated by this news, and at once summoned Andelot, on his return from Brittany, to come to him at Monceaux, the country house of the queen-mother. As soon as Andelot appeared, the king reminded him of all the benefits he had heaped upon him, and told him that on this account the very last thing he expected was that he should revolt from the religion of his prince. Then growing warmer, he reproached him not only with favouring the preachers of the new doctrine, but with having taken part in the Lutheran assemblies at Pré-aux-Clercs, with having forsaken mass, at which he had not been seen during the whole affair of Calais ; and finally, with having sent Genevan books to the Admiral in his prison.

To this Andelot replied with calm dignity, acknowledging all that he owed to the king, and saying that in return he had spared nothing for the king's service. " Your Majesty will scarcely deem it strange," he went on, " if after doing my duty in your service, I study to seek my own salvation." Then, taking up the heads of the accusation brought against him, he boldly confessed that he had caused to be preached a doctrine holy and good, taken from the Old and New Testaments, and which had been approved by holy councils and by the early Church. He had not taken part in the assemblies at Pré-aux-

Clercs, but he highly approved of them. As to mass, he said, "If your Majesty had sought to learn the truth, you would feel as I do, that you could not sufficiently praise and magnify the goodness of God, who has so taken from my eyes the veil of ignorance, that by His grace I purpose never more to go to mass." As to the last charge, he owned he had sent his brother a book full of consolation. In conclusion he said, "I pray you therefore, sire, leave my conscience alone, and let me serve you with my body and worldly goods, which are wholly yours."

Theodore Beza, who gives us the account of this interview, says : "The king thought this a very strange proposal." It was the first time he had met a Protestant who dared to speak out boldly to him. This wretched heresy, the followers of which he was hanging or burning in all the streets of Paris, dared then to lift up its head in his very presence, and the man who represented it was one of the chief lords of the kingdom. The scandal was great for a king who could never understand what the rights of conscience meant, and in whose eyes it was the first duty of the subject to follow the religion of his prince. The Cardinal of Lorraine was present at the interview. He did not let slip the opportunity, and pressed Andelot to the utmost, telling him that he was in a very bad way, till at last Andelot said impatiently : "I am very certain of my doctrine, and you know better than you say, M. le Cardinal. I appeal to your conscience to witness if you have not heretofore favoured this holy doctrine." (Andelot was evidently alluding to the part of peacemaker between the two sides, which the Cardinal had often affected to play.[1]) "But," he added, "worldly honours and ambition have turned you aside, so that you are even become a persecutor of the members of Christ."

This was too much for the king. Pointing to the collar which Andelot was wearing, he said : "I did not give you that order to be used thus." And on Andelot's replying that he had not accepted the order at the price of his conscience, the king, in a fury, seized a dish which was standing before him, and dashing it to the ground, wounded the Dauphin who was sitting beside him. Then he bade the archers arrest Andelot and have him imprisoned at Melun. When the pope heard this, he complained that the king had been too lenient, and in a conversation with the French *chargé d'affaires* in Rome, he expressed bitter indignation that Andelot had not been burned at the stake on the spot.

The Guises had gained their end. The office of Colonel and Captain-General of the French infantry, which had for a long while been in the hands of the Châtillons, was taken from them and given to Blaise de Montluc, the sworn enemy of the Protestants.

Andelot meanwhile remained unmoved, and in his imprisonment received letters from Calvin. He wrote to the king a full exposition of his beliefs, declaring himself ready to serve his majesty in everything which did not touch his conscience. "But the Cardinal of Lorraine sent to him in prison a doctor of divinity, named Ruzé, the king's confessor, a man well

---

[1] Brantôme says : "He was often heard to discuss the Confession of Augsburg half approvingly, and even to preach it, more to please some of the Germans than anything else."

skilled in the arts of flattery, and in the casuistries of
the Sorbonne." So says Beza. The efforts of this
personage, who proved himself well worthy of his
name, were at first abortive ; Andelot stood firm.
He even wrote to the members of the church of
Paris, under date of July 1st, 1558, a letter full of
courage.[1] The eyes of all the Protestants in the
kingdom were turned to his prison. But Ruzé went
on conversing with him day after day, and at length
succeeded in persuading him that he might at least
be present at the sacrifice of the mass, and so satisfy
the king's requirements. Andelot's conscience could
not accept this compromise without a dull protest, but
the urgent entreaties of his wife overcame him. When
it was known that he was about to yield, a cry of grief
and shame rang through all the Protestant ranks.
The specious distinctions drawn by the casuistry of
the Sorbonne were hateful to the upright Huguenot
soul. To attend mass at such a crisis was virtually
to desert the good cause. Macard, the pastor of
the church in Paris, sent Andelot an earnest remonstrance. He reminded him that the eyes of a
whole nation were upon him, and exhorted him to
finish faithfully his course, which was but for a
moment compared with eternity. But the exhortation failed. Andelot, as Theodore Beza says,
consented that mass should be said in his presence,
and without making any other verbal abjuration, he
received his release from prison. " But," adds the
historian, " he afterwards acknowledged this to have

---

[1] See *Le bulletin de la société d'hist. du protest. français*, vol. iii., p. 245.

been an act of great weakness, which to the day of his death he condemned, and sought to atone for by all the means in his power. Nevertheless his defection caused a great scandal at the time." The pastor of the church in Paris reproached him, with stern fidelity, for his weakness, and nothing short of the unshaken devotion which Andelot thenceforward displayed to the cause of " the religion " could have effaced the memory of the fault which he himself never forgave.

The Admiral meanwhile still remained a prisoner in Ghent. But the time was approaching when peace was to be concluded between France and Spain. The successes of Francis of Lorraine, at Calais and at Thionville (June 23rd, 1558), had been balanced by the defeat which, on the 13th of July, Count Egmont had inflicted on the army of General de Termes at Gravelines.

Philip II. was anxious to put an end to hostilities, and his great idea at this time was to crush heresy by a union of the Catholic powers. The Constable, on the other hand, who still retained a great influence over Henry II., had grown utterly impatient of his captivity, feeling that every day it was prolonged the Guises were gaining ground. The Guises were anxious at first that the war which did so much for their private interests should be continued. Francis of Lorraine made desperate efforts to incline the king to this course. Henry II. wrote to Montmorency : " Francis of Lorraine is constantly trying to persuade me that I am better prepared to go to war now than I ever was, and that I could not possibly lose so much in carrying on the war as I shall by making peace." [1]   But the Guises saw that the mind of the king was towards peace.   Moreover, the Cardinal of Lorraine had come to an understanding with Granvelle, and as he wished to assure the greatness of his house by placing himself at the head of the Catholic party, the co-operation of Philip had become a necessity to him.   While the negotiations with Spain were in progress, therefore (September 1558), he contrived to take part in them.   On October 17th a suspension of arms was concluded at Cercamp. This had to be several times renewed.   The death of Queen Mary of England somewhat interrupted the negotiations, but they were soon resumed.   As a pledge of his good will, Philip II., on consideration of a ransom, granted the Constable his liberty. He left the Low Countries December 14th, and went directly to St. Germain, where he received the heartiest welcome from the king.   He took advantage of this friendly reception to present to the king his nephew Andelot, whom Henry recognised gracefully, as though nothing had happened.   Diane de Poitiers, who began to be made seriously uneasy by the ambition of the Guises, now turned to Montmorency.   During this time Coligny was treating with Philibert Emmanuel touching his ransom, which the Duke of Savoy had fixed at the enormous sum of fifty thousand gold crowns.   Charlotte de Laval was obliged, in order to raise this sum, to appeal to the devotion of Coligny's vassals.   At length, in the

---

[1] See in Delaborde (vol. i., p. 345) the curious letter which shows how completely Henry II. felt himself to be in the power of the Guises.

beginning of February 1559, Coligny was able to set out for France. His captivity had lasted a year and five months.

On the 24th of April, in this year, the famous treaty of Cateau-Cambrésis was concluded between the belligerent powers. Mary Tudor, wife of Philip II., had died with these words on her lips : " Open my heart, and you will find Calais written on it." The Protestant Queen Elizabeth was her successor. The alliance between Spain and England was thus practically broken. Philip II. was weary of the war, as we have seen.[1] On the other hand, the king, the Constable, and the Guises were equally eager (each for private reasons) that peace should be concluded. No one on this occasion was thinking really of the honour of France. If Coligny had had any part in the negotiations, we may be sure they would have taken another direction, and that at Cateau-Cambrésis, as at Vaucelles, Coligny would have staunchly guarded the interests of the country.

As it was, the treaty of Cateau-Cambrésis was a very hard one for France. She was to keep Calais, but to soothe the sensitiveness of England she engaged to restore it in eight years. This was a clause in which no one really believed. The Empire left to France the Trois-Evêchés. Henry

---

[1] On February 12th Philip wrote to his minister Granvelle: "I have already spent one million two hundred thousand ducats which I have drawn from Spain, and I want another million between now and March. . . . Spain can do no more for me. I seem to be in such a case that I shall be ruined if I do not make peace. Let there be no rupture at any price" (H. Martin, *Hist. de France*, vol. viii., p. 476).

and Philip swore perpetual amity, and pledged themselves to hasten the calling of a general Council
to bring about the unity of the whole Christian
Church. Philip was to marry Elizabeth of France,
the king's eldest daughter, then aged thirteen
years.

Philibert Emmanuel, Duke of Savoy, enriched by
the ransoms of so many French officers, became
brother-in-law to Henry II., by his marriage with
the king's sister Marguerite, and recovered almost
all his estates—Savoy, La Bresse, Bugey, and more
than half Piedmont. This was leaving the enemies
of France at the very gates of Lyons.

Henry abandoned, moreover, all his allies in Italy
who had compromised themselves in his cause. He
gave back to Philip, Thionville, Yvoi, Domvilliers,
Marienbourg, and Montmédy. The best French
generals, Moulin and Brissac, protested vigorously.
Francis of Guise opposed his brother, the Cardinal
of Lorraine, and said to the king: "Sire, you will
give back in one day that which could not be taken
from you by thirty years of reverses."

Nothing was said of secret stipulations, but the
sequel proved that one of the points on which
Granvelle and Charles of Lorraine had most strongly
insisted, was the union of the whole forces of both
kingdoms, for the extermination of the Huguenots.[1]

---

[1] "As soon as ever the peace was concluded, the Cardinal
of Lorraine, who had been one of the principal actors in it,
declared, in full parliament, that it had been the will of the
king to make peace at any price and on any terms whatsoever,
in order that he might have more leisure to attend to the
extermination of the heresy of Calvin" (Pasquier, Book IV.,
Letter 3, quoted by M. Delaborde).

Such was, for France, the humiliating close of the sanguinary duel, which had been going on for more than forty years between the house of Austria and the Valois.

CHAPTER XIII.

THE year 1559, which witnessed Coligny's restoration to his country, opened under sinister auspices for the cause of the religion that lay already very near his heart. He was on the eve of openly espousing the reformed faith, but for the present he was still holding himself in reserve. In order to be more free, he offered to resign his office as Governor of Picardy, but the king would not consent. When the English envoys came to assist at the administration of the oath to Henry II. for the ratification of the peace, Coligny accompanied them to the door of the cathedral, but would not go in to mass. This was a very marked step.

In the spring of this year the Protestants of Paris were cruelly entrapped. They had been repeatedly surprised in their assemblies, and visited summarily with barbarous punishments. *"Death to the heretics!"* is the monotonous refrain of all the edicts of this age. Death was the penalty for speaking against the mass; death for taking part in Protestant

gatherings; death for distributing the works of the
Genevan press. For brief intervals the parliament
would relax the persecution, but on the violent
denunciation of some preacher the penalties were
again enforced; and yet the number of the Protestants
increased day by day.[1]

It was on May 25th of this year (1559) that
the delegates of the Protestant churches met in
a narrow street of the Faubourg St. Germain, to
deliberate on the possibility of holding their first
national synod.[2] It was an act of heroism to meet
at all, for the life of all present was at the mercy of
any spy, and to be burnt alive at the stake was the
penalty annexed by law to this offence. We can
but be struck with the calmness of their deliberations under these circumstances, and the wisdom of
their decisions. The president was a young pastor,
François Morel, aged twenty-two. In four days
they traced the grand lines of their confession of

---

[1] The government was sometimes alarmed at the effect
produced by the public executions, and began to strangle the
prisoners secretly in their cells, as Philip II. was about to do
in Spain. Our readers should note among many other trials
of the period that of Gaspard de Heu, Seigneur du Buy, formerly sheriff of Metz; a friend to France, but a Protestant.
He was denounced by the Cardinal of Lorraine. He professed
himself willing to die with Christ, but not with the holy Church.
He was strangled in the Castle of Vincennes while repeating
the Apostles' Creed; and the document adds, "This done,
we caused the said executioner of justice to retire secretly,
and forbade him and his valet to tell or reveal anything of the
said execution" (*Bulletin de la Société d'hist. du prot. français*, vol. lxxv., p. 164). Gaspard de Heu was brother-in-law
to the famous La Renaudie, who, as we shall see, did not
forget what had happened.

[2] Only ten churches were represented beside the Church of
Paris, so dangerous were the times.

faith ; the same confession which already, for more than twenty-five years, their martyrs had repeated before their judges, and which they held with a unity of faith which no cross-questioning could baffle. In the same conference the bases of ecclesiastical discipline were settled. The laity—that is, all Christian people—were guaranteed their rights in the Church. But side by side with the great principles which have formed the strength of Protestantism from its very beginning, we trace the mistakes of the age, especially in relation to religious liberty. The sword of the magistrate was still held to be a lawful weapon · in defence of the truth.

Immediately after this assembly of the proscribed religionists, Paris hailed the arrival of a deputation sent by Philip II., and headed by the Duke of Alva, who came in the name of the King of Spain to marry Elizabeth of France, daughter of Henry II. The princes of the house of Lorraine went to meet him, and there were splendid festivities in honour of the occasion. Among the envoys of the Spanish monarch was a young lord, whose valour had been remarked at St. Quentin, William of Nassau, Prince of Orange. He himself afterwards narrated an incident which happened at this time, which made a profound impression on his life. Going one day with Henry II. to the chase, the king taking him for a good Catholic (as indeed he was at this time), began to unfold to him " the real designs of the King of Spain and the Duke of Alva." These designs aimed at nothing less than the complete extermination of all those suspected of the religion in France and throughout all Christendom. " I confess," adds the prince, " that I was greatly moved with pity and compassion towards so many good people all devoted to slaughter, and generally towards this whole country, to which I owed so much, and into which they are seeking to introduce an Inquisition worse and more cruel than that of Spain. . . . Seeing, I say, these things, I confess that from this time I set myself in good earnest to help to hunt out these vermin of Spaniards from this country."[1]

It was then at the same time, and under the influence of the same feelings excited by the san- guinary projects of Philip and the Guises, that William of Orange and Coligny, without as yet knowing each other, both formed the determination to join the Protestant party.

Henry II., who was always weak-minded, fell more and more under the influence of the Cardinal of Lorraine. He was angry with parliament for its occasional indulgence towards the Calvinists. There were in the parliament three distinct parties, diverging more and more from each other. There were, first, the Catholic fanatics, like the first president, Gilles Lemaistre, who regarded heresy as a crime worthy of death. Then there was a moderate or *political* party, as it began to be called, which believed in the possible co-existence of two religions in the kingdom; lastly, there were the Protestants, some of whom had declared themselves, like the famous Anne du Bourg.

One of the parliamentary chambers—that of La Tournelle—had commuted a sentence of death passed

---

[1] Apology of William IX., Prince of Orange, in La Pize (*Tableau de l'histoire des princes d'Orange*; p. 485).

upon three of the reformed faith, into banishment. As this chamber comprised eminent judges, such as Séguier and Harlay, the king's attorney resolved to convoke the *Mercuriale*, or Assembly of Remonstrance, for the last Wednesday in April. In this way the king's advisers would be obliged to give their opinion on the question of "the religion." Some had the courage to speak of reform and of the necessity of calling a general council. Hereupon arose violent protestations from Lemaistre, President Minard, and others. After the meeting broke up, Lemaistre and Minard went further; they went to the king and besought him to interfere. The Cardinal of Lorraine, who had planned all this campaign, joined his entreaties to theirs. "Yes, sire," he said, "come to the parliament, if only to show the King of Spain that you are firm in the faith." He even ventured to advise the king to take advantage of the presence of the Duke of Alva, and of the great lords who had assembled to witness the marriage of his daughter, to make an example by executing half-a-dozen Lutheran councillors.[1]

On the 15th of June, Henry II., yielding to these detestable counsels, repaired to the Augustins, where the parliament was sitting, the Palais de Justice being occupied at the time by the workmen who were preparing it for the marriage celebrations. He commanded his attorney-general to pronounce the *Mercuriale* against the renegade councillors. The first president, Lemaistre, then spoke of the piety of

---

[1] This fact is attested by Marshal de Vielleville (*Memoires,* Book VII.), who in vain endeavoured to dissuade Henry from going to the parliament.

Philip Augustus, who had had six hundred Albigenses burned in one day. But these threats did not intimidate some of the offenders, who gave proof that day of their heroic courage. These brave men were Claude Viol, Dufaur, and foremost of all, Anne du Bourg, who calmly defended the Lutherans, paying no heed to the storm of anger aroused by his words. He pointed to the vices and crimes which went unpunished day by day, and showed that the Protestants had been no law-breakers nor disturbers of the peace; that what they demanded was the reformation of the Church according to the law of God, and he concluded, "It is no small thing to condemn those who in the very midst of the flames call upon the name of the Lord Jesus Christ."

The king, made furious, ordered Anne de Montmorency, the Constable, to arrest Anne du Bourg and four of his brave colleagues on the spot. The Constable entrusted the work to Montgomery, who afterwards became so prominent a leader of the Huguenots.

These councillors were thrown into prison. Four days later the king sent letters patent from Écouen, commanding the judges to deal with them after the utmost rigour of the laws against heretics. On the 24th of June, at the instigation of the pope, Paul IV., he made a proposal, through Montmorency, to the Duke of Alva, to come to an understanding with Philip II. for the destruction of Geneva, "that sink of corruption." [1]

On June 29th, in a tournament given on the occa-

---

[1] Letter from the Duke of Alva to Philip II., published by M. Mignet in the *Journal des Savans*, 1837, p. 171.

sion of the marriage, he was wounded by Montgomery's lance, which pierced through his visor right into the brain. D'Aubigné says that as he was being carried to the Hotel des Tournelles, he expressed his regret for having persecuted so many good people.[1].

On the 18th of July he died. Coligny was one of the lords who watched over his mortal remains. " And finally there happened unwittingly a very remarkable thing, namely, that in decorating his bed of state, after the fashion of deceased kings, they hung over it a rich tapestry containing the history of the conversion of St. Paul, with these words inscribed in large letters : ' Saul, Saul, why persecutest thou me ? ' The which was seen and remarked by so many that the Constable, who had charge of the body, on being told of it, caused it to be removed, and another piece of tapestry to be placed in its stead." [2]

---

[1] *Histoire universelle*, vol. i., book iii.
[2] Theodore Beza, *Histoire ecclés.*, edition 1883, p. 226.

CHAPTER XIV.

THE unexpected death of Henry II. left the reins
of government in the hands of a youth of
sixteen, Francis II. He was entirely under the
dominion of the Guises, who ruled over him through
his young queen, their niece, the fascinating Mary
Stuart. But while this alliance had brought them
very near the throne, it could not cancel the claims of
the true princes of the blood, that is to say, of the
Bourbons. It was at once evident that there would
be a sharp struggle for power between them and the
Lorraines.

Ever since the revolt of the famous Constable
Charles, the Bourbons had been suspected by the
Valois. Henry II., following in the steps of Francis I.,
had systematically excluded them from all high offices.
They were at this time represented by three princes:
Antoine, who five years before had been raised to
the throne of Navarre by his marriage with Jeanne
d'Albret ; and his two brothers, Charles, the Cardinal,
who was so ardent a Catholic that he subordinated

everything else to his religion, and who, after serving
the Guises, died as king of the League ; and Louis,
Prince of Condé, at·this time in all the fervour of
youth, and already famous for his heroism at Metz,
Renty, St. Quentin, Calais, and Thionville. It began
to be rumoured that Antoine and Louis had joined
" the religion." The report was true, but the issue
was cruelly to belie the high hopes which the French
Calvinists based upon it. Antoine was so unstable
and pliant that he was incapable of any stedfast
course of action. He became a convert to Protestantism before his brave partner in life; but while
Jeanne d'Albret served the cause with her whole
soul, her lord betrayed it shamefully. Condé had
stronger convictions, a chivalrous character, and
heroic aspirations. But his natural levity often let
him be carried away by any access of passion, and
made him fail of his true destiny.

As soon as the Guises came into power with
Francis II., the Constable Montmorency ought to
have allied himself with the Bourbon princes. But
there were old causes of estrangement between them.
Languedoc, which formerly belonged to Navarre, had
been taken away by Henry II., who had given the
government of it to Montmorency ; and quite
recently the Constable, who was the chief negotiator
of the treaty of Cateau-Cambrésis, had made no stipulation for the restoration to France of the portion of
Navarre still held by Spain. Moreover, if the princes,
whether from policy or from conviction, or through
the influence of their wives, were inclining to " the
religion," the Constable, then almost a septuagenarian,
was still a strong Catholic, and was animated by so

blind a hatred of the innovators that he became in the end the ally of the house of Lorraine.

On the death of Henry II., however, the Constable found himself in no enviable position. He whom the late king was wont to call his compeer, saw the two brothers Lorraine at once mount guard over Francis II., " suffering no one to come near his person, still less to speak to him, unless in the presence of one of them ; and they kept so close a watch that they never let him out of their sight." [1] The old Constable, however, so long accustomed to changes at court, bore himself so discreetly, that he contrived to gain honour from that which was planned for his dishonour. A week after the king's death, " having dined early, he made an appointment with his sons and his nephews the Châtillons, and unexpectedly presented himself at the Louvre so as to meet Francis as he was coming away from his dinner. The Guises had read Francis his lesson. The Constable wishing to obtain from the king a word confirming him in his dignities, spoke of his past fidelity and of the services rendered by his nephews, hoping that the king would be pleased to retain them in their offices. " As for himself . . ." Here Francis " stopped him short, saying that he granted his request ; and principally with regard to the Admiral de Châtillon, of whom he hoped to make use. That as to the Constable himself, he confirmed him in his estates, and desired that he should enjoy his pensions during his life." But

---

[1] La Planche. The reader should refer to the whole scene which follows as described by La Planche. There could not be a racier account of this court comedy. St. Simon gives us nothing better than this.

just as the Constable was beginning to breathe again, the king added that desiring to give him rest in his old age, he had decided to divide the principal offices of state between his two uncles, the Guises; "that he had given to one the charge of the finances and of affairs of state, and to the other the command in the war department;" so that if the Constable desired rest he could take it; but that he would be always welcome when he liked to take his place in the Council. The affront was hard to bear, but Montmorency immediately changed his front, declaring that he had come for the very purpose of being released from the offices he held, and then added: "As to your Majesty's good pleasure to retain me in your council, I pray you to have me excused, since for two reasons it cannot be. In the first place I could not be placed under those whom I have always commanded; and second, being full of years and almost in my dotage (so they say), my counsel could be of little or no avail."

After thus solacing his wounded pride, Montmorency went to Catherine, from whom he might hope for a more favourable reception, especially as in the past he had often maintained her cause. He was fond of reminding her that he had brought about her marriage, and had saved her from being repudiated on the ground of sterility. Catherine had been falsely told by the Guises, that immediately after the death of Henry, the Constable had written to the King of Navarre summoning him, and this had irritated her. She was angry with him too for having been the intimate friend and compeer of the late king. In order to justify her coldness, La Planche says she referred to some trifling things that the Constable had said about her in conversation; at length she assumed so distant a manner that the Constable decided to retire to his estates and wait for better days.

The Guises thus remained masters of the young king, and Theodore Beza was not exaggerating when, writing to Bullinger, September 12th, 1559, he said: "The Guises have so parcelled out the power between them, that they have left the king nothing more than the name."

It began to be remarked, moreover, that the partisans of the Lorraines insisted upon the fact that they were descended from Charlemagne by their wives, and that consequently they had an eventual claim on the throne.

And now we note a change in the attitude of the Guises, the importance of which historians have sometimes failed to observe. It cannot be denied that hitherto they had all, and especially the Duke, been strong patriots, and resolutely opposed to Spain. But in 1559 this attitude suddenly changed, and their great aim seemed to be to secure the favour of Philip II. To those who look below the surface this is easily explained by the close alliance between the Cardinal of Lorraine and Granvelle. It was Granvelle who directed the attention of the Guises to the necessity of exterminating heresy, and who urged them to put themselves boldly at the head of the Catholic party, and to lean henceforth on Spain. In no other way can we understand how it was that as soon as ever the Guises came into power, they tendered to Philip II. the homage of veritable vassals. The Cardinal writes to Philip in the month of August, that he "is prepared to serve him with no less affection than the King of France;" and the Duke expresses himself in equally servile terms.[1] Philip II. accepts the honour conferred on him, and writes to Francis II. "that he bears him such affection, that he declares himself tutor and protector of him and of his kingdom ; as also of his affairs, which he holds in no less consideration than his own." As we read these words we see how completely, under the influence of Granvelle and of the Cardinal, everything had changed since the days of Metz and of St. Quentin.

The year 1559 marks then a decided change in the attitude of France. Hitherto her policy had been anti-Spanish ; henceforth it will be anti-Protestant. Charles V. was her enemy ; Philip II. becomes her adviser. From the time that Granvelle and the Cardinal of Lorraine met and understood each other, an alliance was entered into between them, and Coligny truly says upon his deathbed that nothing is done in the counsels of France of which the King of Spain is not at once apprised.

In the depths of the Escurial the sinister son of Charles V. is silently weaving the web in which he hopes to entangle all Europe. That which his father failed to do by force of arms, he will effect by diplomacy. Historians have sometimes spoken of Philip's political genius. Where do we see it ? He misread his age, and led Spain on a downward path from

[1] See the text of these two letters in Delaborde (vol. i., p. 387).

which she has never been able to retrace her steps.
Hating the light of day, eschewing public discussion
as he shunned the battle-field, Philip wrought his
works of darkness in the gloomy solitude of his
palace-prison. Here rigid etiquette barred the access
to any new ideas. No free and honest words could
vibrate in that heavy air. But every day, and almost
every hour, couriers arrived, bringing the reports of
the emissaries whom he had scattered all over Europe.
Never was espionage practised on so vast a scale.
Philip trusted no one. In conference with his council,
he weighed every word. He had the timidity of
pride which feared to compromise itself by betraying
the hesitation and indecision of his mind. He never
directly contradicted anyone, but would seem to
approve what was said, and the next morning the ill-
fated speaker would learn that the king had doomed
him to death.

With every one of his emissaries was a secret
agent, whose duty it was to keep watch over the
emissary. Indefatigable and slow, the king would
collate and compare all the letters of his messengers.
He himself dictated the answers, couched in language
full of reticence and *double entendre*. He never
pledged himself to anything without reserving a way
of escape, concealing a snare under a promise, betraying his friends themselves, and he was forced, in order
to thread his way through this labyrinth, to note in
the margin of the minute of such and such a letter,
that the thing it affirms is false, thus registering his
lies and perfidies with a cynical candour more frightful
than the fiercest access of rage and hatred. Indeed
Philip was never in a passion. In the portrait of him

by Titian, the cold dry glance of his eye only too clearly reveals his soul. Sallow and cold, this Spaniard is as phlegmatic as a Dutchman. He has inherited from his father an inflexible belief in his rights as sovereign, which make him supreme even over the pope himself. He has the haughty pride of his race, and the hard fanaticism which nothing softens. Without remorse he gives the order for assassination; without a quiver of emotion he delivers to the torture the man whom but a day before he called his friend. In all his voluminous correspondence this man, who caused so much suffering and instigated to such fearful tortures, utters no single word of pity or regret.

Granvelle was throughout his chosen counsellor, and Granvelle, in order to keep himself the better informed of all that was going on in France, had sent his own brother, Perrenot de Chantonnay, as ambassador to Paris. These two brothers were worthy of each other, and the ill they wrought to France cannot be measured. Born on the frontier, using French as their native tongue, possessing all the subtlety of the Franche-Comtois, and concealing it under an affectation of brusqueness, they served the purposes of Philip better than any true Spaniards could have done. Spaniards, by their pride and Castilian obstinacy, were prone to show a blind persistency in any cause they took up. But these semi-Frenchmen knew how to accommodate themselves to circumstances, and to supplement force by finesse. Chantonnay, as soon as ever he was settled in Paris, began to work on the *noblesse*, and to create a Spanish party, thus secretly inaugurating that system of corruption which thirty years later led all the chiefs of the League to sell themselves to Philip, and to offer to him the very crown of France.

The new attitude of the Guises could not fail to arouse national resentment. Antoine de Navarre arrived at Vendôme, and summoned thither his brother, the Prince of Condé, the Châtillons, the Count de la Rochefoucauld, the Vidame of Chartres, Antoine de Croy (afterwards Condé's nephew), and other lords attached to Montmorency's party. The meeting was a very excited one. Condé and the Vidame urged an instant appeal to arms, to deliver the king from the tyranny of the Lorraines. Coligny feared anything that might look like a revolt. He recommended that they should try the effect of grave remonstrances and representations addressed to the king and the queen-mother. Antoine de Navarre was commissioned, as a prince of the blood, to demand for himself and his brother a share in the direction of affairs, and a position worthy of their rank. This wise project was unhappily rendered abortive by the incapacity and cowardice of the husband of Jeanne d'Albret.

Coligny and his nephew Condé decided at the same time to interpose, for the first time, on behalf of the Protestants.

The Church of Paris, which was suffering cruelly from persecution, had decided to appeal to the Admiral and to his eldest sister, Madame de Roye, mother-in-law to Condé. On their advice, the Church addressed a letter direct to Catherine. In this letter it was urged that " during the life of the late king, Henry II., and for a long time, they had hoped much from her gentleness and benignity, insomuch that beside the prayers ordinarily offered for the king's welfare, they prayed God continually that it might please Him so to strengthen her in spirit that she might be a second Esther ;" that now they addressed themselves to her and prayed her " not to permit this new reign to be sullied with the innocent blood, which had so cried aloud to God that His anger was manifestly kindled ; and that it could only be appeased by giving respite to those who were suffering wrongfully, and by hearing them in their own defence." Catherine was pleased that the Protestants had addressed themselves to her, for she felt that this was a party which she might, as La Planche says, gain to her side in any pressing extremity.

At the same time (August 26th) she received a letter from a gentleman, named Villemadon, formerly attached to the service of Queen Marguerite of Navarre, and this letter made some impression upon her.[1] He reminded her how once, when she was forsaken by the late king, she had turned to God, reading His Word, and singing with great delight the Psalms translated into French verse, and how she had chosen as her own, Psalm cxli. (although it was not Marot's translation),[2] which ran thus :

" Vers l'Eternel des oppressés le père,
Je m'en irai, lui montrant l'impropère[3]
Que l'on me fait, et lui ferai prière
A haute voix, qu'il ne jette en arrière
Mes piteux cris, car en lui seul j'espère."

---

[1] This is given in the collection of documents published in the seventeenth century under the title, *Mémoires de Condé*.

[2] We must note these words in passing. Marot was the fashionable poet. To quote or sing Marot would not imply anything ; but to sing a psalm which was not translated by Marot was a much more serious thing, and a sign of inclining towards heresy.

[3] *Impropère*—affront, annoyance ; English *improper*.

"Your Majesty," said Villemadon, "must remember how God heard your cry and gave you children." Since then everything was changed. The Cardinal of Lorraine had corrupted the court, and now France was given over to the enemies of God. The only succour possible must be looked for from the princes of the blood, and he entreated her Majesty "to bring up her children in the way of the good king Josiah."

This mention of the princes of the blood made Catherine think. She wondered whether the letter had been written at their instigation. She resolved then to use artifice, "and promised the Prince of Condé, his mother-in-law, and the Admiral, that she would put a stop to the persecution on condition that the Protestants did not hold meetings, and that they all lived quietly and without creating scandal."

She went further, and taking aside her friend, Mademoiselle de Montpensier, whom she knew to belong to the reformed party, she pretended that she was compelled, to her great regret, to yield to the pressure of the Guises, complained of the contempt in which she was held, and promised that in time she would show "all favour to the poor persecuted ones."

Yet the weeks rolled by, and there was no sign that the queen-mother meant to keep her promises. Persecution raged with unabated severity, and it was even rumoured that Anne du Bourg was soon to be led to the stake. Preparations were in progress for the consecration of the young king, and this might possibly be made the occasion for measures of clemency. The Church addressed another letter to the queen-mother. She was

reminded that in accordance with her desire that
they should give no room for scandal, they had met
in such small numbers as scarcely to be noticed, lest
they should give occasion to their enemies to direct
a fresh attack upon them ; but they saw no result
from the queen's promises.   The letter was couched
in sufficiently bold terms.   It was announced that
if Du Bourg was executed, "there would be great
danger that men, pressed by too much violence, might
be like the waters of a reservoir, breaking down its
banks and rushing over the neighbouring lands, carrying ruin and desolation with them."   Not that they
themselves would ever have counselled revolt, but
there were many who did not recognise the discipline
of their Church, who yet could no longer endure
the abuses to which they were subject, and that
" they had thought it well to warn her Majesty, lest
if any mischief came she should think it proceeded
from them."

This kind of threatening greatly irritated Catherine.
She spoke of the letter as " very sharp and hard,"
and added : " They threaten me thinking to make
me afraid, but they will find they are not yet
where they think they are."   Softening, however,
she said " she understood nothing of this doctrine,"
and that if some weeks before she had been " moved
to wish them well, it was rather from pity and the
compassion natural to woman, than from being
instructed or informed if their doctrine were true or
false.   For when she thought of these poor people
being thus cruelly murdered, burned, and tortured,
not for larceny, robbery, or brigandage, but simply
for holding their opinions, and being ready to go to

death for them as joyfully as to a wedding, she was inclined to believe that there must be something here passing natural reason."

The Protestants believing Catherine to be sincere in what she said, were encouraged to make another appeal to her, and this time the Admiral undertook to be their spokesman. Since Catherine had been left a widow, he, seeing her often in great distress, had, among other counsels, admonished her to betake herself to prayer, and to read the Word of God, where she would find sure consolation, without troubling herself about the doctrines of monks and doctors of the Romish Church, who, by their sophistries, plunged souls into despair instead of comforting them. He had told her that in order to receive this consolation she should communicate with some minister of the Reformed Church, and that if she thought well he would send her one from the Church of Paris, who would content her well, and that her Majesty would then have a better opinion of the Protestants than before. The queen-mother feigned to approve of this proposal, and begged him to do as he said, assuring him that she would suffer no harm to happen to any one whom Coligny sent. Indeed, from the demeanour of the queen it would seem that she had a singular desire for this interview.[1]

Madame de Roye, who was at Villiers-Cotterets, where the Court was at this time, sent a messenger on horseback to carry this great news to the Church in Paris.

---

[1] *Opera Calvinii*, vol. xvii., p. 632. M. Athanase Coquerel (fils) has given the translation in his *Histoire de l'église réformée de Paris.*

We know from a Latin letter which François Morel, one of the pastors of that Church, addressed to Calvin (September 11th), that the Consistory was at once convoked to deliberate on this important question. Madame de Roye begged that they would send Laroche-Chandieu, one of their most able ministers, to the queen. " Let her have talk and conversation with our Chandieu," she said, "and it is to be hoped she will change her opinion and become favourable to us." The pros and cons were debated for a long time. Dare they trust the queen? Would it not be denouncing Chandieu, and exposing him to certain death? On the other hand Madame de Roye entreated that they would not let slip such an opportunity. Finally Chandieu settled the question himself, declaring that he was ready to depart. They prayed God to keep and direct him. His departure left his friends in terrible anxiety.

It was the very time of the king's consecration. The queen-mother had just gone to Rheims, and had left word that Chandieu would find her in a certain village in the environs, and that she would see him without any one's suspecting anything. He went to the place appointed, remained a whole day, and received no message. On her return to Paris, Catherine refused to see him. From this time the Protestants knew that they had nothing to hope for from her.

They could place no more dependence on Antoine de Navarre. He had come to the court to fulfil the mission with which he had been entrusted by the Assembly at Vendôme. But hardly had he arrived when he let himself be overruled by Catherine's honeyed speech, and even submitted to the affronts which the Guises heaped upon him, without seeming to feel his dignity wounded. No one was sent to meet him. When he arrived at St. Germain he found his baggage in the courtyard. No apartment had been prepared for him, and he had to accept the hospitality of Marshal St. André, which was offered with a very bad grace. He was treated like a play-king. And finally, in order to get rid of him, he was entrusted with the mission of conducting Elizabeth, the young wife of Philip II., to the frontier of Spain.

This moral abdication of Antoine, which Calvin in his correspondence characterises as shameful treason,[1] made Condé the real leader of the party of resistance. Hence, after his brother's departure, Condé summoned to the Castle of La Ferté most of the lords who had already taken part in the Assembly at Vendôme. There was the same division of opinion, and it was concluded that for the present a recourse to arms was not feasible. Coligny then retired to Châtillon, where he was joined by his brother Odet.

---

[1] " Quum ejus ignavia nihil fuerit turpius, accessit tandem et proditio." (*Calvin to Peter Martyr Vermigli*, Oct. 4th, 1559.)

CHAPTER XV.

THE close of the year 1559, at which we have now arrived, may be considered as the time when Coligny made his first public avowal of adherence to the reformed religion. His earliest biographer says that his courageous wife, Charlotte de Laval, took the initiative in this great decision. He says, "The Admiral, being so often and affectionately pressed by her on the subject, resolved to speak to her once earnestly about it, which he did at great length, showing her how for many years he had never heard or seen, whether in Germany or France, of any who had made an open profession of "the religion" without being overwhelmed with calamities and woes. That, by the edicts of the kings Francis I. and Henry II., which were rigidly observed by the Parliament, those who were convicted of "the religion" were burned alive by slow fires in the public streets, and their goods confiscated to the king. Nevertheless, if she was prepared for her part with so much confidence to accept the conditions common to all who embraced "the religion," he would not be lacking in his duty. Her reply was that these conditions were no other than the Church of God had been subject to in all ages, and she doubted not they would so remain to the end of the world. Wherefore having pledged their faith one to the other, the Admiral began little by little to attempt by pious conversation to bring his household and friends to the knowledge of God, etc.[1]

One question of doctrine had somewhat stumbled Coligny on the threshold of the Reformed communion. He had abandoned the dogma of transubstantiation, on which for a long time he had held discussions with the most learned pastors of the Churches of France (says the same writer). But he inclined to believe with Luther in " the presence of the body of Christ," that is to say, " His flesh, bones, and blood, were in a manner mingled with the bread and wine." One day, being present at a preaching held secretly in a place called Vatteville, and at which the Lord's Supper was to be observed, " he asked the company of the faithful not to be offended at his infirmity ; but to pray God for him, and requested the minister to speak with a little more clearness on the mystery of the Lord's Supper." The minister then set forth the Calvinist doctrine, according to which there are in the Lord's Supper two elements, the one terrestrial, the other spiritual. In the terrestrial element no change takes place. The bread and the wine remain as they were. But

---

[1] *Vita Gasparis Colinii*, 1575, p. 221 *seq*. We generally quote from the translation made in the 17th century, which reproduces very accurately the simplicity of the Latin text.

the faithful believer partakes of the spiritual body of Jesus Christ, "crucified, risen, and glorified." The minister added : " St. Augustine has well said that to eat of the bread which perisheth not, but endureth unto everlasting life, is to believe in Christ. Wherefore," said he, " preparest thou thy teeth and thy stomach ? believe and thou shalt have eaten. Prepare not the throat but the heart." The Admiral, instructed by these words, first of all rendered thanks to God and to the whole Church, and from this time was fully minded to partake of this sacred and holy mystery on the first occasion. This being divulged throughout France, it is impossible to say what joy and consolation the churches received therefrom.

In order to appreciate the heroism of the decision so simply arrived at by the Admiral and his wife, we must call to mind the persecution which at this time was raging with new fury through the whole of France.

In spite of the fine promises made by Catherine to Madame de Roye, the government was putting the edicts into force with remorseless severity. It was needful indeed for the authorities to look twice before striking a blow at Protestants of high rank, because they were anxious to make out that heresy gathered its disciples only among the common people, the working classes.

This was no doubt true at the beginning. Nothing could be more erroneous than to attribute to the French noblesse the first rapid advance of the Reformation in France. For one or two nobles mentioned in Crespin's martyrology, we find thousands of the common people. But as a very Catholic historian, Florimond de Rémond, has remarked, those who joined the Reformation were " mainly painters, clockmakers, picture dealers, jewellers, book-binders, printers and others, who in their trade have some nobleness of spirit."[1]

In 1549 special chambers had been created in the parliaments for crimes of heresy, " for its speedier despatch." In 1551 Chateaubriant's edict had referred these crimes to the secular tribunals as well as to the ecclesiastical judges ; absolved by the one, they could be condemned by the other. The sentences were to be executed without appeal. The law offered the most shameless baits to greed ; those who denounced heretics were to have a third of the possessions of their victims. If the accused were exiled, their property was sequestrated to the king. Diane de Poitiers owed a large part of her immense fortune to these confiscations. The Cardinal of Lorraine had organised a vast system of espionage, for the purpose of discovering the secret assemblies of the Reformed. Wretches were found to pretend that shameful deeds were done in them. The ignorant populace was only too ready to believe it. There was no crime which was not laid to the charge of the heretics. In times of public danger they were made the victims. It was so after the defeat of St. Quentin.

The Protestants were easily recognised by certain outward signs,—the simplicity of their dress, their hats without plumes, their doublets of sombre colours. It was observed, too, that they never swore. " *Surely*

---

[1] Florimond de Rémond, *Hist. de l'hérésie de ce siècle,* vol. vii., p. 931.

or *verily* was their ordinary oath."[1]   But the name
of the Lord was ever on their lips.   Their austerity
gave offence, and was set down as hypocrisy; so
was their contempt of the Church's commandments.
Men jeered at their grave demeanour, mimicked.
their tones and biblical expressions.   The Reformed
retaliated by ridiculing the monks and their crass
ignorance, the luxury of the prelates and their irre-
gular lives, the Latin of the Church, the worship of
saints and relics.   This was indeed a well-worn
theme from the middle ages; but that which only
excited a laugh in the pages of Rabelais, became a
crime on the lips of the Reformed.   Their pamphlets
circulated everywhere, and were greedily read by
their adversaries themselves, to whom it was a *bonne
bouche* to find some great lord or bishop touched up
with a vein of irresistible satire.   These writings
often rose to a rude kind of eloquence, as for example in *L'Épître au tigre de France,* aimed at the
Cardinal of Lorraine.   Hotman, in writing it, had
drawn his inspiration from the first of Cicero's
Catilines.   The Cardinal moved heaven and earth
to discover the author, seized the work, and caused
the printer, and a poor bookseller who happened to
have a copy, to be strangled.

Anecdotes circulated even more freely than pamphlets, and introduced a note of gaiety into this
concert of violent controversies.   Thus at the beginning of Lent it was said that the Sorbonne sent two
messengers to the Admiral's niece, the Princess of
Condé, who was in Paris, to know if she really did

---

[1] Florimond de Rémond, p. 865.

not keep the fast. They were to admonish her on the subject, and well note her replies. The messengers were two corpulent doctors. "In the hall which they entered," says La Planche, "there happened to be a gentleman named Séchelles, from Picardy, who liked them just about as much as one likes a thorn in the flesh, for the ill they had done him. They however, not knowing who he was, explained their errand." Séchelles, at once turning to the princess, said, "Madame, the doctors of the Sorbonne have been afraid you might be short of meat this Lent, and here are two fine fat calves they have sent you." Whereupon "these venerable doctors" took to their heels, to the great diversion of all present. We can imagine how the Court would relish such practical jokes as this.

But the scenes enacted were far more often tragic. In constant danger of betrayal, no one was sure of the morrow. There were endless devices, says De Thou, for ensnaring the Reformed. Statues of the Virgin and the saints were placed behind gratings at the corners of the streets, and candles or wax tapers were lighted before them. Crowds congregated at these wayside shrines, and sang hymns. There was a plate into which the passers-by were expected to drop their offerings. If any one refused to pay or to uncover his head, or tried to slip away, he was denounced as a heretic and arrested.

Death was the almost certain doom of the heretic, and the prison which preceded it was a living death. The accused was thrown into the damp dungeons of the Châtelet. He was kept in close confinement in a cell without light. The ground of the cell was often sloping, so that the unhappy man could neither stand upright nor lie down, but was obliged to hold on by his heels, to save himself from rolling into the mud at the bottom. This was called "*La chausse à l'hypocras.*" There was also the common prison into which were thrown promiscuously nobles and, peasants, men, women, young girls, and the very outcasts of society, all huddled together in a state of filth and wretchedness too horrible to picture.

From this place they were led to trial ; that is to say, to the torture-chamber. Spies were shut up with the prisoners to listen to their conversation, and try to discover where they held their meetings. These counterfeited the language of the faithful, heaving groans and sighs, and lamenting over their woes.

In the public trials the accused often seemed to change places with the judges. They would quote Scripture with singular aptness, appealing to the words of Christ and His Apostles, and arguing better than many theologians. Here and there one would denounce the evils of the Court ; as, for instance, the tailor whom Diane de Poitiers attempted to . cross-question, and who accused her of infecting the kingdom with her poison. The king was so indignant that he meant to witness the man's trial by torture ; but the sufferer fixed upon him a gaze so steadfast, sad, and penetrating, that the king was terrified, and declared he would see no more such scenes. As they were dragged to the stake, the condemned would exhort the crowd, or sing their psalms, the sad or stirring melodies of which moved the hearts of all present. So great was the effect

I 2

produced, that often the executioners were obliged to cut out the tongues of those who were to be burnt. Even then they spoke by look and gesture, their faces sometimes shining with so bright a joy, that the people said with Catherine, " They go to death as to a wedding."

Such a spectacle was to be presented in the sufferings of Anne du Bourg. There had been some talk of executing him secretly ; but his name was too well known, and they dared not do it.

Kept a prisoner in the Bastille from the month of April, Anne du Bourg had ample opportunity to save his life by equivocation. But instead of this, he gave a full exposition of his faith, and his confession is one of the most interesting monuments of the age.[1] It is given with all the calmness of strong conviction, combined with an exactness of theological knowledge which is surprising in a magistrate.

This trial moved not Paris alone, but all Protestant nations. The Elector Palatine resolved to interfere, and to ask for Du Bourg, that he might place him in a chair in the University of Heidelberg. The Cardinal of Lorraine felt that he must hasten on matters. On December 21st, the Parliament condemned Du Bourg " as an obstinate heretic, to be gibbeted in the Place de Grève, and then cast into the pile of blazing faggots beneath, to be burnt and consumed to ashes." The great magistrate, after hearing his sentence, prayed God to forgive his erring judges, and rejoiced for himself that " the day he had so long desired had come."

---

[1] It is to be found entire in Crespin, and in the article in *La France protestante* on Anne du Bourg.

Then turning to the councillors, he addressed them in a loud voice, exhorting them to think of their responsibility before God, and to turn to the Lord. He bore himself in the same manner two days later before an immense crowd, who could only be kept back by a large display of the military. As he mounted the scaffold he repeated several times, "My God, forsake me not, lest I forsake Thee !" He addressed the people from the top of the scaffold. The impression produced by his death was immense. One of those who witnessed it, the future historian, Florimond de Rémond, then only a student, says, "We burst into tears in our college when we returned from witnessing this execution, and pleaded Du Bourg's cause after his decease, cursing the judges who had wickedly condemned him." His preaching on the scaffold and at the stake did more harm than a hundred ministers could have done.

Nevertheless the persecution went on with unabated fury.

At the beginning of January 1560, Coligny came to Blois, where the Court was sitting. He had determined to give in his resignation of the government of Picardy, and to concentrate all his efforts on his duty as Admiral.[1] He had hoped to be able to hand over the government to the Prince of Condé, as was only natural, since Antoine of Navarre, brother to the Prince, had held it for a long time before Coligny. But by the advice of the Guises, this important post was entrusted to Brissac. Coligny retired to Châtillon.

---

[1] " This act of the Admiral's created much astonishment, inasmuch as it was the habit of the other courtiers to be always asking for post upon post."—*La Planche.*

CHAPTER XVI.

WE come now to the famous conspiracy of Amboise, which was rather a patriotic than a religious demonstration, and the great object of which was to deliver the young king from the tutelage of the Guises. It has never been known who were its real originators. Condé certainly took an active part in it, and it was no doubt he who was designated by the name of the "*chef muet*" or dumb leader, whose orders all the conspirators obeyed. We have seen that in the conferences of Vendôme and La Ferté, Condé had declared himself very decidedly in favour of an immediate recourse to arms. But in this case he kept in the background, acting only through his lieutenants, so that he was able afterwards to disavow all knowledge of the affair. The conspirators were not all Calvinists, and d'Aubigné says that Michel de l'Hospital took part in the enterprise.[1] It seems to have been at

---

[1] D'Aubigné does not say this without reason, for with this fact was associated a very dramatic episode of his youth. Having retired to Talcy shortly after the massacre of St.

this time that the name *Huguenots* began to be used to designate the party, at once political and religious, which entered upon the contest with the Lorraines.[2]

The apparent leader of the conspiracy was Godefroy de Barry, seigneur of La Renaudie. The conspirators met at Nantes on February 1st, 1560. La Planche says they took advantage of the fact that the parliament was sitting at the time in Brittany, and had bags full of papers carried by their

---

Bartholomew, and having in his possession the original documents of the conspiracy of Amboise, among which was found *one paper bearing the signature of l'Hospital*, he was tempted to hand them over to the Sieur de Talcy, whose daughter he loved. Talcy burned the documents, lest they should burn him. (*Mémoires*, edit. Lalanne, p. 24.) What could these documents be? Probably a legal opinion defending the royal authority against the Guises. It would be impossible to suppose l'Hospital guilty of a positive act of rebellion.

[2] The name *Huguenots* appears for the first time officially in a royal edict April 5th, 1561. It was after the conspiracy of Amboise that it began to be used commonly in France. Etienne Pasquier says that, eight or nine years before, he had heard it used in Touraine. M. Soldan says that this name, even under its French form *Huguenots*, was used in Geneva before 1530, and was the equivalent of the German *Eidgenossen*, confederates. (*Bulletin de la Soc. d'hist. du prot. français*, 1860, p. 12 and following.)

The origin of the name has been discussed in numberless dissertations (see *Le Bulletin*, 1858, p. 287; 1859, pp. 13, 122, 266, 378; 1860, p. 12; 1862, p. 328; 1876, pp. 388). Ménage, in his *Dict. hist.*, article "Huguenots," mentions the various etymologies given to it. Setting aside those which are decidedly fanciful, we may mention the following:—

1st. The Protestants assembled at Tours by the gate of King Hugo (La Place, followed by Popelinière and Davila).

2nd. The people of Tours believed in an evil spirit which appeared in the night, and was called King Huguet or Hugo. They gave this name to the Protestants who met at night. (Régnier, La Planche, Beza, De Thou.)

3rd. In Touraine small pieces of money, not worth a farthing, were called *huguenots*; the name was derived from Hugh

valets, as though they had suits to plead. It was decided that on the 10th of March following, each leader should march his troops rapidly upon Blois, where the Court was sitting ; that they should seize the Guises, and proclaim the independence of the king, placing the administration of the kingdom in Condé's hands.

The Guises heard through Granvelle, Philip II.'s minister, that something was on foot. In Paris, a lawyer named Des Avenelles, with whom La Renan-

---

Capet. It came to be used as a term of contempt. "So and so is not worth a huguenot" (Castelnau).

4th. The Guises, basing their claims on a direct descent from Charlemagne, the opposite party maintained the rights of the Capetians, and were thus called Huguenots, as the party of Hugh Capet. This explanation has against it the objection that the name Huguenots was from the first in France a term of reproach (the use of it is forbidden in the above-mentioned edict of 1561), and it is hardly to be supposed that the Guise party, who were at the time of the conspiracy of Amboise the protectors of Francis II., would have used as a term of reproach for the Protestants a name which implied their loyalty to the king. It is easy, on the other hand, to see why the Protestants should have been glad to assign such an origin to the name. We may mention here a singular fact which has not, as far as we know, been alluded to elsewhere. When, after the failure of the conspiracy of Amboise, Maligny tried to take possession of Lyon, the watchword of the Protestant conspirators was "Christ and Capet." The choice of the name (Hugh Capet) was evidently made with a view to mark their attachment to the reigning dynasty.

5th. Lastly at Geneva, those who opposed the Duke of Savoy and sought the alliance of Berne and Fribourg were called *Eidgenossen*, *Eidgnots*, *huguenots* (the *h* originally mute). The word came afterwards to designate the Protestants in opposition to the partisans of Savoy, who were called Mameluks. When we think of the close relations that existed between Geneva and the Protestants of France, it will not seem in any way strange that the name should have passed into France, and been used in the valley of the Loire, where the Churches were very numerous. At the time of the conspiracy

die lodged, turned coward and betrayed the plot. The king was hastily removed from Blois and taken to Amboise, where there was a strong castle that could not be surprised, and as it was learned that movements were commencing in many parts of the kingdom, Catherine at once endeavoured to divide the enemy by proposing a measure of pacification. She sent the Châtillons to Amboise, being well assured that they were no parties to the conspiracy.[1]

---

of Amboise, the Guise party took it up eagerly as the synonym of the conspirators; it is used in this way in a pamphlet issued by them in 1562. As early as 1560 the Guises accused the conspirators of Amboise of seeking to overthrow the king, and to form themselves into independent confederate states like the Swiss cantons (see La Planche, *passim*). This explanation, adopted by Mignet, is supported by M. Soldan on very strong evidence. On the other side it may be urged that if the name originated in Geneva, Theodore Beza would not have been ignorant of its etymology, and would have adopted it himself. But it has yet to be ascertained whether the page of the *Hist. ecclés.*, relating to the word *Huguenot* is by Beza himself, or whether it is one of the many documents collected in his name.

For our own part, we believe that the name *Huguenots* was at first an opprobrious epithet to designate those who had become confederates after the Swiss fashion; that the French Protestants early gave it an etymological derivation from Hugh Capet, in order to denote their attachment to the king. La Planche, in a passage that has been too much overlooked (p. 95, Coll. i., edit. Mennechet), says that the conspirators of Amboise, in the remonstrance published by them in 1560, gave to the word *Huguenots* its etymological derivation from Hugh Capet.

We leave the reader to decide for himself, simply observing that in reference to these popular appellations the true is not always that which seems true on the surface. The name Huguenot lost its opprobrious character in the seventeenth century. Balzac uses it as an entirely honourable epithet.

[1] This fact has been denied, but it is well established. Coligny disapproved of the conspiracy. Brantôme says: "The Admiral knew nothing of the said conspiracy of Amboise, as I have been told by some of the oldest members of 'the religion,' and by La Vigne, valet to La Renaudie,

La Planche says : "The said lady had such confidence in the virtues of the Châtillons, and bore such an affection to the Admiral, as having been always the faithful servant of the king, that she thought herself safe with such a wise knight, and hoped through his prudence to appease all." The Guises, who distrusted the Châtillons, felt reassured when they had them in their hands.

When, in accordance with the queen's summons, Coligny arrived on February 23rd, they spoke to him of the necessity they were under to have recourse to his good offices as Admiral, in order to keep open the communications between France and Scotland, and to be ready, if need were, to withstand England. Catherine, for her part, preferred to go direct to the question that was pressing ; she told the Admiral of the anxiety she was in, and implored him "not to desert the king, her son."

Having thus an opportunity of speaking, Coligny did not hesitate. He remonstrated gravely with the queen-mother (says La Planche),[1] and told her plainly

---

who was in the whole secret. The conspirators knew well what opinion Coligny had expressed at Vendôme and at La Ferté. Coligny was in agreement with Calvin, who wrote at this time to the faithful in France on this subject as follows : " Remember what weapons are given us from above. All our help is to come from Him who has granted us this privilege and honour—to hold ourselves in His keeping, and thus to possess our souls in patience ; *for it is not lawful for us to gain anything by force.*" He was very severe on the conspirators. " Quod stulte agitaverunt, pueriliter deinde agressi sunt."

[1] It is from this usually accurate historian that we take most of the details relating to the conspiracy of Amboise. M. Meune says with justice that La Planche, though he often judges of things and persons from his own Protestant point of view, is impartial in the statement of facts. " He never sacrifices truth to his religious preferences."

of the dissatisfaction felt by all the king's subjects, not only with the religious position, but with the state of political affairs generally. " He represented that the king was governed by people who were hated worse than the plague ; and he asked for an edict, which, . pending the holding of a Council, should assure to the Reformed the free exercise of their religion."

Such a demand was sure to exasperate the Lorraines, but to refuse it summarily would have been fraught with danger. The Admiral had said : " I know no other means to avert a great rising of the people." Catherine manœuvred, as she always did. An edict was hastily drawn up, the object of which evidently was to disarm the Protestants without making any important concessions to them.[1] The past was to be forgotten. Persons guilty of heresy (excepting the ministers) were not to be brought to trial, provided they promised henceforth to live as good Catholics. The text of the edict, published March 8th, contained moreover many curious declarations.

The king said that at his accession he had found great disturbances in his realm on account of religion, and certain preachers come from Geneva, for the most part mechanics and people of no education [2]

---

[1] Hence it was called by some of the Councillors " *un attrape-Minault* " (La Planche).

[2] In this way in court circles they explained away the great movement of the Reformation. Observe this allusion to the low origin of the first propagators of "the religion." The charge of ignorance brought against them was absurd ; but it is certain, as we have said, that at first the movement spread chiefly among the working classes.

were accused of causing these disturbances. He admitted that the sect had developed to such an extent that if "it were punished according to the letter of the law and of our ordinances, there would be a marvellous shedding of blood of men, women, maids, and youths in the flower of their age, which we should view with singular regret and displeasure, and which would be against our nature and ill-suited to our times." The king therefore gave a general pardon, remission, and cancelling of the past. "Nevertheless," he added, "we do not include in this remission the preachers nor (and this clause opened the door to any arbitrary exceptions) those who have conspired against the king, his brothers, and *principal ministers.*" These last words, which clearly pointed to the Guises, gave them the opportunity of avenging themselves.

Coligny, and his brother the Cardinal, had signed the edict with all the members of the Council,[1] the Guises also endorsing it. But De Thou says that in presenting it to parliament for registration, they used an unworthy subterfuge, and inserted a secret article, which was to serve as the rule of its interpretation.[2]

As soon as the edict was published, the Guises, assembling forces from all parts for the service of the king, had the country thoroughly searched, and succeeded in surprising the various companies of conspirators before they had had time to reach the

---

[1] One is surprised to find Coligny's name to an edict which urges the Reformed to abjure or conceal their faith. The very rapidity with which it was published inclines one to think he was surprised into it.

[2] *Hist. univers.*, vol. ii., p. 764. The Guises lost not a moment. The registration took place on March 11th.

appointed place of meeting. All who were arrested were either put to death on the spot, or carried to Amboise to be tried.[1] In vain they declared that they meant no evil to the king ; it availed them nothing. Several of them tried to get petitions placed in the king's hands, setting forth their attachment to his person. The Guises kept from Francis II. all knowledge of such facts. Their whole tactics consisted in saying that the conspirators sought to overthrow royalty, and to organise an independent community like the Swiss. The young king said to them : " But what have I done to my people that they are thus turned against me ? I will hear their grievances, and will give them satisfaction. I know not ; but I hear that it is only you they are offended with. I would that for a time you were away from here, that I might see whether it is against you or me they have a grudge."

Alas ! his pleadings were vain. The conspiracy was put down with a pitiless hand. The Guises, taking advantage of the exceptions named in the edict, entered the houses, and proceeded to summary trials and executions. For several months France groaned under a reign of terror and blood. At Amboise alone 1,200 Huguenots were put to death on the charge of conspiracy. The ordinary modes of execution proved too slow, and the prisoners were tied hand and foot and cast by scores into the Loire.

These fearful scenes remained impressed on the

---

[1] La Planche mentions a curious fact here. Villegagnon, the old leader of the Protestant colonists in Brazil, who had abandoned his party and sworn deadly hatred to it, wished to bring up a fleet on the Loire to fight against the conspirators, but this " fanciful naval war " was treated as a jest.

memory of the people who lived by the river. In 1793 the Commissioners of the Convention copied them at Nantes, at the suggestion of Carrier. The chiefs of the conspirators were executed after dinner as a sort of a pastime for the Court. Catherine and the lovely young queen, Mary Stuart, attended by their gentlemen in waiting and maids of honour, were present at these spectacles, and the Cardinal of Lorraine kept count of the sufferers " with evident enjoyment." The young king, who had been made to say a few weeks before that a massacre of the Protestants would be contrary to his nature, was educated with his young brothers in this school.

La Renaudie was one of the first to fall. He was attacked on March 18th in the forest of Château-renault, and was killed with a shot from an arque-buse. His body was hung up on the bridge at Amboise with this inscription : " *La Renaudie dit Laforest, chef des rebelles.*" His death put an end to the enterprise.

Of all the victims the most illustrious was the Baron de Castelnau, whose exploits in Flanders had rendered him famous. He had advanced with his company into the neighbourhood of Amboise, when the Duke de Nemours, who was in close alliance with the Guises, came up and summoned him to lay down his arms, "vowing on the faith of a prince that he would do him and his companions no harm, but that they should all be set at liberty." Hardly had Castelnau and his followers done as he demanded, than he arrested them as guilty of high treason. There was nothing before them but certain death, preceded by torture, then the necessary accompaniment of every criminal trial. But the old soldier kept his judges upon thorns. He questioned the Chancellor Olivier, and reminded him of the evangelical exhortations which he had long before heard from his lips. " Do you not remember," he said, " that formerly you counselled me to frequent the holy assemblies in Paris, and to visit the Reformed Churches of Geneva and Germany ?" Then, continuing his speech, he reminded Olivier of the executions of Cabrières and Mérindol, in which he had acted as judge, and pointing to his white hairs reminded him of the judgment seat of God, before which he must soon appear. He addressed himself in similar terms to the Cardinal of Lorraine, who also at the first had spoken so much of reforming the Church. These words, which were repeated, moved the whole Court. Coligny and Andelot interceded in vain for their old companion in arms.

" The king and the queen-mother being pressed and importuned by them to save his life, as much for his great virtues as for the many services done by his forefathers and by himself to the crown of France, the queen, in order not to irritate the great lords and princes to whom he belonged, did all that she could, even (as she said) going so for as to seek out these new kings in their apartments and ply them with entreaties. But they remained immovable and stern in their anger, and the Cardinal used these words to their Majesties : 'By the blood of God he shall die,.and no one shall prevent it.' In short, the more he was warned of the danger that might result, the more furious did he become. Under this pressure, Olivier signed the sentence of death. Hardly was it executed when the Chancellor (so says La Planche) 'fell ill of an extreme melancholy, in which he groaned without ceasing, murmuring miserably against God.' The Cardinal of Lorraine came to see him. The Chancellor sent him away crying : 'Cardinal, Cardinal, you will get us all damned.' A moment afterwards he expired." [1]

This was the last episode of the conspiracy of Amboise. For a long time the heads of the chief conspirators remained upon poles before the gates of the castle. Agrippa d'Aubigné, as a child, saw them in passing through Amboise with his father, and heard his father exclaim : " The executioners have cut off the head of France ! " The Huguenot added : " My child, thou must not spare thine own head when I have given mine to avenge these honourable leaders. If thou spare thyself, my curse will be upon thee." These words fell into no forgetful soul. The child was one day to become the avenging historian of the last of the Valois.

---

[1] *La Planche* (edit. Mennechet, p. 103).

CHAPTER XVII.

Coligny's mission in Normandy.—L'Hospital is made Chancellor.—
Edict of Romarantin.—Assembly at Fontainebleau.—Convocation
of the States at Orleans.—Attempt of the Protestants to take
possession of Lyons.

CONDÉ, Coligny, and his brothers could not be unmoved spectators of the executions at Amboise. Condé, as we have said, was the *chef muet* of the conspiracy. The Guises had wished to have him arrested. Condé took a bold stand, spoke in the king's Council, defied his enemies to find proof of their accusations, and after this daring but scarcely honest challenge, abruptly left the Court and took refuge in Bearn with Antoine de Bourbon.

Andelot went to Brittany. Coligny was commissioned by the queen-mother to pacify Normandy. "Catherine prayed him very affectionately to enquire into the true cause of the disaffection in that province, and to send her a full and true report." La Planche adds that she promised to keep secret any information that Coligny might give.

The Admiral obeyed. He found in Normandy a number of reformed Churches, with, it was said, fifty thousand members. He wrote therefore to the queen, urging her to put a stop to all the persecutions from which they were suffering. Then venturing

to speak his mind yet further, he referred openly
to the Guises, showing that "they were the real
cause and source of all the discontent and trouble
in the kingdom, through their violence and abuse
of the governing power." He did not hesitate to
recommend the convocation of the States General.
Catherine, of course, communicated all this to the
Guises, who were highly exasperated. They felt,
nevertheless, that it was needful to temporise, and the
Court recommended the various Parliaments to release prisoners who were detained solely on a charge
of religion.

The Reformation was indeed making such rapid
progress in the provinces, that it could not be ignored.
That which Coligny reported of Normandy was no
less true of Nismes, Montpellier, Aiguesmortes, and
many other cities. The Protestants there were numerous enough to take possession of the churches for
the celebration of their worship. Poitou, Saintonge,
Guyenne, Languedoc, Provence, had all received the
new faith. In Dauphiné itself, where Francis of
Lorraine was governor, the reformed worship had
just been set up. Guise ordered his lieutenant,
Mongiron, to hang the preachers and give up to
pillage the towns which had opened their churches
to "the religion." But so soon as this was attempted,
reprisals began, and two Huguenot chiefs, Mouvans
and Montbrun, placed themselves at the head of
large companies, and marched through the south.[1]
The Government was called to be on its guard if it
did not wish to see the country in a blaze.

---

[1] Andelot, in a letter to the Constable, strongly deprecates
this taking up arms.—*Delaborde*, vol. i., p. 489.

Olivier, the chancellor, had died March 30th, 1560. His place must be filled. At this crisis a man appeared on the scene who was to play an important part in history. Michel de l'Hospital, born in Auvergne in 1504, was at this time fifty-six years of age. His family had been looked upon with some suspicion at Court, because of its attachment to the famous Constable de Bourbon; but Michel had early distinguished himself, had been entrusted with various missions, and in 1547 had accompanied the French cardinals to the Council of Trent. Henry II. afterwards made him President of the Chamber of Finance, where he vindicated a character for spotless integrity of administration. The Cardinal of Lorraine took him under his protection, hoping to make him a creature of his own, and it was largely through his influence that l'Hospital was appointed Chancellor. The queen-mother, however, acting with her wonted duplicity, told him secretly " that he owed the dignity entirely to her, and not to the Guises." So says De Thou. L'Hospital was not going to be the creature of any one. The love of country was the ruling passion of his soul, and he always strove to be just in an age when almost all were listening only to party cries. Such a character was sure to find in Coligny a kindred soul.

M. Delaborde justly remarks that l'Hospital was as prudent as he was high principled, as a politician. He knew how tangled a skein he had to unwind. " We must needs accommodate ourselves," he said, " to the manners of the time in which we live. . . . We must sometimes take a few steps backward to

13

get a better leap forward. . . . We must now and again take in the sails a little." La Planche says he always had on his lips the words, " Patience, patience, all will go well!" He used this method to please Catherine ; but if she acquiesced in it as the one way of getting out of her difficulty, l'Hospital had a far different end in view from hers. Under this seeming *bonhommie*, this cheerful optimism, he had a strong will that would not bend to any iniquitous coercion.

L'Hospital's first act was directed against the Inquisition which the Pope was trying to establish in France. The papal court had made the same attempt, it will be remembered, under Henry II. Henry had yielded, and the Parliament, forgetting its great national traditions, had followed his lead. In 1557 the Cardinals of Lorraine, Bourbon, and Châtillon had been designated as the French inquisitors ; but through the opposition of Châtillon the scheme had remained a dead letter. L'Hospital proposed to do away with it altogether by the edict of Romorantin, May 1560.

In presenting this edict, l'Hospital used words which must have sounded strangely daring at the time, and which seem to breathe the spirit of a coming age of freedom. The maladies of the soul are not to be cured like those of the body. When a man holding wrong opinions utters a formula of recantation, his heart may remain unchanged. Opinions are only to be changed by prayer to God, by reason and argument. Such principles as these would have led to religious liberty as their natural consequence, and to the removal of all coercion in matters of faith. But what says the edict? Something entirely different. It assigns to prelates alone the cognisance of all crimes of heresy, and enjoins them at the same time to reside in their dioceses. It prohibits parliaments, bailiffs, seneschals, and other judges from initiating any action in questions of religion. They are only to execute the sentences of the ecclesiastical judges, who will hand over the offenders to the magistrate. How could such enactments as these have been regarded as an advance in the direction of religious liberty? We cannot understand it except by remembering that the rights thus given to the secular French bishops were taken away from the Inquisition, and thus the scheme for establishing an Inquisition on the Spanish model was frustrated.[1] But religious liberty had really advanced not one step.

Reformed Churches rose up nevertheless in all directions. The slight modification effected by the edict of Romorantin sufficed to encourage the Calvinists to celebrate their worship in their own dwellings. The Admiral himself, on his tour through Normandy, openly took part in their assemblies.[2]

---

[1] One word of the Spanish ambassador Chantonnay is memorable. He considers the edict of Romorantin as very favourable to the reformed, for the following reason, "That from fear of the hatred in which the clergy are held, the ecclesiastics would not dare to be severe" (*Letter to the Duchess of Parma*, April, 1540). It is evident also that in the dioceses presided over by Moulin, Marillac, and other moderate bishops, the Protestants would at length enjoy a little liberty.

[2] "The faithful had the consolation, on July 26th, 1560, of seeing the Admiral de Châtillon at Dieppe, and of worshipping God in the house where they went to pay their respects to this pious lord, who for the three days that he stayed in

The queen-mother felt that she must confer with her advisers over this new situation, and at the suggestion of the Chancellor and the Admiral, she decided to convene at Fontainebleau in the month of August an assembly of the greatest lords of France. "The King of Navarre and the Prince of Condé were warned by their friends and dependents not to go on any account, if they did not wish to risk their lives."[1]

On August 21st the assembly met in the presence of the king, Catherine, Mary Stuart, and all the princes of the royal family. That day, after a few words spoken by the king and the queen-mother, the Chancellor explained the object of their meeting.

At the second sitting "the king expressed his will that those of his Council should first give their opinion," and asked the Bishop of Valence to speak first. At this moment the Admiral advanced to the king, and "after reverently bowing twice" he began to say that having visited Normandy, he had seen that the disturbances arose entirely from the persecution of the adherents of "the religion." He added "that he was the bearer of a petition from the reformed, and that although the petition was not signed, there were more than fifty thousand in Normandy who would sign it." That which they asked was that they might have churches and places set apart for public worship and the administration of the sacraments. When Coligny had finished

---

the town had Divine service celebrated regularly with open doors."—Manuscript quoted by M. Vitet in his *Histoire de Dieppe*, vol. i., p. 109.

[1] Castelnau, *Mémoires*, Book II., ch. viii.

speaking, he handed his petition to the king, who caused it to be read at once by the secretary, l'Aubespine. It was an apology in which the reformed repudiated all idea of rebellion, declared that their faith was in accordance with Holy Scripture and with the Apostles' Creed, and concluded by asking that they might be permitted to have churches of their own. They urged that Jews were allowed in some countries to have their synagogues, and they protested their devotion to the king.

The language, moderate as it was, was so new that "the whole company," says La Planche, "was full of admiration, marvelling at the boldness of the Admiral, considering the danger to which he thus exposed himself."[1]

The Chancellor next spoke. He made a grave and eloquent remonstrance, and in pointing out the causes of the present evil evidently offended the Guises, who at once offered to render an account of their offices, Francis of the army, and the Cardinal of the finances.

Two days after, Montluc, Bishop of Valence, spoke. He was at heart favourable to "the religion." He did not fear to speak in praise of the zeal, learn-

---

[1] Chantonnay, in a letter to the Duchess of Parma, August 1560, says that when the king asked Coligny from whom he received his petition, he replied several times over that he did not know, and that the king with an angry look bade him go to his place. The Venetian ambassador says nearly the same thing (Armand Baschet, *Diplomatie vénitienne*, p. 506). This is in direct contradiction to La Planche, La Place, and Castelnau. The truth is Coligny would not name the petitioners, in order not to expose them to danger, but simply said in general terms that fifty thousand persons at least would sign it if necessary.

ing, and integrity of the preachers whom the edict of Amboise had represented a short time before as ignorant rustics and misleaders of the people, unworthy of pardon. " Sire," said the bishop, " the doctrine which seems ridiculous to your subjects has been disseminated not for two or three days, but for thirty years ; it has been taught by three or four hundred ministers, diligent and lettered men, men of a great modesty, gravity, and appearance of holiness, who profess to detest all vices, and principally avarice, and who do not shrink from losing their life in defence of their doctrine. They have ever on their lips the name of Jesus, which is a word so sweet, that it opens the deafest ears, and finds its way readily into the hardest hearts." Then the bishop showed in what state the Reformation had found France, what was the carelessness, covetousness, and worldliness of the clergy and of the bishops themselves. He advised as a remedy the use of the Holy Scriptures, and a return to Gospel preaching, and asked that an œcumenical, or at least a national council might be convened. As to the punishments to be inflicted on heretics, the bishop wished that severity should be shown only to those who had taken up arms. " But," he added, " there are others, Sire, who have received this doctrine, and hold it in such fear of God and bear your Majesty such reverence, that they would not in any wise offend you ; and by their life and their death they show plainly that they are moved only by holy zeal and by an ardent desire to seek the one way of salvation, and who, believing they have found it will not depart from it, and heed not the loss of goods, nor death, nor any tortures that can be inflicted upon them. And must I confess that when I think of those who die with such constancy, my hair stands erect, and I am constrained to deplore our miserable estate who are not touched by any zeal for God or for religion. These men, Sire, meseems should be distinguished and separated from others who abuse the name and doctrine they profess ; these ought not to be counted and punished as seditious persons." After delivering this magnificent eulogium of the reformed, Montluc asked, in concluding, that the State should confine itself to forbidding their assemblies and sending them into exile, so *that they might not have the opportunity of leading the good astray.*[1]

Marillac, Archbishop of Vienne, then spoke, enforcing the necessity of a National Council and of a convocation of the States General ; but he said not one word in favour of granting any liberty whatever to " the religion."

The Admiral followed. La Planche says that " the whole assembly was struck with admiration of his noble and forcible words." He urged the necessity of convoking the States General of the kingdom according to the ancient constitutions. He complained that the king was surrounded with a new and numerous guard, as if he were afraid of his people. He asked for a free and holy Council,

---

[1] The speeches delivered at Fontainebleau are reproduced more or less at length in La Planche, in La Place's *Commentaires*, in Castelnau's *Mémoires*, and in Condé's *Mémoires*, as well as in the *Recueil de pièces originales sur les états généraux* (Paris, 1789).

whether general or national, and meanwhile he claimed for those who belonged to "the religion" the free confession of their faith.

"But the Duke of Guise," says Castelnau, "feeling piqued by the Admiral's remarks touching the new guard placed around the king, said it had only been established since the conspiracy of Amboise, which was aimed at the person of his Majesty, and that it was his duty to see that the king should no more be subject to the annoyance of having a petition presented to him with arms. And as to what the Admiral had said about finding fifty thousand Protestants to sign a petition, the king could find a million of his religion to support the contrary."

The Cardinal of Lorraine strenuously opposed the Protestant petition, saying that if the king gave them churches he would be approving their heresy, "which he could not do without being eternally damned." [1] Then with a sudden reversion, which sounded very strange on his lips, he declared he was of opinion that they should not act with severity towards the poor misguided ones, that they should allow them to go to their preachings and sing their psalms, and that it was for the bishops and other learned personages to rebuke and instruct them according to the Gospel. [2]

---

[1] La Planche.

[2] It has often been asked what position was taken at Fontainebleau by Odet, Cardinal of Châtillon. On this point I find only one indication. Chantonnay, in a letter to the Duchess of Parma (September, 1560), says that the nuncio had just complained to Catherine of the attitude taken by the Cardinal of Châtillon at Fontainebleau, and that Catherine had excused him.

All the members of the assembly had spoken in favour of a convocation of the States General. On August 26th the king decided that a meeting should be convoked for the 18th of December following, at Meaux, and that on the 18th of January an assembly of the clergy should be held to discuss the question of a Council.

Such was the conclusion of the assembly at Fontainebleau. Upon the actual question of the liberty of the Protestants nothing had been decided, but it was a great thing to have had the cause of " the religion " defended in such an assembly by an Admiral of France, and to have ascertained that the Cardinal of Lorraine himself had been brought, from political considerations no doubt, to recommend milder measures.

After such discussions it was difficult to proscribe the manifestation of new belief which had found apologists among the very bishops themselves. How could they forbid religious discussions elsewhere when these had just been carried on so publicly and on so large a scale in the highest circles? For the policy of repression to be successful, every mouth must be stopped, and all free utterance forbidden, as it was in Spain under Philip II. France, happily, was not ready so submit to such humiliation. " *Gens loquax*," said Cæsar, speaking of the Gauls. This irrepressible instinct, free speech, has often been the salvation of the French people, and in the sixteenth century the very *promoters* of religious repression were unable to resist it.

Some weeks later, on October 4th, the Admiral was entrusted by the king with the command of

Havre and Honfleur, an evidence that his courageous and frank behaviour had not brought him into disgrace. These signs of the time were all marked by the public, and it was felt that the cause of the reformation was gaining ground.

While the assembly was sitting at Fontainebleau, Antoine de Bourbon and his brother Condé were carrying on correspondence with the principal Protestant lords in the south, with a view to deliver France from the yoke of the Guises. The soul of this conspiracy was Edme de Ferrières, Sieur de Maligny.[1] He visited the leading Huguenots in Dauphiné and Provence. He arranged with them that they should send soldiers disguised as workmen, in small companies, to Lyons, and that on September 5th they would take possession of the city. In order to mark their loyalty to the dynasty, the conspirators took as their watchword, " *Christ et Capet.*" [2] About two thousand Protestants were in this way assembled in Lyons. But at the last moment, Antoine de Navarre, always irresolute, sent Maligny orders to abandon the project. Maligny left Lyons in despair, and the conspirators dispersed. A gentleman of Béarn, named La Sagne, in the service of Condé, had just been arrested. On him were found letters compromising even the Constable de Montmorency

---

[1] Or Maligny the *younger*, who must not be confounded, as he often is, with his elder brother, Jean de Ferrières, who in this same year became Vidame of Chartres, after the death of François de Vendôme (December 22nd), and who was to play an important part in the affairs of the Protestant party. Edme de Ferrières, after his failure at Lyons, fled to Geneva, where he died from an accident on the lake.

[2] Jean Le Frère, *La vraie et entière histoire des troubles* (1578, p. 180).

himself.[1] La Sagne and some of his companions were put to the torture, and confessed everything.

The Guises kept the affair quiet, however, and urged upon Francis II. that he should summon the princes to Orleans, where it had been decided to hold the States General. The king, with this view, sent to them the Cardinal of Bourbon, their brother. In vain the Châtillons, who suspected danger, warned them not to go. Eléonore de Roye, princess of Condé, and Jeanne d'Albret joined their entreaties to those of the Châtillons. All in vain. On October 31st, the two princes, who thought that by placing themselves in the king's power they would impose upon him, made their entry into Orleans.[2]

---

[1] There was even an angry interview between Catherine and the Constable on the subject. He reproached the queen with wishing to rule the realm, "having had hitherto so little experience, and keeping around her and her son ministers who were incapable, and detested by all." (*Letter from Chantonnay to the Duchess of Parma*).

[2] We find in La Planche the brave letter which Eléonore de Roye addressed to her husband, which shows what a heroic soul hers was. She implored him very humbly not to be of so cowardly a heart as to throw himself into their nets, whatever fine promises the king might make, saying that if she was a man and in his place, she would rather die sword in hand for so just a cause than mount a scaffold and give her neck to the executioner without having deserved it.

CHAPTER XVIII.

WE cannot suppose that in convoking the States General, which had not met formally for three-quarters of a century (1484), the Guises had any intention of really ascertaining the will of the country.[1] Everything goes to prove, on the contrary, that in their false hands this convocation was to be made a means of arresting the princes, crushing the Calvinist party, and reaffirming their own authority. The plan which they had formed, and which we are about to describe, is not referred to only by Protestant historians, such as Beza, La Place, La Planche, and Jean de Serres, whose evidence might be regarded as doubtful; but by Castelnau, by the Catholic Tavannes, the impartial De Thou, Maimbourg, and Pasquier. This plan consisted first of all in preventing the meeting of a national council. Pius IV., alarmed at what was going on in Germany, England, and Switzerland, had just pledged himself to re-open

---

[1] Before the decision of the Assembly of Fontainebleau, the Guises had inspired Francis with a dread of any such convocation. " They gave the king to understand that any one who urged a convocation of the States was his mortal enemy, and guilty of high treason." —*La Planche.*

shortly the Council of Trent, which had been suspended practically since 1552.

It was decided, moreover, that at the opening of the States General, each deputy should be required to subscribe a distinct confession of the Catholic faith ; if he refused to do this, he should be arrested on the spot, deprived of his rank, and sentenced to be burned as a heretic.   It was resolved that the same confession of faith should be subscribed by all who held office in France.   This amounted to organising a general proscription throughout the country, and the first victims would have been the princes of the blood, the Châtillons, and all their adherents.   At the same time the French, combining with the Savoyards, were to invade Geneva and the Vaudois valleys of Piedmont, those two hot-beds of heresy, and Spain was to occupy Béarn.

Monstrous as this plan may seem, it must be remembered that many preachers were constantly recalling the glorious example of the extermination of the Albigeois of Languedoc, and the expulsion of the Moors from Spain.   And Philip II., carrying out the same ideas, was about to place the Low Countries under an interdict.   Why not repeat the exploits of the Middle Ages ?   The Cardinal of Lorraine thought so well of his enterprise, that he laughingly called it *" the rat-trap for the Huguenots."* [1]

---

[1] In reference to this plan, M. Henri Martin has truly said: " The massacre of St. Bartholomew, that is to say, the extermination of the heretics by open force or secret artifice, was always in the heart of the leaders of the persecuting Catholic party " (*Histoire de France*, vol. ix., p. 54).   The cause of the failure of the enterprise at this time was the secret but deep distrust entertained by Philip II. of the Guises.   Fanatic as

We may guess then what were the motives which prompted the Guises to bring the Bourbons to Orleans. When the princes arrived there on October 31st, they felt at once how much reason there had been for the gloomy forebodings of their friends. The city, part of whose population was Protestant, was undergoing a reign of terror. It was filled with troops, and cannon were pointed on the principal thoroughfares.

As soon as the King of Navarre and Condé entered within its walls, they saw themselves surrounded by men with menacing gestures, who openly insulted them. . They were taken to the house occupied by Francis II. But they were not allowed to go in by the chief entrance. The Guises and the courtiers received them with disdainful coldness. The young king took them to his mother's apartment. There he immediately began to question Condé, reproaching him with the various plots in which he had been engaged. Condé had unquestionably been a party to the conspiracy of Amboise, and to the recent rising in the south, of which the taking of Lyons was to have been the first act. But the object he had in view involved no hostility to the king himself; hence

---

he was, Philip dreaded above all things the growing power of the Guises. As the husband of Queen Mary he had defended England against Scotland and Mary Stuart. He so much feared the' latter that he did more than anyone else to save the life of the Protestant Elizabeth. For a long time he defended her, even when she had restored the reformed worship in England. M. Forneron, speaking on this subject, says: "Having to choose between heresy and France at the very time when he had just made peace with France to extirpate heresy, he preferred heresy." (*Histoire de Philippe II.*, vol. i., p. 122.)

he was able to repudiate emphatically the charges
made against him by Francis II. The king replied
that he should clear himself presently, for the moment
he must be imprisoned. He was taken to a house
which was soon turned into a very Bastille. The life
of his brother, the King of Navarre, was seriously
menaced.[1] At the same time Madame de Roye,
Condé's stepmother and sister to the Admiral, and
Grollot, Bailiff of Orleans, who was suspected of
Protestantism, were arrested. La Planche says
Coligny had been warned from various quarters of
the snare that was being laid for the reformed at
Orleans. "But none of these things could persuade
him not to undertake the journey to Orleans without
delay, after reading the king's letters. He went pur-
posing to make a full confession of his faith, and
committing the result to God."

On leaving his home he would not hide from his
wife the danger into which he was going, out of
which there seemed no human probability of his
escaping with his life. He bade her, nevertheless,

---

[1] Very high authorities—La Planche, De Thou, and Beza—
state that the Guises had obtained a promise from the king to
summon Antoine of Navarre into his cabinet, and there to
have him assassinated, himself striking the first blow. At the
last moment the king's heart seems to have failed him. M. de
Bouillé, in his history of the Guises, declares this to be impossible, adducing the hesitating language of De Thou, who after
narrating the fact says : "I dare not pledge myself whether
what I have just narrated is true or false." But further on De
Thou affirms, without a shadow of doubt, that on the first
report of the king's illness the Guises again took up the
project of killing Antoine of Navarre, and that l'Hospital
resisted it in a powerful speech, which De Thou reports. De
Thou could hardly fail, moreover, to be well-informed of all
these facts by his father, who was summoned to Orleans to
act as Condé's judge.

trust in God that He would have pity on His poor
Church and on His kingdom, and he exhorted her,
with her family, to continue stedfast in the truth of
the Gospel which they had been taught, since God
had shown them that this was the true and safe
heavenly pasture. He bade them also esteem it the
greatest honour to suffer for His holy name. He
charged his wife straitly not to swerve from her
course, even if she heard of his imprisonment or
death, but to have the child (whom she was daily
expecting) baptised in the Reformed Church, and
by the true ministers of the Word of God. . . . Such
was his departure from his home.

When he arrived at Orleans the queen-mother
received him with her usual good grace. Then
she warned him that the Cardinal of Lorraine
was about to lay a snare for him ; that he intended
to ask him to answer for his faith in the presence of the king. She implored him then to
think well what he would reply, and not lightly to
put himself in danger. The Admiral answered that
he desired nothing so much as to confess his faith,
and that he hoped God would grant him to do it in
such a manner that the king should be satisfied.
The queen repeated this to the cardinal, who was in
high spirits, thinking that he had found a sure way
to destroy Coligny. He went at once "to the king,
and said to him in jest, before the queen his mother,
that he had this day gained one of the best servants
in the world, who was ready to return to the bosom
of the holy Roman Church." Then, explaining himself, he asked the king's permission to question the
Admiral before him, and in the presence of five or

six doctors of the Sorbonne. The Admiral, informed of this, replied that he had no fear of these doctors, nor of their arguments ; but that he refused to speak before them, knowing that it was their wont to condemn those of his religion, without convicting them of heresy ; but that " if it pleased the king to hear two of them alone, one on each side, he would soon judge which of them was a heretic." In the meanwhile the king fell ill, and " the negotiation was interrupted."

The trial of the Prince of Condé was hurried on with the utmost rapidity. He was tried by a commission, presided over by Christophe de Thou, father to the historian. Sentence was passed by the commission, contrary to all the traditions of the old monarchy, which required that a prince of the blood should be condemned only by the court of parliament. The prince was kept in the strictest confinement. He was not even allowed to see his brave wife, Eléonore de Roye, who had come to Orleans to assist him. She tried to intercede in his favour, but was repulsed. " She went to all those whom she believed to be friends, but no more heed was paid to her than to the humblest damsel in the land. Even the King of Navarre dared not speak to her, so much was he in fear for his own life. In short, there was not a single courtier or citizen who had the courage to notice her, whether in public or private, so closely was she watched."[1] Such was the cowardice produced by the reign of terror in Orleans.[2]

---

[1] La Planche.
[2] It is pleasant to note the indignant protest against

14

The charge against Condé was twofold : he was a heretic and a leader of sedition. His heresy he made no attempt to disavow, for when a priest was sent to him in the prison, he replied " that he had not come to Orleans to hear mass, which he had long since given up." His judges were forced to admit that there was no evidence of Condé's guilt as a leader of sedition ; but his heresy was described as " high treason against God," and the commission sentenced him to death. The execution was fixed for December 10th, the day of the opening of the States General, and it was decreed that Condé should be beheaded in front of the king's palace. Only three members of the commission had the courage to refuse to sign this iniquitous sentence : the Count de Sancerre, Dumortier, and the Chancellor l'Hospital, who asked for a reprieve. " Eléonore de Roye succeeded in gaining an entrance to the king's apartment ; she threw herself at his feet to beg for mercy. The Cardinal of Lorraine, fearing the king might be moved to pity, and eager to show his animosity, drove the princess rudely from the room, calling her importunate and troublesome, and saying that if she was done justice by she would find herself in a dungeon too."[1]

Just at this crisis occurred one of the strangest turns of the wheel of fortune recorded in history.

The rumour got abroad that Francis II. was attacked by an abscess in the ear. The king, still

---

Condé's incarceration addressed at this time to Francis of Lorraine by Renée of France, his mother-in-law, and daughter of Louis XII.
[1] La Planche.

almost a child, was scrofulous to a degree, and in a few days he was in such a state that the doctors gave up all hope. The Guises were beside themselves, for the death of the king would be the ruin of all their plans. The Duke sent for the doctors, and told them that if they let the king die in the flower of his age, the heretics should pay dearly for it ; he threatened them with oaths, that they should be all hanged. The sick boy vowed that if it pleased God and all the saints to restore him to health, he would give himself no rest till he had " purged the kingdom of these wicked heretics, and asked that God would strike him dead if he spared wife or mother, brothers, sisters, or friends, if the taint of heresy was upon them."[1]

The Protestants, in return, met to intercede for the child-king. They asked God to " give to the king not only health, but good and wise counsel, through which they might possess their souls in patience." Catherine saw that all was about to be changed, and that she must be ready to grasp the reins. The Guises altered their attitude towards her ; their haughty and domineering bearing became mild and obsequious. The Cardinal of Lorraine had but one thought at this crisis — to place himself under the protection of Spain. He sent for Chantonnay, and after enlarging on the sad fate of Mary Stuart, and on the misfortunes of his own house, he declared that Catherine was ready to make use of all the strength of the kingdom to maintain her authority, and that she asked the help of the King of Spain to guard against the dangers that threatened

---

[1] La Planche.

religion, if she was not recognised as governing the kingdom.[1] Catherine had given him no authority to speak in this way. The Guises made one final effort ·to get rid of Condé, and to make an end of the King of Navarre at the same time. But the Chancellor l'Hospital saw their design, and strongly advised the queen-mother to rely upon the Bourbons. She agreed, but concealed the game she was playing till the arrival of the Constable, whom she summoned in all haste. He alone, as head of the army, could hold his ground against the Guises. He arrived at Orleans December 5th, 1560. Francis II. had just expired, forsaken by his uncles, who thought only of their own safety, and did not even attend his funeral. "Gentlemen," said Coligny to the courtiers standing around," the king is dead ; let us learn a lesson how to live."[2] A new future seemed opening.

---

[1] Letter from Chantonnay to the Duchess of Parma (Dec. 1560). See La Ferrière, Introd., p. lxxxv.

[2] *MS. Colbert*, fol. 448, quoted by M. Puaux (*Hist. de la réformation française*, Book VIII., ch. xxix.). We borrow a curious anecdote from the same source. "The Admiral, having gone to his house after the death of the king, fell into a profound reverie. He was seated in an armchair, his toothpick in his hand, and his feet to the fire. A gentleman named Fontaine was sitting silently beside him, fearing to disturb his meditations; but seeing that the toes of his boots were almost burnt off, he said, ' Monseigneur, you carry your dreaming too far; your boots are all burning.' 'Ah ! Fontaine,' replied the Admiral, 'less than a week ago you and I would have been glad to get off each with the loss of a leg, and now we are let off with the loss of a pair of boots ; it is a good bargain.'"

CHAPTER XIX.

CHARLES IX., who succeeded his brother, was only ten and a half years old. His accession was greeted with universal gladness. The Venetian ambassador, Michieli, writing of him, says, " He is a charming youth, of quick intelligence, and remarkable vivacity. He is ardent, generous, and kindly. His countenance is pleasing, his eyes are very fine. He is graceful in all his movements and in his deportment, but he is of a weak constitution. He eats and drinks very little, and is apt to over-fatigue himself with horse exercise and the game of tennis, of which he is passionately fond. After any exertion he has to rest a long time. He is not fond of study, but pursues it to please his mother. Much is hoped and expected from him, if God but gives him time."[1] The Protestants formed the same impression. Many

---

[1] *Relations des ambassadeurs vénitiens,* 1st Series, vol. i., p. 14.

hoped that, like the young King of England, he would take up the cause of the Reformation.

The army had yielded to the influence of the old Constable, who, on entering Orleans, had unhesitatingly assumed the military command. The regency might have been claimed by Antoine of Navarre, as the first prince of the blood ; but he lacked the courage to enforce his rights. Catherine made herself regent without assuming the title. She wrote to her daughter, the Queen of Spain, " I am constrained to have the King of Navarre by me, for so run the laws of the kingdom ; but let the king, your husband, not be troubled about this ; the King of Navarre is all obedience to me, and has no authority but such as I give him."[1] Catherine kept the whole control in her own hands. She received the despatches, gave audience to ambassadors, and used the seal royal, the sign of authority. The Privy Council took the management of the finances, which had before been exercised by the Cardinal of Lorraine. Francis of Lorraine still retained the title of Grand Master of France. Condé was set aside on the plea that his honour demanded that he should be formally reinstated. He was told to retire into one of his estates in Picardy—a sort of " graceful captivity." He acquiesced.

Catherine now at length possessed the power she had so long coveted. Under Henry II. she had felt herself set aside by an all-powerful mistress ; under Francis II. her part had been entirely passive, but she had been all the time studying that art of

---

[1] La Ferrière, *Lettres de Cathérine de Médicis*, p. 869.

dissimulation which was one of the distinctive traits of her family.

The task she had set herself was full of danger. She wielded the power of the State in the name of a child whose favour all parties were eager to gain, that his authority might be used in their behalf. She found herself at the head of a nation rent asunder by religious passions more violent than any other. Two foreign powers, England and Spain, were bringing a heavy pressure to bear upon France through their ambassadors, while awaiting an early opportunity to send their soldiers to take part in the internal struggles of the country. At the head of these two great parties who were contending with each other for the direction of affairs, Catherine found leaders who, by birth, military genius and ascendancy over the masses, were almost like so many sovereigns. She herself had but a very slight prestige to set against their influence. A foreigner, descended from a family of *parvenus*, for a long time despised by the king her husband, held recently in humiliating tutelage by the Guises, her sole reliance in this crisis was on the chivalry of the noblesse in both parties (and this might fail her), and on the German and Swiss auxiliaries, whom she found very costly allies, at a time when the States General were beginning to assert their rights and to refuse the subsidies.

When we think of the enormous difficulties which beset her, we can more readily understand the comparative indulgence with which Henry IV. always judged her. Himself of lax morality, Henry of Béarn could but admire the adroitness by which she had so long maintained her power. He who never triumphed himself, except by sheer force of genius, always rendered homage to this faculty of astuteness.

History will be less indulgent. It recalls the unparalleled degradation into which Catherine dragged France ; the systematised perfidy of its rulers, the awful tragedy of 1572, the deterioration of national character, the low morals of Henry III., the saturnalia of the League, the shameful bargains with the Spaniard ; and it cannot forget the weight of responsibility resting upon Catherine for the fatal *dénoument* in which the country well-nigh succumbed.

Undoubtedly Catherine had not the genius of Henry IV. or of Elizabeth, but failing that her influence might yet have been great for good. No one but a fatalist will deny that had there been a firm will at the head of affairs the whole issue might have been different. In 1560 France still retained intact her faith in monarchy and her devotion to the sovereign. When we recall the strange history of the vicissitudes of the English parliament at this time, and the violent crises which had sapped the strength of that nation till Elizabeth restored it to its true place of power and influence, it can hardly be said that the France of that day was in a worse position, or less capable of righting itself under firm and wise guidance. A nation which had then among its sons such men as l'Hospital, Coligny, and so many other noble characters, must have been capable of high destinies. But Catherine had no conception of such possibilities.

Was she incapable of firmness ? We have seen

how, after the defeat of St. Quentin, she showed herself for a moment equal to her task, and for the time rallied, as one may say, the whole nation around her. But it was only a passing greatness.

From the day she was left a widow she began to manœuvre. To retain power was all her aim, and cunning was all her policy.

Throughout her vast correspondence we find no trace of any elevation or breadth of view. Love for her children is the one fine feeling of which she is capable. Sometimes she resents the pressure brought to bear upon her by the Guises and by Spain. Some of her despatches are proud and haughty in tone, but it is a fire of straw which soon burns out. She made use of all parties in turn, and deceived them all. In that tragic quarter of a century when such rivers of French blood flowed, she had no tear for any one of the victims. The terse, cold style of her letters makes one feel that this woman must have looked on many horrors. How different is the language of the true French women of that day, such women as Jeanne d'Albret, Charlotte de Laval, Renée of Ferrara. Indignation, sorrow, pity, is the burden of their letters. Catherine de Médicis has not even the excuse of fanaticism. She would go indifferently to mass or to Protestant preaching just as her interest led her. She influenced men by appealing to their lowest instincts—to their self-interest and avarice. Brantôme tells us how light was the character of those noble ladies who formed her suite, her "escadron volant," and how both gallantry and espionage were called into service to betray to the queen-mother the secrets of the court.

In this heavy and voluptuous atmosphere a subtle poison steals into the soul. Conscience becomes stupefied. Crime itself ceases to shock. French frankness is discountenanced, and gives place to the shrewd perfidy of the Italians with whom the court is peopled. Natures which might have been generous and great, become low and ferocious through that fatal instinct which so often links together sensual pleasure and cruelty, the zest for refined debauchery and the thirst for blood.

Charles IX. becomes, under the tutelage of his mother, the sinister murderer of August 24th. Her favourite son is the future Henry III., the king of minions. Thus she grows old, and death comes at last to carry her away into oblivion and contempt.

But at the stage at which we have now arrived her character was not yet known. The Protestants still believed in her. They loved to remember that in the time of her disgrace she was wont to sing psalms ; that she had cordially received Madame de Roye, the Admiral's mother-in-law, and had often told the Admiral that she depended chiefly upon him. It was easy to believe, moreover, that she had lent herself unwillingly to the enterprises of the Guises against the Bourbons, and that she would gladly have shaken off their yoke. On this last point there was no mistake. What she really thought at this time appears in a letter written by her some months later to her daughter, the Queen of Spain.[1] "I want to tell you, for it is the truth, that all this trouble has grown out of the hatred which this whole

---

[1] April 1st, 1561.

kingdom bears to the Cardinal of Lorraine and the Duke of Guise. It was thought that I should hand over to them the government of this kingdom. I have assured them to the contrary, nor am I under any obligation to do so. *For you know how they treated me in the time of the king your brother*, and even now, when they have no one to look to but me, you know how they are working against me in the matter of your sister's marriage.[1] Hence I have resolved to protect them, so that they shall come to no harm ; but for the rest, to look after your brother's interests and my own, and not to let them mix up their quarrels with mine. For I know well enough, that if they could, they would have made themselves regents, and would have left me out, *as they always do when there is any greatness or advantage to be gained, for this is the one thing they have at heart.*"[2]

These closing words are significant. Never did Catherine pass so severe a judgment even upon Coligny or Condé himself. The sequel shows how ready she was, when she thought her own interests involved, to fall back upon men of whom she entertained such an opinion.

The Spanish envoy, Don Juan Manrique of Lara, in the very first complimentary visit which he paid to the new king, recommended the queen, in the name of Philip II., to be very sedulous in the matter of religion, and, above all, not to have about her

---

[1] This refers to Marguerite de Valois, whom Catherine wished to marry to Don Carlos, while the Guises were anxious to get him to marry their niece, Mary Stuart, as soon as she was left a widow.

[2] *Lettres de Catherine de Médicis*, published by La Ferrière, p. 592.

those who were not steadfast in the Catholic faith. This hint was clearly aimed at the Admiral and the Cardinal of Châtillon. Catherine was hurt by it, and replied to her daughter, the Queen of Spain, in a letter which contained these significant words, " Philip can say to those who advise him to interfere in the choice of councillors for Charles IX., that as he knows no more how the affairs of this kingdom ought to be governed than I do how to conduct the affairs of Spain, he has no intention of meddling in the matter." [1]

But at the same time she recommends Coligny to " put on a good face " to the Guises, who such a short time before were plotting the death of Condé, of the Admiral, and of all the Huguenot leaders. Coligny's reply was frank and fearless. He said that, " As to putting on a good face to those who had compassed his death, attainted his honour, and sought the confiscation of his goods, and the ruin of his whole house, *he could not do it without being double-faced, which was contrary to his profession of religion, and unworthy of any good man.* He was willing indeed to leave God to avenge the wrong, which He would do in His own time, since justice was not to be found among men." [2]

On December 13th, 1560, the Assembly of the States General met at Orleans. In spite of the enormous pressure which the Guises had put upon the country, the majority were far from favourable to them. The clergy numbered one hundred and

---

[1] These words are reported in a letter from Chantonnay to the Duchess of Parma, December 1560.
[2] La Planche.

eighteen, many of whom were inclined to " the religion." The nobility were about the same number; the third estate had two hundred and twenty-five representatives. In the two latter orders—the nobility and the third estate—there was a majority hostile to the Lorraines, and even several Protestants. The " malcontents " joined with the Huguenots to demand a general re-election, on the plea that force had been used ; but two-thirds of the Assembly decided that there was no adequate ground for such a course, and the deliberations began.

Michel de l'Hospital opened with a speech, which has become historical. In simple familiar language, contrasting strongly with the inflated eloquence common to the day, he made the voice of the country itself to be heard, and unfolded with great boldness principles of liberty then new and strange.

" We must not," he said, " listen to those who say that it is unworthy the dignity of a king to convoke the States ; for what is more truly kingly than for a king to do justice to his people ? And how can he do this more easily than by giving permission to all to set forth their grievances with full liberty, publicly and in a place where imposture and deception are impossible ? " Then the Chancellor spoke with indignation of those who kept the truth from coming to the king's ears. He insisted on the necessity of a thorough reformation of the clergy, reminded the nobles of their duty, and set forth the too much overlooked province of the third estate.

When he came to speak of religion, he used words never to be forgotten. Doubtless the ideal he had in view was a return to religious unity ; but he would effect that result only by moral suasion. "The knife," he said, "is of little avail against spiritual error, except to make soul and body perish together. . . . We ought by all means to try to bring back those who are in error, and not be like those who, seeing a man or loaded beast fallen into the ditch, instead of lifting it out, give it a kick. . . . Gentleness will do more than harshness. Let us lay aside those inventions of the devil, the watchwords of party faction and sedition, the names Lutheran, Huguenot, Papist, and let us keep to the name of Christian."

Eighteen days later, January 1st, 1561, the deliberations began. Jean l'Ange, the counsel for the parliament of Bordeaux, spoke first for the third estate. His speech was almost entirely directed against the clergy. He pointed out with much vigour what he called their three principal vices—ignorance, avarice, and luxury. "Ignorance," he said, "has cast its roots so deep that preaching, which is one of the essential functions of the episcopate, is entirely neglected."

The speech of Jacques de Silly, Count de Rochefort, breathed the same spirit. After some biting allusions to the affronts and threats offered to the princes of the blood by the Guises, he pointed to the example of kings who had resisted the encroachments of the clergy ; he demanded a reformation of the Church, and concluded by claiming for the Protestants liberty of public worship.

It was now the turn of the spokesman of the clergy, Dr. Jean Quintin. He stoutly defended the old doctrine of the repression of heresy by the sword. He quoted the example of all Christian sovereigns in the past, from Constantine and Charlemagne to St. Louis. Alas ! he might have adduced the example set by Calvin himself at this very time at Geneva. " No one," he said, " can deny that heresy is an evil and a capital crime, and that the heretic is a capital offender. St. Paul himself has said so, *ergo*, the heretic is punishable capitally, and subject to the sword of the magistrate."[1] Quintin asked that every one who presented a petition on behalf of the heretics should be himself declared a heretic. This was openly pointed at Coligny ; and all eyes, as Theodore Beza tells us, were turned on the Admiral. The Admiral thus directly attacked, complained next day to the king of the wrong that had been done him. Quintin was sent for by Catherine, and compelled to excuse himself. He did so in pitiful fashion, declaring that he had only read the memorial that had been entrusted to him, and in a subsequent speech he protested that he had not intended any reference to the Admiral.[2]

The public discussion then was not unfavourable

---

[1] These are almost the exact terms of the famous pamphlet which sixteen years before Theodore Beza had written against Castalio, who protested against the death of Servetus : ''De hæreticis a civili magistratu puniendis.''

[2] The attitude taken by Coligny at Orleans won for him the congratulations of Calvin, who wrote to him February 18th, 1561 : ''Monseigneur, we have indeed cause to praise God for the singular virtue He has given you to serve the glory and advancement of His Son. It were to be wished that there were many more to aid you. But though others are slow to acquit themselves of their duty, yet you are bound to fulfil the commandment of our Lord, which is that each one of us ought to follow Him at once, without looking to see what others do .

to the Protestants. The States General suspended their sittings on January 31st. The king convoked them for the following May at Pontoise ; but in order to avoid the inconvenience of too large assemblies, it was decided that each of the thirteen great provinces of the kingdom should send only two deputies. This was a grave mistake ; for as the number of clerical delegates was not lessened, these were sure of having a majority on all questions.

Some days after the suspension of the States General, the Protestants held a synod at Poitiers. Here they were guilty of a great error. The ministers unhappily conceived the idea of touching on politics instead of keeping to the affairs of their Churches, and they drew up a memorial demanding the exclusion of women from the government of the State, and the appointment of a lawful regency. This was a direct attack on Catherine de Médicis, and she keenly resented it. We do not know how far Antoine of Navarre was concerned in framing this resolution in his own favour. Assuredly the Protestant cause would not have gained much in having such a protector, as the sequel clearly showed. But the Synod of Poitiers had gone beyond its competence in meddling with politics, and thus creating a pre-

. . . Let each one for himself go where he is called, even if there be none to follow ; and yet I hope that the greatness of soul which God has caused to shine forth in you, will stir up the indifferent to tread in your steps. But even if all the world should remain blind and thankless, and it should seem as though all your trouble were lost, be content, Monseigneur, with the approval of God and His angels. And let it suffice you that you cannot fail of your heavenly crown, having thus bravely fought for the glory of Christ, in which is our salvation.'' Quoted as in *Delaborde*, vol. i., p. 499.

cedent which the Catholics would be only too ready
to turn to account presently at the expense of the
liberty of the Protestants.

The Court, on leaving Orleans, went to Fontainebleau. The Admiral retired to Châtillon-sur-Loing,
where, at the end of February, he had his son Odet
solemnly baptized according to the Genevan rite.
This fact produced an immense sensation. It was
the first public act of Protestant worship performed
in Coligny's house.

CHAPTER XX.

LET us now follow the Admiral to Châtillon-sur-Loing, and see, by the help of authentic documents, what was the home life of a great Huguenot seigneur in the sixteenth century.[1]

Coligny's castle, of which some interesting ruins are still standing, and of which the painter Girodet has preserved a sketch, taken a few days before it was destroyed, was, in its vast proportions, a truly royal residence.[2] Francis I. and Henry II. often

---

[1] Here we cite, in addition to the works of MM. Delaborde and Tessier, a curious pamphlet by M. Becquerel, Member of the Academy of Sciences, who living himself at Châtillon, has collected many interesting details under the title : "Souvenirs historiques sur l'Admiral de Coligny, sa famille et sa seigneurie de Châtillon-sur-Loing." We have seen in M. Becquerel's house some relics of the fittings of the old castle, which was destroyed at the beginning of this century, and some panels inlaid with cameos, which belong to the age of Coligny. M. Jules Bonnet, in his *Bulletin d'histoire du protestantisme français*, May 1882, has described the Admiral's life at Châtillon.

[2] Girodet-Trioson, the celebrated painter of the deluge, was born at Montargis in 1767. In his youth he had seen the castles of Montargis and Châtillon-sur-Loing still standing;

stayed there. From the top of its enormous tower, which is still standing, there is a view of the monotonous plain of the Gâtinais, through which the Loing winds ; to the west are seen the houses of Montargis, where Renée of Ferrara, daughter of Louis XII., and mother-in-law of Francis of Lorraine, openly celebrated the reformed worship. The Admiral, on his return from his long captivity, had rebuilt and enlarged the castle. The new part was in the style of the sixteenth century. Less elegant than Chambord or Fontainebleau, it still formed a

---

he even made a drawing of Châtillon, of which we have a copy —the work of the Count de Castries. It represents the castle as it was at the close of the last century. It is a very imposing pile of buildings, and justifies the enthusiastic descriptions given by travellers in the days of its prime. When the revolutionary administration offered it for sale, some inhabitants of Châtillon tried to purchase it ; but the sum they could offer was too small. It fell into the hands of vandals, who demolished it and scattered all these relics of a heroic past. Girodet was highly indignant at this, and denounced these modern Vandals in a poem (he was a poet now and then). The following verses occur in it ; they are very weak in style, but pathetic in their spirit :—

> "Et toi, pour la vertu décoré par les arts
> Elégant Châtillon, palais des fils de Mars,
> Asile de l'honneur où souvent la victoire
> Allait loin de la cour dissimuler sa gloire ;
> Par le fer abattus, par le feu dévorés,
> J'ai vu tomber tes murs et tes lambris dorés,
> Ces vieux chênes, orgueil de ton parc frais et sombre,
> Qui peut-être avaient vu Coligny sous leur ombre,
> Où sont ils ? Demandez à ces vils acheteurs
> Du palais des héros, sordides brocanteurs.
> O peintre, si tu viens pour en chercher la place,
> La ronce et le chardon t'en dessinent la trace,
> Une tour, comme un roc sur les Alpes assis,
> Montre encore ses flancs nus que la foudre a noircis ;
> Colonne du malheur, par le crime laissée,
> Et qu' attriste le deuil de sa splendeur passée."

Oeuvres posthumes de Girodet-Trioson, vol i., p. 831.

fine and imposing structure, very different in appearance from the gloomy old feudal manors. M. Bonnet says : " Coligny, like a true son of the Renaissance, called in the most famous artists to decorate the castle. One wing on the south side contained a gallery in which the principal military achievements of the family were represented by the brush of Primaticcio and his pupils. Jean Goujon lent the aid of his chisel to produce those marvellous basreliefs and breathing caryatides, of which he alone knew the secret. Several rooms were decorated with fresco paintings from the designs of Giulio Romano. The peristyle of the castle was made to harmonise with the splendours of the enlarged building. Three terraces, one above another, communicated with the great gardens." These terraces are still to be seen, as well as the walls of the conservatories, which were monumental. A covered well is also in existence, the sculptures on which are a good specimen of the style of the period, and the only relics of it remaining. In a panel in the wall of the Admiral's old bedroom, at the foot of the tower, a slab of marble marks the place where lie the remains of Coligny, enclosed in an iron box.[1]

At the time of which we are now speaking, the Admiral was forty-two years of age, of medium height, well proportioned, and capable of enduring great fatigue, though subject to frequent attacks of fever which often endangered his life. His demeanour was grave and almost chilling. His forehead was high, his eyes blue, and beaming with intelli-

---

[1] We have referred already to the sad Odyssey of these remains.

gence. Without the expression of studied grace, which made Francis of Lorraine so fascinating to many, there was a nobleness about his face—the true expression of the noble soul within.[1] In speech, he was slow and grave, but in the presence of danger the whole man was transformed ; he had then the lofty bearing, the commanding look, the stirring tone of the military leader who can revive the broken courage of his men and turn defeat into victory. Kind and gentle to the young and the weak, capable of traits of humanity surprizing in such an age of violence, he never relaxed in matters of discipline. Usually calm and self-possessed, he flashed out in burning ire against all hypocrisy. Holding with an intensity of belief his own convictions, he had an over-mastering sense of justice, an ideal of virtue higher than that of his age, which appeared in all his words and actions, and raised him completely above all vulgar interests and low ambitions. This was the trait which struck all who came in contact with him. Even his enemies admit the greatness of his character.

Charlotte de Laval was the life of his home, and how brave a soul she bore we shall soon see. Three

---

[1] Such is Coligny's appearance in a portrait preserved in the museum at Valenciennes, which must belong to this period. Such is he also in the well-known engraving of the three brothers by Duval. Subsequently in the tragic life of the civil wars which filled him with mortal sadness, and in which he had to witness so many scenes of carnage, and was perpetually threatened with treason, his face assumed a look of habitual melancholy, his brow grew furrowed, and his lips contracted. The terrible wound he received at Moncontour left a deep scar. So he appears in his later portraits. When he was killed they called him an old man. He was fifty-three!

sons and two daughters[1] formed "the whole of his little household," as the Admiral wrote to Renée of Ferrara. The great house resounded with merry life ; for the Admiral was a tender father, and loved to see his children around him leading "a happy life and playing together merrily.[2]

Family worship was conducted every day in the castle by Pastor Merlin, Coligny's almoner ; but the Admiral often took part in it himself.[3] The Scriptures were read, and the psalms sung in the metrical version of Clement Marot, valet de chambre to the late king. Sometimes the letters addressed by Calvin or Beza to the believers in France were also read. The author of the *Vita Colinii* has drawn for us the picture of this family worship.[4] He says : "As

---

[1] His eldest son Henry died at the age of fifteen months. Gaspard, born September 28th, 1554, died at Orleans in 1568; Francis was born April 28th, 1557; Odet, December 24th, 1560. Charlotte gave the Admiral in 1564 another son, Charles, who proved unworthy of the name he bore. Their daughter Louise was born in 1555, and her younger sister Renée in 1561.

[2] These words are taken from a letter which Henri de Condé wrote some years later to Coligny: "I amuse my cousin Louise and my little cousin every evening ; we have fine *times as you like us to*, and play together merrily to try and pass away the sad hours." (Extract from *l'Histoire des Princes de Condé*, by the Duke d'Aumale, vol. ii., p. 415.)

[3] Calvin had this year sent Merlin to the Admiral, and wrote to the latter : "I do not doubt that you have found him all that you wished, and have proved from experience that he tries faithfully to do his duty. . . . Yet I pray you, Monseigneur, not to grow weary in the pursuit of so good and holy and worthy a work, that had we fifty lives they might all be well spent in it. . . . True it is that in order to strengthen ourselves to serve God constantly we must look above the world, even as the Apostle exhorts us to cast our anchor in heaven." Letter, May, 1561.

[4] Page 134. Translation, 1643.

soon as the Admiral rose, which was very early in
the morning, he, putting on his dressing-gown and
kneeling with all the rest who were present, would
offer prayer in the form used by the French churches,
after which, while waiting for the hour for the sermon,
which was given every other day with the singing of
psalms, he would give audience to the messengers
often sent to him by the churches, and would employ
his time in public affairs, which he resumed after
the preaching, and continued till dinner.   Dinner
being ready, his domestic servants, except those who
were occupied in preparing the meal, were assembled
in the hall, where the table was set, before which
stood the Admiral with his wife by his side, and if
there had been no preaching they chanted a psalm,
and then pronounced the usual benediction.   This
custom, a number not only of Frenchmen, but of
German captains and colonels, whom he often asked
to dine with him, can bear witness that he never, for
a single day, failed to observe, not only at home
and in times of leisure, but also in the army.   The
cloth being removed he rose, and standing with his
wife and all present, he either returned thanks
himself or got the minister to do so.   The same
was done at supper, and seeing that all his household were tired at evening prayer, which was late
and uncertain on account of many ˙engagements,
he gave orders that all should gather together as
soon as supper was over, and that after the singing
of the psalm, prayer should be offered.   It would
be hard to say how many of the French nobility
began to establish this religious rule in their own
families, following the example of the Admiral, who

exhorted them often to the true practice of piety, saying that it was not enough for the father of a family to live holily and religiously if he did not, by his example, train up his household by the same rule.   Now it is certain that the Admiral's piety and holiness were so much admired, even by many Catholics, that but for the fear and horror of tortures and massacres, the greater part of France would have been "converted to the reformed religion and discipline."   The same writer also mentions a touching incident which shows how this usually energetic and determined man conducted himself towards the humblest individuals.   He says, " When the time of the Lord's Supper drew near the Admiral called all his household together, showing them how they would not only have to give account to God of their lives, but also of their carriage to each other, and he would try to make up any differences there might be among them.   And if some one seemed to him not sufficiently prepared to understand and revere the holy mystery aright, he took pains to teach him more fully, and if he found any obstinate he would plainly tell them that he would rather live alone than keep unruly followers."

Coligny had chosen for his children a tutor named Le Gresle, who remained attached to them all his life, and whom Coligny mentions with singular affection in his will.   The Duchess of Ferrara, who was one of the most highly educated women of her time, took a great interest in their training, and wished to hear of their progress.   Francis, one of the children, addressed the following letter to her : " Madame, the letter with which you have been pleased to honour us

is a sure pledge of the remembrance which you are
pleased to cherish of us, although we have no means
as yet of doing you the service which we owe you.
But for the affection which you are pleased to show
us, and the good which you wish us, I hope it may
be enough for the present if we give all diligence to
know God, and love and honour Him *by the advancement we make in learning and the sciences,* as of your
singular goodness you are pleased to exhort us; and
we hope to pay such good heed to your words that
you shall see afterwards that your exhortation has not
been in vain by the help of God, whom we pray to
give you, Madame, all happiness and long life for
the advancement of the kingdom of His Son."

Coligny was much occupied with this subject of
education. His first biographer says : "The Admiral
esteemed the institution of colleges and schools for
children as a singular benefit from God, and he
would speak of them as nurseries for the Church, an
apprenticeship in piety. He held that the ignorance
of letters had brought thick darkness not only upon the
commonwealth, but also on the Church ; and that out
of this ignorance the tyranny of the pope had arisen
and grown up. Therefore he built at great cost a
college at Châtillon in a pleasant and healthy situation, where he kept at his own expense very learned
professors of Hebrew, Greek, and Latin, and many
scholars, both children and young people.[1]

This programme of education, which gave special
prominence to the study of the classic tongues, was
new. The middle ages had made the schoolmen
their great study,—that is, they had devoted them-

---

[1] *Vita Colinii* (1575, p. 136).

selves to logic, dialectics, and barren argumentation.

For this thankless task Latin sufficed, and even this became more and more dry and barbarous, bristling with scholastic terms, well suited to the art of disputation, which was then the ultimatum of all learning. The sixteenth century was not yet ripe for the natural sciences. The Renaissance turned attention chiefly to the study of the classics, whose beauty fascinated it. The Reformation cultivated the dead languages with equal ardour, in order to arrive at a knowledge of the sacred text in the original ; hence the importance attached to Greek and Hebrew. For the vaunted art of discussion was now substituted the interpretation of the text, and this stimulated the inventive faculties. One who is a good judge has said : " Through the study of grammars, the Renaissance introduced a general, living, human education adapted to all, which is the same for all, and from which no one is exempt. Henceforward this will be the education of all that part of the nation which is capable of receiving education—the sons of merchants and farmers, as well as of the nobles, the laity, and the clergy."

These observations show that in establishing what we should now call a classical foundation at Châtillon-sur-Loing, in what was after all only a small and unimportant town, Coligny was acting under the same influences which had been at work in Paris, Strasburg, Geneva, and Nismes, producing the reforms introduced by Lefèvre d'Etaples, Jean Sturm,

---

[1] M. Gaston Boissier, *La réforme des Etudes au XVI*[ième] *Siècle* ; *Revue des Deux Mondes* (December 1st, 1882.)

Malhurin Cordier, and Claude Baduel.[1] "We cannot but observe," says M. Gaston Boissier, "that the reformation of study in the sixteenth century was primarily due to the Protestants."[2]

We have mentioned the interest which Renée, daughter of Louis XII., took in the education of Coligny's children. The Duchess of Ferrara had early favoured the Renaissance movement, and her stay in Italy could not but develop her taste for letters. Left a widow in 1559, and from that time taking up her abode in France, she became a devoted adherent of "the religion." Only a year before (July 5th, 1560), Calvin had reproached her for not taking a decided stand. Now the Consistory of Geneva had just sent her, at her own request, a minister, François Morel, Sieur de Collanges, who had presided over the Synod of Paris. Her resolution was the more courageous since her brother-in-law, Francis of Lorraine, was the most prominent leader of the Catholic party. It is easy to understand how her relations with the Châtillons became of the closest. Renée of Ferrara and Charlotte de Laval were kindred souls.[3] Some letters exchanged between them, which have come down to us, show that they were both alike devoted to works of charity.[4]

---

[1] This question is treated at length in the interesting work of M. Gaufrès on Claude Baduel (Paris, 1881).

[2] *Réforme des études au XVI*ème *Siècle.* It must not be forgotten, however, that the nobles were making efforts in the same direction in the republic of Venice, founding free schools taught by persons belonging to the first families in the State.

[3] M. Jules Bonnet, in the article already quoted, gives several touching extracts from Renée's account book, which show her care for the poor.

[4] Porro continentiæ ipsius summum hoc documentum fuit,

The Admiral loved to use hospitality. Singularly temperate and frugal in his own habits, he was so generous that he did not add one acre to his patrimonial estate. He wished that his house should be freely open to those who resorted to him from all parts of France.

At Châtillon the rights of the Catholics were treated with all respect ; this is a point we must not fail to notice. The Admiral, who was supreme as seigneur of the place, was an advocate of liberty of conscience. "Although he was no lover of masses, it could truly be said that there was no place in France where the priests lived in greater liberty than at Châtillon." He added, however, with his wonted candour, not free from a touch of malicious pleasantry, says M. Tessier, "that he did not act thus for his own pleasure, but to obey the king's edicts."

Such, as we look at it from this distance of time, seems the life of the Admiral, in its simple greatness, brightened by the joys of family ties and softened by his own gentle nature. It was but at rare intervals that he could enjoy his home at Châtillon. We must follow him again now into the conflict which becomes ever deeper and more deadly.

---

quod cum maximis honoribus affectus, privatis commodis servire et magnas opes aliorum aulicorum exemplo parare potuisset, tamen ne unum quidem agri jugerum, nullam villam ad paternam hæreditatem adjunxit " (*Vita*, p. 137).

CHAPTER XXI.

Tolerance of Catherine de Médicis towards the great Protestant lords.—
Adhesion of Cardinal Odet de Châtillon to the reformed faith.—
Rupture of the Constable with his nephews.—The Triumvirate.—
The edict of July.—Bold stand taken by the delegates of the States
General at St. Germain.

THE attitude of Catherine de Médicis towards
"the religion" became more and more conciliatory. She had wished to reinstate the Prince of
Condé, and the Parliament of Paris, notwithstanding
its attachment to the Guises, had been constrained
to confirm this act in a formal Council held June
18th, 1561. The Bourbons had become apparently
the real advisers of the queen-mother.

On February 26th the English Ambassador wrote
to his government : "Those who have the greatest
influence in the Court here are the Admiral and the
Cardinal de Châtillon, and *but for them nothing good
would be done.*" The Admiral influences the queen-
mother, the Cardinal the King of Navarre.[1]

Catherine, during a stay which she made at
Fontainebleau at this time, tolerated the meetings
of the reformed, and the prayers, followed by preach-

---

[1] *Calendar of Foreign State Papers*, 1561.

ing, which were performed daily in the apartments of the leading Protestants invited to the Court.[1]

The Court thus offered the singular spectacle of a perpetual violation of the laws of the land. Some bishops, like Moulin and Marillac,[2] shut their eyes to these proceedings ; others remonstrated loudly, and the pope's legate endorsed their complaints. The Jesuit Maimbourg writes on this subject : " It seems to me that taking the most favourable view of it, it may be safely said that if all that the queen-mother did at this time was only a feint, she was very wrong to feign so well that many believed she had gone over to the new sect ; for not only did she allow the ministers to preach in the princes' apartments, where crowds gathered to hear them, while a poor Jacobin, who was preaching the Lent sermons in Fontainebleau, was deserted ; but she even was present herself with all the Court ladies at the sermons of the Bishop of Valence, who preached openly, in one of the halls in the castle, the new heretical doctrines of Luther and Calvin. So sudden and complete was the change that had come over the scene that it seemed the whole Court had become Calvinist. Though it was Lent, meat was publicly sold and served on all tables. No one spoke of going to hear mass, and the young

---

[1] It must be noted, however, that at this very time, on economical pretexts, the king's council put down the Scotch guard, notwithstanding the strenuous remonstrance of Coligny. De Thou gives the real reason for this step. " Almost all the Scotchmen of the guard, beginning with their leader, Hamilton, Earl of Arran, were Protestants."

[2] Marillac died this year. He was a noble man, and well deserves the eulogium pronounced on him by De Thou.

king, who was taken to save appearances, went almost alone. The authority of the pope, the worship of saints and images, indulgences, and the ceremonies of the Church, were all lightly spoken of as mere superstitions." [1]

On the other hand, Coligny seized every opportunity to plead for liberty of conscience. On April 19th, 1561, Michel de l'Hospital issued a decree prohibiting the officers of the king from entering the houses of Protestants "under pretext of former edicts forbidding illicit assemblies." The Protestants who had been condemned on this ground were to be restored to liberty, " provided, however, that they lived henceforth as Catholics and without creating any scandal." The contradiction was palpable, and could but become manifest in practice. The parliament of Paris refused to register this edict, saying, with truth, that its tendency was to increase the number of the Protestants.

L'Hospital braved this opposition. The royal letters giving force to the edict were sent by him to the governors and tribunes of the provinces. In some parts of France they produced great excitement. The idea that the king should command that the persons of the Protestants should be respected, and no molestation should be offered to their houses in which they held their religious assemblies, was so novel, so contrary to all previous edicts, that they would not receive it. From the Catholic pulpits indignant protestations were heard. One sermon delivered by a monk of Provins, which has come down to us,

---

[1] *Histoire du calvinisme*, pp. 192 and following.

expresses with much *naïveté* the feelings with which the clergy received the edict.[1]

"And now, gentlemen of Provins, what ought I, what ought the other preachers of France to do? Ought we to obey this edict? What will you say to us? What shall we preach? "The Gospel," says the Huguenot. To say that the error of Calvin, of Martin Luther, of Beza, of Malot, of Peter Martyr, and other preachers, with their false accursed doctrine which was condemned by the Church a thousand years ago, and since then by the Holy Councils, to say that this is damnable heresy, is not this to preach the Gospel? To say that the Huguenots of France are wicked apostates, who have forsaken the true Catholic Church to follow heresy, is not this to preach the Gospel? To warn men against their doctrine, against hearing them or reading their books; to tell men that these doctrines tend and aim only to incite to sedition, robbery, and murder, as they have already begun to do in the city of Paris and in numberless other places in the land, is not this to preach the Gospel? But does anyone say to me, "Brother, what say you? *You are not obeying the king's edict:* you are speaking of Calvin and his companions, and you call them, and those who hold their opinions, heretics and huguenots; you will be brought to trial; you will be put in prison; you will be hanged as a traitor." I reply that it is possible it may be so, for Ahab and Jezebel put to death the prophets of God in their day, and granted liberty to the prophets of Baal.

---

[1] For this discourse see *Bulletin de la société du protestantisme français* (1854).

" Now, brother, you are going too far ; you will get yourself hanged." Well, be it so ; there will be one Franciscan monk hanged, and they will have to hang many more, for God by His Holy Spirit will inspire the pillars of His Church to uphold to the end the building which can never be destroyed."

A few measures of toleration proposed by l'Hospital had been enough to arouse this storm of anger. The names of Ahab and Jezebel, which the Protestants had so often given to their oppressors, were now taken up by Catholic lips. Catherine was Jezebel, since she allowed the Chancellor to attempt the pacification of the contending parties.

It was at this time that Odet de Coligny, the Admiral's eldest brother, gave in his adhesion publicly to the reformed communion.

Odet, as we have said, had been made a Cardinal at sixteen years of age, November 7th, 1533. At the same time he had been appointed Archbishop of Toulouse, and commendatory of a large number of abbeys. At seventeen he sat in the Conclave which elected Paul III. The year following he was raised to the bishopric of Beauvais, which was one of the oldest ecclesiastical peerages of France.[1] These rapid promotions, and this strange plurality of benefices, strikingly illustrate the corrupt system of patronage which then prevailed in the Church, and against which the Council of Trent was to raise its protest. Nothing could have seemed more unlikely

---

[1] Odet was never made a priest. He remained all his life a deacon, and never performed the functions of a bishop but by proxy. In *La France protestante* (2nd edit.) there is a very complete notice of Odet.

16

than that the Reformation should have found a disciple in a man who had profited so largely by the ecclesiastical abuses of his time ; but in this case the man was better than his fortune, and no accumulation of honours could stifle the voice of his conscience.

His was a gentle nature, opposed to strife, serviceable to all, generous and self-forgetful. " He never wronged any one," says Brantôme," nor blinded any one with court-flattery." De Thou praises his candour, his spirit of justice, the solidity of his judgment. By natural inclination he was fond of study. He made large use of his ample fortune in assisting the scholars and French writers of his age. Rabelais dedicated the fourth book of *Pantagruel* to him. Ronsard and l'Hospital inscribed to him many of their poems. But the stern conflicts in which he was involved proved how strong a soul lay beneath this gentle nature. We have seen how he frustrated by his passive resistance the plan formed by the Cardinal of Lorraine to establish the Inquisition in France. He assisted, without taking any very active part, in the Assembly of Fontainebleau, and in the meeting of the States General at Orleans. The example of the Admiral at length overcame all his hesitation.

Early in April 1561, Odet de Châtillon solemnly abjured Catholicism in the Castle of Werlemont, and in the presence of many witnesses belonging to the French nobility. On Easter Monday, April 7th, he dispensed the Holy Communion in the chapel of his palace at Beauvais, in both kinds.[1] This act set the

---

[1] See the interesting details of the event published by

city in an uproar. The priests organised processions ; the Protestants were attacked in their houses ; many of them were hanged or burned. The Cardinal appealed to Francis de Montmorency, son of the Constable, and governor of the Isle of France, who came at once and severely repressed the tumult. Odet gave up his ecclesiastical dignities, and retained none of his former titles except that of Count of Beauvais, which he held till his death. Men still spoke of him, however, as the Cardinal of Châtillon.

But while the Protestants were rejoicing in this conversion, an event was impending which was to dash all their hopes. The old Constable was about to be reconciled to the Guises, and to break with his nephews.

For a long time the Guises had been compassing this result. They knew that the wife of the Constable, Madeleine de Savoie, hated the Protestants, and made no exception in the case of the Châtillons. The Constable had been very indignant when it was said in Paris and repeated at Orleans, that those who held the great offices of state ought to be made to answer for themselves. He took this as a personal affront. De Thou says that Catherine de Médicis was playing a double game in all this ; that in order to weaken the influence of the King of Navarre she encouraged him to favour the Protestants, but that, on the other hand, she disclosed to the Constable the secret motives of her conduct, and made him understand them. Anne de Montmorency concluded that

---

M. Bonet-Maury in his article "La réforme à Beauvais" (*Bull. de la soc. d'hist. du prot. franç.*, 1874, pp. 732 and following).

since all this favour shown to the Protestants was only a feint, the safest thing for him was to go over to the other party, and to side with the Guises, who were as much exasperated as he was at the idea of having to give an account of their trusts.

De Thou says : " From this time Anne de Montmorency threw off all restraint. He was loud in his complaints that the old religion was being forsaken, that new assemblies, new rites, new ceremonies were being introduced everywhere ; that unknown people were usurping the holy ministry ; that meat was being publicly sold on fast-days, and even in Lent ; that the old worship handed down from our ancestors was being treated with contempt."

One day when Jean de Montluc, Bishop of Valence, who seemed at this time inclining to the reformed doctrines, was preaching in the palace, the Constable could not control his displeasure. His wife urged him on. " You," she said, " are the head of the most illustrious house in France ; it is your duty to maintain religion in all its purity." St. André added that " it was solely through the private hints of the Admiral that anything had been said about the bad administration of the finances, and that this nephew of the Constable, who was as ungrateful for his kindness as he was unworthy of it, had only proposed this article in order to embarrass the uncle who had loaded him with so many benefits."[1]

The Constable's eldest son tried in vain to deter his father, pointing out to him that in seeking new friends he would lose the old, and "that it was safer

---

[1] De Thou, Book xxvii.

for him to leave the Châtillons to fight it out with the Lorraines, and to be himself only an onlooker or arbiter, without taking either side."

" Odet, Gaspard, and Francis de Coligny also sought the Constable and protested, taking God to witness, that their estrangement from the Lorraines arose from no private animosity, but from zeal for the good of the State. They begged him to think whether in abandoning the Prince of Condé he would not be betraying the interests of the king and of the kingdom. All their remonstrances were of no avail."[1] The Constable openly held out his hand to the Lorraines. Diane de Poitiers, who, in her splendid retreat, had heard with indignation the reproaches of the Huguenots against the favourites who had grown rich at the expense of France, reappeared upon the scene at this crisis, and helped to foster the new alliance.

It was she who had sought out Marshal St. André and suggested to him the idea. St. André owed his immense fortune, as did Diane herself, to the ostentatious liberality of Henry II., and to the spoliations of the Protestants. He was one of those against whom public indignation was directed. The Catholics themselves thought his exceptional position out of all proportion to the services he had rendered. St. André, like the Constable, was angry at the idea that the States General wished to call upon the great dignitaries to render their accounts. Diane de Poitiers found no difficulty in persuading him. Davila says that St. André went to Francis of Lorraine and said

---

[1] De Thou, bk. xxvii.

to him: "You see how the Huguenots, sustained by the rebel princes, are turning our divisions to account for the benefit of those who for fifteen years have frustrated their seditious attempts. They mean to strike a blow at once at our honour and our wealth. They will soon have the pleasure of striking at you and the Constable separately, through your own quarrels. Your own danger, your religion, the last wishes of the king, to whom you were both equally dear, all call to you both to make common cause against the enemies of the faith. Do you not see that it is through the queen's devices you are kept apart? Will you disconcert all her policy, and rule in spite of her? Then show yourselves united. March together at the head of all the Catholics, and of all faithful subjects. Believe the warnings of a woman who knows the queen well, the Duchess de Valentinois, your friend and ally; it is she who has sent me to you. She implores you in the name of the king, who loved us all, to see the Constable de Montmorency and to be reconciled to him."

Thus was concerted the famous Triumvirate which was to exert so powerful an influence over the destinies of France. Guise and the Constable formed a close alliance with St. André, whom Brantôme calls " a very Lucullus in luxury and splendour," for the defence of the Catholic cause. This fatal alliance, entered into under the auspices of the old mistress of Henry II., was solemnly consecrated by a religious act. The three leaders partook of the Communion together on Easter Day at Fontainebleau.

One of the first results of this alliance was the promulgation of the edict of July 1561, which forbade, "under penalty of confiscation of person and goods, all conventicles and public assemblies, with or without arms, together with private assemblies in which there should be preaching or the administration of the sacraments in forms other than those received and observed by the Catholic Church." This extreme measure was only passed in the Council by a majority of three. Coligny resolutely opposed it ; saying that " to attempt thus to constrain the reformed to accept the Roman religion against their conscience was a great absurdity amounting to an impossibility." At the same time, however, it was decided that the bishops should hold a conference, in which they should discuss controversial questions with the reformed ministers, to whom safe conduct should be granted. The conference was to begin on August 18th at Poissy ; but the date had afterwards to be postponed, on account of the meeting of the States General, which was convoked first at Pontoise, and then at St. Germain, and only opened on August 26th.

We have already observed that the number of delegates at this session had been considerably reduced, but the spirit which animated them remained the same. The orators of the nobility, and of the third estate, spoke with even more vigour than at Orleans. When we read in the speech of Jacques de Bretagne, magistrate of Autun, and deputy of the third estate, the keen and vehement satire in which he described the life of the clergy, we feel to what a pitch of exasperation the bourgeoisie of the provinces had been driven. Brittany demanded in the name of its constituents, the alienation of the property of the clergy. This it estimated at 120 million livres : 48 millions at 8 per cent. would produce a revenue of 4 millions, which it held to be sufficient for the maintenance of the priests. The 72 millions remaining should be employed either to extinguish the debt or to encourage agriculture and commerce. It will be seen that this is almost precisely the project which the French Revolution was one day to carry out. The spokesman of the nobility took the same ground. He not only demanded the reform of the clergy, enormous reductions in the ecclesiastical revenues, and the convocation of a national council, but just after the publication of the edict of July he ignored it altogether, and demanded for the Protestants the right of assembly. The clergy absented themselves from these sittings, and to mark their opposition resolved to deliberate by themselves at St. Germain.

L'Hospital, however, was not in the least discouraged by their opposition ; and some days later, in the assembly of the clergy, he pleaded with much warmth the cause of liberty of conscience and freedom of worship, which he held to be inseparable. " As to the Protestant assemblies," he said, " they cannot be separated from their religion ; for they believe that the Word of God strictly enjoins them to assemble themselves to hear the preaching of the Gospel and to partake of the sacraments, and this they hold as an article of their faith."

After setting forth their grievances, the deputies of the States dispersed almost immediately, and all attention was turned to the coming Colloquy of Poissy.

CHAPTER XXII.

THE idea of convoking an assembly of the representatives of the two religious communions was not a new one. The thing had been repeatedly done in Germany and Switzerland, and it was often as the result of such conferences that some prince or canton joined the reformed party. The conscience of our age refuses to admit that a change of religion can be enforced by the decision of any prince or any assembly, and to us it seems simply monstrous to appoint as umpires in such a discussion, a woman such as Catherine de Médicis and a child of eleven years like Charles IX. The convocation at Poissy could not be a recognised deliberative assembly, for its members had not been properly delegated, and were not competent, therefore, to come to any valid decision. It was, as its name indicates, simply a colloquy in which the two communions were about to engage in a brilliant but . inconclusive passage of arms. The Protestants, however, accepted it eagerly; for it gave them the opportunity they had so often sought to fully declare their faith, and to show that it was in accordance with Scripture and with the doctrines of the great Councils. L'Hospital was desirous of this demonstration, in order that he might be authorised by it to place the Protestants as Christians under the protection of the law. Certain bishops, such as Montluc, looked on it as a means of bringing pressure to bear upon Rome, so that it should be compelled to grant the reforms which seemed to them urgent. There were others again, such as the Cardinal of Lorraine, whose secret design was to make a split between the Lutherans and the Calvinists or Zuinglians, by bringing into prominence the doctrinal differences between them. This was clearly the only motive which could have induced such strong Catholics as the Cardinal of Tournon to enter the lists in public discussion with avowed heretics.

In view of the coming colloquy of Poissy, the Court met at St. Germain. Never had so large a number of Protestant lords been seen at court before. Foremost among them were the King and Queen of Navarre.

Antoine of Navarre was still regarded as the nominal head of the Protestants; but his perpetual vacillation, and the servile part which he had consented to play on so many occasions, made him distrusted by the reformed party.

A few months previous to this, however (February 7th, 1561), Antoine had written to the Count Palatine "that he had no other aim than to establish the true religion in France;" and throughout the whole of the colloquy he assumed the rôle of protector of the Huguenot party.

Jeanne d'Albret, his wife, had just joined the Reformed Church. Born January 7th, 1528, she was at this time thirty-three years of age. Her father was Henri d'Albret, a man of much energy and vivacity, accustomed to breathe the free air of the Pyrenees, a man of keen discernment, who never allowed himself to be duped by anybody, and of whom Charles V. said, " I have seen but one man in France, and that is the King of Navarre."[1] Jeanne d'Albret inherited her father's quick and impulsive nature, his unfailing good humour, his steadfastness of purpose ; and all these she was to hand down to her son. From her mother, Marguerite de Valois, she received a taste for literary pursuits, an aversion to bigotry, and a large-hearted sympathy with all forms of suffering. But the curious eagerness for novelties, which in Marguerite often assumed the form of a refined subtlety, was tempered in the daughter by a sound and steady judgment. In her early youth she had been much about the court of Francis I., who used to call her " the darling of darlings " (*la mignonne des mignonnes*).

For political reasons it was decided to marry her, while she was quite a child, to the Duke of Cleves. She resisted ; they were obliged to carry her by force to the altar. This marriage was cancelled. In later years, it was she herself who fell in love with Antoine de Bourbon. She was captivated by

---

[1] Palma Cayet (*Chron. novenaire*, vol. ii., p. 218).

his handsome face and chivalrous bearing, and never suspected the nerveless will which dwelt in that manly frame. The opposition offered by his father to the union stimulated his passion. The marriage was celebrated with great pomp at Moulins in 1548. The young couple took part in all the festivities which inaugurated the reign of Henry II. At that time Jeanne was entirely absorbed in worldly pleasure. But trials came. Jeanne lost her first two children by strange accidents, due to the carelessness of those who had charge of them.[1] Her father, angered at this, told her bitterly "that she was not worthy to have children, if she took no better care of them."[2] He demanded that if God gave her another child, it should be entrusted to him to bring up. Every one has heard the story of the birth of Henry IV., and how Jeanne, in order to please her father, sang a Béarnese song amidst the throes of child-birth. Soon after her father died, and she was raised to the throne of Navarre. Her subjects hailed her return with enthusiasm. From this time she took up her abode in her kingdom, and only paid visits, more or less prolonged, to the Court of France.

The Reformation had found its way into her States. Antoine of Navarre was at first favourable to it. He allowed public preaching in the Castle of Nérac, and summoned Beza to come to him. Jeanne had little sympathy with the innovators. She knew that her mother, who had taken them under her protection, had been reproached by them at the

---

[1] See Appendix D.
[2] Palma Cayet., *Chron. novenaire*, p. 232.

close of her life, for her undecided attitude. Their austerity also was displeasing to her. She confessed afterwards that a whole night at a ball appeared shorter to her than an hour at preaching. But the new duties which pressed upon her, the distress which the weakness of her husband caused her, led her gradually to think seriously. Her queenly pride was deeply wounded by the ridiculous part which her husband consented to play after the death of Henry II. From this time she assumed the sovereignty herself, and showed that she knew how to govern. She would preside at her own council, visit her estates, establish useful institutions in all parts of her kingdom, open new roads, multiply schools, and give a welcome to those who were fleeing away from France under proscription. When, in 1560, Antoine was arrested in Orleans and threatened with death, she shut herself up with her son in her citadel, and prepared for a valiant resistance. The death of Francis II., saved the life of Antoine ; but to Jeanne this was only the beginning of fresh sorrows. She learned that her weak husband was allowing himself to be made the tool of Catherine, and that he was the laughing-stock of the Catholics, who thought it a good joke to see such a leader at the head of the austere Huguenot party. In these perplexities Jeanne sought her strength in God. She began to study the Scriptures, sent for a minister named Jean de la Tour, and resolved to join the Protestants. This decision was all the more courageous because Jeanne dared by this act the anathema of Rome. If the pope chose to issue a bull, declaring her to be a heretic, and unworthy to reign, her formidable cousin,

Philip II., might come and lay his hand on her estates.

Catherine de Médicis pressed Jeanne to come to Court at the time of the colloquy. Jeanne started from Béarn, taking with her the minister La Tour. In several cities which she passed through, particularly in Orleans, she did not hesitate to join in the Protestant assemblies. She openly embraced their cause at the very time when Antoine was secretly thinking of breaking off from it.[1] On August 29th she arrived at St. Germain, where she met with an enthusiastic welcome from the Protestants.

She had avoided passing through Paris, where her presence might have excited a tumult. On the day of her arrival there was a great banquet at the Court, with bullfights and fireworks in the evening. Catherine seemed rejoiced to see her. This was taken to be a clear token of reconciliation between the two parties. Everyone, too, was sanguine about the coming colloquy, and Throckmorton, who was usually right in his judgments, expressed the hope that the Duke of Guise and his brother might be led to confess the faith of the Gospel.

Only a few weeks later the martyr-fires of the reformed were burning week after week in Paris, and even now heresy was by law a punishable crime; and yet here was a veritable little Protestant Court assembled at St. Germain, under the auspices of the King and Queen of Navarre, and with the tacit

---

[1] In *La France protestante*, even in the second edition, Jeanne d'Albret is represented as leaving Paris in the middle of July, 1561, and taking refuge at Pau where she embraced " the religion " the following Christmas.

consent of Catherine de Médicis. Louis de Condé and his brave wife, the Countess de Roye, his mother-in-law, the Admiral and Charlotte de Laval, the Cardinal Odet de Châtillon and Renée, Duchess of Ferrara, were conspicuous in the galaxy.[1] All these royal guests were lodged in the castle or in houses adjoining, and, notwithstanding the July edict, the reformed worship was celebrated daily in their dwellings.

Chantonnay, the Spanish ambassador, noted all this with ill-disguised anger. Writing to Philip II., he said : " Religion is going on here in its accustomed way. Every day there is preaching in the house of some lord and lady of the Court ; when I protest, the answer always is that they know nothing about it, and will enquire, but nothing comes of it, and the thing is just repeated. . . . Matters are going on in such sort that I look for no good to come of it. There has been more preaching of late within the Castle of St. Germain, than there ever was before the July edict, and the preachers are as secure there as those of the Catholic Church." [2]

Catherine de Médicis now affected to incline towards the Reformation. Some time before, on August 4th, she had sent a curious letter to Paul IV., pointing out to him the measures to be taken to save the Church.[3] It is easy to trace in this

---

[1] Death had just removed one eminent woman, Jacqueline de Longwy, Duchess de Montpensier, and sister-in-law to Condé. She had considerable influence over Catherine, and always used it in the direction of justice and toleration.

[2] Quoted by M. Delaborde in *Les Protestants au cour de St. Germain*, 1874.

[3] This letter is given by De Thou, Book xxviii.

letter the hand of Montluc, Bishop of Valence, her favourite divine, of whose share in the conference of Fontainebleau we have already spoken. In this letter Catherine referred to the ever-growing number of the Protestants, who had become so powerful that it was no longer any use to think of suppressing them by force of arms. " Yet," she added, " there are among them no anabaptists nor libertines (*i.e.*, freethinkers), nor any adherents of opinions which are regarded as monstrous. All hold the twelve articles of the Creed, as explained by the Œcumenical Councils.[1] Thus many of the most zealous Catholics think they should not be cut off from the communion of the Church, although on some points they differ from her in opinion." The queen-mother went on to advise that special instructions should be given, and a pacific conference should be held with a view to bringing back those who had erred. She thought that some concessions might be made to them. " Images might be banished, at least from the place set apart for prayer and the public worship of God. In the administration of baptism, the exorcisms and forms of prayer which did not belong essentially to the institution of the sacrament might be omitted." There might further be a return to communion in both kinds, and to the use of the vulgar tongue in the liturgy. Private masses without communicants might be forbidden. The queen concluded by protesting her fidelity to the pope and to holy Church. These suggestions of reform in minor points clearly

---

[1] As De Thou remarks, the Protestants acknowledged only the first four Councils—those of Nice, Constantinople, Ephesus, and Chalcedon—to be œcumenical.

show that there was in her mind, or in the minds of those who counselled her, an utter misapprehension of the great movement which was stirring in the hearts of more than one-third of Europe, the pulses of a new religious life. It was a fool's errand to try and stop with feeble barriers like these the impetuous course of a great torrent.

That which proves, however, that the royal family was really influenced by the new ideas is the attitude of two of Catherine's sons, which we learn from the naïve account of her daughter Marguerite.

In the *Mémoires* she says : " I made a struggle to hold fast my religion at the time of the Synod of Poissy, when the whole Court was infected with heresy through the urgent persuasions of many ladies and gentlemen of the Court, and even of my brother of Anjou (since King of France), who, though he was but a child at the time, could not escape the impression of the wretched *Huguenotry*, and who was constantly imploring me to change my religion, often throwing my book of *Hours* into the fire, and giving me instead psalms and Huguenot prayers, and making me use them." She adds indeed that her mother did not admit that things had gone so far, and that she obliged d'Anjou " to return to the true, holy, and ancient religion of our fathers, from which she had never departed." But evidently Catherine had allowed her children to fall, to a large extent, under the influence of the reformed teaching ; for the little king Charles IX. himself, in a conversation with Jeanne d'Albret,[1] declared that when he

---

[1] This conversation is narrated by the English ambassador Throckmorton, *Calendar of Foreign State-Papers*, 1561,

was king he would not go to mass. Meanwhile, my aunt," he said to Jeanne d'Albret, " I pray you keep all this to yourself, and have a care that nothing come to my mother's ears." The Queen of Navarre, in repeating these words, expressed the hope that Charles IX. might be like Edward VI. of England, and might do good service, as Edward had done, to the cause of religion. This opinion was shared by Theodore Beza, who, in writing to Calvin, described the young king as a prince " of singular promise."

It is easy to understand that the leaders of the Catholic party were made profoundly uneasy by this attitude of the Court, and used every influence to counteract it. They saw treason everywhere, and Michel de l'Hospital was, in their eyes, no better than a Protestant in· disguise. Pius IV. sent a legate, the Cardinal of Ferrara, son of the too famous Lucrezia Borgia, to France. The choice was an unfortunate one, for the scandals associated with that name had greatly strengthened the cause of the Reformation. The legate did not dare to make a public entry into Paris ; he even kept as much as possible out of sight. He arrived at St. Germain just in the midst of the colloquy of Poissy.

The old Cardinal of Tournon was the ostensible leader of the opposition. Obstinate and headstrong, he would lend no ear to the party of moderation represented by Bishop Montluc. But the true head of the party was the famous Cardinal of Lorraine, whose share in the proceedings should be well noted.

---

p. 415. It will be found entire in M. Delaborde's book, *Les Protestants au cour de St. Germain*, p. 12, and following.

We have already had reason to remark on his precocious ambition. On his first journey to Rome, when he was only twenty-three years of age, he was already planning the conquest of Naples for his brother. Subsequently his alliance with the adventurer Carafa and the wretched intrigue in which they combined together, brought upon France all the disasters of 1557.

We have seen how baleful was his influence at the time of the signature of the peace of Cambrésis, when in concert with Granvelle, Bishop of Arras, he advised the extermination of the heretics. After the death of Henry II., he, with his brother Francis, had taken the power into their own hands, had treated the conspirators of Amboise with the greatest cruelty, and urged the execution of Condé. The death of Francis II. had, for a brief period, thrown him into the shade ; and during the year 1561 he turned his thoughts to his diocese of Rheims, where he preached with great unction, during Lent, on the necessity of reforming the Church. His zeal was so exemplary that he was accused of leaning towards Lutheranism.[1]

This unscrupulous Lorraine was, indeed, a strange reformer. He owed his extraordinary fortune to Diane de Poitiers. Brantôme tells us that his private life was exceptionally scandalous even for that age of loose morals. He boasted that he could

---

[1] " Cardinalis Lotharingicus a rigidioribus ponteficiis accusatur lutheranismi " (Languet, *Epist.*, xliv.) Languet says afterwards on the same subject, "Rhemis ita concionatur ut videatur non multum a nostris dissentire." But he prudently adds, " Sed viderint alii quantum huic sit fidendum." (*Epist.* lxiii.)

triumph by means of gold over the staunchest virtue. Thus the stern old chronicler says of him " that his very soul was besmutched " (*l'âme barbouillée*). The Jesuit Maimbourg, who is his apologist, cannot deny that he had all his life " an immoderate passion for the aggrandisement of his house." He says also, " that being of an extremely keen and penetrating spirit, impetuous and violent by nature, and with a rare gift of eloquence, he was yet the most timid and feeble of men when it came to carrying anything out at a risk to himself." Mézeray mentions the same characteristic. He speaks of him as " loud and vindictive in word, but crafty, cautious, and fearful in deed." At times he was foremost in advocating pacific measures for France ; at other times no one was so urgent as he for stern and violent repression. The Protestants knew him but too well. They called him the Lorraine tiger, and shrank from him as their most deadly enemy.

In 1561, at the date at which we have now arrived, Charles of Lorraine was thirty-seven years of age. Of all the French prelates he was the one who had most strongly urged the convocation of the Colloquy. He hoped, by his natural eloquence, to take a prominent part in it. The life he had hitherto led had not at all prepared him for the study of theological questions, but he had an excellent power of grasping the telling points of a subject. Later on, he was one of those who gained the best hearing at the Council of Trent. At this time, he relied mainly upon certain skilful tactics of his own for overwhelming the Protestants. The Colloquy must, as he thought, end in splitting up the Protestants into parties. With a view to this end, the discussion must be adroitly made to turn on some points on which they were not agreed, as for instance on the Holy Communion. The reformed must be led on to state their doctrine, and if possible to exaggerate it in the heat of controversy, so as to shock and offend the German Lutherans.[1] Charles of Lorraine, from the position of his diocese, was well acquainted with the German Lutherans. He was a neighbour of theirs, and he used much tact in dealing with them. He kept up a close correspondence with Duke Christopher of Würtemberg, and took every opportunity of praising the Augsburg Confession. It was at his request that the Lutheran princes of Germany had decided to send their divines to Poissy. They did not arrive till after the colloquy, but we shall see what use the Cardinal of Lorraine tried to make of their doctrine.[2]

The Court of Rome placed, however, but little confidence in Charles of Lorraine. It was afraid that he might really take up the part of mediator between the Catholics and Lutherans, and that, strong in the influence which such a position would give him, he would use the occasion to vindicate the

---

[1] This was the snare which Calvin dreaded. Hence he wrote to Coligny, September 1561 : " Above all, I pray you, Monseigneur, have a care that the Confession of Augsburg is not brought forward, for it will be only a torch to kindle a fire of discord." He added this unjust criticism on it, " In fact, it is so poorly constructed, so pliant, and so obscure that it cannot last."

[2] We have mentioned above that when the little Duke of Anjou, the future Henry III., was playing the Protestant and trying to convert his sister Marguerite, it was the name of the Cardinal of Lorraine and the Confession of Augsburg which he had constantly on his lips.

privileges of the Gallican Church, and to assert that relative independence which had always been the dream of a part of his clergy and of the French Government. Rome had therefore sent with her legate to France another person upon whom she could place absolute reliance, the Jesuit Jacques Lainez, one of the early companions of Ignatius Loyola, who three years before had succeeded him in the leadership of that famous society. It was Lainez who, from the work begun by the ardent enthusiasm of Loyola, evolved the Jesuitism with which we are familiar in history. Intelligent, prudent, methodical, he gave the order its first practical initiation, and while he allowed it to be a militia entirely devoted to the pope, he laboured to commend it at the same time to the confidence of the bishops. His zeal in maintaining the infallibility of the pope made him at first an object of suspicion to the French clergy ; but the zeal he displayed at Poissy and at Trent against the Protestants speedily disarmed suspicion, and enabled him to secure for his order the liberty he so ardently desired for it in France. The presence of Lainez foiled all the efforts of Charles of Lorraine to give a Gallican turn to the controversy. It was equally fatal to the attempt at conciliation which was to have been made by Montluc, Bishop of Valence, Catherine's favourite prelate, whose conduct reflected the undecided tactics of the queen-mother. This diplomatic bishop, who had succeeded in his youth in cementing the alliance of France with the Turks, and who by his intrigues was subsequently to secure to the Duke of Anjou the throne of Poland, had warmly defended the cause of the Reformation in the Assembly of Fontainebleau. Blaise de Montluc, his brother, notwithstanding this, boasts of the aid which the bishop gave in exterminating the Huguenots in Guyenne. Catherine counted upon Montluc to give the Colloquy a favourable direction in support of her authority.

Such were the principal representatives of Catholicism in the Colloquy of Poissy. To oppose them the Protestants had sent some of their best divines. At one time they thought of summoning Calvin himself. But the Admiral, who had to secure the safe conducts for the Protestant ministers, declared this to be impossible. La Rivière, one of the pastors of the Church of Paris, wrote to Calvin to this effect: "As for you, sir," he said, "as we have never yet seen any chance of having you over here, so we fear it cannot be now without grave dangers, because of the rage which all the enemies of the Gospel have conceived against you, and the disturbances which your very name would stir up in this country, if they knew you were here. In fact, the Admiral is not at all of opinion that you should undertake this journey, and we are well assured that the queen has no wish to see you here either, and she says frankly that she could give no security for your life here, as for others. As for the other side, the enemies of the Gospel say that they will willingly hear all the others speak, but you they will neither hear nor see. You see, sir, in what esteem you are held by these venerable prelates," etc.[1]

---

[1] This curious letter, the original of which is in the Library of Geneva, was published in the *Bulletin de la société d'histoire du protestantisme français*, vol. xvi., p. 602.

The arrival of the ministers at St. Germain must have been a curious spectacle. " They are easily to be known by their faces," writes Chantonnay, ironically, to the Duchess of Parma. " In the midst of courtiers clothed in silk and velvet, their doublets decked with ribands and laces like any woman, in the midst of the great ladies arrayed in damask and gold and silver brocade, and bending under the weight of their long trains, it seemed strange to see these men of grave carriage, sombre dress, and austere countenance."[1]

" They were better received than the pope himself would have been, had he come," writes Claude Hatton, indignantly.[2] Chantonnay says that the Cardinal of Châtillon prepared to lodge twelve of them. The Admiral received into his house Jean Malot, pastor of the Church of Paris. The others were Theodore Beza; Jean Raymond Merlin, the Admiral's Almoner; Jean de l'Espine; Marlorat, who the year following was strangled in Rome; François Morel, sieur de Collonges, who, though still quite young, had presided two years before over the first Synod in Paris; François de St. Paul; Nicolas Follion; Jean Boquin; Nicolas des Gallards, seigneur de Saules, pastor of the French Church in London, who came at the Admiral's request; Claude de la Boissière, of Saintes; Nicolas Thobie, of Orleans; Jean Viret. From day to day Peter Martyr, the most eminent divine of the Italian reformation, and one of the chief compilers of the Anglican liturgy, was expected. He was then Professor at Zurich, and it was hoped that he might have special influence over his countrywoman,

---

[1] La Ferrière, Introd., p. c.
[2] *Journal*, vol. i., p. 155.

Catherine de Médicis, who had herself insisted on his coming.

Of all the reformed doctors, the one on whom all eyes were turned was Theodore Beza, Calvin's *alter ego*. Beza was then forty-two years of age. "He was well made," writes the Jesuit Maimbourg, "with a pleasing face, of refined and courteous bearing, with all the manners of a man of the world, which made him a favourite with the great, and especially with the ladies, whom he was very careful not to displease. In mind it must be admitted that he was much gifted, lively, easy, versatile, playful and polite."

In another passage the same author attacks Beza with extreme vehemence, and reproaches him with the irregularities of his life. Beza had had a stormy youth. Designed first for the law, then endowed with ecclesiastical benefices, he only thought at that time of shining as a poet, and of imitating Tibullus. His youthful works were well known, and it was only too easy to find in them causes of scandal. But the Protestants had the right to reply that since he joined them he had thoroughly reformed his life, and that this change was the best proof of the sincerity of his faith. In our day we should bring another charge against him,—that of accepting blindly the opinions of his age as to the punishment due to heretics, and of having made himself the apologist of the death of Servetus.

Beza, who had been living twelve years in Geneva, had already come back to his country once on an important mission to Antoine of Navarre, whom he had helped to win over to the reformed faith.

Some difficulties arose now about his leaving

Geneva. The magistrates of that city were afraid that his life would be endangered. It was not till Antoine wrote for him that he was allowed to come.

Beza left Geneva on August 17th, and after paying his respects, as he passed Montargis, to the Duchess of Ferrara, whom he was to meet again at the French Court, he proceeded to St. Germain, where he arrived August 23rd.

In a letter to Calvin[1] he gives an account of the way in which he was received. The King of Navarre, Condé, the Admiral, and the Cardinal of Bourbon, all gave him a hearty welcome. The day after his arrival he preached in the house of the Prince of Condé. In the evening he was invited to visit the King of Navarre. He says : " I was astounded to find there the queen-mother, the king, the prince, Monsieur d'Étampes, the Cardinals of Bourbon and Lorraine, Madame de Crussol, and another lady. I was so surprised that I could not but betray it, but, thank God, this did not prevent my declaring to the queen in a few words the cause of my coming. She replied very graciously. Then the Cardinal (of Lorraine), taking up the discourse, and beginning with fine compliments, went on to say that as I had troubled France, so now I could comfort it."

Beza, as may be believed, did not let this pass without protesting that he had not troubled France. The subject was changed. He was asked about Calvin, his age, and the state of his health. Then the Cardinal introduced the question of the Holy Communion. He said that for his own part he did

---

[1] *Bibliothèque de Genève*, vol. cxvii.

not attach much importance to transubstantiation. This was a trap skilfully laid to draw Beza into a public discussion of the subject, and thus to touch on the point of divergence between the Reformed and the Lutherans. Catherine seemed highly satisfied with 'this first interview. The Cardinal, on leaving, said to Beza : " I adjure you to confer with me, and you will find me not so black as I am painted." Upon which Madame de Crussol, interrupting him abruptly, said : " You are hail-fellow-well-met to-night, but what to-morrow ?" And, in truth, the next day the Cardinal went about saying everywhere that he had brought Beza over to his opinion. The Constable, dining with the queen-mother, repeated this. " I was present," said Catharine, " and I assure you it was nothing of the sort."

The week following Beza preached several times. Chantonnay, writing to the Duchess of Parma (September, 1561), says : " He preached yesterday the most abominable sermon that was ever made, and the people flocked in by doors and windows with marvellous eagerness."

The reformed wished that the colloquy should not be turned into a council, and that the bishops should not be admitted as judges or partisans. In this they were right enough ; but they went too far when they asked that all questions should be decided solely by Scripture, consulted in the original. From the Catholic point of view this was equivalent to begging the question. Catherine promised vaguely to have these conditions observed, but refused to give any engagement in writing.

CHAPTER XXIII.

BEFORE the opening of the Colloquy an assembly of the clergy was held at St. Germain for the purpose of voting the king's subsidy. The financial position of the kingdom was very serious. The States General at Orleans, and at St. Germain itself, had spoken strongly of the necessity of demanding from the great lords an account of their trusts. They had even talked of selling the estates of the

---

[1] For the history of the Colloquy of Poissy see Theodore Beza's full account (*Hist. eccl.*), and his letters, and those of Peter Martyr, and the narratives of La Place, De Thou, Castelnau, and Fleury. We shall have occasion to refer also to the journal of Dr. Despence, one of the Catholic divines who took the most prominent part in the colloquy, a thoughtful and moderate man (MSS. 309, 451, Dupuy's Coll. *Bibliothèque nationale*. The *Mémoires* of Hatton the Curé, written from the ultra-Catholic point of view, contain some curious details, but he sometimes becomes purely fanciful, as, for instance, when he puts into the mouth of the Cardinal of Tournon, in the first meeting, an utterly improbable discourse. Baum, in his *Theodore*

clergy. The clergy at that time possessed two-fifths of the revenue of the kingdom.[1]

The common danger drew together the great dignitaries, Montmorency, St. André, the Guises, and the whole episcopate. The Court did not fail to press this argument upon the clergy, in order to induce them to vote the subsidy, which was only reluctantly done at the end of October. This position of affairs will account in part for the advances made by Catharine to the Protestant party. She hoped in this way to intimidate the clergy.[2]

The Colloquy was opened on September 9th, 1561, in the great refectory of the convent of Poissy. The Court repaired to it in solemn procession. The king, surrounded by his mother, his brother Henry, his sister, the King and Queen of Navarre, sat on a throne, behind which stood the nobility. The prelates sat on either side. There were among them forty bishops, and the Cardinals of Tournon, Châtillon, Lorraine, Armagnac, and Guise. The ministers and deputies of the Reformed Churches, who had left St. Germain under a guard of a hundred cavaliers, arrived at Poissy a little before eleven o'clock. They were placed in front of a barrier, which separated them from the rest of the Assembly. There they

Beza (Leipzig, 1851), treats this subject with great ability. We would call attention also to Klipffel's interesting work entitled *Le Colloque de Poissy* (Paris, Librairie Internationale); also to the chapters relating to it in Soldan's *Geschichte des Protestantismus in Frankreich*, and Ranke's *Französische Geschichte* (vol i. p. 236).

[1] So M. Soriano thinks, *Ambass. vénit.*, vol. i., p. 505.

[2] Despence says that on August 4th there was a report that the king's council had in readiness an edict relating to the election of curés by their parishes.

stood like prisoners at the bar ; but their resolute attitude showed plainly enough the position they meant to take.

The little king read an address which had been prepared for him. " Gentlemen," he said, " I have called you together, from various parts of my kingdom, to know your mind on that which my Chancellor will bring before you ; and I pray you to lay aside all passion, in order that we may gather some fruit which shall be for the good of my subjects, the glory of God, and the quieting of men's consciences, and of the public generally. This I have so much at heart, that I purpose that you shall not move from this spot till you have restored order to my kingdom ; that my subjects may henceforth live in peace and union the one with the other, as I hope that you will do ; and so doing that you will give me occasion to extend to you the same protection as did the kings my predecessors."

The Chancellor l'Hospital spoke next. He justified the idea of a national council, saying that in a general council there would be present a number of foreign bishops, who could not judge of questions arising out of the particular position of things in France. He addressed himself to the prelates, and enjoined them to receive the ministers " as a father does his children, and to take pains to inform and instruct them." If they could not succeed in doing this, at least it could not then be said in the future, as had been said in the past, that they had been condemned without a hearing. The prelates were clearly recognised by him as judges in the cause. This principle being laid down, he urged on them

moderation, and counselled them "to conform themselves as far as possible to the Word of God." This
language was doubtless very conciliatory, but it took
it as an accepted fact that the ministers were in the
eyes of the Government nothing better than accused
persons standing before their judges, with whom
their sentence must rest. Under such conditions
the conclusion was foregone.

The ministers then came forward to the bar, and
Theodore Beza spoke as follows : " Sire, since the
issue of all enterprises, small or great, depends on
the assistance and favour of our God, and most of
all when it is a question of His service, and one
which passes our capacity to understand, we hope
your Majesty will not take it ill, or deem it strange,
if we begin by calling thus upon His name." Then
kneeling, he repeated the well-known confession of
sins which is still used in the commencement of the
reformed worship.[1]

The Assembly listened to this prayer with respect.
The queen knelt. The Cardinals remained standing,
but uncovered. Beza, having risen from his knees,
set forth with great dignity of speech the aims the

---

[1] We give it here in the form in which it was used by Theodore Beza, which is substantially the same as that used in the
Forme des prières, introduced by Calvin at Geneva in 1542.
(*Calvinii Opera*, vi., 173). "Lord God, Father Eternal and
Almighty, we confess and acknowledge unfeignedly before
Thy Divine Majesty that we are poor sinners, conceived and
born in iniquity and corruption, prone to do evil, unable to
do good, and that through our sinful nature we do constantly
transgress Thy holy commandments, by doing which we bring
upon ourselves, by Thy just judgment, ruin and perdition.
Nevertheless, Lord, we are grieved with ourselves for having
offended Thee, and we condemn ourselves and our sins with
true repentance, desiring that Thy grace may come to the

reformed had in view. "Do not think," said he, "that we are come to maintain any error, but to discover and amend all that may be found wanting on our part or on yours. Do not deem us so presumptuous that we would seek to destroy that which we know to be eternal—the Church of God. Think not that we are seeking how we may make you like to us in our poor and low estate, in which nevertheless, thank God, we find a singular contentment. Our desire is that the ruins of Jerusalem should be built up ; that this spiritual temple may be restored ; that this house of God, which is built of living stones, may be again made whole ; that these flocks, so long scattered and dispersed by the just vengeance of God, and the heedlessness of men, may be gathered again into the fold of the one great Shepherd. This," he added with thrilling earnestness, "this is our aim ; this, gentlemen, is all our desire and intention. If you have deemed otherwise hitherto, we hope you will believe us when, with all patience and gentleness, we shall have set before you that which God has given to us. And might it please our God that, without going further, and instead of arguing one against another, we might all with one voice sing a

---

help of our infirmity. Be pleased then to have pity on us, O God and Father most merciful and gracious, in the name of Thy Son Jesus Christ, our Lord and only Redeemer, and blotting out our sins and transgressions, grant to and increase in us day by day the graces of Thy Holy Spirit, so that we, confessing with all our heart our unrighteousness, may be filled with godly sorrow, which worketh true repentance, and mortifying all sin, may bring forth fruits of righteousness acceptable to Thee, through Jesus Christ our Lord." Beza then implored the blessing of God on the Assembly, and its labours, and on the king, and concluded with the Lord's Prayer.

hymn to the Lord, and hold out the hand of friendship to one another, as has sometimes happened
even when armies of unbelievers have been ranged
in battle array against each other."[1]

It is pleasant to dwell upon noble, peaceable words
like these, spoken in such troublous times, and in
this singular meeting between the representatives of
the two parties, on the eve of a conflict which was
to deluge France with blood. Perhaps it was to
these words, and to the impression produced by
them, that the Cardinal of Lorraine alluded the next
day, when he exclaimed, " I would either that he
had been dumb, or we had been deaf! "

After this exordium, Beza began his exposition of
the reformed faith. He first set forth the doctrines
common to both Churches. Then passing to those
on which they differed, he mentioned three : the
basis of faith, the Holy Communion, and the government of the Church.[2] The basis of faith he held to
be Holy Scripture, to which all the teaching of the
fathers and the decrees of the Councils should be

---

[1] Were this a literary study, we might call attention here
to the beauty of Beza's language. The sixteenth century had
undoubtedly greater writers than Beza. Calvin expresses clear
and strong thought in language singularly incisive and telling;
Montaigne has exquisite grace of style, and a wealth of expression corresponding to the richness of his thought. Rabelais
has his powerful vein of humour ; d'Aubigné his grand and
picturesque manner. But none of them excels Beza in
breadth and force and harmony of diction. In this respect
only La Boëtie in *La servitude volontaire* can be compared
with him.

[2] One cannot help remarking that if Beza, instead of taking
up this ground, had dwelt, as Luther did in his first conferences,
on the more central question of justification, he would have
carried with him at least the secret sympathies of the whole of

18

subordinated. When he came to the Holy Communion, wishing to indicate that the presence of Christ in the Sacrament could be only a spiritual presence, he expressed his thought in the following manner: "that the body of Jesus Christ is as far removed from the bread and wine as the highest heaven is from the earth." This was to present the Calvinist doctrine in negative and certainly in not happily chosen terms, for the confession of faith of the reformed Churches affirmed " that those who brought to the sacred table of Christ a pure faith, veritably received that which the symbols set forth, and that the body and blood of Jesus Christ were as truly meat and drink to the soul as the bread and wine were to the body."[1] Since then, according to the Calvinist doctrine, the spiritual communion of the soul with the glorified Christ corresponded to the believing reception of the bread and wine in the Holy Communion, it would have been better not to use an expression which seemed to say exactly the opposite. If Beza had confined himself to affirming that Jesus Christ was not in any degree present in a

---

that part of the Church of France which had held fast the tradition of St. Augustine, and out of which the powerful Jansenist movement was soon to spring. Upon the question of the Communion, the divergences among the reformed were already showing themselves. Thus where the Catholic Church ever since the middle ages had seen a material transubstan-. tiation of the bread and wine into the body of Christ, Zuinglius saw simply a symbol. Luther believed in a real presence of the body of Christ in the wafer and the wine, but not in a change of substance. Calvin affirmed that here was a mystery of a purely spiritual order, and that in the moment of Communion the soul of the believer was united to the glorified Christ.

[1] *Confessio Gall.*, Art. XXXVIII.

material sense in the sacramental bread and wine, he would not have furnished his opponents with the opportunity they eagerly sought of raising a cry of scandal. "*Blasphemavit,*" was the indignant exclamation of the old Cardinal of Tournon, and it was echoed by almost all the prelates.

Beza nevertheless went on with his discourse, and showed that the reformed rejected traditions which they found to be contrary to the spirit and letter of Scripture. When he had finished Beza knelt down and prayed silently. Then rising he came forward and presented to the king the confession of the reformed Churches, saying: "Sire, may it please your Majesty not to have regard to our rude and unpolished speech, but to our hearty affection to youwards. And inasmuch as the points of our doctrine are clearly and fully contained in this confession of faith, which we now present to you, and upon which this conference will turn, we humbly beseech your Majesty to do us this favour to receive it at our hands, hoping, by the grace of God, that after having considered it with all sobriety and reverence for His name, *we may find we are of one mind.* But if, on the contrary, on account of our sins, we receive not this blessing, we doubt not that your Majesty, of his good counsel, will order all *without prejudice to one party or the other,* according to God and reason."

It is clear from the last words that Beza distinctly repudiated the idea that the reformed were accused persons brought before the bishops as their judges. In his view, the colloquy was a conference between two parties pleading before the king.

The Cardinal of Tournon could hardly restrain himself to this point. As soon as Beza had finished, "trembling with rage, he as cardinal and president of the Assembly (of the clergy, that is), spoke in the name of the Assembly, addressing himself to the king, and entreating him to give them a day to reply, adding that saving for the respect they had for his Majesty, they should all have risen on hearing the blasphemies and abominable words that had been spoken, and should not have suffered Beza to continue." [1] Then he implored the king to forget the words which he had heard, and to *return* (here he hurriedly corrected himself, seeing the blunder he had made), or rather to remain faithful to the faith of his fathers. The word which had escaped him showed that the clergy were aware of the sentiments which the young king had secretly expressed to Jeanne d'Albret. Catherine seemed wounded, and replied drily that what was true or false, should be determined according to the pure Word of God, and that the Assembly had no other end in view.

The bishops, who were very loath to enter into discussion with heretics, decided simply to draw up a confession of faith which the Protestants should be bound to subscribe ; but Michel de l'Hospital having refused to consent to this, the discussion was resumed at the sitting on September 16th.

In the interval between the two meetings Peter Martyr arrived, bringing to the aid of the Protestant cause a scientific knowledge of theology more extensive than that of any of his colleagues. In the

---

[1] La Place, *Commentaires*, Book VI.

meeting of September 16th, which was again presided over by the king, the Cardinal of Lorraine
opened the discussion.   He spoke of the obedience
due to kings, an oratorical prelude which cleared
the way for him to lay down the principle that in
spiritual matters the king was not competent to
judge.   He drew a graphic picture of the Catholic
Church and its unity, and showed that it must be
the judge of the meaning of Scripture, and consequently of controversial questions.   When he came
to the Eucharist he carefully avoided speaking of the
mass as transubstantiation, and confined himself to
insisting on the fact that in this mystery the very
body and blood of Christ are given to us in a real
manner.   This discourse, which lasted an hour and a
half, was very moderate in form, and produced a
great impression.   As they were returning to St.
Germain in the evening, Condé and the Admiral
urged Beza and Peter Martyr to observe a like
moderation.[1]   This Peter Martyr did not fail to do
in an interview which he had next day with the
queen-mother, who wished to know what he thought
of the Cardinal's discourse.[2]   Peter Martyr took a
very fair view of it, pointing out where he agreed
with the Cardinal.   As Catherine was urgent that
he should suggest some plan of conciliation, he re-

---

[1] Letters of Beza, 17th September, and of Peter Martyr, 19th
September (*Arch. de Berne*).

[2] Catherine often had interviews with Peter Martyr during
the Colloquy.   Hubert Languet, whose clearsightedness was
well known, expresses this opinion in his correspondence:
"What shall I say of her ?   Truly I know not, but of this I
am sure, that whichever way fortune turns she will turn.   Her
great anxiety is to rule, and she will not sacrifice herself for
either papists or reformed. (*Arcana seculi*, Book II., p. 141).

plied, with the subtlety of the theologian, " that they should not touch on the article of the Eucharist, but allow everyone to believe and to preach on this point the doctrine that seemed to him most in harmony with the word of God. Diversity of belief should not make Christians forget brotherly love, and lead them to brand each other with the opprobrious name of heretics."

The queen warmly approved this language. Then a moment after she walked to the fire where Antoine of Navarre, the Prince of Condé, and the Admiral were talking with Theodore Beza, and before taking her leave of the two ministers she urged them to labour to bring about an agreement between the reformed and the Catholics.[1]

If we suppose Catherine to have been sincere in this wish, she was prevented from carrying it out by the advice of the papal legate already mentioned, who had just arrived at the Court. He could not prevent the Colloquy, but he suggested the idea that the king should not be present any more, and that only a very limited number of delegates should be admitted. This was to take away from the assembly all the solemnity which had hitherto made it so remarkable.[2]

In fact, at the third sitting, on September 24th, there were present beside the Cardinals only sixteen Catholic doctors and twelve reformed ministers, with the queen, the King of Navarre, and a few lords.

Beza introduced the question of the Church, and

---

[1] Letter from Peter Martyr (*Arch. de Berne*).
[2] This fact is attested in the " Discours des actes de Poissy " (*Mémoires de Condé*, vol. ii., p. 490).

pointed out that beside the ordinary there might be an extraordinary vocation, the gift of the Spirit of God not absolutely contingent on the consecration imparted by the laying on of hands. He showed that the Councils had often fallen into error, and that the ultimate appeal must be therefore to Holy Scripture.

Doctor Despence replied with gravity. He disputed the legitimacy of the Protestant ministry, maintained that Scripture by itself was inadequate, and insisted on the importance of tradition. Thereupon ensued a prolonged discussion till the Cardinal of Lorraine suggested that they should revert to the question of the Eucharist, and asked the reformed if they were prepared to subscribe the articles of the Augsburg Confession on this subject; to which Beza made a very apt rejoinder, asking the Cardinal if he himself approved of it.

The next sitting took place on September 26th. The same questions of the ministry and the Holy Communion were brought up again. Beza, Despence, and Peter Martyr spoke. The discussion was grave and dignified till a new actor appeared on the scene. This was the Jesuit Lainez, of whom we have spoken, and who now for the first time took part in the debates. Lainez, who knew well with what suspicion his order was regarded by the French bishops, wished to curry favour with them by flinging opprobrious epithets at the Protestant doctors. He designated them wolves, foxes, monkeys and assassins. Directly addressing the queen-mother, he told her that it was her duty to expel the reformed from the kingdom. Catherine was annoyed at this language.

Theodore Beza replied with much force, and the
debate was prolonged till night. It became more
and more evident that these public discussions would
lead to no conclusion. Catherine abandoned them,
and a new plan was tried.

It was proposed to draw up a set of articles
relating to the Holy Communion. A commission
composed of the more moderate representatives of
both parties assembled and drew up the following
fomulary : " Inasmuch as faith apprehends that which
is promised and renders present things absent, and
inasmuch as this faith in very truth receives the body
and blood of our Lord Jesus Christ by the virtue of the
Holy Spirit, we therefore confess the presence of the
body and blood of Christ in the Holy Communion,
in which He presents and exhibits to us in very
truth the substance of His body and blood by the
operation of the Holy Spirit, and we therein eat
spiritually and by faith of His proper body which
was broken for us, that we may be bone of His bone
and flesh of His flesh, so that we may be quickened
thereby and understand all that is necessary to salvation." This confession is radically equivocal. It
does not express candidly either the Catholic or the
reformed doctrine. The adherents of the reformed
faith modified it, and presented finally a new rendering,[1] which was submitted to a large Catholic Com-

---

[1] It is as follows : "We confess that Jesus Christ in the Holy
Communion presents and exhibits to us in very truth the substance of His body and blood by the operation of His Holy
Spirit, and that we receive and eat sacramentally, spiritually,
and by faith this proper body, which was broken for us, that
we may be bone of His bone and flesh of His flesh, so that
one may be quickened thereby and understand all that is

mission, of which all the doctors of the Sorbonne present at Poissy formed part.

On the 9th of October these doctors read to the General Assembly their report on this formula, which they declared to be "insufficient, captious, and heretical." They proposed a strictly Catholic confession of faith. The Cardinal of Tournon then declared the discussion to be at an end. The bishops and cardinals rose and repeated the words of the Catholic confession, and the Cardinal of Lorraine pronounced an anathema on all who did not accept it. Thus closed the Colloquy of Poissy.

As might be expected, each party pretended to have gained the advantage over the other. In reality the discussion had been cut short, unfinished. Only one point, that of the Eucharist,[1] had been treated

---

necessary to salvation. And inasmuch as faith based upon the Word of God makes and renders present to us things absent, and that by this faith we do indeed and in truth receive the true and natural body and blood of our Lord by the virtue of the Holy Spirit ; in this respect we confess the presence of the body and blood of this our Lord in the Holy Communion." One is grieved in reading this declaration, to observe the equivocations used in the hope of conciliating men, some of whom believed in transubstantiation and worshipped the host, and others of whom were as fully persuaded that no change was effected in the substance of the bread and wine, and that the presence of Christ in the Eucharist was a purely spiritual fact which faith alone could apprehend.

[1] We have only been able to give a brief sketch of the history of the Colloquy in its general features ; but it is well to remember two things: first, simultaneously with the Colloquy was held a real Synod of the Catholic clergy, in which they discussed twelve articles, on which they agreed that a reform was necessary in order to satisfy public opinion. These articles had no reference to doctrine, but solely to abuses in ecclesiastical order. Secondly, after the Colloquy Catherine de Médicis tried to organise fresh conferences between the Catholics and the reformed in presence of the Privy Council. These

at any length.   The moderate Catholic party, represented by such men as Montluc and Despence, had
been defeated by the Cardinal of Tournon, and still
more by Lainez, who was to be rewarded by seeing
the order of the Jesuits recognised in France.   The
idea of uniting Catholics and Protestants in one
common creed was henceforth abandoned.   Two
courses only now remained open ; either to proscribe
the new Communion by force (this they had been
attempting to do for forty years), or to admit the
legal coexistence of two religions.   The latter was
the policy recommended by l'Hospital.

The impression produced by the Colloquy had
been rather favourable to the Huguenots.   They
had gained several distinguished additions to their
party.[1]   Their books were freely circulated every-

---

conferences were prolonged even after the edict of January.
The question of images was specially taken up.   Several
Catholics—Salignac, Montluc, Despence, and others—voted
with the reformed for their suppression.   But the majority
were vehemently opposed to it.   The debate was unhappily
embittered by the destruction of statues and sacred ornaments
wrought by the Protestants in the provinces, in spite of the
stern protests of Calvin, Beza, and Coligny.   The conferences
produced no result.   It was altogether an illusion to suppose
that such reforms of mere details could arrest the great Protestant movement.

[1] Among others they were joined by La Place, President of
the Cour des Aides, who was deservedly known afterwards as
the l'Hospital of the Protestants.   He was one of the men so
rare in that day who understood the meaning of religious liberty,
and always defended the cause of humanity.   To him we owe
the *Commentaires de l'état de la religion et de la république
sous les rois Henri II., François II., et Charles IX.*, a
work remarkable for its impartiality.   La Place fell in the
massacre of St. Bartholomew.   Beside La Place we may
mention among those who attached themselves after the Colloquy to the cause of the Reformation, Carraccioli, Bishop of
Troyes.   He was son of the Prince of Melfi, a Marshal of

where.[1] · For the first time a queen, Jeanne d'Albret, was seen openly avowing the reformed faith in the very precincts of the Court, and inviting the highest lords to the preaching in her apartments.   At the close of these services Protestants and Catholics met and discussed the subjects treated in the sermon. In this familiar intercourse many prejudices were removed.   It was discovered that these odious sectaries were not so black as they had been painted.[2] Doctrines which a few months before would have

France; but he was a man of no consistency or steadfastness of character. He went back to the Church of Rome, and then oscillated for the rest of his life between the two parties.   The Protestants gained a more valuable recruit in the person of Pierre Ramus, the most celebrated philosopher of his time. He wrote to the Cardinal of Lorraine some time after: "It is no thanks to myself, but to you (and it is the greatest of all benefits you have conferred upon me), that I have learnt that precious truth, so well set forth in your discourse at the colloquy of Poissy, that of the fifteen centuries which have passed since the coming of Christ, the first was truly the age of gold, and that in proportion as it has receded, have all other ages become more and more vicious and corrupt.   It was then that, having to choose among the various ages of Christianity, I chose the age of gold."   Ramus, like La Place, fell a victim at St. Bartholomew.

[1] On this subject we refer the reader to the lamentations of Claude Hatton, curé of Provins, who in his *mémoires* mentions "the psalms of Marot and of Beza," as well as the "Catechisms, the Shields of Faith," etc., and other books full of the doctrine of their so-called religion, printed at Geneva, at Lyons, and in Dauphiné, all well bound in black and red calf, some finely gilt, of which they made presents to the princes and princesses of the Court, and even to the king himself, and the rest of the said books were exposed for sale in the Court and in the city of Paris by permission of the king.   There passed through the town of Provins four carts full of the said books, which were taken to the Court in large pine-wood cases. (*Mémoires*, vol. i., p. 160, quoted by Klipffel).

[2] In the letters addressed to Calvin by Beza we are conscious sometimes of a sort of repressed humour, and something laughable slips into the midst of these grave discussions.   One day,

condemned those who professed them to shameful
tortures in the Place Maubert, or the Place de Grève,
were now openly avowed in the presence of the king
himself. In the end of September, at Argenteuil,
close to St. Germain, Beza had given his benediction
on a marriage celebrated after the Genevan mode,
the marriage of Jean de Rohan, cousin of the King
of Navarre, to Diane de Brabançon, niece of the
Duchess d'Estampes. Jeanne d'Albert, the Admiral
and his wife, the Prince and Princess of Condé, and
a number of great personages were present. Such
a ceremony, celebrated without any protest on the
part of the Court, was really a great public event.

"In fine only the reformed gained anything by
the Colloquy."[1] Unfortunately their triumph was
soon marred by excesses. In many provincial towns,
at Orleans, Blois, Tours, Angers, Lyons, Montpellier,
they took possession of the churches, destroying the
images and stirring up tumults.

Philip II. was alarmed at these symptoms. He
sent threatening letters. It was said in Paris that
certain French Catholics had entered into relations
with him, even going so far as to claim his promise
of armed intervention against the heretics if occasion
arose. The national sentiment was deeply wounded,
and Catherine felt obliged to interfere. She was
expecting the arrival of Jacques de Monbéron, sieur

---

for example, when the Admiral was giving a dinner, there was
a parrot in the room which kept on crying out, "Life! life!
the mass is abolished. We may dare to speak of God everywhere. Let us speak of God everywhere." (See Jules Bonnet,
Lettres de Calvin, vol. ii., p. 426).

[1] La Ferrière, *Introd. aux lettres de Catherine de Médicis*,
p. cviii.

d'Aussance, whom she had sent to Philip II. to justify herself for having convoked the Colloquy. The
ambassador returned on the 14th of October, and
reported that Philip II. said openly that "it would be
better worth his while to extinguish the fire in his
neighbour's house than to wait for it to reach his
own." The queen asked what Philip II. thought of
her children. Monbéron replied, " The king thinks
that the young Charles IX. will do all that his
mother commands ; but that, as for M. d'Orléans
and Madame Marguerite, it would not be easy to
pervert them." Monbéron added that Philip II.
boasted of knowing all that was done in the French
Court better than Catherine herself.[1]

The attitude of Chantonnay, the Spanish ambassador, only confirmed Monbéron's statement. He
said openly that the king his master had offered all
his forces to the queen-mother to be used against
the heretics, and that if she refused them, he would
offer them to the Catholics.[2]

Catherine took no heed, and when Chantonnay
came to her levée on October 16th, she spoke to
him with such boldness that he concluded she had
been consulting with the Admiral, the Cardinal of
Châtillon, Bishop Montluc, and the King of Navarre.
She said to him, " If any subjects of the king were
to call in foreign aid, the king would know how to
deal with it, and to punish them in such sort that

---

[1] *Letter from Chantonnay to the Duchess of Parma*
(October 1561), quoted by La Ferrière. However well informed
Philip may have thought himself, he did not know that it was
that same little Duke of Orleans who was at this very time a
pervert, and trying to pervert Marguerite.

[2] Same letter.

they should repent it." The interview grew angry. Chantonnay accused her of favouring the heretics, and giving his impression of the queen in writing to the Duchess of Parma, he said that Catherine had no real confidence in any one but Coligny and those of his party.

A trifling event tended still more to exasperate Catherine. Nemours, who belonged to the Guise party, offered to take the little Duke of Anjou into Savoy. Thereupon the queen's imagination set to work. She persuaded herself that the Catholic party meant to take her son from her, and she wrote freely to this effect. She dictated to Charles IX., on October 21st, a letter addressed to the Bishop of Limoges, French ambassador at Madrid. The language of Charles IX. was proud, almost threatening. Replying to Philip II., who had declared that Frenchmen belonging to the old religion had asked him to assist them in its maintenance, and if they were compelled to take up arms in the cause, to succour them, and to bring his power and his forces to their aid, Charles IX. wrote thus: "Whereupon, I pray you, thank him very affectionately on my behalf for his good will, etc.; but as to the second point, which touches the rising of my subjects, I cannot but deem it a strange proposal, inasmuch as it is not lawful for any subject to rise against his prince on any occasion whatsoever. I cannot believe that, in a common cause which touches and regards all princes and potentates, those of my subjects who should have so forgotten themselves would find favour, support, and aid against those who should have continued faithful to me." And a little further, speaking of the friendship which the King of Spain bears to him, he says : "This friendship makes me hope that, knowing such to be mutinous rebels and enemies to me and my crown, if they address themselves to him, he will not only reject them as enemies and disturbers of the public peace, but will advertise me of their names and positions, that I may inflict such punishment and chastisement as their malice deserves ; otherwise he will show how little sincerity there is in his words, and often repeated offers of good will, in which, if there is no truth, I pray and conjure him by the friendship he bears me, that as I refrain from intermeddling in his affairs more than he wishes, he will leave me to manage mine, hoping, without let or hindrance from any one, to come out of them so well that there shall be no need to employ him or any other of my neighbours." [1]

We see what was Catherine's state of mind at the close of the colloquy of Poissy.

A few days after, all the Protestant ministers had left St. Germain, with the exception of Peter Martyr, Theodore Beza, and De Gallars. Coligny had just taken De Gallars into his service as almoner, in the absence of Merlin, who had been recalled to Geneva.

At this time arrived the German divines, sent to Paris by the Elector Palatine and the Duke of Würtemberg, at the request of the King of Navarre. The Elector belonged to the reformed faith ; the Duke was a pronounced Lutheran. The Duke had recommended his divines, Drs. Beurlin, Bidenbach,

---

[1] This letter is to be seen in the British Museum, vol 19, 272, fol. 23, 24.

and Andreæ, to make all possible concessions to the
Catholics, and to try and use the Augsburg Confession as a platform on which they could meet.   It is
easy to see that if these divines had arrived in the
middle of the Colloquy, their presence would only
have helped to make the discussions more bitter and
complicated.   Beza congratulated himself that they
had come too late.[1]   The King of Navarre complained to them that the Guises feigned adherence
to the Confession of Augsburg.   At this time he
still spoke as if he were a Protestant by conviction.

The mission of the German divines thus fell to
the ground.   Before leaving, they visited the principal Protestant lords.   " We paid our respects to the
Admiral," said one of them (Peter Boquin), " and told
him we were about to return to Germany.   In language full of his habitual dignity and kindness, he
gave us his best wishes.   Then, speaking of the
Christian religion, to the service of which he devotes
all the energy of his soul, he urged us earnestly to
labour to extend its salutary influence, and warned
us to avoid above all things a spirit of discord."[2]   He
said that in everything that depended on him he
would not fail to strive for the advancement of the
Kingdom of Christ, as a sacred duty nearer to his
heart than ever ; that he was assured that on this
subject the Elector Palatine shared his sentiments,
and he prayed us instantly to repeat to that prince

---

[1] *Letter to Calvin*, October 23rd.
[2] It is in these little things that the greatness of Coligny's
character comes out.   While Beza regarded the Lutheran
divines only as *Eutychians*, and almost as enemies, the
Admiral tried to reconcile the two communions, and won
golden opinions even from the Lutheran Andreæ.

this expression of his cordial sympathy.[1] Andreæ, writing of this interview, says : " If God is pleased to bring the welfare of the state out of the troubles which are now desolating France, it will certainly be by making this man the instrument of His designs." .

---

[1] Klackholm, *Briefe Friedrichs des Frommen*, vol. i., p. 554.

FROM the time of the Colloquy the reformed
party became more and more powerful. It
gained accessions from the great nobility. In spite
of the edict of July, which was still valid, in spite
of the repeated protests of the legate, the French
prelates and the Spanish ambassador, the king was
compelled to grant to the Huguenots the right of
public worship in the faubourgs of Paris. " He did
so," says Languet,[1] " on the condition that the number assembling should not exceed two hundred ; but
at the first meeting we were more than ten thousand."

The two places chosen for worship were the close
of the Patriarche in the faubourg St. Marcel, and the
church called Popincourt in the faubourg St. Antoine.[2]
The Prince of La Roche-sur-Yon, governor of Paris,
sent troops to protect the assemblies. The people

---

[1] In a letter written on the Eve of St. Martin, 1561.

[2] The regulations passed at this time by the Consistory for
the "distribution of alms to the poor of the reformed church
in the city of Paris have been preserved." *Bulletin de la
société du protestantisme français*, vol. i., p. 254.

marvelled to see the crowds who attended the meetings, among whom were representatives of the oldest families in France.

But fanaticism could not long brook such a scandal. The day after Christmas day, while Pastor Jean Malot was preaching in the Patriarche at three o'clock in the afternoon, the clergy of St. Michel had peals rung out on the bells of all the churches adjoining the close. It was impossible to hear the voice of the preacher. He suspended the service, and had the sixteenth Psalm sung. Meanwhile two Protestants went to beg the curé of St. Médard to stop the clangour of the bells. They were assaulted, and one of them was killed on the spot. The reformed, rendered furious, surrounded the church. The priests barricaded it, and a struggle began, which was only put a stop to by the arrival of the military. Thirty-six Catholics were taken to the Châtelet as instigators of the tumult. But the next day the people avenged themselves by surrounding the close of the Patriarche and sacking it. The parliament decided against the Protestants, and had Gabaston, the captain of the guard, hanged, because, though a Catholic, he had faithfully discharged the duty entrusted to him. Two days later, Anne de Montmorency, at the head of a company of troops, destroyed all the furniture of the church of Popincourt, and by this ridiculous act gained for himself the nickname of *Brûle-Bancs*.

It was a crying necessity that a stop should be put to such outrages, and the protection of the law assured to the reformed. Coligny and l'Hospital set themselves actively to work.

We are now coming to a momentous date in the history of France. The edict of January was considered by its promoters to be a very important step. We must pause to enquire more closely in what light the question of religious liberty was regarded by the men of that age.

Liberty of conscience, with its logical consequence —the free manifestation of religious opinion—may be demanded on two distinct grounds.

First, it may be said that the State owes to all creeds which do not infringe public order, equal protection or equal sufferance, because no creed is self-evident, and as such has a right to be enforced. This is the view taken by Locke and his successors, which gradually asserted itself in the eighteenth century, and is accepted, at least in theory, in our day.

Second, there is a higher point of view which we hold to be the Christian standpoint, namely, that the relation between men's consciences and God is exempt by its very nature from all legislative control, that religious convictions are of no value except as they are free, and that if we must choose between truth enforced by authority and the liberty of error, the latter is the more truly moral, for liberty does at least respect conscience, while he who yields to the truth an enforced adherence, is governed not by truth but by force.

Now it is evident that neither of these principles was recognised in the sixteenth century. Nothing can be more misleading than to apply to the men of that age our thoughts, and our modern modes of speech. To say that the Reformation was wrought in the name of religious liberty, or of that which was afterwards called free enquiry, is to enunciate a theory absolutely contrary to fact.

The claim advanced by the reformers was that they had found the truth of Christianity, and their aim was to substitute this truth everywhere for the errors of Rome. Holding, as they did, that the magistrate was armed for the defence of the truth, they taught that he could and ought to defend it by force. When the sovereign of a State, or the majority of a Swiss canton, had declared for the Reformation, no alternative was left to the Catholic minority but submission or exile. This view, monstrous as it seems to us to-day, was then common to all. If the minority resisted, it was pitilessly dealt with. If the Protestant magistrate found himself confronted, not simply with a recalcitrant Catholic, but with a declared heretic,—an anti-Trinitarian, for instance, like Servetus,—then exile was not deemed sufficient, and he was handed over, without mercy, to the executioner. For denouncing these proceedings, Castalio was exiled from Geneva, and placed under the ban of Christendom.[1]

When, therefore, Bishop Montluc, at the assembly of Fontainebleau, after paying an eloquent tribute to the piety of the reformed, concluded by asking that they might be exiled, unless they were willing hence-

---

[1] It is idle to advance, in opposition to this, the admirable words on liberty of conscience to be found in the writings of Luther, Zuinglius, and the persecuted Anabaptists. The oppressed have always used such language. Tertullian uttered magnificent sentiments to this effect, but who can suppose that Tertullian, who was so severe on the heretics, would have counselled toleration under a Christian emperor?

forward to live as good Catholics, he was only
applying the principle which the reformed themselves
applied when they were in power.

Let us suppose that Francis I. or Catherine de
Médicis, supported by their parliaments, had, as
was at one time thought possible, declared themselves on the side of the Reformation, can it be
believed that they would have inaugurated a system
of religious liberty? They would have done just
what Elizabeth and the sovereigns of Germany did,
and assuredly Calvin and Beza would have been
the last to blame them. Thus, when at Poissy
the ministers were discussing the question of crosses
and images, they wished the *king* to put them down
altogether.

Since the Protestants could not be masters in
France, what was it they asked? To be tolerated,
protected by the law, and allowed to hold their
assemblies. But did they ask it in the name of the
high claims of conscience? Not at all. What they
said was this: "You ought to recognise us, for we
are Christians. We accept the Apostles' and the
Nicene creed ; the law cannot touch us."

This was the plea advanced by Coligny and
l'Hospital, and if this principle had been accepted,
the result would have been the legal coexistence of
the two religions in the kingdom—obviously a very
different thing from liberty. But even this was an
ideal not understood at that period. This was made
very clear by the resistance everywhere offered to
the edict of January, a resistance which could have
been overcome only by the firm determination of
the king. And here again we must not blame

Catholic France alone. Let us ask ourselves, in good faith, whether Elizabeth in England, or Calvin at Geneva, or the magistrates of Zurich and Berne, would have allowed the mass and the reformed preaching to go on side by side in their territory? Much blood would have to be shed before the true principle of religious liberty would become triumphant, and William of Orange in the Low Countries, and the Edict of Nantes in France, gave it its first legal sanction. If we would do justice to the sixteenth century, we must frankly recognise that intolerance was then the error of all parties. While admitting that those who practised it were sincere, the historian is yet free to condemn the perfidies and crimes which the men of that time often added to it, for the prejudices of the age can be no excuse for deeds which conscience must have condemned then as loudly as to-day.

In drawing up the edict of January, l'Hospital and Coligny were in advance of their age. Coligny was afterwards to make yet further advances in this direction, and to form a grander ideal of liberty.

In the end of December, 1561, the Admiral had sent up to the king a petition, from 2,050 churches,[1] asking for the right of public worship. In the beginning of January, 1562, an assembly composed of the princes of the blood, the members of the Privy Council, and Councillors chosen from the various parliaments, was convened at St. Germain by order of the king, and under his presidency.

---

[1] MM. Haag have given as complete a picture as possible of the Protestant Church of that period (*La France protestante,* vol i., p. 52). The petition presented by the Protestants is found in Condé's *Mémoires,* vol. ii., p. 575, and following.

Michel de l'Hospital opened it. He referred to all the attempts made hitherto to secure religious peace; to the edicts of Amboise, Romorantin, Fontainebleau, to the meeting of the States General at Orleans, and the Colloquy of Poissy. He said that Protestantism went on spreading, and might, like a mighty tree, crush its enemies in its fall.

He urged, with much feeling, that the king could not take either side, for that would amount to saying " that he ought to assemble one army to destroy another, a thing repugnant not only to the name of Christians, which we bear, but to our very humanity. And, moreover, who could fight when in the opposite camp he saw his father, his son, and nearest kindred ? The victory, to whichever side it fell, could not but be quite as damaging to the victors as to the vanquished, just as if the different parts of the body were warring against each other." He showed that it had been impossible to execute the edict of July, and that new remedies must be devised. " The king," he said, " does not desire you to enter into a disputation, which opinion is the better, for it is not here a question *de constituenda religione, sed de constituenda republica.*" A man who is excommunicated does not cease to be a citizen. " If a Catholic can live in peace with a member of his family who belongs to the new religion, why should it not be the same with the State ? " This is liberal and generous language which the age could not understand.

The debate was continued on the following days. The result was impatiently awaited in Rome as well as in Paris. The Sorbonne in alarm sent delegates to the king. They declared that if his majesty yielded to the innovators, he would lose Paris ; that the recognition of two religions would overthrow the State ; that there would, then, need to be two kings in France, etc.

On the other hand, many of the Councillors from the various parliaments were in favour of the idea of granting the Protestants the liberty they asked. On the 15th of January the Assembly dispersed, and the next day but one was signed the famous edict of January, which for the first time recognised the right of the Protestants to a legal existence, and to the public celebration of their worship.

A letter from the legate Hippolyte d'Este to Cardinal Borromeo, dated January 17th, shows the spirit in which this concession was made : " The permission granted to them to hold their services is but temporary, for as soon as the Council of Trent has closed its sittings, it is proposed to drive them out of the kingdom." In the same letter he announces that the King of Navarre had just left the Protestant party, and had spoken openly against the edict in the Privy Council. We shall have more to say presently of this conversion, which produced a considerable effect. Let us attempt first to give some idea of the edict.

In the first place, it required the Protestants to restore all the churches and all the ecclesiastical revenues of which they had taken possession. They were forbidden to build any place of worship at all. They would be compelled, therefore, to hold their services in the open air, or in private houses. They were not to be allowed to assemble in any town, but only in the environs, under the surveillance of officers appointed by the king, and these were to have the extraordinary power of sending away " any whose life, habits, and condition did not commend itself to them." So much for liberty of worship.

The ministers were to be bound by oath to preach only doctrine in harmony with the Scriptures and the Nicene Creed, and to abstain from attacking the mass and the Catholic rites and ceremonies. So much for the freedom of the pulpit.

No assessment or fixed rate of payment for the maintenance of public worship was allowed ; voluntary contributions alone were authorised.

No consistory or synod could be held without permission of the officers of the king, and in their presence.

On the other hand, the edict *recommended* the Catholic preachers to avoid invectives against the ministers and their followers.

All these conditions were, moreover, provisional ; it was stipulated that they were passed pending a Council which was to bring all hearts and minds into unity.

We can see clearly that there were restrictions underlying each seeming concession. Thus the pope's legate was right when he said that the edict had only one end in view : to disarm the Protestants, to take away from them the many churches they occupied, and to prevent their meeting any more in the towns. It would then be decided what next.[1]

---

[1] *Letter of the Legate to Cardinal Borromeo*, February 6th, 1562. The legate states that he has all this from the queen-mother herself. A curious parallel might be traced between the correspondence of the Cardinal of Ferrara with the Pope,

Many of the Protestants murmured, feeling sure that a snare was being laid for them, and seeing clearly what the end would be. Coligny and l'Hospital tried to calm them. Under the influence of the Admiral, the pastors of Paris wrote a circular to the Churches enjoining submission, saying, that "if the king is persuaded of our obedience, he will be the more inclined to hear us patiently, and to do us justice in all that we propose to his Majesty." This noble confidence appeared touching at the time, and makes us smile now as we read the letters from the legate to the pope, and see the hope expressed in them that the kingdom would soon return to the pope, "like the prodigal son to his father.[1]

The Protestants were entirely obedient, and restored without hesitation the Church buildings and property which they had in possession. But, as the legate announced, the parliaments either refused to register the edict, or did so only with secret stipulations which were direct breaches of faith with the reformed.[2]

Faithfully carried out, the edict of January might

---

and that of Chantonnay with Philip II. Both speak alike of Catherine. But while Chantonnay, as the faithful interpreter of the haughty and despotic policy of his master, is irritated at the slightest concession made to the Protestants, and looks upon the queen-mother as their secret ally, the Cardinal, with his Italian penetration and his keen and subtle genius, sees deeper into things. He knows that Catherine is an Italian like himself; that she is feigning and manœuvering, and that all will end right.

[1] *Letter* of February 14th.

[2] One of the stipulations which was made use of to overcome the resistance of parliament was (unknown to the Protestants) to the effect that the edict was only of a provisional character, that the assemblies were always at the mercy of the governors

have secured religious peace. In a few weeks, thanks to the ambiguous interpretations put upon it, it everywhere excited distrust and hatred. Antoine of Navarre, who had great influence, did more than any one to bring about this lamentable result.

We have seen that at the time of the Colloquy of Poissy he was still looked upon as the head of the Protestant party, and openly protected Theodore Beza. On January 24th, 1562, he repaired to the parliament to enforce the registration of the edict of January. But at this very time he was already negotiating his return to the Catholic Church. For three months Manriquez, who had been joined to Chantonnay as Spanish ambassador extraordinary, was labouring in concert with the pope's legate to effect his conversion. He assured him that Philip II. would be disposed in such a case to restore Navarre to him, or if not that, to give him the island of Sardinia. To entice him he gave a fanciful description of the island, praising its fruits, its climate, its ports, its nearness to Tunis, of which Antoine might make himself master. He even went so far as to promise that his marriage with Jeanne d' Albret should be annulled by Rome, and a new alliance contracted for him with Mary Stuart. In a letter to the pope, dated January 10th, 1562, the Cardinal of Ferrara assured the pope that the King of Navarre was won over. A week later he announced that in the Privy Council of January 15th Antoine had for the first time declared himself on the side of the

---

of the province, and that all the king's officers must be of his religion.—*Letter from the Cardinal of Ferrara to the Pope*, February 28th.

Catholic party, and that this conversion, seemingly so sudden, had made even the queen-mother uneasy. The legate, however, while he praised the prince, was under no illusion about his sincerity; for in a letter to Cardinal Borromeo, dated the beginning of February, he insisted upon the necessity of giving the king some compensation for his return to the Church. "One must not imagine," he says, "that in order to commend oneself to him it is enough to represent to him that the approval of conscience is the highest of all rewards, since it is only too plain that pleasure, interest, or shall we say the agreeable and the useful, are the only two things which satisfy worldly souls." This melancholy reflection upon the necessity of pandering to the evil tendencies of human nature, and of supplementing spiritual arguments by reasons of a very material order, shows that the legate was a master of casuistry, but it shows also what opinion he held of his new convert.[1]

As for Catherine she openly favoured the passion of the King of Navarre for one of her maids of honour, Mademoiselle de Rouet. Jeanne d'Albret, wounded in her wifely dignity and in her deepest convictions, could not bring herself to endure such humiliations any longer. She resolved to quit the Court, and to return to Béarn, taking her son with her. From this time Antoine made no secret of his hatred of Coligny and of the other Protestant chiefs, whose upright life and fidelity to their cause seemed a perpetual reproach to him. He carried his malice

---

[1] We see from the report of the Venetian ambassadors in how slight esteem they held the King of Navarre. See Michieli and M. Soriano, *Rapports*, vol. i., p. 429.

so far as to denounce Coligny to the King of Spain, on the ground that he encouraged the depredations which the Spanish marine suffered at the hands of the corsairs. Philip II. eagerly availed himself of this excuse. He wrote to Chantonnay to ask that Coligny should be dismissed from the Court, and Antoine promised to second the request. Catherine was very indignant at that intrusion on her authority. She took up the defence of Coligny, and when he offered to retire to Châtillon, to avoid causing any difficulty, she declared that she " knew him to be so faithful a servant of the king and so affectionate also towards herself, that if necessity called him to Châtillon he must use all diligence to guard her against the intrigues of the Guises."[1]

While these things were passing at Court, every week showed that the edict of January was to remain a dead letter. Scenes of violence and murder were being enacted all over the kingdom. These had been attributed to the exasperation which the Catholics felt at seeing the Protestants so favoured at Court; but it must be admitted that Catherine made no serious attempt to put a stop to the riots. The legate clearly spoke the truth when he said that the edict need give the pope no serious uneasiness, and that it would not last.

---

[1] This is the statement of Theodore Beza, who in a letter to Calvin, dated February 26th, declares that Coligny and Andelot *regi et reginæ gratissimos discessisse.* The legate's correspondence on this subject gives a different impression, however, and makes us doubtful of the interest taken by Catherine in the Admiral. It is certain, nevertheless, that Catherine was much offended at the part taken by the Spanish ambassador in the affair, and let him see it very plainly. See Chantonnay's despatch of February 25th.

CHAPTER XXV.

THE Guises were now about to reappear on the scene, and to show how much they thought of the edict. But it will be well for us to note the singular negotiations by which they prepared the way for the tragedy of Vassy.

The Cardinal of Lorraine had not succeeded in pitting the reformed and Lutherans against each other at Poissy ; but he nevertheless continued active negotiations with the Lutherans. His brother assisted him, and had been carrying on for several months a regular correspondence with Christopher, Duke of Würtemberg.[1]

Francis of Lorraine professed much admiration for the Confession of Augsburg, and Christopher replied "that it had been a great joy to him to hear that in matters of faith the Duke of Guise desired nothing more than to have his conscience enlightened." The Duke of Guise, in a letter of the 11th of July,

---

[1] In the *Bulletin de la Soc. du Prot.*, vol. xxiv., very interesting extracts are given from this correspondence. See also M. Delaborde's work, vol. ii., p. 17 and following.

1561, tries to show that the Lutherans in Germany have nothing in common with the reformed, the latter being nothing better than despisers of the king and of the Church. The letters exchanged become more and more affectionate, and an interview at Saverne is arranged for February 15th, 1562. We know from the Duke of Würtemberg himself, who has left us a very naïve account of it, what took place at this conference.[1]

On the 16th of February the Cardinal preached at Saverne, in the presence of Christopher and of other invited guests. The purport of his discourse was to show that there is no other Mediator or Intercessor but Jesus Christ, and that man is not to trust in his good works.

The next day, while the Cardinal was conferring with the German divines, whom the Duke had brought in his suite, Francis of Lorraine took Christopher apart and gave him his own account of the Colloquy of Poissy, showing that nothing was to be hoped from the Calvinists, who were intractable, but

---

[1] Most of our historians have ignored these facts, which throw so much light on after events and on the conduct of the Guises. The narrative of Duke Christopher, which no one has impugned, was published in its original form (German and Latin mixed) in Sattler's *Geschichte von Würtemberg unter den Herzögen*, 1771, vol. iv., p. 215 and following. Baum refers to it, but it was translated for the first time by Muntz, *Bull. de la Soc. d'hist. du prot. fran.*, vol. iv., p. 184 and following. It is noticeable that De Thou, Sandray de Courtils, and Bayle had spoken, in passing, of the snare laid by the Guises for the Duke of Würtemberg, and that no credit was given to their statements. M. Felice, in his *Histoire des protestants de France*, does not mention the interview at Saverne ; but M. Puaux, whose *Histoire de la réformation française* is more recent, gives an account of it in his second volume.

that he desired to know the faith of the Germans. He added, with many words, that he wished to be enlightened, and to have his conscience set at rest ; that he had been brought up in the faith of his ancestors ; that having been a man of war from his youth, he had remained ignorant on matters of religion; and that assuredly if it could be shown him that hitherto he had been in error, he would willingly and heartily embrace the new teachings.

The Duke of Würtemberg expounded his faith. Francis of Lorraine assured him that he held the same. " I worship no God but the true God," he said. " I trust solely in Jesus Christ. I know well that neither the mother of our Lord nor the saints can help me. I know well also that I cannot be saved by my good works, but by the merits of Jesus Christ."

" What you say fills me with joy," exclaimed Christopher. " May God help you to hold fast this confession ! "

The mass was spoken of. Guise quoted the words of Beza at the Colloquy of Poissy. Christopher justified them by saying that Beza had doubtless meant to combat the " papistical opinion " which makes a god of the host. Guise evaded the point, alleging ignorance in these matters. Christopher then said : " Since we are now talking freely with one another, I cannot refrain from saying to you that you and your brother are strongly suspected in Germany of having helped, after the decease of Henry II., and even during his lifetime, to cause the death of thousands of persons who were cruelly massacred for their faith. As a friend and as a

20

Christian I am bound to warn you beware, beware of shedding innocent blood ! The punishment of God will fall upon you either in this life or in another."

He answered with deep sighs : " I know well that my brother and I are accused of many things, but people do us wrong. We will both explain it all to you before we leave."

Then abruptly changing the subject, Guise asked the Lutheran prince why the Protestants were so divided, while the greatest unity prevailed among the Catholics. Christopher replied that the unity among the Catholics was primarily hierarchical, while among the Protestants it was a true and living thing, since, however, diverse their forms, they all marched under the same banner and followed the same leader —Jesus Christ.

The next day (17th) the Cardinal again preached like a true Lutheran, insisting on the sole mediatorship of Jesus Christ. After the sermon the Cardinal and the German divines entered into conversation. One of the Germans named Brenz [1] asked the Cardinal whether it was right to worship Christ in the host, and to carry it about in procession. The Cardinal answered : " I admit we have gone too far in this." In reference to masses for the dead he made the same admission. He then asked Brenz whether he believed that the Church ought to have a pope, cardinals, and bishops. Brenz rejoined : " Jesus Christ has no vicar ; He is the one Head of the Church. The Scriptures say nothing of cardinals. We grant that there should be bishops, but they

---

[1] John Brenz, called Brentius in the duke's narrative, was one of the greatest divines of his Church.

ought to be canonically elected." The Cardinal said that they could soon come to an understanding on this point also. Then he reverted to his great idea, that of inducing Christopher to break with the Calvinists. Christopher, however, while he held them to be mistaken on some points, would not consent to do this. The Cardinal returned to the charge, praised the Augsburg Confession, and said if that had been presented at Poissy it would have settled all.

The Duke of Würtemberg then said : " If Beza and his friends were to sign the Confession, would you sign it ? " " Certainly," replied the Cardinal ; " nay more, I take God to witness that I believe and think as I have said, and that by the grace of God I will live and die in this faith. I have read the Augsburg Confession. I have read what Melanchthon, Brentius, and others have written ; I entirely approve their doctrines, and I shall be ready to meet them on the matter of Church discipline ; but it is necessary I should still dissimulate for a time, that I may gain over many others who are as yet weak in the faith."

When the conference was finished, the Cardinal repeated his brother's protestations with regard to the sentences passed upon the French heretics. " I swear to you," said he with strange audacity, " I swear to you in the name of God my Creator, and as I hope to be saved, that I am not guilty of the death of any man who has suffered for his religion." The Duke of Guise made the same affirmation with solemn oaths. They both promised " not to persecute, either openly or secretly, the adherents of the new doctrine."

They separated on the 18th of February, pledging

themselves on both sides to do all in their power to secure the peace of Christendom.

Ten days after these solemn protestations (February 28th) Francis of Lorraine wrote to Lamothe-Gondrin, his lieutenant in Dauphiné : " I think that if any notable assembly should be convened over there at which a number of people were present, it would be well to seize the minister and have him hanged or strangled on the spot, as an abettor of sedition and tumult." And he added : " You will do me a favour by sparing no effort in this matter, for I believe there is no other way of putting an end to it." [1]

The Duke did not fail to practise himself that which he enjoined on his lieutenant. On his return from Saverne, he found at St. Nicolas in Lorraine a poor pinmaker, who had had his child baptized after the Genevan mode, and he had him hanged on the spot.[2] On hearing of his return, more than sixty Protestant farmers fled in terror from the neighbourhood of Joinville.

At Vassy, in a part of Champagne, which had been removed from the jurisdiction of the house of Lorraine to form part of the jointure of Mary Stuart,[3] a little Protestant community had sprung up, the existence of which was profoundly irritating to the mother of the Lorraine princes, the old Antoinette de Bourbon, who lived at Joinville. She had sent thither the Bishop of Châlons-sur-Marne. He had

---

[1] Theodore Beza (*Hist. eccl.*). See M. Jules Bonnet's articles on the massacre of Vassy (*Bulletin*, vol. xxi., p. 56).

[2] Crespin (*Hist. des martyrs*). The same fact is mentioned in Condé's *Mémoires*.

[3] This was, therefore, on French soil, and within the jurisdiction of the edict of January.

had a public discussion with the Protestants, had
retired from the encounter much mortified, and had
gone to narrate his discomfiture to the Lorraines,
who were unsparing in their taunts. The Lorraines
had addressed to the privy council of the King of
France a request "to the effect that a commission to
deal with the delinquents should be given to the
Duke of Guise.[1] But the privy council could not
see that any crime had been committed. The meetings were therefore continued, and the number of
the faithful increased continually. At Christmas
they had as many as a thousand communicants.

On the last day of February, 1562, Francis of
Lorraine, accompanied by his wife and his two sons,
went from Joinville to sleep at Donmartin-le-Franc,
where his mother was. On Sunday, March 1st, he
left, after being present at mass, and went on to
Vassy. What for? The district was peaceful, but
the Duke took with him two hundred arquebusiers,
who were joined by a company of archers from
Montier-en-Der. When he came within about a mile
of Vassy he heard a bell sounding, and asked what
it was. He was told that it was the bell calling the
reformed to service. "March, march!" exclaimed
the Duke, "we must have a look at these people
while they are gathered together." On reaching
Vassy the Duke ordered his people to march to the
preaching, "which was held in a barn,[2] in exactly

---

[1] These are details of which history should take account, if
it would apprehend the true character of the massacre of
Vassy. How can it be maintained, in view of such facts,
that it was merely the result of an accident?

[2] The famous engraving of the massacre shows that by "the
barn" was meant a sort of shed, or rather a large covered
building with wide windows.

the opposite direction from that which the Duke should have taken to reach Esclaron, where he was to dine."[1]   The Duke at the same time advised the Catholics not to be found in the streets.

In the barn were assembled about twelve hundred Huguenots, some of whom were seated on the window-ledges.   Two or three of the Duke's people entered ; they were invited to sit down.   They replied, with an oath, " Death to you all !"   At the same time the windows were fired at from without.   The unhappy Protestants, totally unarmed, would have closed the doors, but the soldiers pressed in, crying, " Kill, kill !"   A veritable slaughter began.   Those who attempted to escape by the roof were riddled with balls.   The massacre lasted for an hour.   There were sixty dead and two hundred and fifty wounded, but not one victim on the Catholic side.[2]   The Duchess of Guise interfered, to beg that they would spare the women with child.   This shows that they took time to choose their victims, and that it was not, as has been said, just a scuffle, in which people were struck at blindly.

The minister, Leonard Morel, was on his knees in the pulpit.   They fired at him.   He tried to come down, stumbled over a corpse, fell, and received several sword-thrusts.   " Lord," he exclaimed, " I

---

[1] Crespin.   In M. Jules Bonnet's articles, from which we have quoted, we shall find that the assertions of Brantôme, De Thou, La Popelinière, and Castelnau, in reference to these facts, are disputed.   The defence of the Duke of Guise was that a quarrel arose between his men and the Protestants. But by the admission of all, the Protestants were at service at the time, and were singing their psalms.

[2] Crespin, who was evidently an eye-witness, gives the names of those who fell.

commit my soul into Thy hands." They raised him up, for he could not stand, and carried him to the Duke of Guise. "Minister, come hither," said the ·Duke. "Art thou the minister? What makes thee so bold to teach these people sedition?" "I am no teacher of sedition," replied Morel; "I have preached to them the Gospel of Christ." "Does the Gospel preach sedition then?" exclaimed the Duke with an oath. "Thou art the cause of the death of all these people; thou shalt be hanged by and bye." There was no time to set up a gallows, and the minister was thrown into prison.

The Duke had taken possession of the Bible, and showing it to his brother the Cardinal, said, "Here, brother, see the title of the Huguenots' books." The Cardinal seeing it said, "There is no harm in that, for it is the Bible and Holy Scripture."[1] The Duke, angry that he did not reply as he intended, fell into a greater rage than before, and said, "How now! Holy Scripture by my troth! It is fifteen hundred years since Christ suffered His death and passion, and these books have not been printed one year. How call you that the Gospel? I swear it is all worth nothing."[2]

Davila, the Catholic historian of the wars of "the religion," quotes in reference to this a very characteristic fact. Guise, after the massacre, sent for the judge of the place, and reproved him sharply for having let the Huguenots assemble. The judge having appealed to the edict of January, Guise laid

[1] This was the youngest brother, Cardinal Louis de Guise and must not be confounded with Charles, Cardinal of Lorraine
[2] Crespin's narrative.

his hand upon his sword, and answered angrily, "The edge of this sword will soon cut the tight knot of that edict."[1]

Some days after, Guise wrote both to Antoine of Navarre and the Duke of Würtemberg, to tell them of what had passed. According to him, the Protestants were the aggressors. We are to suppose, then, that these poor people assembled to hear preaching, became the assailants of three hundred men armed to the teeth! In the tumult a stone was thrown at Guise's face, and his soldiers, furious at seeing his blood flow, fell upon the Protestants and killed some of them. Such is the bare assertion which we have to set against the clear and detailed account of eyewitnesses of the massacre. The Duke of Würtemberg believed not a word of what Guise wrote. Since the interview at Saverne, Christopher had been reflecting, and after inquiring minutely into what happened at Vassy, he wrote at the close of the account he had already drawn up of the conference these significant words, "May God, whose cause it is, be the avenger of deceit and perjury!"[2]

Some months later, hoping to appease the prince, Francis of Guise sent his own valet, named Rascalon, to him, with some hunting dogs, for Christopher loved the chase. "But the said Duke of Würtemberg, instead of receiving them, had them killed in the presence of the said Rascalon, whom he put in

---

[1] Book III., 1562. "Now," adds Davila, "as these words, which he spoke in the heat of passion, did not escape those present, they caused many to believe that the Duke of Guise was the author of the wars that followed."

[2] "Deus sit ultor doli et perjurii, cujus namque res agitur."

prison for the space of seven or eight days, and kept him on bread and water." On his departure he said to him : " Go tell thy master that if I had him, I would do to him as I have done to his dogs."[1]

We have thus narrated the facts which occurred at Vassy, and which some historians have described as a skirmish and some as a massacre, according to their respective points of view.

But as all admit that this event gave the signal for the civil wars, we must pause a moment to bring out its true character.

That it was nothing more than a chance encounter between the soldiers of Guise and the Protestants of Vassy is a statement which may have been maintained in good faith in ignorance of the facts which preceded it, but it can no longer be held in the face of those facts. Francis of Lorraine wished to punish severely the Protestants of Vassy. He had asked for a commission from the government to this end ; and it was upon the refusal of such a commission that he resolved to act for himself. For this purpose it was that on March 1st, when the country was perfectly peaceful, he left Donmartin, accompanied by several hundred armed men, and turning aside from the main road which he should have followed, he went at the hour of preaching to the barn where the Protestants were assembled. What other object had he in this premeditated[2] act but to deliver a

---

[1] Extract from a MS. of the sixteenth century, *Bulletin de la société d'hist. du prot. français*, vol. xxix., p. 119, quoted by Jules Bonnet.

[2] This premeditation is acknowledged by the last historian of the Guises, M. de Bouillé, who is otherwise a great admirer of Duke Francis : " The whole country was set in a blaze as

district which had till recently belonged to his family, and over which his niece was suzerain, from the presence of those Huguenots whom Antoinette de Bourbon execrated? Had he any other object? This is the real question before us.

In order to answer it we must go back a few months and recall what happened immediately after the Colloquy of Poissy. We must bear in mind the astonishing progress of Protestantism, the services now publicly held, the ever increasing number of noble families joining themselves to "the religion," and the necessity that had been felt to pass the edict of January, that is, to recognise the legal existence of the two religions.

The Guises saw all this. Their strength, the secret of their power, lay in their remaining at the head of the Catholic party. They knew the indecision and vacillating nature of Catherine. They saw that the only way to arrest the movement which was carrying the country with it, was by some bold stroke to cut, as Francis himself said, the knot of the edict of January.

What was wanted for this purpose? With his keen soldier's eye Guise saw this too from the first; the enemy must be weakened by division. If the Protestants resisted, the possibility of resistance must be taken from them. At this moment there was no forming an army without the aid of Germany, that great market of men of war. What would happen if the Lanzknechts and famous Reiters from beyond

---

the result of a conflict more or less fortuitous, *which the Guises had but too skilfully prepared and foreseen*, and which was hastened by the servants of the prince.

the Rhine were to come riding over the border under
the banner of Condé? At all costs this alliance
must be prevented. The Lutherans must be persuaded that they had nothing in common with the
odious sacramentarians of Geneva, those enemies of
king and holy Church. Hence that conference of
Saverne, the importance of which historians have
failed to recognise. Hence that artful and odious
comedy in which the great conqueror of Metz and
Calais plays the part of theologian, expresses his
admiration of the Augsburg Confession, hints at his
approaching conversion to Lutheranism; in a word,
acts his part so well that he does not deserve to be
believed when he afterwards declares his innocence
of that which was done at Vassy. At the same
time his brother the Cardinal, the bloodthirsty instigator of the tortures at Amboise, swears by the
salvation of his soul that he has never put one
Huguenot to death. The Lorraines, after duping
Duke Christopher, tried also to levy troops in Germany, and on March 18th Sturm writes to Calvin
that they have raised a complete army.

And now the moment has come for a bold stroke,
by which the queen-mother will be forced to take one
side or the other. Since the government is hesitating, since it is making advances to the Huguenots,
and there seems a likelihood of peace being concluded between them and France, it is necessary at
once to create an impassable gulf of separation.
When once blood has flowed between the two camps,
the separation will be made; all hesitation will be
at an end. The two contending armies will stand
confronted, on the one hand old Catholic France,

arrayed under the banner of the Guises, on the other the rebels.

Let us look at history. In critical moments we shall always find daring leaders casting the die. In 1792 France was hesitating between the monarchy and the republic. By the massacres of September Danton compelled it to make its choice. In 1804 Bonaparte wished to separate the old régime from the new dynasty he was about to found. He had Enghien shot at Vincennes.

Thus, in all ages, the ambitious and the violent have understood that in order to divide men past all reconciliation, there is nothing like bloodshed.

And that such was the thought present to the Guises is evident from the fact that at the very time when Francis was trying to blind the Germans by telling them that the affair at Vassy was a mere skirmish quite undesigned, and for which he was very sorry, he was marching upon Paris. In vain the queen tried to stop him, and commanded him to lay down his arms. He knew that Catholic France understood him, that it would hail as its true leader the man who had unsheathed his sword to hew in pieces the edict of January, and his instinct did not mislead him. He seemed already to hear the acclamations with which he would be received in Paris, and saw in anticipation the king and the queen-mother compelled to march behind his banner.

This was the real meaning of the drama of Vassy.

And so the Protestants understood it. They felt at once that this thunderbolt was but the first burst of the storm which had long been gathering over-head.

While these events were passing at Vassy, the parliament of Paris was resisting the registration of the edict of January, and it was only on March 6th, at the peremptory command of Catherine, that it consented to the registration, with the following reservation : " In consideration of the urgent necessity, and in obedience to the will of the king, the whole being only provisional till it can be otherwise ordered, and in no wise expressing approval of the new religion." There can be no doubt that Antoine of Navarre had secretly favoured this resistance. This is proved by the fact that at the same time he sent letter upon letter to the Duke of Guise, praying him to come and join him, " that they might make themselves the stronger party with the king."[1] Catherine de Médicis, alarmed at what was coming, left Paris, carrying the young king with her, and took up her abode in the castle of Monceaux, where she commanded Antoine to come to her.

Hardly was she settled there when she heard of the massacre of Vassy. This event threw France into a blaze. While many of the Catholics received the news with frantic delight, the Protestants everywhere cried " Vengeance." They saw at once, as we have said, that the thing could not stop there, that this example would be followed everywhere. Agrippa d'Aubigné has faithfully translated their feelings in his own powerful way. He says : " It must be ever remembered that hitherto the reformed had been put to death after some form of trial, however iniquitous and cruel it may have been. But when the magi-

---

[1] Castelnau.

strate, the representative of law, weary of burning heretics, threw the knife into the hands of the people, and casting off the venerable mask of justice, let neighbour slay neighbour to the sound of trumpets and drums, who could forbid the unhappy people to meet blow with blow, sword with sword, and to catch from an unrighteous fury the contagion of a righteous anger?"[1] D'Aubigné speaks truly. Hitherto there had been legal repression; now under a seeming reign of liberty, violence took the upper hand. Instinctively it was felt that the Court, whether through impotence or secret connivance, would fail to repress this violence.

The fact proved only too clearly that it was so. The slaughter of Vassy gave the signal for other massacres on a much larger scale, but less widely known, because they were forgotten in the midst of the tumult attending the outbreak of the religious war. In a few weeks the explosion of fanaticism spread over the whole country. At Sens, more than a hundred corpses were thrown into the river. At Amiens, at Épernay, at Châtillon-sur-Loire, at Moulins, at Blois, at Angers, at Tours; in the south, where the Protestants were unable to defend themselves, they were exterminated one by one with the utmost refinements of cruelty. Blaise de Montluc, brother of Catherine's favourite bishop, began at Cahors that series of atrocious executions of which in his memoirs he has himself given the black chronicle. Michelet does not exaggerate at all when he says that what might be called the massacre of

[1] *Universal History*, vol. ii., p. 628.

St. Bartholomew in 1562 was worse than the more famous one in 1572 so far as the number of its victims was concerned. Never was the soil of France reddened with so much Protestant blood.

The queen-mother, nevertheless, made a semblance of receiving with graciousness the Protestant deputies who hastened to her to complain of the massacre of Vassy. But Antoine of Navarre, who, as we have seen, had just been negotiating with the Spanish ambassador the conditions of his return to the Catholic party, suddenly cast off his disguise.

"The King of Navarre," says Beza, "declared himself openly, saying that whosoever should touch with the tip of his finger the Duke of Guise, whom he called his brother, would touch him to the quick. Whereupon Beza, having humbly entreated him to hear him with patience as one whom he had known for long and whom he himself had caused to return to France, to help to secure the peace of the country, pointed out to him that kings were debtors to their poor subjects, and that to ask for justice was to do wrong to no one. And since the said King of Navarre had excused that which had happened at Vassy by saying that the mischief had come from stones being thrown at the said Duke of Guise, who could not thereupon restrain the fury of his people, and that princes were not to endure having stones thrown at them, Beza, after replying that if it were so, the said Duke of Guise would clear himself by representing who they were who had been guilty of such a fault, concluded with these words: 'Sire, it is for the Church of

God, in the name of which I speak, to suffer
blows, not to give them, but may it please you
to remember that it is an anvil that has worn out
many a hammer.'"[1]

---

[1] *Hist. eccl.*, This saying became popular, and was the
origin of the famous device, "Tant plus à frapper on s'amuse,
Tant plus de marteaux on y use"; underneath which was an
anvil struck by hammers.

CHAPTER XXVI.

Condé in Paris.—Advice sent by Elizabeth of England to Catherine de
Médicis.—Guise comes to Paris in spite of Catherine's prohibition.
—Doubtful conduct of Catherine.—Violation of the Edict of
January in Paris.—Condé leaves Paris.—He calls together the
Protestant leaders in Meaux.—Attitude of the Admiral in March,
1562.—The famous dialogue between Coligny and Charlotte de
Laval as given by d'Aubigné.—Was it possible for the Protestants
to avoid the war of religion?—Causes which decided Condé to
throw himself into it.

IT might have seemed probable that the defection
of Antoine of Navarre would draw away his
brother also. But Condé stood firm. As soon as he
had recovered from a serious illness, by which he
was laid aside at the time of the proclamation of the
edict of January, he used all his energy to secure
the observance of the edict in Paris itself, where the
populace, greatly excited by the report of what had
occurred at Vassy, were openly threatening the
Huguenots. Elizabeth of England tried to encourage
Catherine not to yield to the instigations of the
violent party, but to enforce the edict. She wrote to
her ambassador in Paris: "Tell the queen-mother that
so long as she has no other end in view but the welfare of her son and the tranquillity of her realm, she
has nothing to fear, provided she does not lend herself

to the intrigues and designs of those who, from ambitious motives, are seeking only their own glory and advancement. . . . Greet the Admiral affectionately in our name, and assure him that the wisdom and constancy which he has displayed hitherto, and his whole behaviour have deserved and have won for him the admiration of the world. Let him not now, therefore, neglect the cause of God, of which his conscience assures him he is so good a witness, but let him use his wisdom in the furtherance of that cause."[1]

This language of Queen Elizabeth seems to us to describe with singular exactness the very part Coligny was playing at this moment : truly devoted to the Protestant cause, he was resolved to uphold it only by lawful means. It was by his firmness and moderation that he gained such an ascendancy over Catherine. But as Catherine was constantly alleging the pressure put upon her by the Guises and the Catholic party, the Admiral had commissioned a young French noble, Louis de Bar, who had studied in Germany, to see the Elector Palatine and the Duke of Würtemberg, and to induce them to promise to lend Catherine military assistance if it became necessary. Calvin wrote to the same effect to German Switzerland. At this time, when Germany and Switzerland were the great depôts of mercenary troops, each party was anxious to be beforehand in securing their aid.

Francis of Lorraine, meanwhile, was not losing time. Notwithstanding Catherine's injunctions that he should not come to Paris, he advanced upon the capital a few days after the massacre of Vassy,

---

[1] Despatch of Queen Elizabeth to Throckmorton, March 31st, 1562.

and made a triumphal entry on March 16th. Antoine joined him in Paris, as also did the Constable and St. André. This was the triumvirate which carried all before it, and made itself master of France.

At this moment, when it was more than ever necessary to assume a firm and decided attitude, Catherine had recourse to her usual tactics. She manœuvred.

She wrote several times to Condé, from the 16th to 28th of March, imploring his aid.[1] The history of these letters is curious. None of them are explicit. Catherine was too prudent to betray herself in this matter. The clearest phrases in the letters are such as these : " My cousin, I have spoken to Ivoy (de Genlis) as freely as I would to yourself, relying on his fidelity, and that he would say nothing to anyone but you, *and that you would never say anything, but would only think how you might save the children, and the mother, and the kingdom,* as one whom it nearly concerns, and who may be assured he will never be forgotten. *Burn this imprudent letter.*" And in another : " My cousin, I see so many things that displease me that if it were not for the affiance I have in God, *and the assurance I have that you will help me in preserving this kingdom and the service of my son, the king, in spite of those who are seeking to ruin all,* I should be still more grieved ; but I hope that with your good counsel and aid we shall soon remedy all."

---

[1] She sent Condé seven letters, or, rather, seven notes (see the discussion on this subject in Condé's *Mémoires*, vol. iii., p. 213 ; four are given in the *Lettres de Catherine de Médicis*, published by La Ferrière, p. 281 and following.

It must be remembered, however, that every one of these letters was intrusted to a messenger who was charged to declare aloud the wishes of the queen, and that these letters were only the pledge of the reality of his mission. But Condé, who knew what value to place on the queen's word, did not destroy the letters, as she bade him. On the contrary, he made copies of them, and left the original in the hands of Spifame, whom he sent to the emperor to vindicate his taking up arms. When Spifame afterwards handed over the originals to the emperor, Catherine wrote to the Bishop of Rennes, her ambassador at the Court of Ferdinand, and to the Duchess of Lorraine, to explain the meaning of these letters. She had copies of them made with postscripts intended to show their true meaning.[1]

She pretended that her sole object in writing to Condé had been to get him to leave Paris, to avoid the danger of a conflict. But this miserable subterfuge could deceive no one. If this had been her object, why not have said so openly? Why these secret messengers? Why the urgent entreaties to Condé not to compromise her? Why did she tell him to burn the letters? Whence the desire, she so often expressed afterwards, that she could get hold of the originals again?

It is certain that at one time Catherine thought of leaning upon Condé, but that under the pressure of Guise and the King of Navarre, who came upon her unexpectedly at Fontainebleau, she yielded to the

---

[1] These postscripts are to be found in M. de la Ferrière's collection.

stronger influence, and tried afterwards to forget that she had ever desired to be independent.

At the same time that she was secretly addressing herself to Condé, she sought to reassure the Catholic party, and made the Cardinal of Bourbon governor of Paris, in place of Montmorency, eldest son of the Constable, whose sympathy with the Protestants made the Lorraines fear him. The Cardinal inaugurated his entrance into office by forbidding the Protestants to celebrate Holy Communion at Popincourt. Antoine of Navarre who, as Throckmorton said, was all for Spain, went to Paris to enforce this prohibition. This was a flagrant violation of the edict of January.

Condé's position was most critical. It was vain for him to think of remaining in Paris to defend the rights of the reformed.[1] The few soldiers he had at command would have had no chance against the populace supported by the soldiers of the Duke of Guise. Lanoue's words have often been quoted on this point. "What would they have been against an enemy almost *numberless*, but as a little fly to

---

[1] Paris was at this time altogether hostile to the Reformation. "Everyone," says Lanoue, "knows that in Paris is the seat of justice, which gives marvellous authority, and just as the favour of Paris would have greatly strengthened the reformed, so its disfavour brought them great annoyance. All this senate, however, (*i.e.*, the parliament) and its followers showed themselves, with few exceptions, mortal enemies to "the religion." The clergy, which in this city is very powerful, and held in much veneration, was enraged at seeing the reformed worship, which it detested, openly observed, and was constantly plotting against it in secret. The city corporation, also fearing the changes that might arise out of the diversity of religion, sought to banish or to repress the Huguenots. The majority of the University, and almost all the low and small

a great elephant ? Why, if only the novices from the nunneries and the chambermaids of the priests had presented themselves suddenly with faggot-sticks in their hands, I trow it would have been enough to make them draw rein." Lanoue thinks that nothing but the presence of the king supporting his edict could have ensured the rights of the Protestants in Paris.

On March 22nd, Condé left the capital and went to Meaux, where he begged his two uncles, Coligny and Andelot, to join him.

Guise, St. André, and the King of Navarre urged Catherine to come to Paris. She refused, on the plea of the young king's health. Seeing which, the three leaders, feeling there was not a moment to lose in making sure their power, went with a military escort to Fontainebleau. This was on Wednesday the 27th of March. Catherine received them very coldly, but she was obliged to yield to the stress put upon her. They urged the necessity of putting the young king in a place of safety, and Catherine and her son allowed themselves to be carried away to Melun.

The message from Condé found Coligny at Châtillon-

---

people, and the partisans and servants of the great Catholic princes and lords, laboured to the same end. . . . As to the Court, it was notorious that at the time of the Colloquy of Poissy the evangelical doctrine was freely proclaimed there, which led many, both high and low, to take a liking to it. But just as a fire of straw blazes up into a great flame, and as quickly dies down for lack of proper fuel, so after the novelty of these things had somewhat worn away, their affection cooled, and most of them returned to the old cabal of the Court, which was a much more jovial and profitable life from a worldly point of view. Even some Huguenots drew back for the same reason.

sur-Loing, where he was with his two brothers and several Protestant lords, among them Genlis, Boucard, and Briquemault.

They deliberated what steps to take. Must they arm themselves to resist the Guises? That was the point. There was no thought for a moment of rebelling against the queen-mother. On the contrary, the letters she had addressed to Condé were asking for his help. One thing was clear, namely, that the edict of January was becoming a dead letter; that is, that the Government felt itself incapable to enforce it, and that it was necessary to uphold it with a strong hand against the Guises if "the religion" was not to be swept away. No one entertained the idea of a rebellion against the authority of the king. This explains the fact (attested by the veracious Lanoue) that from all sides the Protestants flocked in, without waiting for Condé's summons. He says, " Some have thought that this had been long premeditated by them, or that it had been brought about by the diligence of the leaders; but I can affirm the contrary, having been a witness of it all, and curious to inquire into its causes.[1] It is certain that the greater part of the Protestant nobility, hearing of the execution of Vassy, and urged on partly by good will and partly by fear, thought they would come to Paris, in case the Protestants might chance to need them. And in this way those who were most renowned left the provinces with ten, twenty, or thirty of their friends, carrying arms under their clothes, and lodging in hostelries or in

---

[1] Lanoue, then twenty-one years of age, was in Paris when the news came of the massacre of Vassy.

the fields, paying well and waiting till they found themselves a large body just when the occasion arose. Many of them have assured me that this was the only reason of their coming together. "[1]

We have then every indication of a spontaneous movement of the Protestant nobility. The nobles felt themselves threatened as soon as the report spread of the massacre of Vassy, and they took up arms, not as insurgents, but in self-defence.

This appears in a letter which the Admiral addressed to Catherine on March 27th from Meaux, whither he had gone at Condé's summons. The queen-mother had sent him two letters, the originals of which are missing, and Coligny replied as follows: " Madame, I have received the two letters which it has pleased your Majesty to write to me, both bearing date the 25th of this month; the first handed to me by a courier sent by the prince, and the second by your *valet de chambre.* To reply to both. I know not how the King of Navarre heard that I was levying soldiers, but I answer upon my honour, Madame, that I have had no such thought. I have, indeed, warned some of my neighbours and friends, and prayed them to bear me company in going to join the prince; and if perchance some armed men are found in my company, it seems to me it should no more be thought strange than that others should go to join the Duke of Guise bearing arms openly, and of this I can speak, having seen them. More-over, I am informed from various quarters that the Duke of Guise is using menacing words against me,

[1] Lanoue, *Discours politiques et militaires,* p. 547.
[2] *Lettres de Catherine de Médicis,* by Count de la Ferrière.

as the prince himself has further assured me, having heard it on good authority. Therefore I entreat you very humbly, Madame, not to take it amiss that I stand upon my guard. Your Majesty's second letter makes further mention that you have heard that I had left my house with a great company of men fully armed (*armés d'armes crues*),[6] and that I am thus marching my company, having called out my reserves. As to having a good company, I confess I have, and the best I can get together for my own defence. As to carrying arms openly, I have nothing in my army but pistols and guns, such as are common throughout the kingdom of France. As to having called out my reserves,[2] I have issued no such order, and principally for this reason, that I knew well that there were not so many as to do me much service; but, Madame, even if I had called them out, I should only have done what others have done. In answer to your question, whether I have made my company take an oath without mention of the king's name, let me inform you of the truth of the matter. It is more than four years since I held a review of my company, on which occasion it is

---

[1] *Armé-à-cru* is an expression used for armed *cap-à-pié*; but we cannot understand Coligny's use of the expression here. The parallel with bearing arms openly seems to indicate a reference to the defensive armour used, the various parts of the cuirass.

[2] This seems to contradict the statement above, "If some armed men are found in my company." The contradiction is only apparent. Coligny left his house in company with several neighbours and friends, and he admits it; but he had not called out the regular company, of which he was the head, which would have meant taking up arms. This he only did later, acting in concert with Condé when the Guises had taken possession of the young king.

customary to take the oath of allegiance. If you find that I have done anything of the sort since, in any manner whatever, I pray you to look on me as infamous and dishonoured. For the rest, Madame, I entreat you very humbly to believe that there is not a gentleman in France who more desires to see you in repose and contentment than I myself, as I will the more particularly assure your Majesty by Captain Breuil, whom the prince is sending to your Majesty. I humbly pray God, Madame, that He will be pleased to give you health and long life.

"Your very humble and obedient servant,

"CHASTILLON."

Written from Meaux, March 27th, 1561 (1562, new style).

We have given this letter as a whole because it is of special importance, and enables us to judge what was Coligny's real feeling on the eve of the Huguenots taking up arms. Condé left Paris March 22nd. On the 23rd he summoned Coligny and the Protestant leaders to Meaux.[1] On the 25th Catherine sent the Admiral two letters, in the second of which she says she has just heard "that Coligny has left his house with a great company of armed men." This conclusively proves that the Admiral responded at once to the summons of Condé,[2] and, in fact, it is from Meaux that he writes in reply the letter to Catherine given above. His language is perfectly sincere. He never thought of making a levy of

---

[1] " Being there (at Meaux) the Prince sent at once to the Admiral and Andelot, begging them to come to him with all speed."—Lanoue.

[2] This point must be noted, because it is clearly in contradiction of d'Aubigné's assertion, which we quote presently.

troops, but he does not mean to be duped. He has seen Guise enter Paris with an army at his back, in spite of the queen's orders to the contrary. He knows what are the designs of the Guises in reference to himself and the Protestant leaders. He comes therefore to confer with Condé, and he is accompanied for the sake of safety by a certain number of gentlemen. If these are armed, the queen cannot think it strange, for their enemies are armed, and have been so for a long time. For the rest, Coligny and his friends never for a moment thought of rebelling against the authority of the king and his mother. This he affirms unhesitatingly, and it is beyond a shadow of doubt.

We may observe that Lanoue, who was an eye-witness of the taking up of arms, expresses himself in the very same way. After saying, in the passages we have quoted, that there had been no premeditated rising, he affirms that Coligny and the other Protestant nobles came to Meaux " without at any rate carrying arms openly, as those of the league (the partisans of the Guises) had already done." At Meaux they stayed five or six days, both that they might deliberate on the course to be pursued, and that they might celebrate the Holy Communion together on Easter-day. During this time, Guise and the King of Navarre had gone to Fontainebleau, and had forced the king and the queen-mother to follow them. It was then that " the Admiral, who was no novice in affairs of State, foreseeing that the struggle was about to begin, pointed out that either they must make an earnest effort to reinforce themselves at once, or they must prepare for flight, and he much feared that even now they had delayed too long." It was only when he saw the Huguenot gentlemen coming up on all sides, that Coligny felt they might hold their ground and offer resistance.

There can be no doubt that a large part of the Protestant noblesse would feel their hearts beat high with hope and enthusiasm at the prospect of entering upon a campaign against the Guises. They would recall the cruel sufferings inflicted upon their Church for more than thirty years, the bitter memories of Amboise, the long scroll of Huguenot martyrdoms in which were inscribed so many of their family names. The Reformed Church was, moreover, then in its ascending period. For two or three years it had been receiving numerous additions from the ranks of the highest noblesse. It had the avowed sympathy of all who hated the Guises. Elizabeth of England and the Protestant princes of Germany would not withhold from it their support. Catherine de Medicis herself was thought to be secretly their ally. Finally they were arming to defend an edict which had been guaranteed by oath.

Coligny saw more clearly than the rest. He entered into the conflict with enthusiasm, at the imperative call of duty.

Agrippa d'Aubigné, in his well-known pages, the finest he ever wrote, has described the conflict which went on in the soul of the great Huguenot. Is the dialogue we are about to quote, genuine? No one will ever be able to say.[1] If we observe carefully we

---

[1] We cannot go so far as M. Delaborde, who says that d'Aubigné had the privilege of being the confidant of the noble influence which Charlotte de Laval exercised over her

shall find that the interview of the Admiral with his wife, published fifty years later, bears a distant analogy to that which they held in 1559, at the time when they joined the persecuted Church.[1] Even then it was Charlotte de Laval who urged the Admiral to take the decisive step. It was he who then pointed out to her "at great length" all the obstacles to be surmounted, all the suffering and ignominy to be undergone; to which she replied simply that she was ready for all. It is but too evident that no one could have reproduced this interview at Châtillon, and that d'Aubigné has put into Coligny's lips prophetic language which could not have been exact at the time. This touching picture is one of those creations of genius in which d'Aubigné often indulges. But with this reservation, the dialogue is unquestionably true in the sense that it does not put into the lips of the Admiral and his wife one word which is not worthy of them, and which does not faithfully represent the strength of their moral heroism. One may say that the words used breathe the very soul of the Reformation in its noblest and most genuine inspiration.

Let us listen to d'Aubigné : "At the Admiral's house at Châtillon-sur-Loing were assembled his brothers, Odet, the Cardinal and Andelot; Genlis, Boucart, Briquemault, and others, to urge him to take up arms. This old soldier saw so much danger in crossing the Rubicon, that for two whole days he

husband at that time. D'Aubigné was then twelve years old; he was twenty-two at the death of the Admiral in 1572, and it is very doubtful if Coligny ever confided to him the incidents of that memorable night.

[1] We have given it above from the *Vita Colinii*.

disputed with them, and showed such wise and cogent reasons for restraining their violence, that they were astonished at his fears, and had given up almost all hope of moving him,[1] when that happened which I am about to hand down to posterity, not as a tissue of fable such as poets weave, but as a true history which I received from those who took part in it.[2]

In the night as Coligny lay awake and sadly pondered these things, he heard his wife sobbing by his side, and by degrees led her on to speak thus :

" It grieves me sore, sire, to disturb your rest by my disquietudes, but when the members of Christ are torn in pieces as they are now, how can we who are part of the same body remain insensible ? You, sire, have not less feeling than I, but more strength to hide it. Will you take it amiss of your faithful wife if with more of frankness than of respect she pours her tears and thoughts into your bosom ? Here are we lapped in luxury, while the bodies of our brethren, bone of our bone, flesh of our flesh, are cast alive into dungeons or as corpses into the open fields at the mercy of dogs and ravens. This bed is a grave to me while they lie unburied ; these sheets are as my shroud while they have no winding-sheet. Can we lie here sunk in sleep while there is no one

---

[1] This is in direct contradiction to the much more probable statement of Lanoue, and to the fact that the Admiral responded at once to Condé's appeal.

[2] This oratorical preamble of d'Aubigné's shows that he felt his readers would be likely to ask how, at such a distance of time, he could have reproduced this interview. What seems most likely is that Coligny may have told his guests that his wife had urged him on to resistance, and may have quoted to them some of her words which are too noble to be pure inventions.

to catch the death-sighs of our brothers? I have been thinking of the counsels of prudence with which you have closed the mouths of your brethren; will you also take from them all heart, and leave them stripped of courage as well as of arguments? I fear me that such prudence is of the children of this generation, and that to be so wise towards man is not to be wise towards God, who gave you the skill of a general. Can you in conscience refuse to use this His gift in the service of His children? You have owned to me that conscience has sometimes kept you sleepless thinking of these things. It is God's interpreter. Do you fear that God will hold you guilty for following it?[1] Do your bear the sword of knighthood in order to oppress the afflicted, or to snatch them from the clutches of the tyrants? You have admitted the justice of the contest; why then should your heart forsake the cause of right through fear of ill success? It is God who has taken away the sense of those who have resisted Him under pretext of unwillingness to shed blood. He knows how to save the life of those who would lose it for His sake, and to destroy the life of him who seeks to save it. Sire, I have upon my heart all the blood of our people that has been shed. That blood and your wife cry to heaven against you that you will be the murderer of those whom you do not save from being murdered."

The Admiral replied: "Since I have failed to convince you by my arguments of this evening

---

[1] In words like these we feel the true glory and strength of the Reformation in its early days.

showing the vanity of popular tumults, the doubtful
wisdom of joining a party not yet formed, the
difficulty of taking the first step, not against the
monarchy, but against the possessors of a state
which has cast its roots deep into the soil,[1] which
has so many people interested in its maintenance,
which is enjoying a new and general peace entered
into with neighbouring nations, alas! for the express
purpose of combining to crush us ;[2] since the recent
defection[3] of the King of Navarre and of the Constable which means so much added strength to the
enemies' cause and added weakness to ours. Since
so much power on the side of our enemies and so
much weakness on our part cannot make you pause,
lay your hand on your heart, sound your conscience
and see if you are prepared to face general disorders,
to bear the reproaches of your own partisans as well
as your enemies, to hear of the treason of your friends,
to bear exile into foreign lands, shame, nakedness,
hunger, not for yourself only, but, which is worse, for
your children, to expect your death at the hands
of an executioner after that of your husband ? I
give you three weeks to consider, and if you are
then prepared to brave all that may come I will go

---

[1] D'Aubigné did not mean to say that it would have been
easy to begin to attack the monarchy; his idea rather is that
it was difficult to attack the possessors of a state which had
taken such deep root, and he adds the words *not against the
monarchy*, to show that the Protestants had no quarrel with
royalty as such.

[2] We have referred to the secret stipulations of the Peace of
Cambrésis aimed against the Protestants.

[3] The word defection is truly applicable to Antoine, who had
shown himself a faithless turncoat. It is more difficult to see
how it applied to the Constable, who had never made any
promise to the Protestants.

to meet death with you and your friends." "The time is gone already,"[1] she replied. "Do not bring upon your head the deaths of those three weeks, or I will myself bear witness against you before the judgment-seat of God."

Pressed by these urgent entreaties of his beloved and faithful wife, Coligny mounted his horse and rode to join the Prince of Condé and the other leaders of the party at Meaux.

We have come to the end of our book, to that date, April 1562, which marks the beginning of the sanguinary era of the wars of religion. Before we close, one question remains to be considered.

It has been asked if the conflict might not have been avoided; if the French Protestants would not have acted a nobler part if they had refused to appeal to arms at all, and had suffered themselves to be struck down to the last man.

For more than thirty years the history of the reformed Church of France had been one long, sublime, sad monotone of martyrdom. At certain times, as under Francis I. and Henry II., the number of executions had reached a terrific height. Yet the Church had gone on growing. In 1562, at the time of the January edict, some of the noblest families in France had joined it Would not the outbreak of war check this steady progress ? Instead of a proscribed religion, which nevertheless carried on its conquests even in the ranks of its persecutors, was it not about to constitute itself a party, that is to

---

[1] There is something sublime in these words, Ste. Beuve says, "Corneille has nothing grander."

say a military and political faction ? Parties at war
with each other are anxious, above all things, for
victory. They are dependent on political alliances,
money, and force ; and how can all this be secured
without recourse to diplomacy, intrigue, and the
methods which in all time have been used to ensure
worldly success ? The Church had hitherto been
jealous of the equality of her members, and had
gathered most of her adherents from the ranks of the
common people. But in the event of war the pre-
ponderating influence must belong to the military
leaders and to the nobility. What would become of
the stern Huguenot morality, when the ministers must
needs be subordinate to the great seigneurs so free in
the use of bribes, so little accustomed to self-control ;
when the soldiery must be called in, at a time when
soldiering was almost synonymous with pillage and
open license ? Truth would be staked upon the
success of arms, on the support of the Swiss Lanzknechts, the German Reiters, the English mercenaries.
France would be torn by contending factions, ruin
and malediction following the steps even of the
victorious, not to speak of the terrible possibility of
defeat, the pitiless destruction of those who, having
taken up arms, would no longer be looked upon as
martyrs to the faith, but as rebels who had well
deserved their fate. How much more glorious than
this, death at the stake, prayer the only weapon used
in self-defence, and the only war-cry that sound of
psalms chanted by dying lips, which had so often
aroused troubled thoughts in the crowd of onlookers,
and awakened the conscience even of the executioners
themselves.

So felt many Christian souls in the first generation of the French Huguenots. So always thought
Calvin. In his voluminous correspondence with the
persecuted, there is not one line inciting to revolt.
He always urges submission to the powers ordained
of God, without recourse to carnal weapons. Looked
at in this aspect, such resignation has in it something
sublime. But how strangely the impression changes
when we see Calvin, on the same principle, vindi-
cating the right of the magistrates of Geneva to
repress heresy and to have recourse to the arm of
flesh to chastise those who did not believe with
him! Calvin altogether disapproved of the conspiracy of Amboise,[1] and Coligny was for a long time
of the same mind. But the question no longer
presented itself in this simple form. The Protestants
had shown that they could not be stamped out.
The public conscience had recognised their claims,
and those claims had been vindicated in a law
solemnly proclaimed, which the government had
promised to observe. The point now to be decided
was whether, as citizens, they would passively submit
to the violation of their rights.

On the other hand, the Guises had just committed
an open and flagrant violation of the edict of
January, and no one could, for a moment, be blind
to their intention to carry on by force of arms the

---

[1] We have already referred to this. To the proofs given on
p. 184, we may add the following passage (*Opera*, vol. xviii.,
book iii., 174). Calvinus Sturmio, "Quum me principio con-
sulerunt, qui primi ad hoc negotium agitandum aliis fuerunt
auctores, libere respondi *mihi non placere totam agendi
rationem, rem vero ipsam multo minoris probari*" (Letter
of March 23rd, 1560). Beza took quite another view.

course of procedure begun at Vassy.[1]   Catherine
herself had appealed to Condé, complaining of the
oppression of the Guises.   She represented the
young king as a captive.[2]   The Protestants then
armed themselves to defend the law.   To this
enterprise they might legitimately feel themselves
called by the king, and Theodore Beza truly expressed their thought when he wrote subsequently :
" It would be too daring a calumny to give the
name of a rising and rebellion against the king and
the peace of the country, to so just and purely
defensive a warfare undertaken against the unscrupulous violators of every right human and divine, who
yet dared to cover their acts by the authority of the
king, who was a minor, and who with his mother was
a captive in their hands. The parliaments were packed
and tampered with by them, all those having been
got rid of who might have stood in the way.   I say
again it was a defensive measure fully justified, since
there is no country in the world where all loyal
subjects, even to the humblest, may not lawfully take
up arms to defend the common right against the
aggressions of those who cannot otherwise be repressed." [3]

---

[1] On March 18th Sturm wrote to Calvin from Strasburg,
that on the initiative given by the Guises, troops were
preparing in all parts of Germany: " Supra sexaginta signa
peditum conscripta jam habere nunciatur octo et amplius
millia equitum conquiri."
    [2] " Nos accepto captivi Regis nuncio (neque enim hoc aliud
est quam miserrima captivitas quam etiam Rex cum lacrymis
testatus est)," etc. Letter from Beza, *Calvini Opera*, vol. xix.,
p. 389.
    [3] The *Mémoire* of Beza, from which these words are taken,
was published in 1594, *Bull. de la soc. de l'hist. du prot.
français*, vol. lxxi,, p. 28.

From these words of Beza we see by what a logical progression even the most loyal subjects, such as Coligny, were led into a policy of resistance. At first, the theory of absolute submission prevailed. At the time of the conspiracy of Amboise, most of the Protestant divines, with the exception of Calvin, gave their approval on the understanding that the rising was not against the king, and that the enterprise was conducted by a prince of the blood.[1] Since then the rights of the Protestants had been recognised by law. The government had sworn to respect them. Condé was supposed to be secretly upheld by the queen. The insurrection ceased to be an insurrection.[2]

In truth, what was the point at issue? Was it to secure by the sword the triumph of their religion? Possibly some of the Protestant leaders may have had such a thought. But Coligny desired only one thing—to secure the liberty of the reformed worship. We cannot blame him for this. Every people has a right to see that religious liberty is recognised in its laws, and having secured this recognition, to defend it as it would defend any other liberty.

To establish or to propagate religion by force is contrary not only to the spirit of Christianity, but to

---

[1] La Planche.

[2] What right has the party of the Guises to accuse the Protestants of rebellion against the king? They themselves had repeatedly declared that they would not accept a heretic as king. On the 15th of May, 1561, Catherine de Médicis had asked Francis of Lorraine what the triumvirate meant. Going further, she asked whether if she or her son changed their religion, he would at once withdraw his obedience. The Duke replied plainly that he should. Letter from Chantonnay to the Duchess of Parma. June, 1561.

the most elementary dictates of conscience. St. Paul, speaking of the apostolate, said : " The weapons of our warfare are not carnal;" yet we know how stoutly he vindicated in his own person the rights of a Roman citizen. To defend liberty of conscience is an imperative duty no less for a nation than for an individual.

History, alas ! gives ample proof that, notwithstanding the beautiful saying of Tertullian, " *Sanguis martyrum semen Ecclesiæ,*" religious persecution can succeed, and that the more atrocious it is, the more successful. All the Christian Churches have had bitter experience of this. The sword of Mahomet wrested from the Eastern Church Alexandria, Jerusalem, Antioch, Ephesus, and Constantinople itself. In China and Japan the Catholic Church lost for centuries ground that had been richly watered with the blood of the martyrs. By the same means the Reformation was stamped out in Italy, in Spain, and in Bohemia.

Doubtless, in a general and higher sense, Tertullian's words are true. Unless we are prepared to admit that an ironic fatalism governs all human things, we must believe that no suffering undergone for the sake of truth and righteousness is really lost. The author of the *Tragiques* compares the ashes of the martyrs to a precious seed which the wind of persecution wafts to other climes, where it is sure to germinate. This is the firm hope of all who believe in eternal righteousness. The facts show that this hope is often realized on earth, and that humanity, as a whole, profits by the devotion and self-sacrifice of its lowliest members. But that which is true of the whole is not true of each nation, taken separately. A nation may stifle thought within its own borders. It may quench the light, and pass into the night on which no morning breaks again. Woe to the religions which proselytise by the sword! But woe also to the nations which are not ready to take up the sword in defence of liberty of conscience and the right of the oppressed! The Huguenots were not willing that France should become a second Spain, and they resolutely rent in pieces the network which was being thrown around them. Charlotte de Laval was not mistaken, and in the thrilling words which fell from her lips we hear the voice of Protestant France herself avowing that on her own head would be the blood of those she had not sought to save from death.

When Calvin recommended passive submission, it was well for him that the people of Geneva had not strictly adhered to his principle, but had defended themselves against the machinations of Savoy. Neither Scotland, Holland, nor the Protestants of Germany, had reason to repent defending their rights by the sword. The conscience of man must have fallen low indeed when the name of William of Orange ceases to be honoured. For the French Protestants the struggle was a terrible one, and fraught with dangers; but in sustaining it they deserved well of God and of their country. Doubtless the cause they defended was often compromised by the ambition of its leaders; and we must deeply deplore the fact that in the conflict, the Church sometimes became entangled with and well nigh merged in a political party. But let their enemies

do them at least the justice to confess that these
so-called rebels never dreamed of overturning the
government of the country. They became afterwards
the defenders of the rights of Henry III. himself,
the instigator of the St. Bartholomew massacre, when
the chiefs of the league offered the throne of France
to Philip II. of Spain. Never was there witnessed a
more touching instance of loyalty than that of
Châtillon, the son of the Admiral, when, at the head
of his Huguenots, he marched upon Blois under a
terrible fire, with a calmness which won shouts of
admiration from his enemies themselves, and defended against the leaguers the very king who had
been the murderer of his father.

If the one word *religious liberty* had always been
inscribed upon the Huguenot banner, their cause
would have been irreproachable. To the honour of
Coligny be it said that this was his one aim. He
said so when he took up arms, and ten years after
he could repeat it in all good conscience, when,
wounded by Maurevel, he assured Charles IX. that
he had never carried arms but in defence of the
edicts.

FINIS.

APPENDIX.

A.

(Page 12.)

ANECDOTE OF COLIGNY AS A YOUTH.

COLIGNY and Andelot gave their governor Prunelay plenty to do. One day, in a fencing match, Morin, their master at arms, broke his foil, inflicting so severe a wound on a young gentleman from Poitou that he died. "This gentleman had two brothers, who were no sooner told of this sad accident than, without knowing anything of how it happened, they were eager to revenge themselves upon the master, who was more dead than alive. M. de Châtillon, who had been present at the affair, was anxious to stop them, and to tell them how it all happened. But, not being in a state to listen to reason, they thrust at him, and would have killed him if most of the students at the Academy had not ranged themselves on his side. By this means he saved the life of the master, at which the two brothers were so enraged that they resolved to avenge themselves on him. The elder of the two spoke to M. de Châtillon, telling him that he thought him too much of a gentleman to refuse to give him satisfaction. Nothing was then more common than duelling, so that so far from having a horror of such things, as reason and the service of God would dictate, it was a matter of boasting to have been often engaged in such affairs of honour. M. de Châtillon, falling in like the rest with the custom of the time, promised this gentleman to give him the meeting he desired, and as his brother was to be his second, Coligny sent for Andelot, so that the sides should be two brothers against two brothers. But Parini, their squire, suspected what was going on, and when these two young gentlemen went out and did not return, he warned Prunelay and urged him to see into the matter. Châtillon and Andelot, to escape him, arranged a tennis party, on leaving which they tried to evade him, for he generally left them when they were at this sort of exercise, and they hoped that he would do so now. But he was on his guard after the warning he had received, and they, seeing that he was watching them, said nothing, but told one of their valets de chambre to go and buy a large basket and bring it in so cunningly that their governor should not notice it. The valet carried out their orders to the letter, and having hidden the basket in a cupboard by the side of their bed, without knowing what they wanted it for, he told them what he had done. They were charmed, and after making him all sorts of promises, they told him that they wanted him to do them a service for which he should be well rewarded. He was to conceal himself in the hayloft, which was two or three stories above their room, and when the governor was asleep, he was to let himself down with the rope used for drawing up the hay, because they wanted to tie this to the basket, and to get into it one after the other, and he must let them down in the basket by the rope. The valet trembled at this proposition, guessing well, after what had happened, what was their intention. Nevertheless, alarmed by their threats never to do anything for him unless he obeyed, he agreed, and let them down one after the other. The meeting was fixed for the morning, so they betook themselves to an inn, in St. Germain, where they passed the remainder of the night. The night over, they had not much difficulty in awaking, for they had had only a hard mattrass to sleep on; and going to the Pré-aux-Clercs, they found there the two gentlemen, who were at their prayers waiting for them. They inspected one another, after the custom of the time, to see that they had no weapons about them, and having found nothing which was not according to rule, they took their swords. The combat was short, but sharp. Châtillon wounded his man at the first stroke, and having made a pass at his throat, forced him to ask for his life. Andelot was not so fortunate. His assailant, who was one of the best swordsmen in Paris, having made a feint of giving way, watched his opportunity to throw himself upon him, and, in fact, had already seized his sword when Châtillon thrust the point of his sword into his loins and made him cry for mercy like the other."[1] The thing did not end here. The vanquished parties tried to take their revenge in an unfair way. Some time after, having heard that Coligny and his brother were hunting at Juvisy, near the estates of one of their friends, they seized the occasion to watch them and set upon them, under pretext that they had gone beyond the boundaries of their chase. This dastardly trick ended in a real fight, in

---

[1] Sandras de Courtils, bk. i., p. 15 and following.

which the Châtillons again had the advàntage. The thing
was rumoured at Court. Louise de Montmorency gave information of what she regarded as an attempt at assassination ;
but Coligny generously hushed up the affair, and thus raised
still higher the reputation for chivalrous courage which he had
already won.

B.

(Page 19.)

At the siege of Arlon, an incident transpired which, if the
account be true, brings out conspicuously Coligny's stern
morality. The town was given up to pillage, and, according
to the barbarous custom of the time, the inhabitants became
the property of the conquerors. A remarkably beautiful girl
was brought to Coligny. Distrusting himself, he offered to
have her honourably escorted to some place of safety, or, if
she preferred to remain in his house, he offered to leave it at
once. He gave himself no rest till he knew that she was on
her way to some neighbouring convent ; but the escort he
gave her was attacked by a party of soldiers, who violated her.
Coligny demanded of the Duke of Orleans the punishment of
the offenders. The Prince was surprised at such virtue, which
was not common in the army, and attempted some remonstrance ; but as the escort had been dispersed by violence,
the infraction of discipline was flagrant ; and two of the
offenders were put to death.[1]

C.

(Page 29.)

Coligny's elevation of fortune made no change in the serious-
ness of his life. The following is an account of the way in
which he usually passed his days at this time, taken from
Sandras de Courtils, who says he had it direct from the
family :—

"The first thing he did on leaving his bed was to throw
himself on his knees before a crucifix, and there he remained
for a quarter of an hour, not allowing himself to be interrupted
for any cause whatever, except when he was in the army.
When there he said it was the will of God that what was due
to Him should be deferred till necessary duties were done.
After prayer he used to dress himself and go into his stable,

---

[1] Sandras de Courtils, bk. i., p. 29.

where he looked at his horses one after another, trusting much
more to his own eyes than to the care of his groom. He was
so good a horseman that he always rode the horses most
difficult to manage, and used to spend an hour and a half
each day in this exercise. . . . He then retired to his chamber,
where he read regularly for an hour, and to so much purpose
that there was never a man better versed in history than he.
When the hour was over he went to mass, to which he listened
kneeling ; for although he never failed to attend mass with
the king, he thought that most went there only to pay their
court to royalty, and as people were stumbling over one
another, passing and repassing all the time, it seemed to him
a poor opportunity for private prayer. After mass he went to
the king's levée, and having spent the rest of the morning
with him, he went to dinner, where he remained longer than
he would have done if he had been quite alone ; but as everyone was welcome at his house, good manners compelled him
to yield in some measure to the customs of society. After
dinner he read again for an hour, and in order not to be disturbed, he had cards given to those who had dined with him.
This hour over, he returned to the Louvre, where he generally
had a game of tennis with the dauphin. If he did not play
tennis he would play mall or billiards ; but he would have
nothing to do with games of chance, saying that it would be
well if that sort of amusement was forbidden throughout the
kingdom, and he did all that he could to discountenance it.
But to return to my subject. Coligny spent the rest of the
afternoon with the king or the dauphin, and when eight
o'clock came, he returned home, where he read for another
hour, after which he took some fruit or a biscuit in some wine,
for he never made a regular supper. After this he returned
again to the king, and stayed till he had retired to rest. He
went to bed himself when he came home, but not without
having spent another quarter of an hour at the head of his
bed, in the presence of his household ; for while he believed
that true devotion does not consist in any mere form of worship,
he yet felt that masters are bound to set an example to their
domestics.''

The same writer tells us of a trait in his character at this
time, which is well borne out by the care which Coligny often
showed afterwards for the poor, and which is the more notable
in a man of war in an age of rude manners, when the great
were very indifferent to the sufferings of the common people.
He says : " I must relate what happened to Coligny in the
Church of the Jacobins, whither he had gone to hear mass on
St. Dominic's day. He had put into one of his pockets some
money to give to the poor, and a poor man having come up to him

while he was deep in his prayers, instead of feeling in the pocket where he had put the small money, he thrust his hand into the other pocket, in which were gold pieces. He took out a handful, without counting, and gave them to the poor man without looking at what he gave. The poor man was much astonished at the largeness of the gift. He must have been a good man, as appears from what he did; for, waiting at the door of the church till M. de Châtillon came out, he said to him : 'I know not, Sire, if it was your intention to give me so large an alms, but if it was not, I do not wish to take advantage of it.' M. de Châtillon was not so much surprised at his own mistake as he was at the generosity of this poor man, and, looking at him with admiration, he said : 'No, my good man, it was not my intention to give you that which you have in your hand, but since you have had the generosity to wish to return it to me, I shall certainly have the generosity to let you keep it.' Nor was he content with this. He took the man to his house, where he kept him as long as he lived. . . . And indeed this man proved a model of virtue, as was seen even more after his death than during his life, for no sooner were his eyes closed than an old woman, who had been accustomed to come begging every day, began to sob when she was told that God had taken him to Himself. It was thought that she must be his wife, since she took such an interest in him, and they asked her the question. 'No,' she replied, 'he was not my husband, but if he had been he could not have taken more care than he did of me and my family.' She then told how, since he had been in the house, he had brought her every day the meat and wine that were given him for his own food, and it was she who had benefited by Châtillon's generous alms. The case having been reported to M. de Châtillon, he could not believe it without hearing it himself from the woman's own lips, but when he was convinced of its truth, he could not keep back his tears, saying that he had lost a treasure he had not been worthy to possess. He took pains to enquire about the woman, and finding that she was a poor unfortunate, burdened with children, he took charge of her and her family.

"He had no greater joy than these deeds of charity, and it was observed that young as he was, he had so much compassion for the unfortunate that he would willingly have ruined himself to put them at their ease. He had an especial pity for the poor noblesse, saying that he felt most for them because others could work and these were not accustomed to it. As his kindness of heart was well known, all the poor were looking out for him when he went to the Louvre, and not one went away without some gift. . . . There was no ostentation about his charity, and there could be no doubt that he was really touched when any poor persŏn came to him. . . . Once when he went to Châtillon with Andelot, a poor gentleman came to him, who lived four or five leagues from there, and was introduced by some one whom Châtillon knew. Turning to Andelot Coligny said: 'Ah, my brother, what are we to be so well clothed and so much at our ease, while this poor gentleman is destitute of the barest necessaries? He is of the same rank as ourselves in the kingdom. If we are gentlemen, he is a gentleman also; and if there is any difference it is that God has been pleased to favour us, while He allows him to remain in poverty.' Nor did he stop short at kind words. Deeds followed closely, and he gave orders not only that the poor gentleman should be clothed, but that his own bailiffs should allow him each year a certain sum towards his maintenance. His estates were heavily charged with pensions of this sort, and he had such a care for the poor that he engaged a number of women to nurse them in illness, and give them all possible attention. But as it would be of no use to get them nurses, if they could not have proper food, he gave two hundred francs monthly for soup to be made for them on his estate at Châtillon, and he did the same thing on all his other estates, whether large or small. He took care, moreover, not only of their bodies, but of their souls, and it is remarked that before he embraced the reformed religion, he used to keep priests at Châtillon and founded schools for the education of the young. He did not discontinue this good work when he was brought to the truth. All the difference was that then he employed ministers instead of priests."

D.

We have said (p. 252) that Jeanne d'Albret lost her two eldest children by strange accidents. This is the account given in the *Chronologie Novenaire* of Palma Cayet (Petitot edit., vol. ii., p. 230 and following).

"These two fine young princes were not to be reared. Unhappily they both died early in the following manner:— The Duke de Beaumont was placed in the charge of the wife of the bailiff of Orleans, who was grandmother of the Marshal de Matignon, and lived in the said city of Orleans. This lady was very old and crotchety, and extremely sensitive to cold. She used to keep herself shut up in a room with a great fire, and closely hung with arras. She kept the little prince even warmer still, making him pant and sweat with heat, never suffering a breath of fresh air to enter the room. She persisted in doing this in spite of all that was said to her, until at last the little Duke de Beaumont was gradually stifled by the heat and died. To the last the old lady said; ' Let him alone, it is better to sweat than to shiver ! '

"The Count de Marle (Jeanne's second son) came to his end in another way. M. de Vendôme and the Princess, his wife (Antoine de Bourbon and Jeanne) had gone to visit King Henri d'Albret in Béarn. They found him at Mont de Marsan, where they stayed. They had brought with them the Count de Marle in his long clothes, as the king wished to see him, and they presented him to his Majesty, to his great contentment. The little prince was very beautiful, and every one wanted to hold him. One of the gentlemen ushers of the Court began to play with him one day as his nurse held him in her arms by an open French window. The nurse and the gentleman passed him from one to the other several times outside the window, sometimes only pretending to take him, which was the cause of the accident. For the gentleman pretending to take him, and not really doing it, the nurse let him go, and he fell out of the window down on the steps below and bruised one side. The gentleman at once leapt down out of the window, which was on the first floor, and carried him, crying bitterly, to the nurse. She quieted him as well as she could with the breast. The king, M. de Vendôme, and the Princess were out hunting, and no one told them of the accident. I have heard some of the old servants say that if the nurse had told, something might have been done for the child, but as it was, he grew worse, and at last died."

Printed by Hazell, Watson, and Viney, Limited, London and Aylesbury.